For Ca
you en
it!

With love
Ness

# The Matchmakers

## VANESSA EDWARDS

CH00925930

Copyright © 2024 Vanessa Edwards

The moral right of the author has been asserted.

All rights reserved.

This is a work of fiction. Names, characters, businesses, places,
events and incidents are either the products of the author's
imagination or used in a fictitious manner. Any resemblance to
actual persons, living or dead, or actual events is purely coincidental.

Author cover photo © Nick Gregan

ISBN: 978 1036903 565

# PROLOGUE

## Honeymoon Tragedy of Bride in the Bath –
## Exclusive

### West Cornwall Times

*This past weekend, tragedy has struck the quiet village of Polpen. On Saturday, James Anderson married Stephanie Faulkner and on Sunday they drove from London to Polpen to start a fortnight's honeymoon at a pretty holiday cottage. James had never felt so happy, but that evening, on the second day of his marriage, his bride drowned in the bath while alone in the cottage. Prostrate with grief and even though he felt unable to talk face to face, James bravely agreed to give your local paper an exclusive interview by telephone from the room in the White Hart where he's staying until he can make his sad, lonely journey back to his empty home.*

*As he wept, James tried to explain what happened, but his account was constantly interrupted by his obvious heartbreak. 'I'd run her a bath,' he said, and stopped, choking on his tears. 'She loved her baths. She was about to add some bath oil and foam before getting undressed when I realised I'd forgotten to pick up eggs when I was in the village earlier getting the papers. Stephanie loves — loved' — James stopped again, his voice a hoarse croak when he resumes — 'a cooked breakfast as a special treat. So I popped back to the shop, except of course when I got there it was closed. I'm used to London shop hours I suppose. I was only away for five or ten minutes.'*

*James paused, clearly needing time to control himself. He blew his nose and continued. 'I called up the stairs to say I was back. She didn't reply but I just assumed she hadn't heard. She often puts headphones on in the bath, she has some relaxing playlist on Spotify I think. So I didn't worry, didn't go up to check.'*

*James stopped for a third time. 'Sorry. I — I'll never forgive myself. If I'd gone straight up, maybe ... Anyway I went up after about ten minutes I suppose. I thought I'd take her a glass of champagne for her to sip in the bath. But she was ... she was under the water. She'd drowned. I think she must have slipped. To be honest we'd been drinking off and on all afternoon — it was the first day of our honeymoon for god's sake. She'd put lots of bath oil in and there was also a small bar of soap that looked squashed, as though she'd trodden on it. So she must have slipped and banged her head, lost consciousness long enough to drown.'*

# PART ONE – STEPHANIE AND VIVIEN

# ONE

## THREE MONTHS EARLIER

I brush my fingertips over the brochure for the umpteenth time while I wait. *MadeInHeaven MatchMakers* — the raised gilt letters feel smooth and full of promise. It took a lot of courage for me to make the phone call. I don't have much courage anymore, but I did it.

The knocker raps. I glance around the sitting room — I've decided it's the best place for the interview, tasteful and welcoming but also comfortable — smooth my skirt and square my shoulders. I've lost the knack of relaxing in the company of strangers. I lost a lot in my marriage, though I suppose that ultimately I gained a lot also.

When I first spoke to MadeInHeaven MatchMakers, the owner, Vivien Harrison, spelt out her first name. 'With an "e", but only one, like Vivien Leigh.' And I see now, as I open the front door, that she has something of the actress's striking beauty. Raven dark hair, perfect skin, glossy red lips. I realise I've forgotten to check my lipstick and run my tongue over my teeth, hoping to sweep away any stray flakes.

'Mrs Faulkner?' she asks with a smile. I nod and she follows me to the sitting room where I hesitate, briefly stranded. 'Erm, I thought … Maybe the sofa? Or would you prefer that we sit at a table?'

'This is perfect. What a lovely room.' Her eyes sweep the lush swagged curtains, the art, the Persian carpet, and she settles herself on the leather Chesterfield, crossing one elegant leg over the other. She pulls a silvery pen and a hardback notebook with a Liberty-print cover from her bag. 'This is a very informal meeting, my dear. Stephanie. Is that how you prefer to be addressed, the full name?'

I nod again, feeling awkward and tongue-tied, and offer coffee, which Vivien declines. I would have liked a shot of caffeine — it's my form of Dutch courage — but sit down on the other sofa, angled and close enough for easy conversation. I hope it will be easy.

'As I said when we spoke,' she begins, 'I always like to meet a new client in their own home. So much more relaxing than an office. And I know that meeting, even making the first contact with, a matchmaker — I prefer the term to "dating agency", it sounds so much more personal — can be very stressful. Is this your first time, Stephanie?'

I nod, then swallow. I need to speak, to participate. There's no one here now to tell me to keep quiet, to know my place. Or not to do something I've decided to do. I take the plunge, and once I start talking it's hard to stop.

'My husband passed away a few months ago. It may seem soon —' Vivien smiles, and shakes her head — 'but it was … not a happy marriage. I want to try again, but I want to get it right this time. So I thought maybe a dating agency was the answer. I didn't want to just sign up to some app though.'

Vivien gives a slight but eloquent shudder. 'You are so right, my dear. We don't even have a website, as I'm sure you know. I believe you said you found us through one of our discreet notices in *The Lady*?'

I nod. Get a grip. 'Yes. I thought that might be a safer bet than Tinder or whatever it's called.'

'There are lots of them. And lots of horror stories also. But we vet our clients, both male and female, very carefully indeed. Not only so we have the best chance of introducing people who have similar interests, but also to be absolutely sure that there are no …' She pauses, as if searching for the word.

'Gold-diggers?' I suggest.

Vivien smiles. 'Precisely. Such a vulgar term, but exact. And there are a lot of them out there, believe you me. Which is why I need to ask what might seem to be searching questions. I know you'll understand — it's for your own protection, and also gives you the reassurance that anyone I introduce you to will have gone through the same wringer. So let's just rattle through my list. The sooner it's done, the sooner I can leave you in peace and start the hunt for your perfect man!'

I offer coffee again, and this time she accepts, perhaps realising that I need a break. She seems sensitive to moods. A good matchmaker must need that quality, and a good matchmaker is what I need.

I put the tray with the cafetière, mugs and a plate of biscuits on the small table between us. Robert couldn't abide mugs, always insisted on cups and saucers, but they're tricky if you're sitting on a sofa with a notebook and pen. And he's not here anymore anyway. If he were, Vivien wouldn't be.

'I'll start with the most intrusive question,' she says, putting her mug down after sniffing the coffee appreciatively and taking a sip. 'Can you tell me a little — as much as you feel comfortable with, given that you know that the more information I have the better — about your financial circumstances?' She glances around again and gives a small, seemingly satisfied sigh.

'My husband, late husband, was a wholesale trader in precious stones. Gemstones, he called them. He always said it wasn't as lucrative as people think but … well, he must have been good at it. I didn't realise how good until he died. So no, you can rest assured I'm not a gold-digger.'

Vivien makes a note, her pen swooping and dipping. 'Thank you for your honesty, Stephanie. And of course none of this information gets passed to potential matches; I just need to be able to say, hand on heart, that you're not after their money. Most of our male clients are, well, very rich I suppose, no point beating about the bush, and it's often the first thing they ask.' She takes another sip and a delicate nibble of a brittle speculoos biscuit.

'Delicious, thank you. So the next thing they ask is about family and friends. As part of the question why you've come to a matchmaker.'

I give a short laugh. 'That's easy. No family, no friends.'

She raises an eyebrow. 'None?'

'No close family. We — my husband never wanted children. My parents died ten years ago, within a short time of each other. They were in their eighties and not in good health.'

'I'm sorry.' Vivien makes another note. 'Siblings?

'No.' It's strictly true after all, though I wish it wasn't so. 'I'm an only child. A late one — my mother had turned forty when she had me. I have two cousins but we lost touch.'

'And no friends? You poor lamb.'

I sigh. It's hard to think back, to articulate it. 'My husband was … very controlling. I think it's called coercive control now, but really, if I'm honest, it was just bullying. It was only once he'd … gone that I realised quite how bad it had been. He was never physically violent but —'

I trail off and Vivien picks up the slack. 'Let me guess. He didn't like you having friends. Wanted you for himself. Gradually persuaded you to let them go. Along with the cousins.'

I nod gratefully. 'It was exactly like that, yes. And now I want — company. Someone kind. I don't even care what they look like, or not much anyway. Just kind. Someone who'll be nice to me, look after me. I think I deserve some happiness.' I feel my voice start to quaver, and stop.

Vivien reaches across and pats my hand. 'I understand. I'm sure I can find you your soulmate. Give you a second chance at happiness.' We chat some more, batting little questions to each other, but it's clear that she has what she needs. Or almost.

'Just one last thing,' she says. 'I have to check your ID. Irritating interfering regulation — KYC they call it. Know Your Client. It's to prevent money laundering. So would you mind if I took a look at your passport?'

I find my passport and pass it to Vivien, who gives it a cursory glance and hands it back to me. 'Thank you. Faulkner's your married name, I assume?'

I nod, and Vivien makes a brief note then slips the notebook and pen back into her bag as she stands up. 'That's all, my dear. Thank you so much for your time. I'll be in touch very soon with some suggestions.'

There's something that's bothering me and I need to clear it up before Vivien goes any further. It's true that Robert left me a lot of money, but according to the solicitor handling the estate most of it was tied up in the precious stones or in accounts in his own name. We had a joint account which was mainly used for what Robert called 'housekeeping money', and his monthly infusions, though more than adequate for that purpose, stopped once his other accounts were frozen pending some official milestone called probate. So ironically I'm having to watch the pennies for the time being. When I began to research dating agencies, I was horrified at the mouth-watering amounts they charged upfront.

I swallow, but force myself to speak. I feel my shoulders tense and my colour rise as the words stumble out, part question and part explanation. 'It's … about the money. I just need … I'm not sure I can —'

Vivien steps in smartly.

'My dear,' she says. 'I know exactly what you're going to ask. Don't be embarrassed. I too am shocked at how most agencies operate. It's another way in which MadeInHeaven differentiates itself. I'm demanding about the clients I take on, as you'll have seen. I meet them, in their home, and ask a lot of intrusive questions. And I have good intuition. I know if a potential client is a good fit for MadeInHeaven. And if they are, that means I'm sure I can find them that match made in heaven. Maybe not with the first or even the second introduction, but

I'll find you your Mr Right. And I'm so confident about that that, for some clients, I don't ask for payment of our fee until it happens.'

Some clients. Not all, it seems, and Vivien asks me, delicately, not to enter into any discussion about fees with potential Mr Rights.

I see her out then flop back down onto the sofa. I'm exhausted but exhilarated. And proud of myself for having taken this step, daunting as it was. But MadeInHeaven was a good choice, and I'm clearly in a safe pair of hands with Vivien.

*

'She's perfect. It's so good to have a new client who's going to be easy to place. We could do with the fees.'

Vivien takes the glass of champagne that Max hands her. He pours another for himself and raises the flute, dipping it towards her. 'I'll drink to that.'

'Widow. Recent widow, can't wait to find Mr Right. By all accounts her late husband was Mr Wrong. Coercive controller.'

'Who weaned her off her friends?'

'Got it in one. So no one to put her off the idea of matchmaking, like so many potential clients. And she's an only child and her parents are both dead. A couple of cousins, but they were never close even before Mr Wrong and they lost contact a while ago. And she's sweet, and so keen.'

Max touches Vivien's elbow and they move out of the kitchen towards the love seat that has pride of place in the sitting room. It's an S-shaped one, which Max said was strictly called a tête-à-tête seat, but they've always called it their love seat. They sink into the two semi-circular halves, upholstered in soft rose velvet, and twist a little to face each other across the divide. They kiss, but it's complicated when they're holding nearly full glasses so it's just a tender touching of the lips. There'll be time for more later.

'A pretty widow?' asks Max.

Vivien laughs. 'Pretty enough,' she says. 'But what you really mean is —'

'A rich widow?'

'Very, it seems.' And this time it's Vivien who tilts her flute, scarlet lipstick on the frosted rim.

*

I'm drifting round the house, trying to see it with Vivien's eyes, with the eyes of the Mr Right she's promised to find, when my mobile rings. It's a number I don't recognise, but it turns out to be Vivien. She'd had No Caller ID on our initial call, but tells me she's cancelled the ID block for me now I'm a client so I can call her whenever I want. I start to gabble my thanks for yesterday's interview.

'You're so welcome, Stephanie.' Her voice sounds softer, sweeter, as though she's smiling. 'You're a perfect client. Open about all that annoying personal information. You wouldn't believe how difficult it can be for me to find out what I need. But that's a sign in itself — if someone resents the questions, I suspect they have something to hide and don't go further with them.'

'You were very polite about the questions,' I say, thinking some reply is needed. 'Explained very clearly why you needed to know.'

'Thank you my dear. I just wanted to follow up — I stopped when I did yesterday because I could see you were getting tired. Just a couple more questions. Much lighter and easier than before! Can you give me an idea of your likes and dislikes? Culture, sport, anything that springs to mind really.'

I rack my brain but nothing springs to mind. I used to enjoy going to the cinema but Robert preferred to watch films at home. And I used to go to art galleries but Robert didn't like me to mingle too much, so that petered out too. The silence becomes heavier. Eventually I say, 'Opera. We used to go to the opera.'

'Was that your choice?' Vivien's voice is gentle.

I hear the whisper of a sigh and realise it's mine. 'No. I hated

9

it to be honest.'

Vivien laughs, but it's a kind laugh. 'Don't worry. I've had clients before who've been in that sort of relationship. We'll manage. The main thing is, you've taken this big step towards a better future. I admire your courage, I really do.'

\*

Vivien is leafing through her client list. She keeps it in longhand, reassuring her clients that she makes no digital record of them, leaves no digital trace. Some of the younger ones find it quaint while most of the older ones thank her effusively.

She turns a page towards Max, sitting opposite her at the dining table. 'I think maybe Harry would work as a first date for Stephanie?'

'The new one,' says Max. He scans the page. 'Hmm. From what you said we know so little about what she wants, what she likes —'

'*She* knows so little,' Vivien corrects him. 'The poor lamb. She's had everything washed out of her by Mr Wrong. But you're right, she's a bit of a blank canvas so in a sense it doesn't matter who we try.'

'Harry seems OK. Easy. But almost certainly not quite right.'

'A bit too bluff, too hearty,' agrees Vivien. 'But we have to start somewhere.'

# TWO

I can't believe Vivien has already found me a date. She laughs when I say that, but again it's a kind sort of laugh. Not like Robert laughing at me.

'It's what I do, Stephanie,' she says. 'Nothing is more important to me than making my clients happy. I hope you'll like Harry. It's hard to be sure with a client like —'

'Like me?' My voice catches. 'Difficult to match?'

'I don't mean it like that,' she says swiftly. 'As I've said, I've had clients before who've come out of an abusive relationship. It's hard to know yourself after that. It takes time. But I thought you'd want me to start looking for introductions sooner rather than later.'

'I do. Of course I do. Thank you.' It sounds like a prayer.

I spend ages getting ready for the date. How long is it since I've been out without Robert? Apart from the funeral of course. I push the thought away. I'm careful with my make-up — not too much, don't want to look tarty, but don't want to look washed out, ghostly, either. And jewellery's another problem. Robert wasn't on the retail side of the gemstone business, but he had opportunities to acquire precious stones at wholesale prices, said they were our pensions. He had some set for me — sapphire earrings, a silver and ruby necklace, diamond rings — before he stopped buying me anything. I love the pieces, the look of them, the feel of them, the necklace running through my fingers like water, and sometimes take them out of the home safe to handle them, stroke them, but I don't like the memories they carry. I wear the necklace none the less, but choose plainer earrings.

But the worst is deciding what to wear. I'm meeting Harry for dinner. I googled the restaurant — not too smart but not too casual, not too bright but not too dark, not (according to the reviews) too noisy but not too quiet. A Goldilocks venue. Perhaps nudged by the memory, I dress childishly. A plain blouse with a Peter Pan collar, a knee-length pleated skirt, a lambswool cardigan, black pumps.

*

Vivien said I should ask to be seated when I arrive at the restaurant; that way there'd be no awkward scanning of faces at the bar. She's told Harry the same. I'm a punctual person, especially since my marriage — Robert couldn't abide lateness. Though of course he was late himself now, I think, with a small private smile.

Harry clearly isn't a punctual person. I sit alone at the table for an uncomfortable fifteen minutes. The waiter asks me twice if I'd like to order a drink while I wait, but I'm not sure what the protocol is so I don't. Eventually a ginger-haired man is shown to the table. He seems bigger than his actual height, I think because he's constantly on the move — shrugging off his jacket, waving away the waiter who tries to take it, hanging it on his chair then pulling the chair out, starting to sit down, getting up again to lean over the table, hand extended to me. I take it and shake it, surprised by the formality. Is this what happens on dates now? Or maybe only on first matchmakers' dates.

'Hello,' he booms. 'I'm Harry. Hello Stephanie! So good to meet you. Have you had a drink? Not yet? Let's see what's on offer.'

He buries himself in the enormous folding card that's laid across his place setting. 'What do you drink, Stephanie? What would you like? A cocktail? White, red, rosé? Or maybe the wine should wait till we've chosen our mains. A glass of champagne?'

Reeling at the unaccustomed onslaught of words and the terrifying range of options — Robert had always been quiet and measured when he spoke, and also usually chose for me — I nod dumbly.

Over the icy bubbles the onslaught continues. 'Let me tell you something about myself. I'm a lawyer. A barrister. You know, the wig and the funny collars and the Dracula cloak. Or maybe Batman, a force for good in the struggle against evil! Though that suggests a criminal lawyer, which I'm not. Or not in the sense you probably think I mean — murder, rape, burglary. But it can be criminal law, what I do, in another sense. Financial shenanigans. Wheeler dealing, sailing too close to the wind. Dodgy transactions. Long complicated trials. Better fees than the murder guys.'

Harry laughs loudly as though he's made a funny joke. And thankfully pauses to take a gulp of champagne, emptying half his flute. I sip mine, relishing the silence. Then realise my eyes are closed, better to enjoy the peace, and snap them open, worried that he thinks I'm rude. But he clearly hasn't noticed, and ploughs on. I tune out most of the detail, picking up the prominent words as if I were skim reading.

'Oxford. Christchurch. Rowing blue. Inner Temple. Notting Hill. Wife. Actress. Unfaithful. Divorce.' He pauses again, drains his glass and beams at me, as if expecting praise. Then gestures wildly to the waiter. 'Another glass of the same please. Susanna — sorry, Stephanie?'

I shake my head. Harry picks up the main menu and the cascade of words resumes. Calamari, chorizo, carpaccio. Magret, medaillons, moules. Rillettes, rognons, Rossini. I zone out again, feeling as though I'm in a language lesson.

Three courses, two bottles of wine (of which Harry drinks the lion's share, I'm not a big drinker) and a much needed espresso later, I'm exhausted. I'm not used to company and Harry is probably overwhelming at the best of times. I worry about the bill then remember Vivien saying that Harry will pick it up the first time. I'm not sure that there will be a second time though.

*

Vivien calls the following morning and suggests that we debrief over a coffee. 'The office always seems so formal. Perfect for the boring stuff — the admin, the paperwork — but for the heart-to-hearts I prefer somewhere more relaxed, more intimate.' She proposes a café in Bloomsbury and we meet a couple of days later.

It's a busy, bustling place, heady with the fragrance of roast beans, cinnamon and almonds. But there's a quiet room at the back, the few customers working on their laptops, their ears cocooned in headphones or stoppered with white earbuds.

I'm nervous, not sure what to say, and sit twisting my rings. I should take them off, these relics of my engagement and marriage, fossils from an earlier epoch. But my knuckles must have swollen slightly over the years, though I'm not conscious of any arthritis, and the rings stubbornly stay when I try to slide them off. Maybe a jeweller would know how to remove them.

Vivien, empathetic and diplomatic as ever, cuts through my silent discomfort. 'I'm sorry,' she says, patting my hand. The one without the rings. 'I have the impression that it didn't work out with Harry. I'd normally suggest persevering, having another meeting or two — both parties are often so nervous on a first date that it flops, but the next time can be fine. Tell me how it went so we can decide whether to do that or try again.'

I try and organise my thoughts. 'He seems very nice,' I concede, determined to start with a positive. 'And friendly. But … this sounds silly, but so noisy, so busy, talking so much.' And all about himself, I think, but don't want to appear overly critical of Vivien's first offering. Harry didn't ask me a single thing about me or my history, at least not that I can recall.

Vivien smiled. 'I can tell you're an only child,' she says. I blink, surprised for an instant. 'If you'd been brought up with

14

brothers, like I was, you'd think it was quite normal. Mind you, it is normal for many men to talk mostly about themselves.' I blink again. Did I say that after all?

'I'm just assuming that's what he did,' she continues. 'I think … As I say, I usually recommend another meeting or two before giving up, but I can quite see that for you someone quieter, more thoughtful would be more suitable. Let me go back to the drawing board, my dear. I'm sorry about Harry, but I'm learning about you all the time. I hope at least you had a good meal!'

I nod. 'I did, thank you. It was delicious.' But I'm pleased she's going to look again.

\*

'So Harry didn't work out then?'

Max is in the kitchen, leaning against the counter as he watches Vivien deftly putting together a salad.

'Sadly not.' Vivien turns to face him. 'As we thought, too loud, too cheery. But it's helped me know her better. I did wonder about James, but I'm not sure. Maybe Thomas next.'

Max agrees. 'Well, he'll certainly be an antidote to Harry. And again, she'll reveal a little more of herself. Another step nearer the perfect match.'

\*

I can't believe Vivien's done it again, so quickly.

'Thomas is very different from Harry,' she explained. 'Maybe too far at the other end of the spectrum. But he's kind and gentle and I'd like to see what you think of him.'

I'm getting ready for dinner with him. With hindsight I think I underdressed for Harry. Too plain, too childish. And even though it didn't work out with him, somehow the evening, or perhaps the fact that I survived it, and Vivien's faith in me as a client, have given me a confidence I haven't felt for a long time.

I flick through the plastic shrouds hanging in my wardrobe

and pull out a clingy dress in what I think is called 'teal' now. Not only clingy but a bit low cut — a sort of cross-over of soft stretchy fabric pulled tight. I haven't worn it outside for a long time. Robert said I looked tarty in it, but then he thought I looked tarty in most things. But he liked me to wear it at home. It was OK to look tarty for him, it seemed.

I'm a bit more daring with the jewellery today also, and complete the look with kitten heels and a short swing coat in bright red with big brassy buttons.

This time I misjudge how long it will take to find the restaurant and arrive early. I'm shown to the empty table and when I'm offered a drink while I wait, I ask for a sparkling water with ice and lemon. It comes in a chilled cut-glass tumbler, beaded with condensation.

'Stephanie Faulkner?'

A tall, spare man is shown to the table. He's handsome in a slightly austere way. Chiselled face, silvering hair. Like Harry, he offers me his hand, then sits down neatly opposite me with much less noise and bustle.

'A drink, sir?'

Thomas asks for a tomato juice, unseasoned. He sees my glass and frowns slightly. 'I assume you don't want another G&T yet?'

'It's just water,' I say hastily, but he looks unconvinced. Perhaps I should offer him a sniff or a sip.

'Shall we order?' he says, and gestures at my menu. I should have looked at it while I was waiting. 'You go first,' I suggest, thinking I may just have what he's having and avoid another language lesson.

He glances at his menu and frowns again. 'I'll have the consommé,' he tells the waiter. 'Followed by the sole. Steamed, no butter.'

'Very good sir,' says the waiter. 'And on the side?'

Thomas scans the list. 'Potatoes, carrots, peas — no, no, I don't mean I want them, I'm looking for something less starchy. Ah, here we are finally. I'll have the spinach and ... yes, and broccoli. Steamed also, no butter.' He puts his menu down and looks at me expectantly.

Whatever else, Robert loved to eat well and had a hearty appetite. Going to restaurants was one of the few things we enjoyed doing together. How could I have forgotten that when Vivien first asked me what I liked? I was nervous, I suppose. And fragments of my marriage come to me randomly, like pieces of a scattered jigsaw puzzle. Eating out with Robert wasn't always relaxing — I learnt quickly not to catch the barman's eye or banter with the waiter. But I'd shared his love of good food, and that did not include steamed white fish or broccoli without butter. I run my eyes over the lists of starters and mains. Thankfully this one's mostly in English.

'I'll have the smoked eel,' I say. A sudden memory, another fragment, surfaces. Robert always said you should never have smoked eel without Gewürtztraminer. But perhaps it would be risky to suggest that, given Thomas's reaction to my reckless glass of water.

The waiter smiles approvingly. 'Excellent choice, madame. Can I suggest a glass of Gewürtztraminer to accompany it? We have a very good Hugel.'

I glance at Thomas whose lips are tight, but perhaps that's because he's looking at my cleavage which I realise is a little more visible than I'd thought. What the heck. I nod at the waiter. He makes a note and looks back at me.

'And for your main, madame?'

'I'll take the slow roast pork belly,' I say firmly. 'With … yes, with the buttery mashed potatoes and roasted seasonal root vegetables.'

The waiter looks happier as he jots down my more decadent order and asks about wine. Thomas says he'll have a small glass of Chablis and glances at me. I ask for a small glass of whatever the chef recommends with the pork. The waiter takes the menus and heads off. Silence falls on our table.

Thomas clears his throat and we both speak at once.

'I have to be careful about my—'

'This restaurant is lovely.'

We both pause, and I let him resume.

'I have to be careful about what I eat,' he explains. 'I have a cousin who died young, of a heart attack, and I'm rigorous about my cholesterol levels.'

Thomas would probably think Robert had invited his own heart attack with his lusty appetite, but I put it down to stress. The relentless toll of all that aggression he held back, at least most of the time, his drive to earn ever more money, the emotional rusting of constant and unwarranted jealousy about his wife.

We make desultory conversation as we wait for our starters. Thomas is a merchant banker. I never really knew what they did and Thomas clearly senses this lacuna in my knowledge and explains at length and in detail. Not that I'm much the wiser.

He does at least ask me a few things about myself, but in fairness I don't have a lot to say. Studied fine art. Had a job at an art gallery which was more boring that I'd expected, mostly trying to persuade prospective buyers to open their wallets for over-priced and indifferent pieces. Stopped work when I married. I don't intend to describe my marriage with any colour, and fudge the cause of Robert's death to pre-empt any further discussion of cholesterol.

*

Vivien leans back in the impressive but not terribly comfortable Chesterfield. It was she who suggested that she come back to Stephanie's house for the Thomas debrief, thinking that it would be useful for her to have one more visit before deciding how to move on.

'I feel I should apologise,' says Stephanie, twisting her hands in her lap. 'Is it me? Am I more difficult, more picky, less attractive than your other clients?'

'Of course not, my dear,' replies Vivien, her voice soothing. 'And if anyone needs to apologise, it's me. As I said at the outset, it sometimes takes me a while to get to know a new client well. Especially when — well, let's say a client who's fresh from an abusive or controlling relationship may have lost track of who they really are, and certainly lost confidence in their own ability to form a new and successful relationship.'

She takes a sip of Stephanie's excellent coffee while she reflects.

'And as for less attractive — definitely not. Both Harry and Thomas commented on how pretty you were, though I do try and discourage the gentlemen from focusing solely on looks. Not always with much success, I have to say.'

Vivien pauses again, returns Stephanie's amused smile, pleased that her client is visibly relaxing. 'Also, I probably rushed you a bit,' she resumes. 'I was so keen to find you the right partner, start you on the next stage of your life in a well-deserved better place than your past, that I pressed on. I should perhaps have spent longer getting to know you.'

'Restaurants,' says Stephanie suddenly. 'And wine. I remembered that that's something Robert and I enjoyed doing together.'

'As long as you didn't flirt with the waiter, I'm guessing?'

'Yes,' admits Stephanie. 'But it's still something I enjoyed that hasn't been spoiled. And art. I remembered when I was telling Thomas about myself —'

'Ah, yes. Thomas I'm sure was much less self-centred in his conversation than Harry.'

'He was. Anyway, I still love art. I gave up my job in a gallery when I married Robert, so that's not tainted either.' Stephanie pauses, chews her lower lip. 'I don't like being negative. Thomas wasn't bad company. And he's very handsome. But … just not for me. We didn't click. He's a bit too — ascetic, that's the word. I don't think it's worth another date.'

Vivien stretches out her elegant legs, then crosses one over the other and settles herself more comfortably on the sofa. 'I agree. And the good news is that I have someone who's much more suitable. I don't know why I didn't think of James earlier. Although to be fair he's been on holiday for the last few weeks, only recently got back.'

# THREE

'So Thomas wasn't a great hit either?'

Max and Vivien have finished dinner. Vivien, who prides herself on her cooking, always makes a special effort on Fridays. Max has ordered in some good wine, spending a little more than usual.

Vivien takes a sip of tonight's offering, a Chambolle-Musigny on the cusp of perfection. She tries not to think what it must have cost. Which makes her think of Stephanie. She's a sweet girl — woman, she corrects herself automatically, she's well into her forties after all, but there's something of the ingénue about her. It's pleasing to see her character gradually emerge from the chrysalis her marriage forced her to build round herself. Vivien tries not to get too attached to her clients, knowing that once they've found Mr Right she barely sees them again, but she doesn't always succeed. She'll miss Stephanie. Vivien is sure that James is The One. And thinks fondly of the whirlwind courtship, the fairy tale wedding, the romantic honeymoon that awaits her client. Stephanie's fee would be useful, whatever Vivien told her, but she's happy to wait.

'No,' she replies. 'As you thought, darling. But I really think she'll love James. Literally, I hope — fall in love, dive in headfirst. She deserves it, the poor dear. I'm so excited for her. She so wants the whole Mills & Boon package.'

'Tell me more about James. He's a new client, I assume?'

'Almost. He had a couple of first dates a few weeks ago. They didn't work out and since then he's been on a break abroad. Italy, was it? Very indulgent by the sound of it. Yes, it was definitely Italy. Restaurants in Piedmont and Rome, culture in Florence and Venice. Anyway, he got back recently and he's really keen to meet Stephanie.'

*

Again, Vivien has really pulled out all the stops. She phoned yesterday to say she'd be in Hampstead this morning and could she drop round for a chat. I'm worried that she's giving up on me and, over coffee, admit that I feel discouraged by the lack of success so far, but Vivien says that's absolutely the wrong approach. Both Harry and Thomas liked me, it seems, and would have been happy to meet again, but I agree with Vivien that there's no point as I hadn't felt that 'click'.

And then, with one of her charming smiles, she says that the client she'd mentioned, James Anderson, is keen to meet me and that she thinks he'll be a much better fit. She also says that the first two dates will have been good for building my confidence — I'll have a better idea of what to expect, be more comfortable going into a restaurant on my own to meet someone for the first time, starting the evening more relaxed. She's right, I'm sure.

She's been so understanding about the money as well. My solicitor's still waiting for Robert's probate and I raise the subject with her before she leaves. I'm hesitant, feeling embarrassed to discuss finance again, but also conscious that she's put so much effort into finding my Mr Right and hasn't had a penny from me yet. I tell her that I'll have control of my money very soon so can pay the introduction fee, or whatever it's called, if she wants.

'My dear, that's sweet of you. But as I said, I don't like to take any payment until I know that I've done my side of the bargain. Let's see how it goes with James. But I have high hopes this time.' She winks at me, a smooth, suggestive flutter of an eyelid, freighted with promise, and I smile back, feeling reassured and hopeful and excited.

\*

I'm quite used now to choosing what to wear for a date. Who'd have thought it! Vivien's right, meeting Harry and Thomas has given me confidence even though they didn't work out. I hope James is a better fit. Now I've had the experience of socialising with new people — three of them in as many weeks! — I thirst for more. But just one more. I shouldn't think in terms of a second husband, but I can't help myself. A second marriage, a good one, to a kind and loving man. I deserve a happy ending, surely?

I leaf through my wardrobe again, the slender sheaths like the spines of books on a shelf. Reading, that's another love I should have mentioned to Vivien. I feel as though my brain is waking from a long slumber, like a fairy tale. Or a long winter, like in Narnia. Always winter, never Christmas. A good description of my first marriage. Giddy with excitement, I text Vivien.

*Am so looking forward to meeting James! And just remembered another interest I forgot - books and reading! Thanks for everything. Fingers crossed for this eve! I'll text you after. Stephanie x*

I remember too late Vivien's no-texting policy. It's part of what she calls her data privacy paranoia. 'It's all in a good cause, my dear. I've got my clients' best interests at heart, and though I know there's not a legal problem provided I have your consent, and that you'd always be sensible, I prefer to have a blanket rule. Some clients are so indiscreet — sending explicit texts, both good and bad. So let's stick to speaking by phone and, even better, face to face.'

James and I arrive at the restaurant at the same time. He's standing behind me as I give my name to the woman at the welcome desk and taps me gently on the shoulder. I look round and see a good-looking man with a friendly smile.

'James Anderson,' he says. He doesn't offer to shake my hand, but touches my upper arm instead — it's a warmer gesture, less formal, and I feel it's a good omen. The evening is already different in two ways from my previous dates.

The woman takes our coats and James's hat — I hadn't noticed he was holding a Fedora — and shows us to the table together. The restaurant is cosy and comfortable but not too crowded. There's a candle on our table and a small posy of yellow freesias, casting a sweet but not overpowering scent, and a background murmur of conversation from the other customers.

James asks whether I'd like a glass of champagne to start. I wonder whether this is a bad omen since Harry did the same, but everything else is so different this time that I tell myself not to be superstitious and accept graciously.

We start talking over the fizz — James doesn't swig it like Harry did, another difference — and have so much to say that I'm aware of the waitress hovering on the edge of my field of vision a couple of times, clearly not sure whether to intrude. She doesn't, and I'm glad.

James asks me all about myself, and I tell him what little there is. But it takes longer than the cursory account I gave Thomas, and I enjoy it more. I feel that I'm describing the real person that I was and hope to become again. Am already becoming, perhaps. And James is listening, seems genuinely interested in what I'm saying.

I pause for another sip of champagne — my mouth is quite dry. 'We should order,' says James, his eyes crinkling in a smile. 'We're chatting so much they might be closing before we've eaten at this rate!'

I stifle a laugh and pick up my menu as James gestures amiably at the waitress, who is still circling our table at a polite distance. I choose scallops and rack of lamb, and am relieved when James orders foie gras and ribeye steak with no mention of cholesterol.

I try and turn the conversation away from me and ask

James about himself. He's an IT consultant. 'Boring,' he says, with a self-deprecatory moue of distaste. 'But it pays well and there's always work. I'm freelance, so I can pick and choose and work when I need to. And not work when I don't. I love to travel. In fact I'm just back from a short break — well, not so short really, I was away for a few weeks, couldn't get enough of it — in Italy.'

The waitress brings our main courses and pours a splash of the red wine that James ordered into his glass. He buries his nose in the glass and inhales deeply with his eyes closed, then lets it roll round his mouth as he savours the taste. All done smoothly and easily. Harry just gulped his tasting portion, nodded vigorously and thrust out his glass for more. And Thomas sipped his Chablis with a caution that appeared to verge on apprehension.

'Delicious,' says James with a nod at the waitress, who fills my glass then tops up his. A Barolo, I see from the label. Italian I think.


Over our demi-tasse coffees, James asks where I live. I'm pleased that Vivien hasn't divulged my address — she said at the outset that the only information she gives one client about another is his or her name and an indication of likes, dislikes and profession, if any. And, I assume from our first conversation, a reassurance about gold-diggers. 'We take our data privacy obligations very seriously,' she'd repeated.

'I'm only asking in case we can share a taxi,' James adds. When I say Hampstead, he looks pleased. 'Just up the road from me,' he says. 'If you're happy to share, we can drop you off en route. I live in Belsize Park. For the moment anyway. I sold my house a few weeks ago, got an offer that was too good to refuse even though I hadn't found anywhere myself by then. So I'm renting. Must start looking again now I'm back.'

James glances at the bill when the waitress brings it over and hands her an Amex card. When the payment's gone through the machine and he's putting the card back in his wallet, he says, keeping his eyes down as if uncertain how to put it, 'Stephanie, I … erm, I'm not actually sure what the protocol is. But I want to say, I'd love to see you again. Do we need to arrange it through the agency do you know? I've never got beyond a first date before. Not that I've had many.'

'Same here,' I say, laughing. 'I don't know. I think we can do what we like as long as we let Vivien — Ms Harrison — know.'

When the taxi coasts to a halt outside my house, James leans forward — he's been sitting opposite me on one of the folding-out seats — and brushes my cheek with his lips. We've agreed to meet again on Friday, and exchanged mobile numbers. James says he always uses WhatsApp as his phone sometimes loses text messages, so I must remember that.

'It's been a lovely evening,' he says. 'Looking forward to the next one.'

'Me too! Thanks so much. Have a good few days.' I scramble — I hope not too inelegantly — out of the taxi and turn on my front step, haloed in the security light, to wave. The taxi waits until I go inside and close the door. What a gentleman.

*

The following morning, I'm about to call Vivien when she calls me.

'I'm sorry,' I get in quickly. 'About the text. I was so excited I just forgot.'

There's a faint echo of a sigh, then Vivien says, 'Don't worry about it, Stephanie. But I'd prefer if we stick to the no-text rule. It's just easier for me to have one rule for all my clients.'

'Of course,' I say meekly. Then I feel my cheeks and my voice warming as I rush on. 'Vivien, we — at least I, and I hope James — had such a lovely evening. Thank you so much for setting it up. I really like him.'

'I'm so glad, though not surprised. I was calling to suggest we meet, but we can talk now if you prefer?'

I hesitate for a moment. I feel gay in the old sense, almost giddy, and leap at the thought of a small excursion with more information about James at the end of it. But Vivien must be a busy woman and probably prefers to save her time. 'Why don't we carry on chatting now?'

'So I've spoken to James,' she says. 'He called earlier. I gather you're meeting again on Friday?'

'Yes.' I feel colour rise to my cheeks in anticipation. 'I hope — is that all right? That we made the plan without you?'

'Of course,' says Vivien, her voice warm. 'I've done my first job, which is bringing together two people who spark. As you know, it can take a couple of attempts. But as I got to know you better, I felt increasingly sure about James. If he hadn't been away I'd maybe have introduced you to him first, but it's not a bad thing to get a feel for other men.'

'Has he — or maybe this is indiscreet, just say if so — had many introductions? He did tell me he also hadn't got past a first date.'

'Until now, by the sound of it!' says Vivien. She sounds as happy as I feel. I can see why she's so successful at what she does. 'But no, he also only had a couple of previous meets. He then got very caught up with selling his house and after that had gone through he went off to Italy to recover. Treated himself by all accounts.'

There's a pause, and I realise my mind has drifted to thoughts of our next date.

'Let me know how you get on, Stephanie. Keep in touch.'

'Of course,' I say, shocked. Surely she doesn't think I'm going to disappear into the sunset without paying her fee?

'I just mean,' says Vivien, in that warm, kind voice, 'I take a personal interest in my clients' happiness. So keep me in the loop.'

I'm sure she'll let me know if and when — I hope 'when', and surreptitiously touch the wooden table leg — she feels it's time to collect. And my solicitor emailed just before Vivien to say that probate had been granted, so I'll be in a position to pay her whenever she asks.

# FOUR

I'm sipping my morning coffee on Friday when my phone chimes with a WhatsApp from James.

*Hi Stephanie, v much looking forward to this eve. I've booked an outside table at The Oyster Shed (on Thames). Let me know if that's OK. NB don't worry if you don't like oysters, there's lots of other stuff on the menu! See you at 8? Jx*

The kiss is nice but I'm not so sure about an oyster shed. It sounds a bit basic but Google is reassuring. The Oyster Shed has, as James suggested, an extensive and tempting range of food, and the river terrace looks inviting. I spent the day agonising over what to wear — I'd had in mind a new dress but decide to keep it for another occasion, somewhere smarter and indoors, and instead choose white jeans and a clingy cashmere sweater in aquamarine. Even with a jumper I guess it might be cool so I fold a soft pashmina into my bag, give myself a spritz of scent, and set off.

As it happens I do like oysters, as does James. We share a dozen for a starter while we decide on the mains. 'There's no rush,' he says. He was waiting when I arrived; I do like punctuality in a man. Even though I feel I'm gaining confidence daily, I'm still uncomfortable in a restaurant on my

27

own.

The Oyster Shed is stunning. Views up and down the river — London Bridge and the ghost of Tower Bridge beyond in one direction, the dome of St Paul's silhouetted against the sky, which is gradually turning more fiery as the sun slowly sinks, in the other, the striking needle of the Shard across from us. It's cool but he's chosen a sheltered table next to a patio heater and I'm wearing exactly the right clothes.

'I just thought,' says James, topping up the New Zealand Sauvignon blanc he ordered to accompany the oysters, 'that you might like to eat somewhere different this evening. I mean different from the more formal, fine-dining restaurants that you — well, both of us—' he smiles ruefully '— have been to on first dates. The ones that didn't work and the one that did.' He touches my hand. 'At least I hope it did.'

'It did for me,' I say softly. 'And yes, this is perfect. It's nice to be somewhere more relaxing. And outside.' I squeeze a couple of drops from the muslin-covered half lemon onto another oyster and tip it into my mouth. I never tire of the silky brine, the taste of the sea.

Later, we walk along the river to the Millennium Bridge. The Tate Modern squats across the river. 'We should meet there one time,' says James, dipping his head towards it. 'For lunch maybe, or an early evening drink. There's a nice restaurant, and I'm a member.'

'What a lovely idea.' I hadn't realised he was interested in art. Then I recall he mentioned spending hours in the Uffizi when he was in Florence recently. I don't think I fully took in everything he said on that first date. Mostly he asked about me, which was sweet of him. Next time — I'm sure there'll be a next time, this evening was so enjoyable and I don't think it was just on my side — I must remember to ask him more about himself.

We walk to Blackfriars station. James suggests a night cap at the Blackfriar pub — apparently there are stunning Art Nouveau mosaics inside — but though I'm tempted I'm also tired; we've lingered companionably over the meal and it's later than I thought. On the tube, James insists on staying on until my stop, even though it's better for him to get off at the one before, and walks me home. I wonder if I should invite him in, but I'm sagging with exhaustion now.

He seems to read my mind. Before we step into the pool of light illuminating the front door, he pulls me towards him, tips up my chin and gives me a long, gentle kiss. 'I won't come in,' he says, and I feel a mixture of relief and regret. But there will be a next time. Before he turns to go, he says, 'This evening was so wonderful. Let's meet again soon. Maybe something around Blackfriars and Tate Modern; it'll seem like a continuation. I'll message you tomorrow.'

I murmur my thanks and let myself in as he waits and watches. I almost blow him a kiss before closing the door but decide it might be too forward, so just give a little wave, a ripple of my fingers.

*

We return to the City on the following Saturday. James says the only evenings the Tate Modern restaurant is open are Fridays and Saturdays and we plan our excursion around an early supper. We drift enjoyably, if uncomprehendingly, round an exhibition of baffling modern art involving coat hangers, then repair to the restaurant for a light meal with a superb view over the river. And this time we agree to stop at the Blackfriar to round the evening off with another glass of wine.

We sit inside — and what an inside it is! Sitting under the curved vault which glows with extraordinary rich mosaics, I almost feel that I'm in an early renaissance church. It's certainly more my type of art than this afternoon's exhibition. And James's also it seems.

He glances around him with satisfaction. 'Every time I come here, which isn't often, I realise I've forgotten how stunning it is. It reminds me of Italy. Torcello in particular — the island off Venice, with a cathedral with amazing mosaics. Somewhat older than these of course!'

I have a vague recollection from my history of art course.

29

'I've never been to Venice.'

'Oh, you must,' says James, taking my hand. 'We —' He breaks off. My heart skips a beat. Was he about to suggest we go together, that he show me the artistic sights? But then I think that maybe he was talking about a trip he made with another woman. Which reminds me that I planned to ask him more about himself.

'You were so thoughtful,' I say, 'on our first date. So interested in me. Drawing me out. Not like, well, one at least of my previous first dates. But I never got the chance to ask about you. I know you're an IT consultant, that you're between houses and currently renting a flat in Belsize Park, that you like art and food and wine, but what else?'

'What else do I like?'

'What else everything!'

'Hmm.' James gazes reflectively into this glass. 'It's a fairly brief everything. Computer science at uni, hence the IT. Not very interesting sometimes, but there's always work around for someone who keeps themselves on top of the changes.' He pauses for more wine, then adds, 'I was married. And then we split up a couple of years ago.'

I murmur something vague and ambiguous, not sure what the protocol is. I certainly don't want to offend James, say something out of turn.

He smiles, if a little ruefully. 'You don't need to say anything. It was a marriage that was never meant to be. Not particularly bad but not good enough to last a lifetime. It took us a while to work that out and then to extricate ourselves. It was as amicable as a divorce can be. No children, which helped. But it dragged on because I wanted to buy her out of the house so I could stay there. I loved that house, but she wanted her half share in cash. I had enough investments to raise the money, at least I had until Fred Linwood went belly up. I'd stupidly put almost all my money into various funds of his, so most of it evaporated overnight, and what was in the more robust funds was frozen.'

I vaguely remember Robert talking about Linwood, and crowing about his own canniness in having nothing invested with him. It sounds as though he'd been right.

'Anyway,' James resumes, 'Laura needed her share of the money ASAP, she'd found somewhere to buy. So I — we — had to sell the house after all. But we had a good offer and at least I've got my share, for when I start house-hunting. And the frozen funds will thaw and there should be some compensation eventually for the others.'

'And MadeInHeaven?' I ask. 'What made you approach them? Did you try others? How did you hear about them?' James was so attractive, such easy company that I would have thought he'd have no problem finding a new woman. Not that I'd say as much, of course.

James sipped his wine, looking thoughtful. 'One day I suddenly realised that, what with the job and the divorce and the investments and the house sale and the move, I hadn't met anyone new for years. And also realised that my opportunities for doing so were limited. IT's still very much a male-dominated field. There are some women, of course, but they're few and far between.'

James pauses, glances up again at the glittering ceiling. 'We should …' he trails off and takes my hand.

'Stephanie, I don't want to crowd you. But I just want to put it on the table — I so enjoy our time together. I love being with you. I'd love to show you Venice. Other places too of course. When — I hope not if — you feel ready.'

We take the tube again, and again James walks me to my door. This time I invite him in. I serve us each a small glass of Robert's excellent Armagnac and then taste it a second time when he kisses me, long and hard, his hands on the curve of my buttocks. I feel stirred in a way I haven't for a long time, and wonder whether I should suggest he stay the night. Too forward? Too formal? Sex on the sofa? It's all so confusing, and I so want to get it right.

He lets me go, steps back and rests his hands lightly on my shoulders. 'I'm going to head home,' he says. 'It's late and you're tired. I can't think of anything I'd rather do right now than take you to bed, but I want to be sure it's what, and when, you want.'

'I — I do. But maybe …'

'Exactly,' he says easily. 'Let's go for deferred gratification. I have to be away for a few days next week I'm afraid. It's an in-house IT audit in Leeds. I signed up to it before I met you. I wish I hadn't now, of course, but I can't cancel at this short notice. I'm back on Thursday, but late. Are you free on Friday?'

A question with an easy answer. I'm always free except when I'm with James.

'Come to my flat?' he suggests. 'It's not very exciting, just a serviced rental so it's all a bit bland and corporate. Fortunately it's only temporary. But the kitchen's not bad, I can try and cook for you. It'll make a change from restaurants. Though it might not be a change for the better — I'm a lousy cook!'

'I'll cook for you!' I can hear the excitement and anticipation in my voice. 'I love to cook. I'll plan a menu and buy the ingredients. I'll keep it simple, nothing that needs obscure utensils or anything.'

James draws me towards him in a long, warm hug. 'That would be wonderful, Steph. I'll get some good wine. And I'll come and pick you up so you don't need to bother about a taxi.'

I kiss him again, then reluctantly pull back.

'Until Friday,' I say. 'I hope your travel and work go OK.'

'Until Friday,' he echoes. 'And Steph—'

I raise my eyebrows.

'Bring, you know, whatever you need. In case you want to stay the night. But only if you do.'

I feel my face creasing in a wide smile, which I hope hides the apprehension I feel alongside the excitement. It's a long time since I had sex with someone for the first time. And long enough since I had sex at all.

'I will,' I say.

*

Vivien is in the home office, poring over the agency's accounts, when she hears a faint ringtone.

'Darling,' calls Max from the sitting room. 'Your phone. The Stephanie phone.'

He comes in and hands it to her, just in time for her to answer.

'Stephanie, how lovely to—' she starts automatically, but her client's excited babble cuts across her.

'Vivien, I just wanted to say — I've had this wonderful delivery of flowers from James. He's away for a few days, on a work thing, and it was so sweet of him, and it reminded me that I've been meaning to call to say how well it's going and how perfect he is and how grateful I am. And—'

Stephanie grinds to a halt, presumably needing to draw breath. Vivien seizes her opportunity.

'My dear, I'm so thrilled for you. And I know James is very happy also. It sounds as though you're really enjoying each other's company.'

'Yes, very much. And we're finding interests in common — art, travel, food and drink. I'm cooking for him on Friday. I can't wait!'

Vivien wonders whether Stephanie is looking forward to more than preparing a meal. They may only have met a few times but judging from her client's fevered tone they're already contemplating the next step.

'I'm so pleased for you. I thought the two of you would hit it off. And thanks for keeping me in the loop, it's always lovely to hear from you. Enjoy your meal.' And the dessert or digestif. Vivien tries to be happy that they've progressed so quickly, but somehow can't muster the enthusiasm. Must be the accounts; Excel spreadsheets and numbers always give her a headache.

Max comes back in once she's finished the call, bearing two mugs of fragrant, frothy coffee. He sets them on her desk and gestures to the chair opposite hers. 'A quick break?' he suggests. 'Now that your concentration's been broken already? Even though by our favourite client.' He winks.

'Thanks, my love.' Vivien takes a long draught of coffee,

leans back and breathes out a long sigh.

'You look tired,' says Max, a slight frown puckering his forehead.

Vivien shakes her head. 'I'm fine,' she says shortly. 'Bloody accounts. Not that we're not going OK, but book-keeping always makes me wonder whether we shouldn't call it a day. We always said we'd work hard at it until we'd made enough to stop. And play hard instead, for the rest of our lives. Somewhere exotic. I'm sure we're nearly there now. I'll go over the figures with you.'

Max grimaces. 'If you must. I think I hate that part of it even more than you. But yes, I agree, we mustn't lose sight of the master plan. We — you, in particular — have worked so hard to build up the agency. Let's take stock after Stephanie. We can't bale on her now. Not with that bonus we're expecting.'

Vivien drains her mug, sets it back on the desk and rolls her shoulders, smoothing out the knots of tension. The coffee, or maybe just the hot liquid, has put some colour in her cheeks.

'You're right,' she says. 'Sorry darling, you just caught me at a bad moment.'

Max watches her, his eyes narrowed. 'It's not just the accounts, is it? You always find this stage of a new match stressful. Will they won't they …? And will it work if they do? It's out of your control, my love. Let's hope for the best. I'd say the signs are good.' He reaches across the desk for her hand and brings it to his lips.

Vivien smiles. 'Let's hope so, as you say. I'd better get back to the bloody spreadsheets. But the finances are looking OK. And, fingers crossed, Stephanie will be a big help. She's off the books, of course.'

'Of course,' says Max, smiling in turn.

# FIVE

I lift the glass vase, heavy with water and the exuberant floral display. Tasteful and fragrant: snowy lilies, royal blue irises and golden freesias, framed by the feathery emerald fronds of asparagus fern. I brought it up to the bedroom last night so it would be the first thing I saw when I woke this morning. And now I'm carrying it carefully downstairs to give it pride of place in the sitting room.

I felt a bit foolish yesterday after I'd called Vivien. Babbling away as if she were a good friend. But she didn't seem to mind. And I realise that, apart from James, she's the closest thing I have to a friend. After Robert died, or at least after I'd got over the — shock, I suppose, if I'm honest, rather than grief, but it was so sudden and unexpected — and navigated the administrative challenges of death certificate, funeral and solicitor, I resolved to do two things for myself, to help make my life better again. I would make new friends and I would try and find a partner.

I think back to my wedding. I almost thought 'my first wedding.' I mustn't get ahead of myself — I'm behaving, or at least feeling, like a giddy teenager at times. I had a number of friends when I met Robert; several from university, a couple more who I'd met through the gallery. And there was Lucy, of course. But Robert gradually drove a wedge between me and them. I've researched 'coercive control' and realise I was a

35

perfect victim. I let Robert essentially take over my life. He persuaded me my friends were moving in a different direction from me, from us. They were obsessed with their careers or their children, wouldn't have time for me, would resent my making claims on them. Or their husbands were unpleasant and he didn't want me around them. That was a fine irony, the last one.

I may have been a perfect victim but Robert was also a perfect controller, and he'd excised them all from my life by the time he died. I knew it was too late to rekindle the former closeness, though I did try briefly with Lucy but that went very pear-shaped almost immediately. So I gave up on that front. It was easier to prioritise my other promise to myself; if I could find a good dating agency, they'd know what to do. And if it worked out I'd find new friends through my new partner. Killing two birds.

I turn my thoughts back to tomorrow's meal and decide to focus on food I can cook in advance as much as possible. Blinis to start with; I just need to make the little pancakes and buy the toppings, then I can put everything together at the flat. And coq au vin. It'll be easier to transport if it's cold; I'll cook it this afternoon. And a dessert, or maybe cheese? I'll ask James what he'd prefer. I feel excitement mount; it's been months since I cooked for anyone else. I'm looking forward to seeing James's flat also. Particularly the bedroom. I cross my fingers.

*

It's the first time I've seen James's car — like most Londoners, we've used cabs or public transport for getting into and around the centre. I'd somehow expected something flashier than the grey Peugeot in the drive. Embarrassingly, I think he must have seen my surprise because he gives a slightly bitter laugh and says, 'My last car was a Jag. Sounds like a stand-up comic's line but it's true. Had to sell it as part of the divorce arrangements.'

I've packed a Le Creuset casserole containing the coq au

vin into a sturdy tote bag, together with containers full of blinis, smoked salmon, crème fraîche, chopped chives, caviar, scrubbed new potatoes, butter, washed and shredded spinach and chard leaves, slivered carrots, and a selection of cheeses and savoury biscuits. My steamer's tucked on top, just in case. The bag's ready waiting by the front door and James carries it to the car and carefully sets it in the boot, wedging it with a couple of folded blankets so that it's stable. Then, ever the gentleman, he opens the front passenger door and waves me in with a little bow.

James lives in a 1930s block, the original Art Deco features well preserved on the exterior and in the vestibule with its sweeping staircase and lifts like gilded cages. The flat itself though, down a narrow corridor on the third floor, is beige and characterless.

'It's just a corporate serviced job,' he says with an apologetic shrug. 'It's fine for now, until I find somewhere to buy. I must start looking.'

'What happened to all your stuff?' I ask. 'From your house, I mean?'

'Laura and I divided it up. My share's all in storage. Everything. So finding a serviced flat was perfect. I didn't have to buy anything, not even a teaspoon!'

Looking around the tiny kitchen I'm glad I prepared almost everything at home. And that I brought my steamer, since I can't see one in the cupboards. I put the casserole on the stove to start heating and set water to boil for the potatoes and, later, carrots and greens, then find a big plate and open the boxes with the blinis and toppings.

'Let me,' says James. 'And then we can sit down with a glass of bubbly. This all looks amazing, thank you so much!'

He tips the blinis onto the plate and starts to carry it through to the table in the sitting/dining room. 'Wait,' I call, laughing. 'I have to warm them, then put them together.'

'I have a better idea,' says James. 'So you can sit down and relax. Let's do DIY blinis. We'll put the toppings on the table and we can each make our own. Much more fun. More intimate.' He comes back into the kitchen, puts his arms round me and gives me a long, hungry kiss.

He's right about the blinis. I give them a blast in the microwave, turn the toppings out into bowls, find cutlery and two more plates, and we settle down at the table. He's a tall man and our knees touch companionably.

'To us,' says James, handing me a flute of champagne and lifting his own in a toast. 'To this evening. And to many more, I hope!' I'm happy to drink to that.

But we're sensible, and don't drink too much. The prospect of what's to come fizzes like the champagne. The meal is delicious, if I say it myself, but I can't eat much. James serves a red Burgundy with the coq au vin, and because we're drinking slowly there's enough left for us to have a glass with the cheese.

'You're a fabulous cook,' says James, leaning back and stretching his legs out in front of him so they gently jostle mine. 'It's been lovely to eat together at home. More relaxed than a restaurant. Even than the Oyster Shed. I can't think of anything I'd rather be doing. Except ...' He takes my hand. 'Let's go to bed.'

I'm disorientated for a moment when I wake early the next morning. I open my eyes and immediately wonder where James's flowers are. Then I remember where I am and roll over, and think that seeing James first thing is even better than seeing the fabulous bouquet. He's awake, lying on his side watching me. 'Good morning my love,' he says softly, then pulls me into a kiss.

Later, when we're showered and dressed and sipping coffee from the Nespresso machine in the kitchen, I drift round the flat, curious. Not that there's much to drift around, just the rooms I've already seen. All, as James said, bland and corporate. There are a couple of books on the coffee table; I recognise the titles from the recently announced Man Booker longlist. And the latest Tate magazine; of course, he's a member. That's about it for personal touches, except — a photo catches my eye, on the small, empty bookcase. It's a house. A beautiful Georgian townhouse, arranged like a child's drawing — steps up to a bright red door with a half-moon fanlight, neat sash windows on either side and on the two floors above. It's very similar to mine, sharing the harmonious symmetry, though mine's much smaller. It's another omen, I think. Another good one, that we share this taste in houses.

James comes up behind me and wraps his arms round me. 'That's my old house,' he says with a sigh.

'You must be really sorry you had to sell,' I say.

'I am. I'll never find anything to compare. Bloody Fred Linwood!' He gives a short laugh, then picks up the photo. 'You know, it's quite like yours, isn't it? Not that I've seen much of yours, especially in daylight.'

'I hope that will change,' I say, hoping also that I'm not being too forward. But I think I can stop worrying so much about that now. 'And yes, it's very similar. Same period.' It's going to be impossible for him to match his old house, I think, on half the proceeds. But if we get — whoa, Stephanie, stop thinking about that word. If we did, though, we could pool our resources. Or he could move in with me, but if I'm going to get … I'm doing it again. But if I were, I'd want to start somewhere new. I love my little house, but it's tainted with the memory of my first husband. I mean my husband. I must try and discourage James from starting to house-hunt, at least until I know whether our relationship is going to move in the direction I now can't stop thinking about.

We have another coffee before James has to go to work. I'm wondering whether he'll suggest a next date now or message later. He answers that question by reaching across and taking my hands.

'Stephanie, I have an idea. I've got some more out-of-town work coming up — next week and the week after, two or three nights away each time. I thought of inviting you to come too but it would be insufferably tedious for you; I don't usually get away until early evening and sometimes the client wants to discuss stuff over dinner. But then I had a better idea. If it's not too soon, too intense—'

It won't be, I'm sure. I bite my lip in anticipation.

'I'd love to take you away for a weekend. I can't spare longer at the moment, so it can't be Venice, or even anywhere very far in England — I was thinking maybe Dorset or Somerset. What do you think? A small hotel or luxury Airbnb. We can go for walks, have good food and wine. And I'm sure we'll think of something else, something even more pleasurable!'

He squeezes my hands and beams at me, and I feel myself beaming back.

\*

Vivien ends another call and puts the phone down on the kitchen table, a little harder than necessary. Max glances up; he's been arranging smoked salmon slices on a plate.

Vivien sighs. 'Stephanie again,' she says.

'Good news I hope?'

'Yes. It's always good news from that one. Which is great, but the sugar-coated enthusiasm is a bit relentless.'

Max delicately extracts a sliver of salmon and extends it towards her. She smiles and opens her mouth, and he feeds her like a fledgling.

'Confucius say — better a happy client than an unhappy one,' intones Max, leavening the monotone with a wink.

'Of course that's right, darling.' Vivien helps herself to another slice, takes two wine glasses from a cupboard and puts them on the counter next to Max. 'It's just — a difficult time at the moment.'

'Will they / won't they?' agrees Max. 'Everything hinges on that.'

'Oh, they've already done the deed,' says Vivien. 'Not that she said as much, but it was pretty obvious.' She takes a bottle of Chablis from the fridge and puts it pointedly, and, like the phone, a little harder than necessary, beside the glasses.

'Nothing escapes you, my love.' Max pulls her towards him, rubs her neck. The tension begins to ebb.

'I was thinking,' he says, continuing to move his hand

rhythmically over her shoulders, kneading out the stiffness. 'About what you said the other day. You're getting tired of it all, I can see that. It takes too much out of you. Perhaps you're right, we should call it a day. Take that early retirement we've always planned for. Dreamed about.'

Vivien tilts her face up at him, kisses him softly. 'You're a dear. I know you understand that it all gets on top of me sometimes.'

'Especially when you're doing the accounts,' Max says with a smile.

'Especially when I'm doing the accounts. Like last time she called. Talking of accounts, Stephanie's fee will come in very handy. Let's wait a bit before taking a decision. See whether wedding bells ring.'

'I believe they will,' says Max. 'You're such a witch, my love. Your instincts about James were absolutely right.'

Vivien sighs. 'We'll see. Soon enough I hope. In the meantime I'll doubtless continue to be plagued with regular Mills & Boon updates from Stephanie. But if there are wedding bells — and the nice fat fee — maybe we should get away for a bit, even if we decide to carry on with the agency.'

'You're sounding more positive already,' says Max, and kisses her on the forehead.

'It comes and goes,' agrees Vivien. 'We've been at this for a while and it takes it out of me. The constant attention, the cosseting, the encouraging, the worry that the match isn't right.'

'The matches are almost always right. You're made to be a matchmaker. You've built the agency up to what it is. We should think carefully before we decide to sell up and sail into the sunset.'

'Well, let's see what happens with James and Stephanie. We actually don't have many other clients at the moment. It could be a good moment for us to take a break.'

'We could have a pretend honeymoon,' agrees Max. 'Go somewhere luxurious. Give you a break. No constant phone calls.'

'After they've had their real one,' says Vivien, 'if they do,

41

of course,' and they kiss again.

*

The drive down to Somerset goes smoothly. The car is laden — James suggested we bring most of the food and drink we'll need for a long weekend so I'd arranged a Waitrose delivery while he sorted the wine. 'We don't want to waste time shopping,' he said. 'And it's only a small village, there probably won't be a lot of choice anyway.' We're planning to eat out in the local pub on the Saturday but there are still a lot of bags and boxes in the boot and wedged on the back seat.

We arrive late afternoon. James has taken the day off work so we can avoid the rush-hour traffic. Not that I imagine there's much of a rush hour here — a scattering of pretty cottages, a couple of shops, the pub. James originally thought we should stay there, but then he found an Airbnb which looked stunning. Huge double bed. Amazing bathroom with an enormous free-standing bath as well as a shower that looked big enough for two. A cosy sitting room with a wood burner if the evenings are cool, and a sun-trap patio garden with a sea view if it's warm enough to sit out. And a kitchen diner that, at least in the photos, married practicality with vintage charm.

The reality lives up to the website. We unload the car and I organise the food and wine, making sure everything that needs chilling goes into the fridge.

'I can't see the champagne,' I say, assuming he'd have included his favourite aperitif, and am surprised when he says casually that he must have forgotten it.

'I was probably distracted by the thought of a whole weekend with you,' he says easily. 'Never mind, there are a couple of nice whites.'

I follow James as he carries our cases upstairs. I pause as I take my wash-bag into the bathroom — it is as vast and luxurious as it looked online. They must have combined the original one with what was probably a small second bedroom. I look longingly at the bath; James knows how I love to soak in bubbles.

He comes up behind me and wraps his arms round me, kissing the nape of my neck. 'Later, darling,' he says. 'There's plenty of room for two!' I shiver in anticipation, and not just for the bath. It's the first time he's called me that.

I put away the clothes I brought — not many, it's only a long weekend. The dress I bought for our second date but didn't wear when I discovered we were going to the Oyster Shed. I think back fondly to that dinner, getting to know each other better over oysters on a river terrace. Jeans and a fleece and boots for walking — James showed me some easy routes marked on the website map. Otherwise casual wear for relaxing in the cottage. And a new negligée, which James doesn't know about, for relaxing in the bed.

We decide to start our stay by doing just that, though I save the negligée for later. Then James runs a bath, sloshing in some of the bath foam that the owners have provided. The room fills with the fragrance of rose geranium.

I ease myself cautiously into the tub and sit down happily in the hot, silky water. There really is room for two, as James demonstrates. We laugh as the water level rises dangerously near the lip, and he lets out enough to stop it overflowing.

We realise once we're dry and dressed that it's after six, and decide to leave the walk and the pub dinner till tomorrow and relax over a drink and an early supper in. James goes down first, and I'm surprised when I go into the kitchen to see two champagne flutes on the table.

'Ta ra!' he says, opening the freezer compartment and bringing out a bottle of Dom Pérignon with the air of a magician whipping a rabbit from a hat. 'Oops, better not wave it around too much.' He fiddles with the foil and the wire, and pours us each a glass.

The evening's still warm and we take our drinks out to the patio. I feel as though I might overflow with happiness as I sit down, looking across the table to my handsome man, and beyond him to the sea that's reflecting the colours of the slowly setting sun.

James fiddles with something in his trouser pocket. He

seems nervous, almost awkward, as he reaches across and takes my hand in his. My left hand. It still feels bare after I recently managed to remove my wedding and engagement rings. I didn't need to ask a jeweller in the end: I used soap and a thread after reading up on Google.

'Stephanie,' he says, his voice a little croaky. 'I hope this isn't too soon. But I'm just—' he pauses, clears his throat and rubs his eyes '—so in love with you. Will you marry me?'

And he opens his other hand to reveal a ring. A stunning ring with a large emerald and two smaller stones — diamonds? — set in a distinctive arrangement, gold claws gripping the stones.

# SIX

Vivien holds the phone away from her ear to dilute Stephanie's burbling effervescence. She can barely make out one tumbling, fevered word in two, but has no problem picking up the gist.

'My dear, I'm so thrilled for you. For you both. You do realise this is every matchmaker's dream? We so yearn for our happy endings. I don't mind telling you, I have tears in my eyes.'

Stephanie chatters on and Vivien puts the phone down while she lights a cigarette. 'so romantic … no idea … beautiful ring … antique … his mother's … fabulous Airbnb … so happy …'

Vivien inhales a much needed rush of menthol and nicotine, her eyes closed. She breathes out a long, fragrant plume, and with it releases what she realises is tension that has been mounting for weeks. Another satisfied client. Wedding bells and confetti. And a welcome infusion of funds in due course.

*

James is adamant that he wants a very small, quiet wedding. 'My first was a huge affair,' he explains. 'Laura had a big family. Parents, uncles, aunts, cousins, even three rather elderly grandparents. And numerous godchildren. And that's before I

45

count the friends … It was very formal, very traditional. Church, morning suits, bridesmaids, telegrams. The whole nine yards. After the divorce I promised myself that if I married again it would be the complete opposite.'

I'm disappointed at first, but the idea grows on me. My first wedding wasn't huge — my family was small, as was Robert's — but I had a fair number of friends. At least I did then. Lucy refused to come, of course. It wasn't an especially formal wedding, but it was traditional. Now I like the thought of just the two of us in a register office. Witnesses from the street. It sounds romantic. Gretna Green for grown-ups. And who would I invite anyway? The only person who springs to mind is Vivien, and I make a mental note to ask her; surely James can't object if she wants to come? I'll call her when he's not here; I'm sure I can talk him round later if she accepts. Thinking about Vivien reminds me that I never did ask James how he found the agency. MadeInHeaven — a perfect name for the perfect matchmaker!

The one thing I try to hold out for is a photographer. But James has a phobia about being caught on camera.

'It's because of an IT job I did,' he says. 'An employer who thought some of his staff were using the office computers to run a porn ring. It was a while ago; they wouldn't get away with it now, with better security and filters and alerts and so on. But …' He pauses, swallows. 'I found it and identified the employees and they were fired. Prosecuted also, and I think some went down. But I wish I'd never taken that job. It was very lucrative but I can never unsee the photos. And ever since I can't face a camera. Even the idea of being photographed.' He shudders, and rubs his forehead, kneading between his eyes as if he has a piercing headache.

'You poor thing,' I say, stroking his hand. 'How horrible. Of course, no photographer then.' But privately I decide to ask one of the witnesses to sneak one pic of us, or even just him, and send it to me, so I have a record of my perfect day.

*

46

'Stephanie dear, that's so sweet of you,' croons Vivien. 'It's such a lovely idea. But it's another of my little policies. It probably seems perverse, but a lot of happy clients invite me to their special day and I always say no. I worry that my being there might remind the radiant bride of an unhappy previous marriage, a bitter divorce, a tragic bereavement, even of the dates that didn't work. And I would never want to risk tainting what I hope will be the happiest day of their lives.' She lights another cigarette, cradling the phone between her neck and shoulder as she stretches up to crack the window open, takes a long drag, and adds, 'I can't wait to hear how it goes. I know about James's photo phobia of course, he was considerate enough to tell me, but you can describe every moment to me. Enjoy your happy ending, my dear. I'm thrilled it's all worked out so well.'

*

Later, in fact it's the day before the wedding and I'm fizzing with excitement and anticipation, I suddenly remember something I've been meaning to talk to James about. I need to do it before we're married, though it may be too late now. I shouldn't have left it so long, but I've been so busy with even our minimal arrangements. And, if I'm honest, daydreaming about the future Mrs Anderson. I don't like to talk about money but I feel I must, so I raise it over our last unmarried aperitif. I'm fretting, the excitement and anticipation eclipsed by worry.

'Darling,' I start. The word is like honey, or silk, in my mouth. I never called Robert 'darling', or any other endearment come to that, nor did he me.

James cocks his head. I'm reminded of a puppy, a dear, playful puppy, and stroke his hair.

'I've been meaning to ask you about this but it's so boring and I've been so happy these last few weeks that I've just kept putting it off. But it's about my will.'

He raises his eyebrow in a question.

'I need to make a new one. If anything were to happen to

me, I'd want you to have everything.'

James moves over to sit next to me. He puts an arm round my shoulders and pulls me towards him.

'Don't think about it,' he says. 'There's no time to do anything before the ceremony now anyway. I don't want you worrying about money, or about me, or about horrible things that might happen to you. Not on our wedding day, not on our honeymoon. We can sort it out when we're back.'

I feel my shoulders relax, the knot in my stomach easing, and push all thoughts of wills and money out of my mind. James is right, we can sort it out after the honeymoon.

*

James was so right. The simple ceremony is perfect. He comes to my house that morning — I didn't want him to spend the night with me, some old superstition. I'm wearing red silk — he asked me not to wear white, he'd be reminded of Laura. And it would hardly be appropriate anyway.

'You look fabulous,' he says, leaning forward to kiss me, but I point to my freshly applied lipstick and blow him a kiss instead, then tuck a white carnation in his buttonhole — the florist delivered it earlier, together with my bride's posy. He puts his hat on — 'Auto-pilot, darling! I feel naked without it outside, but I promise to take it off for the ceremony!' I laugh, but I don't mind — and, holding hands, we head out of the front door and into the taxi James ordered. I thought we'd drive to the register office but he says he's booked a very special lunch after the ceremony.

'It was supposed to be a surprise,' he says ruefully. 'But you're too clever. You'll love it. And I want to be able to drink. To toast you, us, our marriage.' He raises an imaginary glass and I laugh again.

We need two witnesses, and the registrar, a brisk woman in a smart suit, confirms that we can ask any passing person. 'It's not that uncommon,' she says, with a kind smile.

I say to James that I'll have my private interview with her

first and then pop out and find two willing passers by while he's having his. The interview only takes a few minutes, she just checks a few details, then I skip down the sweeping steps outside the main entrance, fumbling in my clutch bag, and approach a young couple. They're strolling at a leisurely pace so are presumably not in a hurry and they smile when I ask them if they'd mind witnessing my wedding.

'We'd love to,' says the woman. She's black, her skin the colour of strong coffee, her ebony hair in swinging ropes beaded with vibrant colours. Everything about her shines. 'You look radiant,' she says, touching my arm.

I take a deep breath and, keeping an eye out for James and trying not to garble, say quickly, 'Would you do me a huge favour? I mean another huge favour. My husband-to-be' — I can't stop myself smiling at those words and have to pause briefly, despite the urgency — 'has a camera phobia so we don't have a photographer but I so want one photo of us. Or of him if it's easier. Would you mind? If you get a chance without it being obvious.' I slip her the sliver of paper I put in my bag before we left the house. 'This is my mobile number. If you could send it to me after …?' I trail off, worried that I've asked something unreasonable.

But the woman beams. 'I'd be delighted! Of course you must have a pic. I'll be very careful.' She mimes looking furtively left and right, like a spy, her fingers raising an imaginary camera to her eye. I laugh. It's going to be all right after all. I thank her effusively and they follow me back to the private room where I'm about to become Mrs James Anderson.

Apart from the photo, which of course I haven't mentioned to James, there's one other part of my wedding day that I've insisted on. I want the traditional vows. We can't have the references to God in a civil ceremony, but that's fine by me. It's my love for James, and his for me, that I want to highlight, to etch in my memory. He's fine with this very minor embellishment on the minimalist register office wording, so now I can't believe my luck as I stand beside him and listen to those magic, fairy-tale words:

'I, James Anderson, take thee, Stephanie Ann Faulkner, to be my wedded wife, to have and to hold from this day forward, for better, for worse, for richer, for poorer, in sickness and in health, to love and cherish, till death us do part.'

*

I resist the urge to check my phone as we walk the short distance from the register office to the restaurant where James has booked our 'surprise' wedding breakfast. Just the two of us, surely the smallest wedding breakfast in history! But I'm happy enough for a multitude of brides, and don't miss guests, friends, family at all. As I think that, though, I feel a faint, fleeting emotional twitch.

The restaurant is like a jewel, small, neat, bright. I'm reminded of my engagement ring, and stroke it automatically, passing my right index finger over it. Of course it feels different now, rubbing up against its new companion. I squeeze James's arm. 'I love you,' I say. 'Husband.' The word feels strange on my lips — new and shiny and untasted.

The waiter, or perhaps he's the owner, greets us effusively and shows us into a tiny private room, the table laid with white linen and lilies. For a fleeting second it strikes me as funereal and I shiver, but the spectre passes and I'm back to being the newly minted bride, buoyed with happiness bordering on ecstasy.

'I'll be two seconds,' I say to James before sitting down, and I head to the Ladies. I noticed the sign on a door to the left of the entrance when we came in, and find what could only be described as a powder room. Like a Fragonard painting, I think; all it needs is a fake shepherdess on a swing. Flowery wallpaper, deep pile carpet, pinks and fringes, the scent of violet. I lock myself in a cubicle and find my phone. There's a text from a number I don't recognise.

*Here's your pic! You looked gorgeous but I only got one chance and couldn't get you in properly. Or a very good one of the*

*handsome groom, but at least you'll have it as a memento. So
pleased to have been your witness. Have a happy marriage! Grace
xxx*

The picture was a bit lop-sided and as if it had been taken from
low down as well as at an angle, which I suppose it probably
was as the woman — Grace — was trying to be discreet. But
still, it's my husband's face and, as she said, it's a memento of
a wonderful occasion. A keepsake. There's a glimpse of me at
the edge, a vertical sliver of hair and silk scarf and scarlet dress,
but not much.

I text back a quick thank you, then breathe in a long breath,
square my shoulders and text the photo to Lucy. No message,
she'll know who it's from. And she'll see what I've done, how
well it's turned out. Then I realise it's not obvious that the
picture is of a wedding. No white dress, no lace, no confetti.
There's the carnation, of course, but he could be the best man
at someone else's wedding. So I take a photo of my left hand,
my two rings, and text that also. I delete both texts once I've
seen that they've been delivered, and the exchange with Grace
once I've saved her photo, then tuck the phone back in my
bag and join my brand new husband.

\*

We spend our first night as husband and wife — I can't get
enough of those words — in my house. James thought it was
the simplest bridge between the perfect wedding day and the
perfect honeymoon. He's booked another luxury Airbnb in
the West Country, but this time in deepest Cornwall. It'll be a
long drive and it seemed sensible to do it this way. Also we're
taking most of our own food and drink again, so we can pack
the car without rushing. As he says, once we're there we won't
want to leave the cottage unless it's essential.

He wraps his arms round me, lifts me so my feet leave the
ground and twirls me around. 'This time, I want you to myself.
For the whole time. So you won't need smart clothes, Mrs
Anderson. Apart from for bed!' He sets me down but doesn't
release me, instead drawing me even closer and into a long,

deep kiss.

James is right about the drive. Once we're off the motorway the roads get smaller and twistier, the hedges higher and thicker. There are few villages but those that we pass through are charming clusters of cottages, church, pub and green.

As we did for our last break — I'll always think of it as the proposal weekend — we arrive at Polpen in the late afternoon. This Airbnb is further off the beaten track than the previous one; the car has to wend its careful way along a narrow lane edging a field. I gasp when we round the last curve and draw up outside the prettiest cottage you could imagine. Thatch, weathervane, a climbing rose — it really could be a postcard.

'The key should be under a mossy stone to the right of the step,' says James, stooping to look. 'I told the owner that we didn't want to be disturbed. She's used to that, it seems — makes a speciality of honeymoon lets.'

He finds the key and opens the front door, then puts his hand up to stop me stepping in. 'Allow me, Mrs Anderson,' he says with a gallant bow, then sweeps me up and carries me over the threshold.

'I should have done it yesterday really,' he says as he lowers me down, holding my elbow until he's sure I have both feet on the ground. Only literally, though. We're both laughing and I don't think I've ever felt happier. 'But I thought you wouldn't want the neighbours to see us horsing about. And today's the real start of our married life.'

I wouldn't have minded the neighbours seeing, although I barely know them. Robert had, of course, discouraged any socialising with them. But I don't mind. As James says, today we're starting our marriage for real.

The cottage may be traditional on the outside but inside it's clearly been gutted and completely refurbished, though they've kept some of what I assume are original features like ceiling beams, a fireplace with a Victorian grate, and a butler's sink. A bit like the other Airbnb but even better. I start putting the food away while James takes our cases up the steep, narrow staircase.

'Wow,' he calls down. 'Come and see the bathroom, darling. I specially looked for one with a big bath when I saw how much you enjoyed the last one.'

'How much we both enjoyed it, you mean,' I say saucily as I join him. Even after his spoiler, I can't help but gasp. The bathroom isn't as huge as the other one but the bath looks even more impressive, deep and curved and smooth. I can't wait to try it.

\*

The following day is dull and damp, but we don't care. We're tired after not much sleep — the owner clearly hadn't been exaggerating when she said she was a honeymoon specialist or whatever she called herself. The bed is huge and was scattered with red rose petals. There was an ice bucket on the dressing table with a bottle of Bollinger chilling in it and two flutes waiting. We went straight to bed once we'd unpacked, got up after a couple of hours for a brief supper of cold beef, baked potatoes and salad, and retired again with the remains of a bottle of claret.

We spend the next day lounging around, reading the Sunday papers which James picked up in the village earlier and indulging ourselves with Bellini cocktails and a bottle of Sancerre with a light lunch. There's a bit of a diversion when I can't find my phone, but I ask James to call it and track down the ringtone to the bedroom. I'm sure I left it in the kitchen but James laughs, kisses me, says I'm honeymoon-scatty. He sounds a bit brittle, but when I ask him he shrugs it off with another kiss.

'Just a bit tired suddenly, darling. All the excitement of the wedding and then the long drive down. And now I can relax it's catching up with me.'

He lights the fire, though it's not really cold, just a little grey and damp, then starts to open another bottle of champagne. 'I'm going to make you a champagne cocktail. One of my special talents, but I've kept it secret till now.'

I laugh, delighted. Robert would never have done anything

like keeping something secret to surprise me. And I love cocktails, or I used to anyway, when I went out more, before I married for the first time. The idea that my first marriage has been consigned to the past, been superseded, is heady and I feel as though I'm smiling like the Cheshire Cat.

'Let's take our glasses up to that glorious bath,' James says. 'In fact …' he breaks off and puts the bottle back in the fridge; he's only taken the foil off, 'even better — let's get the bath ready then I'll come back down and bring the cocktail up so it'll be really cold for you.'

I follow him up the stairs and he runs the bath, adding oil and bubble bath from the selection of bottles on the windowsill. This time the fragrance of orange blossom fills the room. A bridal bath!

'You first,' he suggests. 'That way I get to undress you.' And he does, lovingly and gently peeling off one layer after another. He hesitates when he comes to my black lacy bra and pants, then says regretfully, 'These too. Seems a shame to get them wet. I look forward to helping you put them back on later.'

I step in carefully — the sides are quite high. All the better for a deep soak for two! The water is silky with oil and I ease myself down and sink back into the pillow of fragrant foam, closing my eyes and thinking that I'm the luckiest woman in the world.

# PART TWO – LUCY AND VIVIEN

# SEVEN

Lucy hadn't intended to sever all ties with Steph, but the row they'd had about the matchmaking agency was a row too far for both of them.

It had been hard enough to mend fences after Robert died, but they'd managed it. They were just getting used to seeing each other again, being civil, catching up with those missing years in the course of which Steph's vile husband had slowly prised her away from the last remaining member of her immediate family. Who was herself busy building a second career as a lawyer, having had as much as she could stomach of being an accountant.

But when Steph told her she was going to some tacky sounding dating agency called MadeInHeaven, Lucy was livid. It wasn't long after Steph had been widowed, and though there was nothing Lucy would have liked more than for her baby sister to find a good man, she knew it was far too soon. Steph was so naive, so trusting, so passive. Not like her. Bossy Lucy, Steph used to call her when they were children, but more in fun than anything. They were very close then, despite the age difference. Or perhaps because of it.

So they fought about the matchmaker and said nasty, hurtful things to each other, and by the time they'd cooled off it was too late to retract the harsh words. The one quality they shared was obstinacy. If it had been their first falling out it might have been easier for both to recover from it, but Steph had never forgiven Lucy for her antipathy towards her first husband, for refusing to attend her wedding — her first wedding, Lucy supposes she must say now — even though Steph must have come to realise that Lucy had been right about Robert.

After Steph first mentioned the agency, Lucy googled it. There was no website for MadeInHeaven, which was odd, even suspicious. But when they next met, Steph explained that the woman who ran it kept it very discreet, very old school. Advertised in *The Lady*. Lucy had snorted derisively — I mean, do me a favour, she thought, and maybe, probably, said out loud. Steph showed her the brochure, which Lucy found quite ludicrous — all embossed gilt on the cover and Mills & Boon style stories with soft focus photos of happy couples in clouds of white lace and confetti. Made her want to puke. She didn't puke, but she was strident and bossy and unkind. No, cruel. And for once Steph, her perfect little sister, the shiny new apple of their parents' eye after she'd conveniently been born eight years after they'd adopted Lucy, responded in kind.

Lucy felt bad, of course, a week or so later. She'd never been able to shake off the feeling, remorselessly inculcated by their mother — well, her adoptive mother, she'd never known her biological one — that she had to look after Steph. So Lucy tried to phone her a couple of times but Steph ignored her calls. Lucy even went round to Steph's neat little town house, so different from her own untidy home in Hackney though she knew which she preferred. She was sure Steph was in, but if she was she didn't come to the door, even after Lucy called through the letter box. Fuck it, she thought then, I've had enough. I never want to see her again. She called that through the letter box too.

But the next morning, still unable to shake off that residual feeling of duty, Lucy did the only thing she could think of. She set up a Google alert for any reference to Steph by either her maiden or her married name.

*

The irony is that the first notification Lucy has is after Steph's second marriage, and the alert wouldn't have picked it up if the article hadn't used her first married name. Lucy knows she remarried, but didn't find out until the day of the ceremony, which it turns out was only a couple of days before the notification. Steph texted her a photo of what was evidently the bridegroom: the white carnation in his buttonhole made it abundantly clear who he was. The photo wasn't brilliant — it had obviously been taken from low down and at something of an angle. Still, Lucy could see that he was good-looking in a conventional sort of way. She was more interested to see her sister, but there was just a slice of her along the edge of the picture. Enough to judge that the groom was tall as well as dark and handsome, if not enough to identify Steph clearly, but of course she recognised the number which had sent it.

And just to make it abundantly clear that the first photo was of a wedding, her wedding, Steph also sent a photo of her left hand. The band of gold and the retro engagement ring with what looked like a vulgarly large emerald and two small diamonds set in gold claws. Weren't emeralds supposed to be bad luck?

Anyway, Lucy gets a Google alert ping a couple of days later. It's for an article from the online edition of some obscure Cornish local paper. Her first thought, before the substance of the piece has sunk in, is that they could surely have managed somewhere better for a honeymoon. Even if he doesn't have any money, she must have plenty since Robert died. In fact maybe her second husband is just a gold-digger. Not that she has any reason to suspect that.

*Honeymoon Tragedy of Bride in the Bath*, the headline shrieks.

*

Lucy's not the screaming type, but she's sure she would have screamed long and hard if she had been. It's bad enough to lose your sister, your baby sister, the one you promised your mother on her deathbed that you'd always look after, the last

59

surviving member of your family. It's bad enough to lose her in such a horrible, unexpected, tragic accident. But it's a trifecta of badness to lose her when you're not speaking to each other because of some stupid sister row. When there's no further possibility to apologise, to make up, to laugh and joke and reminisce about their childhood, to tell her she had good legs, beautiful eyes, a lovely figure. Steph never had any confidence, Lucy doesn't know why. She, Steph, was the cherished baby. Of course Lucy was cherished before her, she was the baby her adoptive parents had been told they couldn't have. But then Steph was doubly that.

Actually, Lucy thinks, if she's honest she's sure it's because of her that Steph had no confidence, because Lucy had it in spades. Probably because she was the first cherished baby. And though she always — well, until recent years — looked out for Steph, she also bossed her mercilessly, made her play Lucy's games, told her off, shut her out of her social life when the age gap got too big. Eight years is a long time once the older one hits the teens, and the difference doesn't shrink again for another decade or more. They had a few years then of being closer again, but only until Steph fell for the horrible Robert.

Lucy reads the article again and again. She's not the crying type either, but she realises that she's been unconsciously weeping and wiping her eyes when she catches herself in a mirror. She looks like a clown, or one of those bandit-masked snuffling mammals of the night, the grey of her irises lost in the dark surrounds of smudged mascara. And she feels as though she's being cut into a thousand pieces inside. My poor baby, she thinks. Drowned in the bath. On her honeymoon.

Lucy knows she's just picking at the scab, making things worse, but she goes back to the article again and again. James Anderson will surely contact her, she thinks. Even if he knows about their rift, it would be the natural thing to do. There's no reason to think Steph will have left her anything given their recent history, but she'd like to meet him, like the opportunity to choose something of Steph's as a memento to have and to hold, to love and to cherish. The old traditional words of the wedding service have wormed their way into her brain and she can't shake them off.

But after a few days she's heard nothing from James Anderson. She goes to Steph's house, which looks empty — no car, some flyers caught in the letter box which she pushes through. No one comes to the door when she raps the elegant knocker. Perhaps he's still down in Cornwall. Lucy scribbles a brief message on an old receipt she finds in her handbag, then crumples it up and stuffs it in a pocket — she'll come back the next day with a neatly written condolence card. Which does, adding her phone number after her name. Again, an echoing silence is the only response to her insistent knocking.

Lucy resorts to Google and spends some time ploughing through the first few pages of the inevitable gazillion hits, but there's no James Anderson with the sort of age and marital status she's looking for. She tries LinkedIn, Facebook and Twitter, but again none of the numerous James Andersons seem to fit the bill. It's unsettling: who leaves no digital footprint in this day and age? And how? And, more importantly perhaps, why? But of course it's a fairly common name.

She supposes she could contact the dating agency, ask for James Anderson's details or leave a message for him to contact her. But she remembers Steph saying that the agency didn't have a website, had some weird notions about data privacy or whatever. Lucy racks her brains for the name — she knows it's something corny, some sort of word play. But she can't find it. She resolves to stop thinking about it, hoping that it will surface unexpectedly once she ignores it.

\*

MadeInHeaven, that's it. Lucy wakes in the night with the name on her lips, and makes a note on her phone.

The agency itself is initially as elusive as the name, and she remembers what Steph said about them being very quaint and olde-worlde, to the extent that they didn't even have an online presence. But she also remembers how Steph found them, and eventually tracks down one of their discreet advertisements in *The Lady*'s classified columns. She rings the number. It's a landline and it's answered by a well-spoken, young-sounding female voice.

'Good morning. You've reached the office of MadeInHeaven. How may I help you?'

'Hello,' says Lucy, thinking that the wording sounds more like a voicemail recording than a real person. 'I'd like to speak to the woman who runs the agency please. I'm sorry, I've forgotten her name.'

'I'm afraid Ms Harrison isn't in the office today,' comes the reply, which at least reassures Lucy that she's not talking to a tape. 'Would you like to leave a message? Or shall I ask her to call you?'

'Please. My name is Lucy Hawkings.' Lucy recites her mobile number and closes the call.

Lucy doesn't have to wait long. Her mobile rings, the screen showing 'No Caller ID'. A silky woman's voice introduces herself as Vivien Harrison and asks how she can help.

'I'm trying to get in touch with James Anderson,' Lucy says.

There's a brief pause, then a puzzled, 'I'm sorry, but I don't know that name.'

'Isn't he one of your clients?' Lucy asks. 'Or ex-clients?'

The woman assures her he's not.

'What about Stephanie Faulkner?' Lucy asks.

'Who?'

'I'm sure she told me …' Lucy stops, thinking fast. Something's not right, but she needs time to work out what.

'I'm sorry,' she says, trying to sound like some ditzy airhead, which doesn't come naturally to her. Although since Steph died she's increasingly felt like one. 'I'm getting confused. I heard the tragic news about Stephanie. Someone I used to know back in the day. I didn't know her well, lost touch ages ago, but I ran into her, oh, a few months ago I think. She told me she was planning to try a dating agency but I must have remembered the name wrong. Or maybe she decided not to use an agency at all, I have to say I advised her against it. So sorry to have bothered you.'

Vivien Harrison graciously acknowledges the apology and Lucy ends the call.

Lucy knows that Steph will have left a fairly hefty estate, though she doesn't know the details beyond the house — small, but on the edge of Hampstead — and that Robert had been wealthy. She assumes James Anderson will inherit and eventually she'll be able to find out his address from the grant of probate — as the lawyer in the family she'd been closely involved in both her late parents' probate, though had delegated the form filling and filing to a specialist solicitor — but it's bound to take a while. In the meantime, there's another thread she can follow. The more she thinks about it, the more she feels there's something wrong with MadeInHeaven. Lucy's sure that it's the agency Steph signed up with. It's possible, she supposes, that Steph met James Anderson independently of it, though it's hard to imagine how — Steph had lost touch with all her friends when she was married to Robert, and she wasn't the type to launch into a lot of group activities in her quest for a new husband. It's also possible, Lucy supposes again, that Steph signed with another agency and met James that way, but she was so rapturous about MadeInHeaven and the woman who ran it. Lucy assumes she's the one she just spoke to. Vivien Harrison. Like a film star, Steph said. But even if she hadn't met James through MadeInHeaven, Lucy knows for a fact she'd signed up and surely the agency would have her name on record? She needs to find out more.

*

It's helpful to know that Vivien Harrison's not in the office today, thinks Lucy, as it gives her the chance to check it out without the risk of running into her. The address is in the advert — if it can be called anything so vulgar — in *The Lady*; it's something called an Office Sweet in Bloomsbury. North Bloomsbury, Lucy would say — it's almost at the Euston

Road. She googles Office Sweet and finds that they rent out office space in numerous locations in London and further afield. Among the options available are various 'virtual office plans'. It seems you don't even need a physical office to have an address that looks like one. That could explain the robotic sounding receptionist; she probably picks up the phone for a number of different firms. Lucy goes to the address anyway. Office Sweet occupies the ground floor and, although there are Venetian-type blinds down in some of them, she can glimpse a series of small, bare, empty cells with rudimentary office furnishings and a couple of larger, better equipped rooms, one set up as a conference room and the other as some sort of business lounge. She goes into the building and asks the receptionist if there's anyone she can talk to about renting space for her start-up company. The receptionist makes a short call and invites her to wait in the lounge for 'Maurice,' who'll be half an hour or so as he's working at their Covent Garden address today.

There's a woman in the lounge, tapping away on a laptop. With an apology for the interruption, Lucy asks if she rents office space here.

'Sort of,' she says with a laugh. 'I basically rent a physical postal address, a landline and a receptionist who answers the phone and sweet talks anyone who walks in looking for me. Not that there are many of those.'

'So you don't actually have an office here? I'm just asking because I'm looking to rent an office for my start-up.'

The woman looks at Lucy as though she's in medieval dress. 'No one has a real office anymore, honey. It's money down the drain. My clients much prefer meeting in a bar or restaurant, and with the money that I haven't poured down the drain I can afford to treat them, to look generous. If a client really wanted to meet in "my" office —' she makes quote marks with her fingers '— I can rent one here for the day. Or meet in one of the lounges, like this one, free.'

Maurice says essentially the same thing, though it's wrapped up in a lot of corporate speak. But the clear takeaway — the corporate speak is contagious, Lucy thinks — is that you pay not very much for even less, with the bonus of a posh, or almost posh, address. It sounds as though Vivien Harrison probably runs MadeInHeaven from her home, wherever that is. And keeps her records there also.

Lucy waves a thank you to the receptionist, who's reciting her robotic mantra into a phone but this time in the name of 'Software Support Solutions', and leaves. She has a yen for a coffee while she decides what to do next. You're never far from half a dozen indistinguishable chains in London, and sure enough there's an EAT across the road. It's busy, but there's a stool free at the bar in the window and she sits sipping her latte, vacantly watching the men and women going in and out of the Office Sweet building. Any one of them, or at least of the women, could be Vivien Harrison, she supposes. Although if she's really only renting a shadow office, why would she need to be there at all? And how can Lucy find her if she never visits?

Lucy thinks back to the fatuous advert in *The Lady*. There's something nagging at her, but she can't remember the wording. She finds it again on her mobile.

> *MadeInHeaven is an old-fashioned agency and discretion is our watch word. We pride ourselves on having no website, and see this as a strength in a world where digital data can so easily end up in the wrong hands. With this in mind, we like to hear from prospective clients by letter addressed to MadeInHeaven, Office Sweet, London NW1 2QS. However, if you prefer the telephone please call 020 7946 0259.*

Jesus, thinks Lucy. Even more fatuous than she remembered. Though she guesses Vivien Harrison has a point about the vulnerability of digital data. But what Lucy had half-remembered was the invitation to potential clients to write a letter. A real letter. Which presumably means that Vivien Harrison will come by the office every day or two to check her post. Just as well, Lucy thinks, that she's due some leave and is a caffeine addict. And that Vivien Harrison is such a dinosaur.

# EIGHT

Lucy gets through a lot of coffee in that branch of EAT over the next couple of days. She's always enjoyed people-watching, and according to a friend who's a birder she's also more observant than most. The friend tried to persuade her to go twitching with him, but standing around silently in mud and rain with no book isn't her idea of fun.

Sitting with a latte while checking the people who go in and out of the Office Sweet building is much more diverting. Well, checking the women at least; Lucy doesn't really notice the men. What had Steph said about Vivien? Glamorous, elegant, well-dressed, that sort of thing. She doesn't recall any further detail, maybe Steph hadn't given any. But Lucy discounts most of the women she sees: they are striding along as if late for an appointment, frowning into their mobiles, faces grey with commuter pallor, wearing ill-fitting trouser suits, struggling to juggle umbrellas, bulging briefcases, carry-out coffees.

It's not till the second morning that Lucy spots Vivien. At least she thinks, and hopes, that it's Vivien. The woman is petite, dressed in an above-the-knee charcoal pencil skirt revealing shapely legs in kitten heels, her glossy black hair cut in a neat bob. She has a compact shoulder bag on a gold chain with a clasp which looks like the Chanel logo swinging against her cherry-red waisted jacket.

She goes into the Office Sweet building. Lucy watches her

pause at the welcome desk and speak briefly to the receptionist — Lucy can't see whether it's the same one she met — who hands her a couple of envelopes. Vivien — surely this must be her, it's probably the only snail mail that's delivered — tucks the letters into her bag and comes back out onto the street. She turns left and gives the impression of following a well worn route as she sets a steady pace.

Lucy's hoping that the woman's heading home and hoping even more that she lives within walking distance of her so-called office. She follows her for twenty minutes or so, along Torrington Place then left and across the Euston Road, up between the station and the British Library, past Mornington Crescent and into a network of backstreets in Camden Town, which, fortunately for Lucy, are busy with shoppers, buggies and reckless delivery cyclists. Not that the woman has shown any sign of having noticed that she's being followed; she walks purposefully, her heels clicking briskly on the pavement, looking firmly ahead.

The woman stops at a narrow house, a maisonette perhaps, set slightly back from the road, finds her keys in her bag, unlocks the door and disappears inside. Lucy makes a note of the address and goes back to her own house, not really sure what her two days of leave have achieved and what she should do next. But she's still driven by the conviction that there's something dodgy about MadeInHeaven, and therefore Vivien Harrison, and that she owes it to Steph to keep on the scent. She books the rest of the week off, thankful that she moved from transactional work to back-room research last year so has no imminent, unmissable company takeovers or applications for injunctions or whatever.

*

Lucy shadows Vivien — she's sure it's her — over the next three days, turning up near her address every morning, sitting in the inevitable chain café within sight of her front door, following her whenever she leaves the maisonette. Lucy's not sure where this is going but has taken to wearing sunglasses and a variety of baseball caps. There's still no sign that Vivien's noticed her though: she walks briskly and rarely glances back.

Over those days Vivien visits three cafés, all within walking distance of her house and all upmarket independent venues. She always goes inside and, judging from the way she checks her watch before she finds a table, has arranged to meet someone. Twice Lucy takes a seat in one of the chairs on the pavement; on the third time there's no room outside and she has to go in. She asks to be seated in a corner where she's not in Vivien's direct line of sight, takes out her phone and props it in front of her, frowning at the screen and making random scribbles on the paper napkin that came with her coffee, while keeping an eye on Vivien from under the peak of her cap.

Vivien meets women — different women, one at a time — at two of the cafés and a man at the other. Lucy assumes these people are clients or prospective clients. The women are in their forties, maybe fifties — well kept, smartly turned out, exuding an aura of comfortable privilege. The man is of a similar vintage and also elegantly dressed and with an air of easy wealth.

Lucy judges the first woman to be a new client. Vivien has a different handbag from the Chanel one, something bigger in what looks like luxuriantly soft leather, from which she pulls a small black notebook, a Moleskine Lucy thinks. She opens it and makes the odd jotting as the woman speaks. At the end, Vivien summons the waiter, settles the bill, places her hand on the woman's arm, and they rise with a smile. As they leave the café they pass Lucy's table and she hears Vivien say, '… to meet you my dear. I'm sure I can help. I look forward to continuing our discussion next week in the privacy of your …'.

The second woman is visibly excited — she's glowing, bubbly, holds out her hand in what looks like a proud display of a ring, though Lucy can't see that much detail from her table. Vivien claps and calls over the waiter, who brings two flutes of, Lucy assumes, something with bubbles. This café is more of a brasserie, perhaps chosen because it has a licence.

The man looks as though he's chatting easily with Vivien, though Lucy can hear nothing though the window. Vivien listens attentively, pausing a couple of times to write something in her little black book. The meeting has the air of a debriefing or similar. When they stand to leave, Vivien shakes the man's hand. They exchange a last few words as they exit the café and Lucy catches the drift from her pavement table. 'Next week … Bernadette … I'm sure,' from Vivien, and 'Let's hope … looking forward,' from the man.

\*

Lucy's not sure where to go next after witnessing Vivien's three apparent client meetings. She's still convinced there's something not right about the agency but doesn't want to approach Vivien. She's confident that Vivien hasn't noticed her — in all three encounters, she appeared to be totally focused on her companion, her attention professionally unwavering. But Lucy can't keep shadowing her in the hope of … what? She has some idea now of her routine though, and is reluctant to give up. She makes an appointment to see someone in Human Resources and ask about compassionate leave. It's still less than a fortnight since Steph died; the firm has been flexible about her days off so far, even the ones not booked as holiday entitlement, and now her formal request is granted readily. Three weeks on full pay; after that she needs to check back in and negotiate what she needs and on what basis. Lucy suspects they'll be happy to let her go half time on half pay for a while, which would suit them both: as she doesn't have a lot of work on at the moment, everyone wins.

Less than a fortnight … Lucy is honest enough to admit to herself that her obsessive tracking of Vivien is driven as much by a need to distract herself from the scalding emotional pain of Steph's death, of their stupid estrangement, as by any real belief that anything will come of it. Though she would like to meet her sister's widower. But the distraction is real and Lucy knows that there's no way she could work effectively — her powers of analysis and concentration seem to have withered. Following someone requires little in the way of brainpower while keeping her occupied, so she continues to flit somewhat aimlessly around Vivien's haunts. Sometimes she waits to see whether she'll leave her house in the morning — apart from the café, Lucy discovers a bus stop just up the road, and who ever notices someone waiting impatiently at a bus stop, constantly checking their phone? She continues to wear one cap or another, otherwise deliberately dressing drably in unremarkable colours and styles, avoiding the arresting, bright colours she prefers.

Vivien goes to the office every couple of days, picking up an envelope on the first visit but leaving the building apparently empty handed the other times. She returns to the three cafés, whether to meet clients or to enjoy a solitary coffee Lucy doesn't know; Lucy doesn't wait to find out, not wanting to loiter too much. One day when Vivien leaves the office she hails a taxi and gives Lucy the opportunity to do something she's always yearned to do, something that fits with the PI persona she seems to be inhabiting now, namely flag down the one behind and say 'follow that cab'. It would have been trickier had Vivien called an Uber, but Lucy imagines that's a bit too hi-tech for her. When Vivien's taxi stops outside a house in Notting Hill and she gets out, Lucy asks her driver to slow down and drop her further down the road. As they pass the house, she sees the front door being opened by a woman who looks like the first one she saw Vivien meet in the café. This must be the promised visit to her house. Lucy wonders why Vivien likes to meet clients in their own homes. Perhaps it puts them at their ease, and doubtless she doesn't want them to see that her office is pure Potemkin.

In the third week, Lucy has what she would probably call a lucky break if she were a real PI.

*

Lucy is sitting outside the café near Vivien's house, keeping half an eye on her front door. It's mid-morning, she's been there for a while and she's wondering whether she can be bothered to follow Vivien if she comes out. What has she learnt so far, after all? That Vivien picks up her mail from her office. That she meets clients at upmarket cafés or in their own homes. That she makes odd notes about them, followed up with a home visit to the one who seemed to be new, congratulated the one who'd got engaged, perhaps apologised to the one whose date had apparently not worked out. It all seems a bit quaint and old-fashioned — the notebook, the snail mail, the black cab — but then it reflects the character of the agency as described in the advert in *The Lady*. Your data are safe with us. No digital footprint. We respect your privacy. Lucy decides to call it a day, or maybe a week or more. She nips into the café to use the loo then does a double take as she's about to step back out onto the street and instead slips partly behind the door.

Vivien is standing on the pavement outside her house, talking to a man. She's turned three-quarters towards Lucy and he's mirroring her so Lucy can only see a sideways-on sliver of his face. They exchange a few words which she can't hear. They don't look like a couple somehow — they don't touch, they're keeping a professional distance from each other. Perhaps he's a new client and for some reason she invited him to her house for an interview? Vivien turns to go, looking as though she's planning to walk to the office, then suddenly swings back and raises a hand to brush something off the shoulder of the man's jacket. And that gesture jars. It's familiar, intimate, almost proprietary. Not the cool, professional formalism Lucy saw between Vivien and the male client she watched her with in the café. She crosses the road, frowning at her phone, hoping she might hear more.

\*

'Do you want a lift?' the man says to Vivien. 'I've got an Uber coming any moment.'

Vivien shakes her head. 'Thanks, but I'll walk. See you later. I'll pick up wine and steak for this eve.' She trots off down the street, heading, as Lucy had thought, in the direction of her office.

Lucy summons an Uber, and for the second time in a week

— in her life, actually — she instructs the driver to follow that car.

Shortly before they arrive, Lucy realises that Vivien's … client? partner? is going to Steph's house. She asks her ride to drop her and wait. She doesn't like to get too close to the man but she has her trusty baseball cap pulled low and is again pretending to be engrossed in her phone.

The man's Uber reverses into Steph's short drive. Lucy can't get much a view of him as he gets out and lets himself into the house. She frowns. How come he's got keys? He reaches behind the front door, to where Lucy recalls there's a burglar alarm panel. The faint bleeping she can hear in the background stops and the front door closes after him.

Lucy takes the opportunity to find a slightly better position where she's partly shielded by Steph's hedge but can still keep an eye on the drive. She adjusts her cap, turning it a fraction to give her face more cover, and resumes staring at her mobile. It's only a few minutes, maybe ten at most, before the door opens and the man comes out. He's carrying a couple of small cardboard boxes and as he opens the boot and puts them in Lucy finally catches a glimpse of his face. There's a ghost of familiarity about it, though she doesn't think it's someone she's met in the flesh. Then she remembers.

*

Vivien walks to the office, where there's no post to pick up. She wends her way back to the maisonette, pausing to do some window-shopping in a couple of clothes shops she passes and some actual shopping at the local butcher, greengrocer and off-licence. It's a sunny day, mild for the time of year, and she treats herself to a coffee and cake at one of her favourite cafés, where she's greeted like the valued customer she is.

She sits outside, permitting herself a few minutes with her face turned to the sun, eyes closed behind her designer sunglasses, basking like a cat. Only briefly though, she's conscious of the destructive effect of sun on skin. After a few minutes she turns her head back into the shadow, stirs her latte, licks the froth. She cuts a delicate sliver of the almond lemon cake and chews neatly, reflecting.

The lack of mail is a little worrying. She's had nothing since … Vivien casts her mind back. It must be nearly three weeks ago now. And it wasn't a promising query, though she followed up of course. A woman who was neither obviously wealthy nor obviously attractive. She was reluctant to pass up a possible new client though, and reminds herself that she must think who to set her up with.

But really, she reassures herself, they must have enough money now to cut and run. Though of course she doesn't know exactly how much as most of it's in Max's name and accounts. When she raised the topic with him after Stephanie's unfortunate drowning, he'd made a case for waiting another eighteen months or so. She'd intended to come back to it, press him again about selling up and getting out, but hadn't. She frowns, then promptly smoothes the lines away with a practised finger. She takes the last fragment of cake, the frown ousted by a beatific smile. Somewhere hot, she thinks. Sun and sea. And Max. They can, after all, have their cake and eat it.

*

Lucy opens the Messages app on her phone and, now genuinely engrossed, finds the two photos Steph texted. She pinches out the photo of the groom, tilts her phone to try and compensate for its slant. The man bringing stuff out of her house could be the man her sister married, but it's not conclusive. But if he is James Anderson, it makes sense. Of course he'd know Vivien, he was a client also. And of course he has keys to Steph's house and knows the burglar alarm code, or has a fob if it's one of those. She's so excited that she's finally found him, that she has the opportunity to meet him, to express condolences, to talk about Steph, that she actually takes a step forward. Then she stops, and shrinks back into the hedge. Why did Vivien say she had no record of James Anderson? And why did she make that small but unmistakably intimate gesture when she was talking to him?

James — for who else could it be, despite her uncertainty? — ducks back into the house, reaches behind the open door, presumably to reset the alarm, then comes out with a couple of smart cases, the sort of thing you might take on a plane as hand luggage. If you were well off. He closes the door behind him, locks it and gets back into the car after putting the cases in the back. In parallel, Lucy returns to her Uber and asks the driver to follow the car. He laughs. 'Twice in a day,' he says. 'Never been asked that before. You a detective or something?'

'Or something,' agrees Lucy, though she's not sure what.

The next stop is a smart, well maintained block of flats in Crouch End called Renoir Mansions. There's no drive to park in and there are double yellow lines on the road in front of the building where the man's — she might as well think of him as James — car pulls up. Again, Lucy asks her Uber to drop her and wait where he can. James hops out of the car and is heading towards the flats when his driver opens his window and calls something out to him. Lucy can't hear what, but it's presumably about the illegal parking because James shouts back over his shoulder as he's letting himself in to the main entrance, 'I'll only be a minute. Oh, maybe a few — I'll have to wait for the doorman to come back to the desk. If there's any problem, just say I'm collecting my post. Number ten.'

Lucy glimpses a tantalising panel of buzzers by the main door, with what could be labels next to them. But she daren't risk it. She doesn't think James has noticed her yet, or if he has it's just as an unremarkable and anonymous woman in the background, but if he walks into her as he comes out of the block that may well change. She's not sure why that would matter but is still driven by her conviction that something's not right, and although she has no idea what that something is or what she might do about it if she finds out, she wants to keep her options open. So she stays well back from the entrance and makes a note of the address on her phone. She can always come back tomorrow and check the buzzer panel.

Moments later, James comes out, a couple of brown envelopes in his hand, and hops back into the car.

Fortunately for Lucy's Uber bill, the third stop is the last one before James returns to Vivien's. It's a self-storage unit on the Finchley Road. In two swift journeys James takes the boxes and cases inside and comes out again empty handed. Another address for her rapidly growing list, matched by her rapidly growing puzzlement. Once she's seen James go back into Vivien's maisonette, and trying not to think about the extra cost, she asks her driver to run her home to Hackney. Might as well be hanged for a sheep as a lamb.

# NINE

Lucy tries to put it all out of her mind once she's home. It's been a strangely tiring couple of hours and she feels somehow sullied by what she's seen, even though she can't make sense of it. She revives after a shower, pours herself an early — well, it's after five by now so not unconscionably early — glass of wine and settles down in front of the latest Scandi noir series. But she can't concentrate. After twenty minute she gives up, takes her wine over to the table and opens her laptop. And her phone at the note she made of the second address James Anderson visited. It's been a while since she did her training contract seat in the property department — even longer since she studied land law — but Lucy remembers enough to know that the Land Registry holds information about property in England and Wales and that its records are publicly available. She googles 'Renoir Mansions postcode' and, having found it in the first result, is about to bring up the Land Registry site when she notices a Rightmove link further down the page, flagging properties for sale in Renoir Mansions. There's a sidebar trumpeting recent sales. Which include Flat 10, a triumphant banner across the lead photo shouting 'Sale Agreed!!'. The asking price is shown as £995,000, though of course the agreed purchase price is not disclosed.

Lucy indulges in a few minutes of property porn (more gripping, she admits, than the Scandi noir). It's clearly a very upmarket apartment in a very upmarket block, and she has to force herself to move on to the Land Registry. She puts the address into the search field and forks out £3 for a copy of the register of title, which arrives promptly in her inbox.

The flat has been owned by a John Allen since 14 November 2021. Lucy scans down the summary on the first page to see what he paid for it, but the 'Price stated' field simply says 'Not Available'. According to a different section on the next page, '(14.11.2021) The value as at 14 November 2021 was stated to be between £500,001 and £1,000,000.'

Lucy tops up her wine on autopilot, frowning in concentration. She can see that James would have had legitimate reasons for going into Steph's house, and presumably the storage unit, but what was he doing going into Flat 10, owned by someone else? Letting himself in, coming out with letters, which she assumed were addressed to him?

Back at the table, she googles John Allen, but nothing leaps out of the first few pages of hits for any of the names. Lucy decides to focus on the property instead, and goes back to the title register. It feels odd to be using her brain again. She wouldn't trust her mental powers in any other context — at work, for example — but surely she can trawl through dry public records even in her still raw and discombobulated state? Like the real-life shadowing, the virtual equivalent is a much needed distraction.

She doesn't understand why the title register doesn't show the price John Allen paid for the property. She shells out another £3 and checks her own title register. Yes, it shows the completion date and the price she paid. Further googling flushes out two Land Registry guidance documents from which, after ploughing through a lot of small print, she gleans that the formulation in the Flat 10 register is for the purpose of assessing the Land Registry fee for registering the transfer of ownership. That fee is based on value, which is normally indicated by price paid, but where no price is paid, for example where property is gifted or inherited, the formulation referring to a price band may be used.

Fleetingly grateful that she never practised land law, Lucy

goes back on the Land Registry site to see who owned Flat 10 before John Allen. Her curiosity is aroused now, and she wants to know who gave or left him such a valuable and desirable asset. But the only extract of title for the property available on the site is the one she already has. With some perseverance she discovers that information about past owners is available, though she has to download Form HC1 to obtain it.

Lucy is tired from too much screen and too many puzzles on top of the constant tides of grief and regret. She's tempted to call a halt for the evening — it's probably a wild goose chase anyway — but decides to take this last step. It turns out to be a wearisome series of steps. She downloads the form as a Word document, fills it in online, prints it, signs it in black ink as specified (she's surprised they don't stipulate a quill pen) and spends twenty minutes searching for her cheque book. She writes a cheque for £7, spends another five minutes tracking down an envelope, addresses it, realises that she doesn't have any stamps, prints the postage and puts the envelope by the front door to take to the post box tomorrow.

By this point she really has had enough. She pours herself some more wine and settles back on the sofa, zapper in hand for another go at the Scandi noir, but instead finds her thoughts turning to Vivien. She would have felt at home with the paper forms, the pen and ink, the cheque book and envelope and postage. Lucy has just briefly re-entered that world, which seems like historical fiction to her now, but Vivien lives and breathes it. And Lucy can think of only one reason for that.

She tries to put all thoughts of Vivien, James Anderson, John Allen, Flat 10, Form HC1 and the private storage facility out of her mind, but again Vivien intrudes. That strangely intimate gesture. Is James Anderson already looking for another wife? Or has he already found one?

*

It takes a few days for the Land Registry to send Lucy the historical title extract for Flat 10, which arrives in the post.

She's gone back to the office for the intervening period; they're happy to be flexible, to have her drop in and catch up on anything outstanding when she feels up to it. She finds she can concentrate in small doses, but disintegrates unpredictably into tears and self-recrimination, suffers from an intermittent headache and makes unwonted and foolish errors. Concerned that she can't assume she'll pick the mistakes up in time to correct them, she talks to HR again and is reassured that she should come back to the office only when she feels able to. She's encouraged to seek medical assistance or bereavement support, but prefers to find her own way through her unaccustomed muddled mental and emotional states. She goes home to find the Land Registry document on the doormat; more mechanical distraction, she hopes.

Lucy had asked for details of the flat on 13 November 2021, the day before ownership passed to John Allen by gift or will. The extract shows that it then belonged to Barbara Ellen Watson, but there is no information about whether she gave him the property or left it to him on her death. Or indeed whether she has died, or if so, when. Lucy's on more familiar territory here having dealt with both her late parents' estates, and navigates to the 'search probate records' page of the GOV.UK website. She enters Barbara Watson's full name and year of death, which Lucy assumes is the year when John Allen became the owner, but the search is fruitless. She's about to try with 2020 then realises that Barbara and John may well have been married when she died. She searches again under Barbara Ellen Allen — what a tongue-twister — and brings up one result. Barbara died on 25 June 2021 and probate was granted a few weeks later. Lucy's invited to add a copy of the grant to her basket, for which she pays the princely sum of £1.50. It won't be available for up to forty-eight hours but still.

Two days later she gets an email with a link to download Barbara's grant of probate. Strictly, it's letters of administration as she died intestate. The administrator of her estate was John Allen.

It's also been a long time since Lucy studied wills and succession; she feels that she's entered a time warp in the last couple of days, taking her back to her time as a student or trainee. She checks the intestacy rules, which have in any event changed since she was at the College of Law. There's a lot of clunky terminology, but the gist is that the administrator of an intestate estate will normally be the surviving spouse if there is one. And the surviving spouse will inherit everything if there are no children. Barbara's everything was a fair amount — according to the grant of probate, the net value of her estate amounted to £1,324,357.

Lucy wonders when Barbara and John Allen were married. She's about to go down the rabbit hole of marriage records when she realises that she may already have enough information to narrow down a Google search. She tries 'John Allen Barbara death 2021'. There are still a ludicrous number of results ('About 16,800,000'), but this time she finds the hit on the second page.

### *Tragic death on celebration holiday*

### *Glamorgan Times Online*

*On Friday, John Allen went from happy husband to grieving widower on the holiday he'd arranged as a surprise celebration for his first wedding anniversary. He and his wife Barbara had just started what should have been an idyllic week at Bwythyn Rhosyn, a pretty but remote cottage outside Cwmwen.*

*'It was a full moon,' said Allen. 'Barbara so wanted us to take a moonlit swim. There was a beautiful cove twenty minutes' drive away; we'd seen it on the Airbnb listing. We drove there and walked down the path. She was convinced the sea would be warm enough, we were only just past the longest day. She pulled off her dress and ran in, naked, laughing and shouting with joy, and started swimming. I went in after her and ...' Allen stops and wipes away a tear. 'She ... I suddenly realised I couldn't see her anymore. There was no sound, no splashing or disturbance of the water. I ran to the car, where I'd left my mobile, and tried to call 999 but there was no reception. We'd chosen that corner of Wales*

*precisely because it was so private, so we could cocoon ourselves away for our special time together, and I'll always feel responsible.'*

*He stops again, struggling to regain composure. 'Her body was found the next morning. Drowned. We'd been drinking earlier in the evening — she, we both, wanted to celebrate our wedding anniversary. Our first, so it was special. We had champagne and wine with the meal. I wasn't drinking much because we'd already decided to swim later and I'd be driving, but she must have drunk more than I realised. She was so happy.' Allen breaks down.*

There's a photo underneath the article. It's not a very good one, almost as if John Allen didn't want to be photographed. It's slightly out of focus and he's looking down, half turned away. But Lucy can see part of his face and she frowns in concentration. His hair's a bit longer and he has glasses and a moustache, but ... She opens her phone and checks the photo Steph sent her. It could be the same man, there's a similarity, but not enough to be sure.

*

Vivien and Max are on the long sofa. She's sitting longways, her legs across Max's lap. He's absently stroking them and she's trying hard not to worry about the risk of his nails snagging her sheer black stockings. They're each holding a glass of red Burgundy, the remains of the bottle they shared over dinner.

Vivien can't dispel the faint shadow of financial concern that has been haunting her since her coffee and cake a week ago. She's tried to shrug it off but has decided to raise it with Max this evening. She's waited till now, knowing that he'll be relaxed and mellow after the excellent — if she says it herself — meal she prepared: oysters (she was reminded briefly of Stephanie), venison steaks and a perfect Vacherin Mont d'Or.

'Max,' she says, 'can we have a word about the money?'

Max raises his eyebrows. 'What about it?'

'It's just — it's been a while since we sat down and looked

at the numbers together. Shouldn't we be planning now?'

'There's plenty there, darling,' he says. 'I don't have the exact figures in my head — there are several accounts, as you know — and I certainly don't feel like sitting down at my laptop and going through all the hoops to check.'

'But surely it's time we made a plan? It'll take a while to organise, you've always said.'

'It will. And we'll start soon. But not too soon. I still think we should wait. One last one. Then we'll be sure.'

'But—'

Max runs his hands further up Vivien's legs, no longer absently, and she stops worrying about the risk of snags, about the money.

*

Lucy googles Bwythyn Rhosyn and finds its Airbnb listing. It's a mile or so outside the village. The owner is Gwen Jones and she lives next door to it. Lucy flicks through the photos. The huge double bed in the only bedroom catches her eye and she wonders whether Gwen specialises in romantic holidays. She can't find any reference to the secluded cove and assumes Gwen deleted it after the drowning. She can see various possibilities though on the site map.

Both cottage and surroundings look stunning and Lucy thinks briefly about booking herself in for a couple of nights. A change of scene might do her good, though perhaps not this particular scene, and in any event it's a long way to drive on a hunch that may come to nothing. Gwen might not even have been the owner when Barbara and John Allen stayed for their ill-fated holiday. Instead she emails via the 'Contact' link, saying that a friend has recommended her cottage but she has a couple of questions and would really appreciate a quick chat.

Gwen calls back that evening.

'Gwen, I wanted to ask you something. I hope you don't mind. Did you own Bwythyn Rhosyn — sorry, I'm probably pronouncing it wrong — when Barbara Watson — Barbara Allen —drowned on her holiday?' She really needs to mug up her small talk, she thinks, as the silence stretches, and hastily adds 'I'm not a reporter' before deciding to go for the truth, or at least some of what she's beginning to think is the truth. 'My sister died on the first day of her honeymoon a few weeks ago. She drowned in her bath in an Airbnb in Cornwall. I'm just wondering whether there could be a connection.'

There's a soft sigh at the other end of the line. 'You poor dear,' she says. 'I'm so sorry to hear that. And yes, I was the owner then. It was a terrible tragedy of course, but no one thought it was anything more than an accident. A stupid, avoidable accident. People who can do twenty lengths in a heated pool think the sea at night will be the same. Well, it's not. Especially if you've been drinking.' She sighs again.

'I can see that,' Lucy agrees. 'It sounds totally different. I just thought I'd ask, I hope you don't mind.' She pauses, thinking. 'Can I ask one question, though. It's a bit of a long shot, but do you happen to know how Barbara and John Allen had met?'

There's another silence. Gwen was probably expecting some more probing questions about the drowning. But it seems that she was just casting her mind back.

'As it happens, I do,' she says eventually. 'The husband had ticked the "do not disturb" option when he booked, and I always take that very seriously, so they let themselves in and I deliberately kept out of their way. But on the Sunday morning — they'd arrived on Saturday afternoon — I was here, at my front door, shaking out my tablecloth and I saw him get into his car and drive away. Probably picking something up in the village. She'd come out with him and waved him off, then wandered round the front garden looking at the flowers. So I went over to the hedge between the two cottages and said I knew they didn't want to be disturbed but, as I'd seen her, I thought I'd quickly check that everything was all right, that there was nothing they needed.'

Lucy hears Gwen swallow and there's a catch in her lilting voice as she resumes. 'She said everything was perfect. She said her husband had planned the holiday as a surprise for their first wedding anniversary. And then I — you see, I have a lot of honeymooners, I make it a bit of a selling point, but even though she wasn't on her honeymoon she was so … so radiant. So I said I hoped she'd have a very happy marriage. She said she'd been widowed a few years before and thought she'd never find happiness again, but she had. And I asked how they'd met. I didn't mean to pry, it's just, well, again I see a lot of recently married couples and I'm always curious. But she didn't mind, Barbara. She looked pleased, even, and said it was through a dating agency.'

Lucy feels herself grow very still, though she wasn't moving in the first place. 'You don't happen to remember the name do you?'

'I'm sorry, no. I don't think she mentioned the name. If she did, I've forgotten. It was a while ago and — I try not to think too much about that time.'

# TEN

After Gwen's call, Lucy pours herself a glass of wine and starts making some notes on her laptop.

### *What I know*

1. *25 June 2021 / remote cottage in Wales (Bwythyn Rhosyn) / Airbnb / wife (Barbara) drowned in sea / husband (John Allen) present / husband and wife met through a dating agency.*
2. *9 October 2022 / remote cottage in Cornwall / wife (Steph) drowned in bath / husband out at time / husband and wife met through MadeInHeaven (NB Vivien Harrison, owner of MIH, denies either was client).*
3. *The man I saw with Vivien Harrison is presumably Steph's widower, James Anderson, on the basis of the fact that he has the key and burglar alarm code to Steph's house, and, less reliably, the photo Steph texted me. But he picked up post from a flat that is currently owned by John Allen, who I think inherited it from his wife Barbara.*
4. *On the basis of Steph's photo and the photo in the article about Barbara, James Anderson and John Allen might be the same person but it's not certain.*

Lucy rubs away the tears that rise as she visualises Steph's lonely death again. Of course it's impossible not to be reminded of the Brides in the Bath case. She skims the Wikipedia entry to refresh her memory. George Joseph Smith murdered three 'wives' in eighteen months by drowning them in their bathtubs. All three marriages were bigamous on his side, along with four others he'd contracted previously. All three drowned brides had made wills in his favour, in one case five days before dying and in the other three hours before. Two had taken out life assurance policies in his favour, in one case three days before the marriage.

Barbara Allen died intestate so she hadn't made a will, or — a faint memory floats to the surface, more from golden-age crime fiction than from olden days legal textbooks — if she had made a will, it would have been revoked by her marriage to John Allen. Another, much more recent, memory, intrudes — if Barbara had no children, John Allen inherited everything. Lucy refines her google search about Barbara's death, including the date and location, but it just throws up the local newspaper piece and a couple of even briefer death notices.

She calls Gwen back. Gwen sounds flustered when Lucy says who it is, but not hostile.

'Gwen, I'm sorry to disturb you again but can I ask you one more question? It'll be the last, I won't keep pestering you.'

There's a pause, then the soft sigh. 'All right. But please don't call again. I feel very sad for you but I'm that upset, remembering all the details of the drowning again.'

'Thanks so much. It's just — I'm still trying to find out more about … the drowning. Barbara Watson's, or Allen's, death. I feel I need to do it for my sister. But there's hardly anything online. Do you know whether it was covered by the press, apart from that article in the local newspaper?'

'I doubt it,' says Gwen. 'I do remember she didn't have any immediate family. I felt terrible for her parents, that's why I asked her husband — widower. I thought maybe I could contact them, tell them how happy she was the day she died. Of course it was awful for him, the husband, but losing a child …' Her voice stumbles, and Lucy hears her blow her nose.

'Anyway,' Gwen continues, 'he was very keen to keep it

quiet. The husband. Didn't want saucy articles about her swimming drunk and naked on their wedding anniversary I imagine. I had a few journalists coming to my door, and phoning, but I refused to speak to them. To be honest I didn't want any publicity either. I had to think of my business. And he, the husband, checked out as soon as he'd dealt with the formalities, and everything went back to normal.'

Not for Barbara it didn't, thinks Lucy grimly, as she thanks Gwen and promises not to call again. She goes back over her brief notes. Two wives accidentally drowned in different places and over a year apart, but possibly married to the same man. And that man, or at least James Anderson, is also connected to Vivien Harrison who runs the agency through which Lucy is almost certain that at least one of the wives met her husband.

*

Lucy reads back over her list, which looks so brief as to be almost meaningless. Irrationally she tries to think of ways to flesh it out, and adds that Barbara had no immediate blood family. As she does so, the thought occurs in passing that strictly that was also true of Steph. But it could hardly be relevant.

Lucy stares at the list. It's like some horrible version of Cluedo. Mr Anderson in Polpen with the bath. Mr Allen on the beach with no reception. Something niggles her. She thinks it's the description of her lovely Steph as 'wife' and changes it viciously to 'SISTER'. But then it hits her. John Allen. James Anderson. JA.

She'd already wondered whether they might be the same person, and this was perhaps further corroboration. She thinks back to George Joseph Smith. If these two names were the same man, was he a serial bigamist? Except neither of these marriages is bigamous unless, like George Joseph Smith, he had married earlier and that marriage was valid each time he went through another ceremony. Neither of the first names or surnames is uncommon, though, so perhaps she's reading too much into the initials. She's aware that she's still not thinking straight, forgetting things, finding it hard to concentrate. Her head is pounding, and she closes the laptop and tries to think of something else, but her thoughts retrace their familiar steps to Steph, her death, their estrangement. She can't let this puzzle, this mystery that perhaps she's just dreamt up, go.

*

Lucy's not sure where all the information she's gathered over the past few weeks is leading her, but she's had enough of paperwork for the moment. She's still waiting for Steph's probate, which should at least give her the address of James Anderson, but has no idea how long that will take. And she'll need to go back to work full time at some point. She decides to try and follow Vivien's mysterious man — James Anderson? John Allen? another variation on the theme? In any event, she's started to think of him as simply JA — again, while she still has the leisure to do so.

It takes three long mornings in the café near Vivien's house, drinking indifferent coffee and unable even to read a book in case she misses something, before she strikes gold again. Vivien comes out of the house, calling something through the front door before she pulls it to and heads off briskly in the direction of her office. Ten minutes later, JA emerges. He's wearing a hat, a Fedora tilted at a rakish angle so she can't get a clear view of his face. He double locks the door behind him and starts walking in the opposite direction. Lucy slips away from her table and strolls casually some way behind him, another of her caps obscuring her face in turn. It's a fine day but there aren't too many pedestrians — just enough to give her some cover if JA looks back, which he doesn't, but not so many that it's hard for her to keep him in her sights. She's hoping he's going to carry on walking to wherever he's heading, but has her hand on her phone so she's ready to summon an Uber if she sees him making a call.

After half an hour or so Lucy wonders whether he's going to Steph's house again, and is proved right. He obviously enjoys walking and she's grateful for that and the weather. She watches him let himself in, then shrinks back to her semi-screened waiting spot.

A few minutes later, a car turns into the drive and a woman gets out. Young, maybe in her late twenties or early thirties, though Lucy can't see her for long enough to be sure. She can see that she's very pretty though, slim and dressed professionally but elegantly in a navy suit with a short skirt, high heels, blonde hair in ripples round her shoulders. The woman raises her finger to the knocker but JA opens the door before she touches it. He must have been waiting in the hall.

Lucy can't hear everything but she catches a few words of the brief exchange before the woman goes in and JA closes the door.

Her: 'Hi there, sorry I'm …'

Him: 'I'm not. Come … garden.'

When Steph and Lucy were still close, in the brief period after Steph married Robert and before he'd succeeded in closing down her other relationships, Lucy had been to their house a few times while Robert was at work, had had lunch with her sister. Even though it was awkward, given all the warnings she'd given Steph about Robert and her subsequent boycott of the wedding, Lucy thinks they both wanted to try and make it work. Which they couldn't, Robert saw to that. But Lucy knows the layout of the property. It has a small, well tended — or at least it used to be well tended — patio garden, and as the house is end-of-terrace the boundary runs alongside the quiet perpendicular road. She jogs round the corner and slows down as she reaches the high, cast-iron railings. She can hear voices, but not clearly. She keeps walking and as she approaches what she thinks is the end of the garden the voices become loud enough for her to pick up most words. It's the sheltered, sunny corner, she recalls, where Steph had had a little cast-iron table and chairs, painted white. Lucy stands against the railings; they're entwined with a climbing evergreen plant so she's screened, but can hear enough to follow. She puts her phone on record and listens as hard as she can.

After a while the conversation stops and she hears the scrape of iron against the patio, glimpses a shadow of movement as JA and the woman go towards the house, registers the soft click of the French windows closing behind them. She imagines, given what she's heard, that they're heading to Steph's bed. Which is at the back of the house, she remembers; the small spare bedroom and narrow home office are at the front, and she can't see the mysterious JA bedding his sexy blonde in either of those. She retraces her steps, pauses as she passes the drive and has a rapid glance inside the car, but there's nothing to indicate who the woman is. A box of tissues, a carry-out coffee goblet, a lipstick, a collapsed umbrella, a bag for life, a pair of flat slip-on shoes she maybe uses for driving.

Lucy makes her way home and plays the recorded conversation a couple of times, typing it up on her laptop as well as she can. The quality isn't brilliant and she has to fill in a few overheard or probable words where she can't catch everything, but the gist is fairly obvious, as it had been from the patchwork she'd heard from the street.

*Him: 'You're looking gorgeous. Very sexy in that skirt. Like an air hostess. You can serve me at my seat any time!'*

*Her: [Irritating giggle.] 'You said to be smart. Professional like.'*

*Him: 'Yes. If we're going to meet here you need to look like an estate agent. The neighbours aren't nosy but you never know.'*

*Her: 'It's a nice house though. Are you selling it?'*

*Him: 'Not yet, but the neighbours won't know that. And I'll need it to sell it before too long.'*

*[Pause with some sickening scuffling sounds.]*

*Her: [Breathless] 'Are we overlooked?'*

*Him: 'Too much for my estate agent to sit on my lap, let alone anything more risqué, darling. We'll go inside soon. But let's stay out here a bit longer. It's so nice to sit in the sun with you. To look at you.'*

*Her: 'You'll be able to look at me all you want soon, Max. In the sun. Proper hot sun. Are we really going to do it? Are you going to leave her?'*

90

*Him: 'Patience, darling. I told you, there are things I need to do first. Preparations, formalities, selling this house, moving money. And I'm hoping to come into some more money, even more, so don't knock it. We're talking eighteen months or so, maybe a bit less if I'm lucky. Don't pout, even if we can't see each other much while we wait it'll be worth it, I promise. Let me show you how much. I've even put a bottle of champagne in the fridge for us to take to bed. To toast our future.'*

*Sounds of patio furniture moving, footsteps towards house, French windows closing.*

Lucy feels faintly nauseous as she rereads her notes. And confused, though she's starting to see a pattern coming into focus. A dark, toxic pattern if she's right. Is JA Max? And is Max Vivien's partner? It certainly looks like that — Lucy sees that gesture again in her mind's eye, affectionate, intimate, almost proprietorial.

Does Vivien know what he's been doing with the brides, if she's right? Stupid question, of course she does, she's the procurer. Procuress — is that even a word? And are Max and Vivien married? If so, Lucy suddenly realises, Stephanie's marriage will have been void. Or does she mean voidable? Another area of law long since forgotten. In any event, surely Max / JA has no legal right to inherit her estate, though if he's uncovered that might be the least of his worries. Would it come to her instead? But it's not the money that's driving her, and she's well enough off in her own right. She'd rather give it to a charity though than see Max / JA's grubby hands all over it.

But does Vivien know what he's been doing with his faux air hostess? Lucy would bet she doesn't. And it sounds as though she's not just a bit on the side — well, quite possibly a bit on the side of more than one woman if you think about it. Max has been, is, cheating on Vivien, and may well have been cheating on Steph with the same woman. And he was cheating on Steph — and presumably Barbara — with Vivien, and on Vivien with Steph and Barbara. But that didn't really count because Vivien must have known about it. Conspired, aided and abetted. What were they called, conspiracy, aiding and abetting, attempt? Lucy's criminal law is also rusty but she dredges it up. Inchoate offences. The minimising term has an almost harmless ring to it, as if the actions are abortive, ineffective, rather than pivotal. But she vaguely recalls that in some cases the sentences can be as severe as for the principal offence.

Lucy stands up, wanders into the kitchen, thinks about an early glass of wine. She feels in a sort of limbo — magpie-like, she's gathered glittering pieces of near-random, apparently unconnected information about property ownership, deaths, marriages, wills and probate, but there's still no coherent pattern, and she can't hasten what she suspects is the one detail she doesn't have. James Anderson's address, which will almost certainly show on Steph's probate. But James Anderson must be Max, and Max lives — sometimes, probably — with Vivien. So Lucy knows at least one of his, or their, addresses. Kicking herself for not thinking of this earlier, she goes back to her laptop, where she now keeps the Land Registry site permanently in an open tab. The maisonette is owned by Vivien Jane Harrison; she bought it in August 2020 for £825,000. There's no mortgage so she must have bought it for cash.

She won't know till she sees Steph's probate — she checks again, still not public — whether James Anderson used that address. It seems unlikely on reflection. He, Max, is obviously very careful. It's not just MadeInHeaven's clients who have virtually no digital footprint. So James probably had, has, another — yet another — address, perhaps a short-term rental, from which he wooed Steph. Bile rises in her throat and she goes back to the kitchen and this time pours herself a glass of chilled white. The flinty, steely Chablis washes away the sour taste.

Probate, brides, addresses — Lucy realises that Max's earlier incarnation, John Allen, would have faced the same need for another address, if her increasingly cartoonish theories have any substance. She brings up Barbara's grant of probate, but his address is the one she already knows, Flat 10.

Of course, Barbara had died sometime after the marriage, so John Allen would have used the so-called matrimonial home for probate purposes. Even though by then he was doubtless cosily ensconced back home with Vivien, just going out now and again to check his properties. But poor Steph — she died on the first day of her honeymoon. James Anderson might have been spending time at her house but he probably wouldn't have moved in completely before the wedding. Steph would have been old-fashioned about that.

Lucy closes her laptop with a sigh, tops up her wine and settles down for the evening with a thriller.

# ELEVEN

Vivien roams restlessly round the maisonette. She ends up in the kitchen, as she knew she would, by the fridge. She needs to cut down on the creamy coffee and cake, on the wine in the evening. She's always been trim, watched her weight carefully, but it's getting harder. Especially when she's on her own, as now. Max is away for the night at some IT event. There've been a few recently.

And she's annoyed with herself for allowing Max to distract her from the money the other day. He was always good at that, she thinks ruefully, though with a smile. She can never have enough of Max. But still. They need to talk.

She finds it hard to admit to herself, tries to bat the thought away, but she worries about his commitment to her. Perhaps not commitment, that's the wrong word, makes it sound like a business investment. She bats that thought away too.

What she worries about is his fidelity, his loyalty to her. Vivien doesn't worry about the obvious lures, the opportunities she knows about. There are aspects she finds difficult, but she doesn't feel threatened, at risk. Well, not most of the time anyway. But she sometimes wonders whether he might find someone younger. She's starting to notice the web of fine lines around her eyes, a slight, shudder-inducing crepiness in the skin of her neck, a softening, even sagging, of her normally tight, flat stomach. With a sigh, she opens the fridge and pours herself a glass of Sancerre.

*

There's not much more Lucy can do now until Steph's probate comes through, so she tries to zip herself back into normal life — makes a couple of appearances in the office, goes out for drinks with colleagues and meals and cinema with friends. But the commiserations and condolences about Steph are hard to bear and, still not convinced there's any meaning to it, she doesn't want to talk about her febrile suspicions, so after a frenetic fortnight she drifts back out of socialising and just focuses on work when she feels able to. And checking the GOV.UK website obsessively.

The following week, and two months after she died, Steph's probate is there. Or more accurately, as with Barbara, her letters of administration; Steph died intestate, which surprises Lucy. Steph was organised and efficient and would surely have had a will? But of course — Lucy checks her earlier recollection — any will made before her marriage, unless explicitly made in expectation of it, would have been automatically revoked when she married again. She must have not realised, or if she had she maybe intended to make a new one in due course.

Lucy reads on. James Anderson is Steph's administrator — no surprises there. The estate is valued at over two million pounds. And of course, she suddenly realises, there would have been no inheritance tax because everything went to the surviving spouse.

Although … Barbara, at least on the basis of what Gwen said, had no siblings, or at least none who were alive when she died. Lucy isn't relying on Steph leaving her anything, but don't close family have some sort of entitlement on an intestacy? Or is it just children? She can't recall the detail from when she checked Barbara's probate — only a few days ago but she's finding it hard to keep track of so much information revealing itself so rapidly, with her head still aching and her heart still sore — so she googles and confirms that, since the

Inheritance and Trustees' Powers Act 2014, the surviving spouse takes the lot where there are no children.

She's disappointed, not for herself but by the unfairness of it all, at least in this context. If her suspicions are correct, the last person who deserves to inherit is James Anderson. There's something still niggling her about the figures though. The bulk of Steph's estate must have been the house. Lucy frowns. She'd always thought that Robert made a lot of money, had a good feel for investments. Was she wrong, or could Steph's ephemeral second husband have somehow siphoned off some of the cash? Or other assets? She tries to recall what Robert did exactly, and realises she doesn't know. Steph had given the impression it was something in the City and that he was very well off, but they had soon stopped talking much about Robert in an unsuccessful attempt to find some uncontroversial common ground, and then they'd stopped talking at all.

Now, Lucy googles Robert Faulkner. She needs to narrow down the search, and tries to remember his middle name; it had been on the wedding invitation that she'd spurned. Terence, that was it. She searches again, and adds 'died' and 'death' and '2022'. Google throws up a brief death notice in The Journal of Gemmology. Thomas had been a wholesaler of precious stones. Further research reveals that the wholesale gem market is not generally as lucrative as it sounds, but presumably provides the opportunity to acquire precious stones at wholesale prices. Perhaps that's where he put his money. In which case perhaps James Anderson, if he knew about it, hadn't been entirely honest in valuing Steph's estate. Had he siphoned off some valuable gems? Maybe Robert kept them in a home safe rather than pay for professional storage. And maybe James Anderson had quietly removed them to his own professional storage. So he could value the estate at less than its actual worth and pay less inheritance tax? But no: again, there's no inheritance tax between spouses, so James Anderson would have scooped the lot anyway. As, come to think of it, would Barbara's widower John Allen. Lucy's mind returns to James Anderson and she wonders briefly whether Vivien knows about the apparent discrepancy in value and about his storage facility, then orders — almost a knee-jerk reaction now, she thinks wryly — a copy of Robert's grant of probate.

She's shaken out of her wondering when she remembers to check James Anderson's address on Stephanie's grant of probate. She'd hoped that he would have used his address before the marriage. But he'd clearly taken the view that giving an address that anyone could connect to him by virtue of his marriage to Steph would be safer than giving another address that could maybe yield more information about him. And anyway, who would question a husband and wife having the same address?

*

Robert's grant of probate and will have arrived, or at least the emailed links to download them. Lucy sees that, as she half suspected, Robert's estate was valued at considerably more than Steph's. She checks his will. Apart from legacies to his brother Brian Matthew Faulkner and to a charity supporting research into something called Fibrodysplasia Ossificans Progressiva, the residue goes to Steph absolutely. At least in his death Robert was generous to his wife.

Lucy can't think of anything more she can do to find out about what happened to Steph or to Barbara. She brings up the brief notes she made a month or so ago and skims through them. The dates stand out from the text — Barbara died in June 2021, Steph in October 2022. Lucy frowns, remembering that Vivien bought the maisonette in August 2020. For cash. She grimaces. Has she been reading and watching too much crime fiction? But she can't shake off a macabre suspicion about the source of Vivien's money. Of course she might have had an entirely legitimate windfall, or sold a previous property, but the dates fall into a horrible pattern.

But Barbara died a year after her wedding while Steph, poor love, died on her honeymoon. If Lucy's noir fantasies have any basis in reality, and both deaths were murder, why did Steph die sooner? Was it the serial killer bloodlust so beloved of thriller writers, driving JA to kill much sooner after the marriage? Perhaps Steph had spotted something, called him out, but Lucy thinks it's unlikely — Steph was naive and credulous at the best of times, and at the very worst of times was wildly in love. With a serial killer? Lucy ponders for a few minutes, but regretfully concludes that she'll probably never know.

Or, she thinks again, jolted by the repetition in her head of 'serial killer', is she letting her imagination run wildly away with her? Since she heard about Stephanie's death, hot on the heels of hearing about the wedding, she's thought of little else. Her mind has been a toxic whirlpool of guilt, regret, self-blame, obsession and grief. She hasn't been thinking clearly, which is hardly surprising. Only the other day she realised that she could have ordered a copy of Steph's death or marriage certificate and checked James Anderson's address that way rather than waiting for the probate to come through, though again maybe he'd used the Hampstead house on those documents also. But still, it shows her state of mind.

Is there even a pattern? Two apparently accidental deaths, fifteen months and many more miles apart. Lucy remembers, with a wry smile, a maths class at school where they were learning to plot a graph, and someone in the class announcing with pride that her first two points made a straight line. More points are needed for a pattern of any significance. She thinks over what else she's discovered since she wrote those notes, limiting herself to facts. Both widowers inherited everything, but that was because Barbara and Steph died intestate, which must happen often after a marriage. Both wives drowned, though in different circumstances. She checks Google and learns that there were 616 deaths by 'water-related fatalities' in the UK in 2021 alone — not a negligible statistic.

And, she realises, she'd read and watched nothing but crime fiction since Steph died. Not for any sinister reason, just as a mindless distraction. But maybe it's done more than distract her. Perhaps she needs to take a step back. What does she know, really? Nothing concrete. A tangle of suspicions, coincidences, assumptions, of widowed women who used dating agencies, of men who look similar, in a generic tall dark and handsome way, from bad photos and brief glimpses, of whom two but not the third, apparently called Max, have similar but not uncommon names, of estates that might have been undervalued. She's not sure she trusts herself to approach the tangle clearly and analytically anymore. If indeed she ever did.

With a sigh, Lucy closes her laptop. She needs to take a break from it. Put it out of her mind and try again to pick up the threads of her professional and social lives for a few weeks, hope she can recover some focus. Then look back at the information she's put together with dispassion and distance. If in the cool light of that day there seems enough there for the police to take over, track down the real Max/JA, bring him and Vivien to justice, she can take it to them.

But before taking that decision, she needs a stiff drink and some mental and emotional time out.

# PART THREE – VIVIEN, KATE AND CAROL

# TWELVE

Vivien hears Max's key in the lock and has opened the fridge before he's opened the front door. She's teasing the foil off a bottle of champagne when he comes in. He pauses, raising his eyebrows. 'What are we celebrating?'

Vivien is twisting the wire now, and Max gently takes the bottle from her. 'Your nails, my love', he says. 'You'll snag them.'

Vivien smiles and flutters her fingers, tipped with blood-red, at him. 'Thanks. I had them done today. I wanted to look my best for tomorrow.'

'You always look your best.' Max takes one of the two flutes from the counter and carefully pours a glass for Vivien, does the same for himself, rummages in the top drawer for a stopper and returns the bottle to the fridge. 'What's happening tomorrow?'

'A new client!' says Vivien joyfully. She tips her glass towards him. 'Perfect timing. We've been quiet for a while. Since … well, since poor Stephanie really.'

Max frowned. 'There were a couple shortly after her, weren't there?'

'Yes, Bernadette and also — what was he called? Stephen, that's it. Anyway she met someone through a friend and he was relocated to Dubai or somewhere. And no real prospects since.'

'Perfect timing then, as you say.'

'And this one  sounds like a perfect client. Rich and lonely.'

'I'll drink to that,' says Max, and does so.

\*

I flick through the brochure again while I wait. *MadeInHeaven MatchMakers* — the raised gilt letters suggest money, image, power. I'd never have thought in a million years that I'd resort to a dating agency, but the time has come.

The doorbell rings as I'm checking that everything's ready in the sitting room, the cushions plumped, the rug straight — I think it's the best place for this meeting, it suggests wealth better than any bank balance could and I want the matchmaker's first impression of me to be as a woman of substance. But also, of course, a woman in need of a man. I'm ready to try a dating agency and on the basis of our phone conversation, Vivien Harrison is just the woman I need — discreet, old-fashioned and professional. I can't face Tinder or whatever it's called (wouldn't Ember be more appropriate for some of us anyway?).

'Ms Lincoln?' she asks with a smile.

'Yes. Delighted to meet you, Ms Harrison,' I reply, and show her into the sitting room.

'Vivien, please. What a lovely room.' Vivien Harrison's eyes sweep the William Morris Roman blinds, the bright modern rugs, the original art on the walls, and she sits neatly down on the corner sofa, crosses her shapely legs, opens her expensive-looking handbag. 'This is a very informal meeting, my dear,' she says as she extracts a silvery pen and a hardback notebook with a Liberty cover. 'Kate. Is that how you prefer to be addressed?'

'Yes, thanks.' I offer coffee, which Vivien declines. I could do with a cup, I have a faint headache behind the temples, a shadow of a hangover compounded by too much poring over the small print of the MadeInHeaven brochure in bad light. But I sit down on the other wing of the sofa, fold my hands in my lap and look at her expectantly.

'As I mentioned on the phone,' she begins, 'I always like to meet a new client in their own home if possible. Much more relaxing than an office. And I know that meeting, even making the first contact with, a matchmaker — I prefer the term to "dating agency", it sounds so much more personal — can be very stressful. Is this your first time, Kate?'

'It is,' I say. Vivien lifts one elegant eyebrow a fraction and I continue. 'I never thought I'd use a dating agency, sorry I mean a matchmaker, but … I turned fifty recently. One of those big birthdays where you take stock. And I realised that I'd given so much time to my job that there wasn't much to fill the out-of-office hours. Not that there were many of those. I had everything I could ever want in terms of possessions, this flat, money in the bank, exotic holidays whenever I could spare a week or two away from work, but no people. I'd lost touch with old friends and the only new ones I ever made were from the office. Which I wanted to get away from. So here I am.'

'Forgive me if I ask what seem to be overly personal questions, my dear,' she says. 'It's for your own protection, of course. And it works both ways — it also gives you the reassurance that anyone I introduce you to will have gone through the same wringer. So shall we rattle through my list? The sooner it's done, the sooner I can leave you in peace and start the hunt for your perfect man!'

I offer coffee again, and this time she accepts. I make two lattes from the state-of-the-art machine in the kitchen and put them on the small table in the angle of the sofa.

'I'll start with the most intrusive question,' she says. 'Can you tell me what you can — as much as you feel comfortable with, given that you know that the more I know the better — about your financial circumstances? I have the impression from what you said when we spoke on the phone that you're … reasonably well off, shall we say?' Her eyes roam the room again and she smiles.

'I am. I'm lucky, though I've made my own luck.'

'Not divorced or widowed then?'

'No. Never met the right man, never had the time to perhaps.' Vivien makes a brief note. 'I know this flat's on the small side—'

'Bijou, my dear,' she says, putting her mug down after sniffing the coffee with apparent pleasure and taking a sip. 'And a fabulous location. I've always loved Chelsea.'

I smile. 'It is. I love it. I was tempted to buy something bigger just because I could, then I realised that that would have been silly. This is perfect for me, living alone, out all day. Easy to lock up and leave if I can ever get away. And …'

I pause. I've given a lot of thought to this. It's important to me, but I don't want to offend Vivien. 'Ms Harrison—'

'Vivien, please,' she says again.

'Vivien, maybe this is also an intrusive question, but I need to know. I don't want to brag about my wealth but I can't deny that I'm a woman of means. Most of my money's offshore, of course, but it's still going to be obvious to anyone I meet that I'm well off. How can I be confident …' I trail off, still not sure how to phrase it.

Vivien smiles knowingly. 'That I won't introduce you to a gold-digger?'

I laugh, relieved. 'Exactly. I didn't want to sound … paranoid, say, at this early stage.'

'It's not paranoid at all. In fact it shows your good sense. And there are a lot of them out there, believe you me. But I promise you that we vet our clients, both male and female, very carefully indeed. Not only so we have the best chance of introducing people who have similar interests, but also to be absolutely sure that no one is just looking for money.'

Vivien takes another delicate sip of coffee. 'Thank you for being so open, Kate, about your means,' she continues. 'And of course I would never pass any of this information to potential matches; I just need to be able to reassure them that you're not after their money. Most of our male clients are, well, very rich, not to put too fine a point on it, and it's often the first thing they ask.'

She makes another note, or maybe she's checking her list of questions before she resumes what is essentially an interview. It's a long time since I was a candidate.

'The next thing clients ask about a potential match is about family and friends. They like to know why you've come to a matchmaker. You've already partly answered that — you've lost touch with old friends through working long hours. Tell me about your family, and also, while we're talking about working, what it is that you do.'

'I'm in financial services,' I say. 'Private equity. I'm a venture capitalist. Specialising in companies in the life sciences.'

Vivien looks impressed and jots something down.

'And as for family, that's a short answer also. My parents died a while ago. And I'm an only child. I have a few distant relatives out there, somewhere, but I lost touch long ago. Same old story.' I heave a sigh. I hope this matchmaking lark is going to work.

'I'm sorry to hear that,' says Vivien. 'I can see why you've come to us. Like many of our clients, you're lonely through no fault of your own. But I'm sure we can help you with that. Talking of which, is there anything I should know about your interests, your taste in men, that could help me find the right match?'

'I've never had time for interests outside the office. Sad but true.' I shrug. 'As for taste …' I chew my lip, thinking. 'As you'll have noticed, I'm very tall. Five eleven. I wouldn't feel comfortable with a man much shorter than me. I fear that might narrow the field a bit.'

'Don't worry, my dear. There are plenty of fish in this particular sea, and plenty of them are tall enough.'

I smile. 'That's reassuring. And apart from height — you're probably not allowed to say this anymore, but I also wouldn't feel comfortable with someone who was … very fat. Obese. I'm sorry. I just mention it because you asked.' I hope I'm not being so picky that she'll give up on me before we've even started.

Vivien's pen twitches as she scribbles a couple of notes. 'Don't worry about it, Kate. We all have our little fancies. I'll see what I can do. Just one more thing before I leave you in peace,' she adds with an apologetic shrug. 'I need to check your ID. Tedious and intrusive legislation — KYC they call it. Know Your Client. It's to prevent money laundering. So would you mind showing me your passport?'

I wonder fleetingly whether KYC rules apply to matchmakers, but why not? They probably have as good an opportunity to launder money as bankers and accountants. Maybe better. But I'm not surprised by the question; I thought the agency might ask for ID just as a routine step.

'Of course.'

I find my passport in the small home office and pass it to Vivien. She runs her eyes over it and hands it back to me. As she does so, I remember I also have one last question.

'Vivien, I hope this isn't awkward, but I just wondered about pay—'

'Paying me? You don't need to worry about that now, dear. I expect you've done some research and seen the obscene amounts which most dating agencies pocket upfront?'

'Yes. With no guarantee of any result. But it's not so much that, it's more that with most of my money tied up in one way or another I can't always raise a large sum instantly. I might need a couple of weeks' notice.'

Vivien smiles. 'I like to think that MadeInHeaven differentiates itself from other agencies in a number of ways, and this is one of them. I'm ... particular about the clients I take on, as you'll have realised. I meet them face to face, ideally in their home, and ask a lot of personal questions. And I trust my intuition. I always know if a potential client fits our ethos, our culture. And if they do, I'm confident that I can find them that match made in heaven. I can't promise it will be with the first or even the second introduction, but I'm sure I can find you your Mr Right. And I'm so sure that, for some clients, I don't ask for payment of our fee until the match has been made.'

Some clients. Not all, apparently, and Vivien asks, delicately, that I don't discuss fees with the dates she's confident that she can arrange. Then she stands up, tucks her pen and notebook back into her bag, smooths her skirt and says, 'Just one last question. Curiosity rather than info-gathering, but I like to ask. How did you hear about MadeInHeaven?'

'Oh, I saw your advert in *The Lady*. I thought it was very discreet, very ... sensitive. That appealed to me.'

Vivien smiles graciously. 'Thank you, Kate. Discretion is our watchword. That's all, my dear. Thank you so much for your time. I'll be in touch very soon with some suggestions.'

*

That woman works fast. She's already found me a date. Maybe matchmakers, or least MadeInHeaven, are worth their outrageous fees. Though that depends on who she finds for me.

'Thank you,' I say down the phone. 'I'm impressed.'

'It's what I do, Kate,' she says. 'Nothing is more important to me than making my clients happy. I hope you'll get on with Archie. It's hard to know with a first date. But I thought I should start looking for introductions sooner rather than later, that that's what you'd like.'

'I do. Of course I do. Thank you again.'

As I close the call I see that Vivien's unveiled her mobile number, her earlier call in response to my letter to MadeInHeaven's office address having been heralded as No Caller ID. At least I can call her directly now, though she has stressed there's a house rule against texting.

The problem with Vivien's efficiency is that I'm not really ready. I wanted to splash out on one of those makeup demonstrations at the weekend, but I'm meeting Archie tomorrow.

And I've got irritating late morning and early afternoon meetings so I can't get out at lunchtime, at least not for the time needed to hop on a bus to John Lewis and cajole one of the Barbies at the cosmetics counters into showing me how to make myself prettier. Though it's not something I've ever really bothered about, I feel I should make an effort for

MadeInHeaven, but it's too late to make an effort for tomorrow. I'll have to make do with my limited range of make-up-even-I-can't-mess-up, mascara, a dusting of powder, a touch of barely noticeable lipstick. At least I had the foresight to go clothes shopping last weekend. I found a whole collection of 70s-style flares in different colours and fabrics, exactly what I'd been looking for for ages, and bought several pairs. And I also found the perfect shoes to go with them, and a fabulous floppy hat — think Carly Simon on the cover of her No Secrets album. I love hats.

*

I'm almost ready to leave the house for my date with Archie. I'm pleased with how I look, though I should probably make a point of getting that make-up tutorial if I'm going to keep going with MadeInHeaven until I meet the man of my dreams. Perhaps that will be tonight, but I doubt it. I don't usually have much luck, but I promise myself not to give up too soon.

The trousers — I choose the russet pair — and shoes are perfect. A cream silk blouse looks good, and I dig out a navy cardigan that completes the look. At least I hope it does, I'm really not good with clothes. I've never worn much jewellery but I have my mother's engagement ring, sapphire and diamonds in platinum, and the silver studs I always wear in my ears. I need something more ideally, but I don't have the necklace I can see in my mind's eye that would complete my outfit perfectly. I find a brightly coloured silk scarf instead.

Vivien said I should ask to be seated when I arrive at the restaurant; that way there'd be no awkward scanning of faces at the bar. She's told Archie the same. I arrive on time and sit alone at the table for a long fifteen minutes. The waiter asks me twice if I'd like to order a drink while I wait. I would, very much, but I'm not sure what the protocol is so I don't. Eventually a fair-haired man is shown to the table. I'm sitting so can't judge his height accurately but he doesn't look as tall as me, and when we leave at the end of the evening I discover that I'm right — he's actually slightly shorter. Not a good match by the matchmaker, but I suppose she did rustle him up pretty quickly. Perhaps she likes to get a date in promptly after the first interview, particularly when she hasn't taken any non-refundable eye-watering payment.

'Hello,' says Archie, trying to shake my hand at the same time as handing his jacket to the waiter and sitting down. It doesn't work and there's an awkward moment while he retracts his hand to pull his chair out further. Finally he's settled, and starts again. We exchange introductions.

The waiter returns, having presumably hung Archie's jacket somewhere, and asks if we'd like a drink.

'Yes,' says Archie. 'A large white wine.' He glances at the drinks menu. 'Picpoul de Pinet.'

He picks up the main menu and studies it. The waiter looks at me. 'I'll have the same,' I say. I'm irritated by Archie's lack of courtesy but my need for a drink trumps the temptation to delay his by spending a long time deliberating over mine.

'So,' says Archie once the wine's arrived and he's had a good slurp of his. As, I have to admit, I have had of mine. 'Let me tell you about myself. I'm an author.' He fixes me with a penetrating gaze and I have a sudden recollection of learning the first few verses of the Rime of the Ancient Mariner at school. I hastily suggest that we order first. He looks disappointed but we choose our entrées and mains and a bottle of wine (well, Archie chooses that with no consultation; I suppose I should be grateful that he let me order my own food) and the waiter bustles off towards the kitchen.

'I write speculative fiction,' Archie resumes. 'More specifically, in the high concept dystopian young adult fantasy genre. I have two series. In the first, my MC is an arch-princess in the Lupine clan. The series is set in the aftermath of nuclear war, in a nuclear winter in the distant future. The princess has to protect …'

He drones on and I zone out. A few words occasionally percolate through, some of which I understand and others not. Wolf. Fight. Sword. Prize. POV. Arc. Inciting incident.

'And then,' he says, and there's such excitement in his voice that I sit up and listen, 'you'll never guess the twist — one of my reviewers described it as jaw-dropping — the princess is an unreliable narrator! She wasn't born into the Lupine clan, she's a Vulpine in disguise!' He leans back, spreads his hands on the table and beams at me as I try — not very hard — to stifle a jaw-dropping yawn. The waiter arrives and I'm saved from having to make any comment.

When we've finished our meal and wine and I've declined a coffee (suggested by the waiter, not Archie), Archie has still asked me nothing about myself. He's told me in similar detail about his second series, which is apparently set in the aftermath of nuclear war, in a nuclear winter in the distant future and involves a prince. This one has a heart-stopping twist. I cannot wait to get away and am wondering how to extricate myself politely when I see the heart-stopping glow of a free taxi. I wave it down, give the driver my address (very quietly), and stumble into the back, casting an insincere 'Thanks so much Archie' over my shoulder as I pull the door to.

# THIRTEEN

Vivien calls and asks whether I'd like to arrange a coffee to discuss how my first date went. 'The office is too formal, I find. Fine for all the boring admin and paperwork, but for the heart-to-hearts I prefer a more relaxed, intimate setting.' She suggests a café in Fitzrovia and we meet a couple of days after the Archie dinner.

The café's doing a good trade against a soundtrack of beans being ground, milk being steamed and cups rattling down on saucers, saucers on trays. We order at the counter and Vivien chooses a table in the corner, an oasis of relative peace.

'I don't like to criticise your first choice,' I start, 'but it really didn't work with Archie.'

'I wouldn't say Archie was my first choice exactly,' says Vivien thoughtfully. 'First date, yes. He joined us very recently and I don't yet know him well, but I thought he might be interesting. Being an author. Bestselling author, apparently. Something different.' She pauses to sip her cappuccino, nibble a croissant. 'I'd usually advise clients in this situation to persevere, meet a couple more times — both parties, or even just one of them, can sometimes be so nervous on a first date that it doesn't work, but then the second one's fine. Tell me more about it.'

I sigh. 'He was just — the opposite of what I'm looking for, I suppose. I know I can't expect you to summon a Prince

Charming for my first date, but I have a bit of a thing against blond men, I don't know why, and he's shorter than me. And he talked about himself the whole time. Well, about his books. Young adult werewolves in a nuclear war or something.'

Vivien's lips twitched. 'Ah. That sort of author. I'm sorry, I should have quizzed him more. I was so pleased that I had someone on the books who was immediately available. I think … As I say, I usually recommend another meeting or two before giving up, but I can quite see that Archie isn't for you. Let me go back to the drawing board, my dear. I promise that I'll find you your prince!'

\*

Vivien's set up another date already, for next week. I'm not easily impressed as a rule but she certainly doesn't let the grass grow under her feet, or whatever the saying is.

'Omar is very different from Archie,' she explained. 'Maybe too far at the other end of the spectrum. But he's attractive and interesting and polite and I'd be interested to see what you make of him.'

I'm getting ready for dinner with him now. I flick through my wardrobe, going straight to the trousers, and choose one of the new pairs in soft blue velvet. The cream silk blouse is back from the dry cleaner and will do for the second date, as will the cardigan, the ring, the earrings and a different scarf.

Cursory make-up again. I still haven't booked one of those sessions. Perhaps I'll set one up for next weekend.

This time I order myself a glass of wine when the waiter asks. I've arrived on time but Omar is late. Not very late though, and he apologises profusely. Problems on the Northern line. We're all used to those.

Vivien's right, he is attractive. Black hair pulled back into a man bun, which I know most women think is naff but I find it cute. Skin the colour of a good cigar. And tall.

But Omar doesn't drink. He doesn't seem evangelical about it, takes my glass of wine and my request for another with the meal in his stride, but still. And when we order it's clear he's a vegetarian.

'Aspiring vegan,' he says cheerfully, 'but haven't made it there yet.'

Again, it's admirable. I know we should all be eating less meat. But I'm just not sure a teetotal aspiring vegan is the man for me.

\*

'Is it me?' asks Kate. 'Am I just being too choosy, too difficult? Not attractive enough?' She sighs, tucks her hair behind her ears — really she should get some strategic highlights, thinks Vivien, the colour can only be described as mousy, a greying mouse at that, not to mention all those split, ragged ends, most unsightly — fiddles with her glasses. She could do with lighter frames too. It's clear she's spent her life in the office.

Vivien leans back in the sofa. It had been her suggestion that she come back to Kate's flat for the Omar debrief; she felt that one more visit would be useful before she decided how to move on.

'Of course not, my dear,' she says. 'And if anyone should apologise, it's me. As I said before, it can take me a while to get to know a new client well. And the first few dates can be tricky, with everyone feeling their way.' She takes a sip of Kate's excellent coffee while she considers what to say next. She decides not to respond to the attractiveness point.

'Also, I fear I might have rushed you a bit,' she continues. 'Apologies if so. But I was so keen to find you the perfect match that I forged ahead. I should maybe have waited to get to know you better.'

Kate frowns. 'I don't mean to be negative, or come across as too fussy. Omar was good company. And very good looking. But … we just didn't click. He's a bit too — abstemious, maybe. Clean-living. I know I drink more than I should — well, more than that measly recommended daily allowance anyway — but I'm so used to unwinding in the evening with a glass of wine after a long and stressful day in the office that I can't really imagine sharing my life with a teetotal vegan. I don't think it's worth another date. I'm sorry.'

Vivien stretches out her legs, briefly admiring their elegance, then crosses one over the other before finishing her coffee. It's time to move on to Jake. Third time lucky, she hopes. 'I agree. And the good news is that I have someone who I'm confident is much more suitable. I don't know why I didn't think of Jake earlier. Although to be fair he's been on holiday for the last couple of weeks, only just got back.'

'Jake,' Kate says, as if she's trying it out for size, rolling it around her mouth. 'Nice name. What's his surname, out of interest?'

'Andrews,' says Vivien.

*

Jake arrives at the restaurant just after me — as I give my name to the woman at the welcome desk, I feel a gentle tap on my shoulder. I turn my head and see a tall, good-looking man behind me.

He smiles, and says, 'Jake Andrews.' He doesn't extend his hand in an invitation to shake it, but touches my upper arm instead.

Jake's wearing a Fedora and we laugh as I have my Carly Simon hat. I'm sure it must be a good omen. The woman takes them and our coats and shows us to a table in a quiet corner. Jake suggests that we have a glass of champagne to start and we start talking once it's arrived.

Jake asks me to tell him about myself. I give him the executive summary that I gave Vivien — there's no way anyone's going to be interested in any detail about private equity, venture capitalism and life sciences. But I'm curious about Jake and ask him about himself. He's an IT consultant. 'Not very interesting,' he says, with a careless shrug. 'But it's good money and there's always work to be had. I'm freelance, so I can decide which projects I'll take, work when I need to, take a break when I don't. I love travelling. In fact I'm just back from a couple of weeks in France. Wine tasting, mostly.

We should probably order,' he adds. 'Plenty of time to continue the conversation over the food.'

I give the menu the most cursory of glances and order without much thought. I'm entranced by Jake. Can't stop looking at him, drinking in his features. He really is handsome. I think I've met my Prince Charming. I hope I can keep him. Third time lucky maybe?

The waitress brings our main courses, opens the red wine that Jake ordered and pours a small amount for him to taste. He sticks his nose into the glass and takes a deep breath in, his eyes closed, then swills it round his mouth, all done with practised smoothness.

'Delicious,' he says with a nod at the waitress, who fills my glass then tops up his. I glance at the label; it's a St Joseph. I take a sip and agree with Jake's assessment.

'I'm not a connoisseur,' I say. 'Just — love the stuff. After a long day in the office, back in the flat on my own, a glass of good wine is the perfect tonic. Relaxes me when I'm stressed — which I usually am after a long day in the office — and revives me, at least if it's a chilled white, when I'm tired and need to go out. Not that I go out much to be honest. It's hard to keep on top of the job and have a social life.'

'Which is why you approached MadeInHeaven, I guess,' he says gently. 'Here's to your social life, Kate. Maybe to ours!'

Over our espressos, Jake asks where I live. 'I'm just asking in case we can share a taxi,' he adds, and looks pleased when I say Chelsea. 'Same general direction as me,' he says. 'And even nearer to where I used to live. If you're happy to share, we can drop you off en route. I'm in South Ken. For the moment at least. I sold my flat recently — it was in Knightsbridge — got an offer that was too good to refuse even though I hadn't yet found anywhere to buy. So I'm renting. I must start house-hunting again now I'm back from my little escape.'

Jake glances at the bill when the waitress brings it over and hands her an Amex card. When he's putting the card back in his wallet, he says, fumbling a little, 'Kate, I … erm, I don't really know what the form is here. But I'd love to see you again. Do you know whether we need to arrange it through MadeInHeaven? I've never got beyond a first date before. Not that I've had many.' He gives a self-deprecatory laugh.

'No idea,' I say. 'I'm in the same boat. But I imagine we can make whatever arrangements we like provided we keep Vivien — Ms Harrison — in the loop.'

When the taxi glides to a stop opposite my flat, Jake leans towards me and brushes my cheek with his lips. We've exchanged mobile numbers and arranged to meet again on Friday. Jake mentions that he prefers to use WhatsApp — something to do with his phone sometimes losing text messages — which is fine by me.

'It's been a lovely evening,' he says. 'I can't wait for the next one.'

'Me neither! Thanks so much. Have a good rest of week.' I manage to get out of the taxi without too much difficulty — it's always a bit of a struggle, given my height — and turn at the floodlit entrance to wave to him. The taxi waits until I'm inside. Such a gentleman.

*

Vivien calls me the following morning and asks how it went last night.

'I hope it was better than Archie and Omar,' she says with a laugh that tinkles like glass. 'I'm sorry about them, Kate. I was too rushed. As I've said, I was so keen to get you started. You deserve to meet Mr Right but I am aware that the first two at least were Mr Wrongs.'

'Don't worry,' I say graciously, trying to disguise my excitement. It somehow wouldn't feel professional to reveal quite how enthusiastic I feel. 'Vivien, we — at least I, and I hope Jake — had such an enjoyable evening. I think Archie and Omar have been eclipsed! Even the memory. Thank you so much for arranging it, for suggesting Jake. I really like him.'

'I'm so glad, but I have to say I'm not surprised, I was sure you'd hit it off. I was going to suggest we meet, but we can chat now if that's easier?'

117

I'm at work, but have slipped out and am on the pavement surrounded by smokers. 'Let's do that. I can't really get away from the office today.'

'So, I've already had a word with Jake,' Vivien resumes. 'He said you're meeting again on Friday.'

'Yes.' My heart flutters in anticipation. 'Is that OK, Vivien? That we arranged the next date without going through you?'

'Of course it is, my dear! I've done my first job, introducing two people who spark. As you know to your cost, there are sometimes false starts. But I felt — confident — about Jake. If he hadn't been away I might have introduced you to him first, but it's sometimes better to get a feel for other men.'

'Has he — this might be indiscreet, but I was wondering — have you arranged many introductions for him? He told me he also hadn't got past a first date, which was reassuring actually. Made me feel … I don't know, safe I suppose. In good hands. He must know what sort of woman he's looking for, not jumping at the first, if you know what I mean.'

'Absolutely, my dear,' says Vivien. 'You've hit the nail on the head.' She sounds as happy as I feel, and I can understand why she's so successful at what she does — she's a natural matchmaker. 'But in answer to your question, like you he's only had a couple of earlier introductions. They were before he got so caught up with selling his flat, and after the sale had gone through he treated himself to a short break in France. To recover from the stress. I must let you get back to your work, my dear. Let me know how you get on, Kate. I'm personally invested in my clients' happiness. So do keep in touch, and don't hesitate to call if you've got any questions, anything at all. No texting though please, you know my quaint views about digital privacy.' She gives another tinkling, silvery laugh.

I promise to keep her in the loop, but only by phone, and head back into the building.

*

Jake WhatsApped me yesterday saying he'd booked a table at Vinoteca for Friday, adding that he was looking forward to trying some nice wines with me. It's their latest branch, in the City, and a new venue for me, though I know and like the one at King's Cross.

It's busy and friendly and we have a drink at the long, curved bar first. But it's a bit noisy for easy conversation and Jake suggests we move to the quieter corner table he's booked. Once we've ordered he starts to talk about wine. He seems to have me pegged as something as a connoisseur, despite what I said on our first date. But I play along, asking where his recent tasting holiday was.

'Rhône,' he says. 'North and South. Mostly Hermitage and Châteauneuf. All delicious.' He's ordered a Crozes-Hermitage and I have to say it's excellent. I say so, and add, 'As I said the other day, I'm not an expert though. I've always thought it would be fun to know more, maybe do a tasting course, but I've never got round to it. Work getting in the way of life as usual.'

'Same here,' he replies. 'I finally got to do my first wine holiday and I definitely want to do more. We should ...' He trails off, and tentatively places his hand over mine.

'Kate,' he says with a smile. 'Listen, I don't want to crowd you. This is maybe too soon and the last thing I want to do is screw this up. But I just want to say — I so enjoy our time together, even though this is only our second date. I'd love to do another tasting break somewhere. With you. When — I hope not if — you feel ready.'

Jake's a fast mover, that's for sure. I smile, and say, 'That sounds lovely. In a while, maybe, when we know each other better.'

After the meal, we take the tube and Jake insists on getting off with me, even though it would be easier for him to go a couple of stops further, and walks me home. I'm not sure whether I should invite him in. We're still early in our relationship, even if I'm increasingly hopeful that he's the man for me. But I don't want to rush things. And to be honest I'm tired. This whole dating lark after a day, in this case a week, in the office is draining.

Jake seems to read my mind. While we're still in what

passes for dark in London, outside the floodlit circle by my door, he pulls me towards him and into a long, gentle kiss. 'I won't come in,' he says, and conflicting relief and regret wash over me. 'Not tonight, anyway. Not yet. This evening's been so wonderful. Let's do it again soon. Maybe try another branch of Vinoteca; it'll seem like a continuation. Shall I message you tomorrow?'

I mumble my agreement and let myself into my flat, Jake waiting to see me safely in, then collapse, exhausted, onto my sofa. I need to face up to what's bothering me. I'm not sure how to deal with it best and have been putting off thinking about it, but things are moving so fast that I might not be able to do so for much longer. Of course I'm really pleased about the heady pace at which our relationship is developing, but I need to make a plan, soon. I decide to call Vivien tomorrow and suggest we meet. She'll know what I should do.

# FOURTEEN

Vivien is pleased when Kate calls. 'Lovely to hear from you, my dear. How's it going? Well, I hope?'

'Wonderful,' comes the enthused reply. 'But Vivien, there's … not a problem, but something I need you to know. It's a bit delicate. Can we meet, somewhere private? Or at least where we won't be overheard?'

'Of course we can. I can come to your flat if you like? Or we could meet in that café again, in Fitzrovia? There's usually a quiet table available.'

They agree to breakfast at the café first thing on Monday. Kate clearly wants privacy for whatever she needs to say and it'll probably be busy over the weekend, but she says she can make time before going into the office.

Vivien's been wondering what Kate's concern is. She hopes it's not a problem with Jake. It's not.

'Vivien, this is awkward.' Kate fiddles with her spoon, tears a small corner off her croissant, crumples her paper napkin in her hand. 'The thing is …' She hesitates, then takes a deep breath and says, quietly enough that there's no risk of being overheard by anyone else, 'I'm still a virgin.'

Vivien wasn't expecting that, but she's so relieved that Jake's not the issue, at least not directly, that she doesn't show her surprise. It's usually the opposite — female clients trying

121

desperately to hide their pre-marital, and sometimes extra-marital, adventures from their dates and sometimes — unsuccessfully, she has a nose for sex — from her.

Kate is flushed, her eyes on the froth of her cappuccino. Really, thinks Vivien, in a moment of near bitchiness, it's hardly a surprise. She's so dowdy. At least she's had her hair trimmed since their first meeting, though she could still use a good colourist, the mouse is stippled with the beginnings of grey. And instead of those awful long bell-bottoms, the hems beginning to show signs of wear and even dirt from dragging along the ground, she's wearing some smarter trousers. Hideous colour, admittedly, and still floor-skimming. Lovely long legs, though, if she'd only not hide them.

'Well,' says Vivien. 'That is unusual, my dear, I venture to suggest. A woman of a certain age as attractive and successful as you.'

Kate heaves a sigh and looks at Vivien, who's reminded of her one other good feature, the intense blue of her eyes. 'I know. It's just … work I suppose. Obviously I've met men over the years, had a few dates but they all petered out early on. Just never met anyone I clicked with, and I certainly wasn't going to go to bed with just anyone. Even when I was younger. Which is why, of course, I eventually came to you. Realised that I didn't want to spend the rest of my life alone and that I wasn't going to meet the right man any other way.'

Kate pauses for a long draught of coffee. 'But the thing is, I really like Jake. Even after only two dates. But now — I hope this isn't too forward, too presumptuous — I want to wait. Because if it works, continues to work, and we … if he proposes, somewhere down the line, I want to wait till my wedding night.' She blushes again, and goes back to fiddling with her spoon. 'And if it doesn't work, I'm not sure I want to have had casual sex after all this time. I'd rather do without.'

Vivien laughs her silvery laugh. 'You know, Kate, woman to woman that's probably the best strategy. Hold off for the moment, make excuses if you need to, and if and when you're really sure Jake's the one for you, tell him exactly that. It worked for Anne Boleyn after all.' She realises, too late, that

Anne Boleyn is probably not a reassuring model. But Kate doesn't seem to have noticed.

'I was worried he'd give up on me,' she says.

'I doubt it, my dear. I know he's very keen. Fingers crossed, and keep me posted.'

\*

Carol is sitting hunched over a cooling cup of coffee, staring at the blank screen of her laptop and willing herself to write something. Anything. Start the article. Write the pitch. Even just a title.

Not that she's got any real subject-matter yet, just an idea. She was laid off a couple of weeks ago — well, not so much laid off, which might suggest an element of compensation, of easing the way out, but just told that her contributions were no longer needed. The editor apologised for his brutality but apologies didn't pay the mortgage. The paper was merging with several other small local North London rags and going fully online. The Ham & High crime reporter was younger and more experienced, which seemed a contradiction in terms to Carol but the editor said that was just the way it was and Carol wouldn't be needed anymore. She was welcome to submit on a freelance basis, of course, but no guarantees. The editor waved a piece of paper at her and helpfully explained that she'd originally agreed to work on a self-employed basis. No redundancy payments, no notice, no nothing.

She didn't have a lot of outgoings, which was just as well. A small mortgage on her small flat in Wood Green. She could live cheaply, was used to that as her salary — or her not-salary, it now seemed — had also been small. But she'd been growing restive, fed up with living cheaply, even before she got the non-sack. And now she would have to get used to living on even less. Well, nothing really, unless she could sell some freelance pieces. But she had an idea that the new paper wouldn't be very receptive. At best, it would be a lot more competitive.

She'd gone home after her interview with the editor, sat in

her tired kitchen with a glass of wine and a cigarette — she'd have to cut down on both of those — and turned things over in her mind. Writing was all she knew how to do. Oh of course she could stack shelves, no doubt — might get her a discount on the booze and the fags — or wait tables or serve behind a bar. But she was a journalist. Always had been, always would be.

Carol spent the next few days skim-reading most of her work from the previous few years, since she'd taken on the crime-beat mantle. She has a couple of ideas for making some money; barely formed, more like inklings really, but jostling in a gentle, leisurely way in her mind. They both involve crime — well, only one would involve any crime on her part and she hopes it won't come to that. The other, though, would keep her hands clean and might net her some decent cash. She'd read an article the other day about the growing interest in true crime. It featured a woman who'd started a podcast on the topic. Even though it seemed it was a crowded field, this woman had rapidly made a name for herself and, it was suggested, a surprising income.

Carol had no idea how to do a podcast, let alone make money from it. But there were other ways to profit from true crime. Perhaps by delving into her past reporting she could see a pattern in the crimes that would be obvious only by looking back. Or somehow find out something incriminating about one of the subjects. The first could be the basis for a good article or series of articles, even maybe a book. True crime books were also having a heyday it seemed. And if that didn't work, the second could be the basis for a bit of careful blackmail.

So she's been going back over her pieces from the last few years. For the most part the only pattern she can see is the soul-destroying frequency of most crimes. Theft, burglary, muggings, driving offences, rape, domestic violence, assault, occasional homicide. Rinse and repeat. Burglars will burgle, rapists will rape, killers will kill. But there's little in the dreary litany suggesting any originality, anything out of the usual depressing run of things, that might imply an unseen hand pulling the strings off-stage.

Carol sighs. She needs to come up with a Plan C it seems. She stands up, stretches and rolls her shoulders, and is about to close her laptop when an email from her friend Heather snakes across the screen: *Drown sorrows / celebrate divorce??*

*Hi Carol*

*Got back from Thailand yesterday. Michael duly cleared his stuff out while I was away — at least he's done one thing he said he'd do! Saw your email re job, so sorry to hear, what a bummer. Do you fancy coming over tomorrow eve? I have wine! Stay the night so you can get hammered if you want.*

*Heather xxx*

Carol smiles. She's known Heather since they were at school. Heather had married late and rich but the marriage broke down when her husband met another woman. She'd come out of it well; Michael had clearly — and justifiably, Carol thought — felt blameworthy and agreed that Heather could take the house as well as a generous lump sum. Heather had immediately spent most of the money on a radical makeover of the kitchen and bathroom and the rest on a luxury trip to recover, as she put it, from the stress of spending so much money. An evening drowning her sorrows with Heather could be just what she needed. And she could run her ideas past her friend — Heather was good at seeing pros and cons and opportunities.

*

Carol has been looking forward since the tour of Heather's bathroom to a long soak in the state-of-the-art bath — a treat compared to her own feeble shower. But by the end of the evening she's ready to tumble straight into bed so defers the gratification until the following morning.

'Take as long as you like,' says Heather as she hands Carol

a huge fluffy towel. 'And help yourself to unguents.' She gestures to a collection of bottles arranged artistically on the windowsill and leaves Carol to it.

Carol duly takes as long as she likes, at least while the water's hot. She's tipped in a generous slug of sandalwood bath oil and soaks in the steamy fragrance, eyes closed as she tries to breathe away her slight headache. She turns over in her mind her discussions with Heather, grateful for her friend's enthusiastic encouragement and suggestions. But she's still not exactly sure where to start, what to write.

The water's cooler now and though Carol is tempted to keep topping it up with hot, she thinks with regret that she'd better get out, get dressed and start the day. She finds the smooth, recessed button that releases the plug and tries to stand up. But her feet slide dangerously as she moves. She reaches automatically for something to hold but there is nothing. There's no handrail and the taps are set in the tiles above the bath, barely jutting out and also smooth and curved, and in any event out of her reach. Even the rim is scrolled over itself, and her hand, wet and oily, slithers as she tries to grip it.

Carol makes another attempt to stand but splashes back down. Jesus, she thinks, she's unfit. No strength, no suppleness. She needs to do Pilates or something. Which doesn't help now. Surely this isn't what Heather meant by drowning her sorrows? She calls out, then realises that she's locked the door; moreover she can hear music from downstairs, loud enough to drown — not that word again.

She lets the water drain out while she crouches on her hands and knees in the bath, cooling rapidly and beginning to feel a glimmer of fear. She looks around and sees the shag pile bathmat. Maybe that would work? She leans carefully over the smooth curve of the rim, struggling not to let her knees slide from under her again on the slippery base. She just reaches the mat and lays it over the bottom of the bath, tucking it under her knees, adding more water and letting it soak in. When the mat is waterlogged, Carol shuffles carefully onto it. To her relief it anchors her as she slowly and inelegantly pushes herself up and clambers out.

Shaken, she dries herself and gets dressed. She makes light of it to Heather but does suggest that a rubber grip mat might be a good idea.

*

Back home, Carol makes herself a coffee — her third of the day, and it's only half ten. At least the caffeine has woken her up and scotched her headache. But she can't shake off the shadow of the fear she felt in the bath. What a stupid, dangerous design, she thinks with mounting anger. She could have drowned if she'd slipped when the bath was full and knocked her head. Or even not knocked her head; she could have slipped under and panicked when she couldn't find anything to grab, couldn't gain any purchase against the sinister smoothness of the base. Admittedly she'd been very free with the oil, but surely a bath should still be safe if bath oil has been added?

She wonders idly whether anyone has drowned in such a situation. Probably not; she knows she's prone to exaggerate, to catastrophise. But if anyone has, that could be the basis for a story. It's something, or could be, and, she reminds herself, she still badly needs something. She opens her laptop, googles 'drowning in bath' and skims through the first page of mostly generic items. Baths are dangerous for anyone with seizures. Or if you fall asleep. Or have drunk in excess (but surely that doesn't include drinking to excess the night before?). Or for unsupervised children. There are examples of suicide by deliberate drowning in the bath. But nothing about unfit middle-aged women with a hangover and no muscle mass being put at risk by a bath doubtless designed by a man who only takes showers and probably thinks oil is just for engines. She flicks to the second page. More of the same, except halfway down …

Carol stiffens, like a pointer dog which has got wind of an interesting scent.

*

127

Carol drums her fingers on the table as the reads the article again and again. *Honeymoon Tragedy of Bride in the Bath*. She googles Stephanie Faulkner and James Anderson, separately and together. Separately there are just the usual overwhelming number of not obviously relevant hits. Together there is the article she's just read. She frowns. OK it had billed itself as exclusive but it's odd that there's apparently nothing else online. She supposes that both the Airbnb owner and James Anderson would have had no appetite for publicity. But it's quite the story. Losing your wife the day after the wedding. It must be rare enough to be newsworthy. Feeling somewhat voyeuristic, she searches Google for other instances within the last few years of deaths of a spouse shortly after marriage. Plenty of examples but nothing quite as emotive as drowning on the first day of your honeymoon. She narrows the search to death on honeymoon. Fewer examples — sudden illness or obvious accident — but again nothing quite as heart-rending.

She turns her mind back to James Anderson. His bride in the bath died in October last year, several months ago now. Perhaps with the passage of time Anderson would be prepared to be interviewed again. And even if he's reluctant, she knows she could persuade him. She feels a surge of energy roll over her. She's on the job again. Or will be, once she's found him.

That, however, proves impossible. She tries all the usual press channels, LinkedIn, Facebook and Twitter, googles him to death — perhaps not an apposite metaphor — searches phone directories and electoral rolls, but there's nothing. But she's loth to let it go. It could be a strong and sellable interview. She'll have to go to Cornwall and see what she can find out.

She googles the White Hart, the pub where James Anderson retreated after his tragedy, and, once she's recovered from the shock of their weekend rates, she makes a booking for early the following week. As she's about to close her laptop, she pauses, opens Google again and sets up an alert for deaths of a spouse on honeymoon — who knows, if there's another instance before she's tracked down James Anderson and persuaded him to give her an interview, she could maybe expand the article. Cold and heartless, but she's a journalist after all. A journalist on the rocks at that.

# FIFTEEN

After the next meal with Jake, I invite him in for a nightcap. I rarely drink spirits and forgot to buy a half bottle of brandy for the occasion, so pour us each a glass of a decent red. I sense him roaming round the flat and see it through his eyes: the high ceilings and sash windows giving a spacious, airy feel, the pale wood floors and white walls a perfect foil for the palette of colours in the William Morris blinds, the colourful rugs and the modern art. 'I know it's quite small,' I call over my shoulder, 'but it's perfect for me. So central, so convenient. I used to travel a lot for work so didn't want anywhere too big. I always thought …' I trailed off, thinking of the family I didn't have.

'It's perfect,' he agrees. 'And how wonderful to be in Chelsea. Not far from where I used to live. I mean, when I had a proper flat.' He sounds bitter. 'I'll tell you about that later,' he adds, his voice softening. 'I don't want to spoil the mood.'

When I turn to offer Jake his wine, he takes the glass from me and puts it down on the counter. He pulls me towards him, leans in for a long kiss. Hungry, thirsty. I respond in kind and feel his hand on my back, following the curve of my spine down to the curve of my buttocks, then sliding round and back up to the neck of my blouse.

I give a small, hectic gasp but pull away. 'Jake,' I murmur. 'Stop. I … I can't. Not yet.'

He steps back, letting out a small sigh. 'I'm sorry,' he says. 'Too pushy. I just … I just find you very attractive. You turn me on. I got carried away.'

I decide to follow Vivien's advice. I'm sure, even after only three dates, that Jake is the man I want to marry. I run my fingers over the contours of his face, the fine cheekbones, the full lips.

'No, I'm sorry,' I say. 'The thing is … It's not the right time. I've never … I'm still a virgin.'

If Jake's surprised, he hides it well. He squeezes my hand then he smiles, a small, rapt smile, and kisses me again, but gently, sweetly.

'I wasn't expecting that, my love,' he says, and now I start in surprise at the endearment. 'Don't worry, I won't push you. You let me know when you're ready. If you're ready. I don't want to lose you over this. It's just sex, after all.'

'And no sex before marriage,' I say playfully, and leave it hanging in the air, to be taken as a joke or not.

\*

Carol checks in, takes her luggage to her small but adequate room and heads down to the uncrowded bar. A small group at one table are talking noisily about handicaps and some excitement at the fourteenth hole. A woman sits on her own, engrossed in *Middlemarch*, and an elderly couple sip their beers in companionable — or perhaps resigned, or bored, or even inimical — silence.

Carol chooses a stool at the bar and orders a small glass of the cheapest red. She takes her phone out of her bag, opens the newspaper article and, when the young barmaid has banked payment for the golfers' round and is unenthusiastically wiping the bar, gasps loudly. The barmaid glances at her.

Carol claps her hand to her mouth, her eyes riveted on her screen.

'You all right miss?'

Carol shakes her head in what she hopes is a gesture

suggesting disbelief rather than negation. 'I'm sorry,' she says. 'If I startled you, I mean. I've got a day to kill—' Not a good start. She clears her throat. 'I've got time to fill tomorrow after something was cancelled. So I googled local news. This came straight up, even though it's a few months old. It's horrible.' She tilts her phone to the barmaid, who edges closer to her, glances briefly at the screen and says in a ghoulish whisper, 'That's for sure. It happened right in this village you know.'

Carol does a double take she's rather proud of. Perhaps she could go into acting as a Plan C.

'What a terrible thing. Really tragic.'

The barmaid flicks her eyes round the room and says, 'Sorry but I have to ask — orders. You a journalist?'

Carol tries hard to look affronted. 'Certainly not.'

'OK, then I guess it can't hurt to share. The guy — the husband, widow, widower, whatever you call him — he stayed here. Right after it happened. Right here at the White Hart.'

Carol stretches her eyes wide. 'Wow. That poor man. He must have been — well, gutted doesn't really do justice to it, does it? Shell-shocked or something.'

The barmaid nods solemnly. 'He wouldn't see nobody. Only agreed to stay here if we promised not to talk to anyone—' She has the grace to flush slightly. 'Journalists, I mean. Even after he left. He gave that interview you saw as a — what do you call it, an exclusion or something?'

'Exclusive,' says Carol automatically. 'I think,' she adds hastily, and takes a sip of the vinegary wine. At least it's good cover — no one would think she was on expenses.

'Exclusive, that's it. It means no other newspaper has the story,' the barmaid explains helpfully. 'But he had to stay in the village for a few days. So we agreed he could keep to his room and we wouldn't take bookings from any journalists.'

'Didn't he come down to eat? Or to drink, come to that. In his position I'd be hitting the bottle I reckon.'

'Room service. Not that we offer it normally, but we said we'd bring up his meals and stuff.'

Carol glances at her watch. 'Talking of meals, can I get something to eat here, or is there a dining room?'

'Here's fine.' The barmaid takes a printed menu from under the counter and hands it to Carol. 'Table four's free.' She gestures at an empty table in the corner.

'Can I stay here?' Carol asks. 'I love sitting at the bar. Makes me feel as though I'm in a film about Chicago gangsters.'

The barmaid looks nonplussed but nods. 'Sure. Just call me over when you want to order. I'm Moll, by the way.' She moves along the bar to serve the *Middlemarch* reader.

*

Carol gleans nothing further from Moll that evening, though she does notice a copy of a bodice-ripper spatchcocked open under the row of optics. Moll has a penchant for romantic fiction, it seems. Carol can't make out the name of the author but the title is in screaming embossed gold capitals: *THEN I CANNOT MARRY YOU, MY PRETTY MAID*.

The following morning Carol makes a point of going down towards the end of the breakfast slot. The golfers have gone. The silent couple are silently sipping their tea, having evidently finished their full English. The *Middlemarch* reader is nowhere to be seen.

Carol orders toast and coffee, this time sitting at the corner table, where she eats and drinks slowly while checking the news on her phone. Nothing of national or local interest. She moves on to conduct some further research of potential relevance to the day.

By the time Carol has finished and Moll comes over to clear her table, there's no one else in the room.

'Thanks,' says Carol. 'Moll, can I ask you something?'

Moll looks apprehensive.

'Don't worry, it's not about the horrible ... thing. Though the thought of that kept me awake in the night. So terrible. Anyway, what I wondered was where the nearest bookshop is? I'm a novelist and like to drop in and offer to sign my latest if I see a bookshop that stocks it.'

Moll gives an impressed gasp. 'A novelist? Wow. What sort

of books?'

'Romantic fiction. Historical, mainly. You know, boy meets girl but the boy wears breeches and the girl has a crinoline. Sort of thing,' she adds hastily, suspecting she's got her eras confused.

'I just love those sort of books,' sighs Moll.

'Well,' says Carol briskly, 'if I do find any of mine I'll buy one for you and sign it. I don't have any with me unfortunately.'

'Oh, Miss ... Ms ...'

'Miss Turner. But please call me Carol. I mean ... erm, I write under a pseudonym.' Seeing Moll's confusion, Carol adds, 'A pen name. I write as Beatrice Hopkins.'

A tide of deep pink washes over Moll's face. 'Ooh, Miss ... Beatrice ... Carol, she's my favourite. There's a Waterstones in Truro.'

*

Carol had hoped that Beatrice Hopkins was the sort of author who went straight to paperback but her latest (*NOBODY ASKED YOU SIR, SHE SAID*) is unfortunately still only in hardback. Another expense that no one else would pick up. Still, it could buy her some information. Carol has the germ of a plan.

Back in her room, Carol signs the book with what she hopes is a suitable florid and curlicued signature, using a violet felt tip she bought for the purpose. *To Moll, with my best wishes and gratitude for your reading!! Beatrice xx*

There are a few people having lunch in the bar when Carol goes down, and Moll looks busy and flustered. Carol sits at her table again and orders a sandwich and a half of cider. When Moll brings them over, Carol says, 'Moll, I've got something for you but I don't want to give it to you when there are other people here — I prefer to remain incognito. Anonymous,' she adds, seeing Moll's puzzlement. 'It's a real pain being a famous author you know. Everyone thinks it's all glamour and interviews, but you get constantly followed and interrupted by people wanting autographs.'

'Of course,' breathes Moll. 'I understand.'

'So when would be a good time for me to give it to you? With no one else around?'

Moll thinks. 'About five, maybe? Usually I'm just tidying up then, there's not much to do.'

'See you then,' says Carol with a wink. 'And not a word about my pen name, OK?'

Moll beams and mimes zipping her smiling lips closed.

*

The bar is indeed deserted at five o'clock save for Moll, who is perched on a stool behind the bar watching the door intently. Her face lights up when she sees Carol.

'Hi Moll. Here, this is for you. I hope you enjoy it!' Carol puts the signed copy of *NOBODY ASKED YOU SIR, SHE SAID* on the bar in front of her and pulls up another stool. She gestures to Moll to take the book.

'Thank you,' sighs Moll, reverently lifting the front cover and tracing the violet message with her fingers.

'You're very welcome. I love meeting my readers. I mean,' Carol adds hastily, 'in this sort of setting. Personal and intimate. Not being harassed for signatures!'

Moll blushes.

'Moll, can I ask you something?'

'Of course, miss. Beatrice. Erm, Carol.'

'I know you're not supposed to talk about the tragedy to journalists, but of course I'm not one of those … vultures. But as a novelist, a romantic novelist, I can't help being interested. It's just so … tragic.' Carol gently dabs the corner of one eye.

Moll looks up from the embossed title of the book, which she's stroking.

'I don't want to ask you any details about James Anderson because I know that might put you in an awkward position. But I'd really like to get in touch with him. Nothing like a phone call or anything, I don't know him after all, but I'd like to write to him. Condolences and just to ask whether he'd like

135

to talk about it. Romantic novelists, you know, can be very good shoulders to cry on. We've seen it all, through our characters.'

Moll nods solemnly.

'Do you think,' asks Carol, 'that you could let me have his address? You wouldn't even have to write it down for me, I'd just need to write it on the envelope.'

Moll chews her lip. 'Well,' she says. 'I suppose … seeing as it's you, and I know you, and you're not one of those — vultures did you call them?'

Carol shudders. 'Absolutely. Vile heartless vultures.' She digs in her handbag and pulls out a sealed blank envelope.

'Here. I wrote the letter earlier, just in case. I thought if we were chatting in private it would be safer … er, easier for you.'

Moll frowns. 'I don't know as I can find it now. Sue will be on the front desk.'

'No worries,' says Carol. 'I just thought it might be on the tablet you use for orders.'

Moll's brow clears. 'Of course! You're so clever, miss. Er, Carol.' She finds the tablet, taps on a few keys and says, 'OK. It's 26 Belsize Court, Belsize Grove, London NW3 4UY.'

Carol scribbles the address onto the envelope, tucks it back into her bag and says, 'Thanks so much Moll. I'll probably see you later for supper.' She glances at her phone and swears. 'No I won't. I've got to head back to London earlier than planned. Family crisis.' She rolls her eyes. 'Thanks for everything, Moll, it's been lovely to meet you. Enjoy the book!'

Back in her room, Carol packs her bag. She'd originally planned to ask Moll which cottage James Anderson and his luckless bride had stayed in and pay the owners a visit, but decided down in the bar that that was risky. Better to bank what she has than risk blowing her cover, and finding James Anderson is the priority now. She checks out, losing yet more money, and sets off back home.

*

Jake is away for a few days after the evening of the nightcap, doing some in-house IT audit in Sheffield. 'I committed to it before we met,' he says when he calls me the following morning. 'I wish I hadn't now, of course, but I can't cancel at such short notice. I'll be back on Thursday, but not till late. Are you free on Friday?'

A no-brainer — I'm always free for Jake.

'Let's do something different,' he suggests. 'I'll book at a restaurant near me — maybe for an early sitting as it's Friday, they'll probably be booked up later by now. Not that that's very different, come to think of it. But we can have an aperitif in my flat. I'd like you to see it. Though I have to warn you that it's not very exciting, just a serviced rental so it's all a bit beige and impersonal. Fortunately it's only temporary. I'll WhatsApp you the details.'

I feel tense, nervous, as I push button 32 to call Jake's flat. It's a modern block in South Kensington and I can see a somewhat clinical reception area through the glass door, with a woman sitting at a desk. Jake buzzes me in, telling me to take the lift to the third floor. He's waiting for me when I step out of the lift and I follow him to the end of the corridor. Once we're through his door he puts his arms round me and gives me a kiss, but it feels chaster, less urgent, than the other night. I hope he hasn't lost interest in me now that there's no prospect of imminent easy sex. I return his hug and he steps back, his hands on my arms, looking at me with a smile. 'Don't worry, Kate,' he says. 'I'm not going to push you. Deferred gratification can be all the sweeter.'

I'm none the wiser and decide to change the subject and see how the evening goes. I really don't want to lose him but nor do I want to have sex with him yet. I glance around. The flat is a bland, colourless box. 'This is … neat,' I manage. 'Practical.'

'It's just a corporate serviced job,' Jake says with a shrug. 'It's OK for now, while I look for somewhere to buy.' We go into the kitchen and he takes a bottle of champagne out of the fridge and starts to open it. There's a dish of olives on the counter, a mix of shiny black and stuffed green. We take the three steps into the sitting room and sit on the pallid sofa.

Jake raises his glass. 'To us.' I mirror the toast and we drink.

'You're wondering how I ended up living here,' he says.

'Well, you said it was temporary. I think you said you'd recently sold your house?'

'Yes. I'm between houses. Or between flats, more accurately.' Jake takes another sip and nudges the plate of olives towards me. 'I was married. And then divorced.'

I'm not sure how to respond — is it better to commiserate or congratulate? Either might be inappropriate. Maybe I should suggest to Vivien that she primes her clients; it must come up often. I'm still trying to decide what to say when Jake smiles again, his eyes crinkling.

'There's no need to say anything, Kate. It was a marriage that should never have happened. Nothing really bad about it, but it wasn't good enough to last a lifetime. It took us several years to realise that and then to bring it to an end. It was as amicable as a divorce can be. No children, which was a blessing. In that context, I mean. But the divorce dragged on because I wanted to buy her out of our flat so I could carry on living there. I loved that flat, but Laura wanted her share in cash. I had enough in stocks and shares to give her the money, or thought I had, but then Fred Linwood went belly up. I'd stupidly put almost everything into his funds, so most of my money disappeared overnight, and what was left was frozen. I'll get some of it back though, it was just bad timing.'

He pauses, drinks some more, nibbles a green olive with a red stripe of stuffing. 'Anyway,' he resumes, 'At almost exactly that time, Laura found somewhere to buy and needed her share of the money urgently. So I — we — had to sell the flat quickly.'

'What happened to all your stuff?' I ask. 'From your flat, I mean?'

'We divided it up. My half's all in storage. Everything. So a serviced flat is perfect. Everything a new bachelor needs — which isn't very much!' He glances at his watch. 'We should head off. The restaurant's very near. We can have the rest of the bottle later, if you like. No strings attached!'

138

Jake takes the glasses and olives back to the kitchen and I explore the flat. Not that there's anything much to explore apart from the rooms I've seen. I glance through the open doors of the bedroom, neat and light, and a second room set up as a small home office. All, as Jake said, beige and impersonal. There are a couple of books on the coffee table — I recognise the titles from last year's Man Booker shortlist — and the latest issue of *The Decanter*. No other personal touches that I can see, except — I notice a photo on the windowsill. Two photos, I realise as I look at it more closely, though I don't like to pick it up. The pictures are opposite each other in a folding silver frame. An elegant redbrick façade in one half, the street sign just visible. Pont Street, just behind Harrods. And a stunning sitting room, light and airy and high-ceilinged, with sash windows and richly coloured rugs and dramatic art, a door in the corner opening onto a hallway with other rooms just visible.

Jake comes up behind me and wraps his arms round me. 'That's my old flat,' he says with a sigh.

'It's lovely. I can see why you so regret having had to sell it.'

'Yes. I'll never be able to afford anything to match it. Bloody Linwood!' He gives a harsh laugh that sounds more like a bark, then picks up the frame. 'You know, it's quite like your flat, isn't it? Not so much the outside, though even that … But I meant the inside. Not that I've seen much of yours, especially in daylight.'

'It is,' I agree. 'It's very similar. Same light, same proportions.' And he's right — he's never going to be able to buy anything comparable with only half the proceeds.

# SIXTEEN

According to Google, Belsize Court is a large 1930s block in Belsize Park with communal gardens and a day porter. The day after she gets back from Cornwall, Carol takes the tube to Belsize Park, walks the short distance to Belsize Court and rings the bell marked 'Porter'. The door's released and she steps into the impressive Art Deco … vestibule is the only word. Among other features is a large mahogany desk with pigeonholes on the wall behind it, like a hotel. There's a man in uniform sitting at it, hastily folding his *Daily Mail*. He looks at Carol expectantly.

'Hello,' she says. 'I'm looking for James Anderson. Number 26. Is he in do you know? He didn't answer when I buzzed him, but he should be expecting me.'

The porter frowns. 'That's not the name in 26,' he says. 'I'm sure because I took a parcel in for 26 yesterday. But I do remember the name James Anderson. I think he moved out a while ago.'

Carol cajoles the porter into double checking, which he does on the screen in front of him, only to confirm that James Anderson left at the end of October.

'I'm sorry,' she says, genuine regret colouring her voice. 'I must have deleted his new contact details when he gave them to me instead of the old ones. I don't suppose …?'

The porter shook his head vigorously. 'Sorry miss, but it's more than my job's worth.'

Back in her flat, Carol thinks gloomily that she's learned nothing useful in the last couple of days and expended a lot of money — petrol, pub, book. She makes herself a coffee and wonders whether there are other avenues to find the elusive James Anderson. There must have been an inquest, but the coroner's detailed report won't be in the public domain. She casts her mind back to the inquests she'd attended on her crime beat. The coroner can issue an interim certificate or some such, she recalls, enabling the next of kin to apply for probate before the coroner gives his or her verdict. Probate! She's occasionally used the Probate Registry in the past to track down wills. Not that she'd ever found anything interesting. But the executor's details will be on the grant of probate and she imagines it'll be the widower. She could also, she suddenly realises, probably find them on Stephanie Anderson's death certificate — she doesn't have enough information to order her marriage certificate — but she knows from previous searches that this will take a few days to arrive whereas grants of probate, once in the public domain, can be obtained more promptly. She opens her laptop, navigates to and around the Probate Registry site and orders a copy of Stephanie Anderson's. No will, though. She must have died without one. No matter, what Carol's interested in at the moment is Stephanie Anderson's address. If James Anderson had moved out of Belsize Court a few weeks after their marriage and Stephanie's death, it was presumably to move into wherever Stephanie had lived when they met and married.

The following day the grant of probate lands in her inbox. Yes!

\*

Stephanie Anderson had indeed died intestate and James

141

Anderson was the administrator of her estate, which was valued at a whopping £2,154,387. His address is in Flask Avenue, NW3. Hampstead. Carol googles it, intending to pinpoint it on the map and plan the best route there. But the top hit is an estate agent.

The house is on the market for £1,800,000. Carol indulges in a few minutes of Windows shopping, looking covetously through the fish-eye lens photos of a small Georgian town house — two bedrooms, a small home office, an open-plan kitchen diner at the back with French doors to a patio garden, a neat sitting room. Compact and quaint and worth a fortune. She calls the agent and asks for a viewing as soon as possible, stressing that she's already exchanged on her sale and is getting desperate. The agent tries to steer her to later in the week, explaining that the owner's away and the cleaner won't be in till Wednesday so the house will be a bit dusty, but Carol replies that she's only in London for a couple of days and really, really doesn't want to miss the opportunity to view such an obvious jewel. The agent rapidly backtracks and makes an appointment for the next day.

*

The house is as pretty as it was in the pictures, though inevitably it's much smaller than it looked. Doll's house rather than mansion. But Carol barely registers the layout and decor and dimensions and Grade II listing and all the other advantages that the estate agent — 'Call me Basil' — relentlessly catalogues, though she feels she's done a good job at feigning fascination, and indeed the detailed scrutiny she gives each room would suggest that. Towards the end of the tour, when Basil draws breath, Carol manages to get a word in edgeways.

'I am interested,' she says, truthfully if not in the sense that Basil would understand the word. 'But before I make a decision I'd really like to speak to the owner. Get a feel for the history of the house, what it's like to live in the area, all that sort of thing.'

'I'm sorry,' he says. 'Mr Anderson is … well, shall we say on the reclusive side. He's not spending much time in the house and I understand he's not in London at the moment.'

Carol looks a question at him. 'That is a shame,' she says. 'I've done a fair amount of buying and selling property and I never buy without talking to the owner.'

Basil looks grave. 'I can try and contact him,' he says doubtfully. 'But — he suffered a terrible tragedy a few months ago. I'm instructed not to divulge the details — his privacy is of paramount importance to him in this period of extended grieving. He finds it very stressful even visiting the house. And he only lived in it briefly anyway.'

Carol frowns. 'Well, I'll have to consider. Thank you for the viewing. I'll get back to you as soon as I can.' She steps towards the front door which Basil is holding open. 'Oh — I've left my bag upstairs. I remember I put it down in the office room to take my phone out. I'll nip up and get it. Shall I see you outside — I wouldn't mind another quick look at the garden?'

'I'll wait here,' says Basil repressively, standing guard firmly on the doorstep. 'I'll need to reset the alarm when we leave.'

Carol runs lightly up the stairs and into the home office. She'd noticed a few papers in the bin. She crams them into her bag then goes into the bathroom, calling down, 'Won't be a sec. I've got my bag but just need to visit the loo. Long tube ride back!'

In the bathroom she checks the cabinet over the basin. There's a women's deodorant and a small box of tampons. Could be Stephanie's, of course, but Carol had noticed the rumpled bed in the master bedroom earlier. She checks the small pedal bin. A pair of tights. Bingo. She flushes the loo and runs back downstairs.

\*

The tights don't really prove anything, Carol thinks, any more than the creased bedspread, the deodorant or the tampons. So what if James Anderson has sought and found solace with another woman? It won't help Carol find him, though it seems at odds with his alleged extended mourning.

The papers, however, are more productive.

They're all empty envelopes, torn across, so at first Carol thinks there'll be nothing to gain, and the first three seem to confirm that — all addressed to James Anderson at the Hampstead address. One, she sees from the branded envelopes, from the estate agent and one from the council. But the third is addressed to a Jake Andrews at an address in SW7. 'Swordfish Corporate Rentals Limited' is on the back flap, over an apparently laughing swordfish.

Carol googles the name. According to their website, they are specialists in London corporate accommodation, trusted by some of the world's most important companies. 'Swordfish differentiates itself from most other corporate rentals by the variety of locations it offers. Many seconded or travelling company employees have no wish to be exiled in the same square mile where they spend their day. Swordfish offers serviced apartments in sizes from studio to penthouse and in areas such as Chelsea, Bloomsbury, Hampstead and many more.' A carousel of photos revolves slowly below the description. Belsize Court, labelled 'Hampstead', drifts across the screen, followed a couple of locations later by a block labelled 'Chelsea' which Carol thinks is probably South Kensington.

She takes out her reporter's notebook, barely used since she'd stopped what had passed for paid work. She'd resolved not to write anything in it until she had some meat for her Plan A or B. Does she have meat now? She's not sure. James Anderson had an address in Belsize Park, which is near Stephanie's house, but is that suspicious? It's probably how they met, a chance encounter somewhere in the area. And in Stephanie's house was an old envelope from Swordfish addressed to a Jake Andrews at a block of flats also owned by Swordfish. It's a bit odd, but again nothing obviously suspicious.

Anyway, she remonstrates with herself, she's not looking for suspicious. Not necessarily anyway. She's still looking at things through her old jaundiced crime reporter's eye. What she should be focusing on is trying to find James Anderson, to persuade him to give her that exclusive interview. Whatever the estate agent said, he obviously does spend some time in Stephanie's house. And maybe he's living in the Swordfish South Ken flat for the moment? That must be it. She feels a spark of excitement. He probably goes by the name Jake Andrews — same initials, after all — in an attempt to put journalists off the scent. Well, it hasn't fooled her. She'll watch the South Ken flat, and some of the time Stephanie's house, until she finds him.

*

The problem with watching the South Kensington flat is that it's a block with one street entrance guarded by a reception desk. Carol enters Jake Andrews' apartment number on the keypad by the door but there's no answer. She hits the key for 'Reception', is buzzed in by the receptionist and tries the same routine that she did at Belsize Court but with the same result.

'Can you let me know at least whether Jake still lives here?' she asks. 'I lost a lot of my contacts when I had a problem with my phone and it's taking forever to piece them back together, and I don't recall whether this is his current or previous address.'

The heavily made-up woman behind the desk gives Carol a withering look. 'Swordfish Rentals prides itself on its discretion,' she rattles off with the air of an oft-repeated multiplication table, the meaning long since lost in automatic recall. 'Quite apart from data privacy legislation,' she adds with the flourish of playing a trump card. She turns back to her iPad. Carol wonders whether to venture that she's not even sure of his name, but abandons the idea almost before it surfaced. She turns and leaves, thinks briefly of stationing herself in the café on the opposite corner then remembers that she still doesn't know what Jake Andrews / James Anderson looks like. Or even whether they're the same person. She'll have to start watching Stephanie's house.

*

It seems that Jake didn't take my comment about no sex before marriage as a joke and Vivien was right about tactics. I guess you don't get to be a successful matchmaker without an instinct for such things. And she was also right about Anne Boleyn, of course — her holding out bought her a crown, if only for a while. And the stakes were a lot higher — at least I run no risk of execution after marriage.

It's our next date after the one that started with aperitifs at Jake's flat. He's booked a table at the Darwin Brasserie in the Sky Garden at the top of the Walkie-Talkie building. I must have picked up something of his mood, because as I'm leaving the loo after the main course, perhaps emboldened by the excellent wine he's chosen, I compose a short WhatsApp to him.

*I love you Jake. Too shy to say so though! xx*

I pause, and add a red heart. I want to see him read it, so to his evident surprise when I come back from the loo I sit down beside him on the bench seat instead of on my chair across the table. I nestle up to him and tell him to close his eyes. He obeys, looking bemused. I have my phone in my hand and touch the 'send' icon. I hear a ping from Jake's jacket, folded beside him. He opens his eyes and glances at me, looking surprised for some reason, but I say, 'Go on, check it, I don't mind.' He gets his mobile out, pecks in his passcode and reads the message. I feel the blush washing over my face, my pulse racing.

Jake's face is wreathed in a wide smile. He looks happy, satisfied, like a cat that's found the cream. He leans across the table and kisses me gently, clasps my hand.

Once we've finished our dessert, Jake suggests we go to the Sky Pod bar for coffee. I'm surprised when he orders two glasses of champagne. When they arrive at our table I raise mine in what has already become our usual toast.

'Wait,' he says, his voice a little croaky. He's fumbling in his trouser pocket, and seems unusually nervous as he reaches across to the hand that's holding my flute and wraps a hand round it, guiding it gently back to the table.

'Kate,' he says huskily. 'I hope this isn't too … too forward, too soon. I don't want to rush you but I'm just—' he pauses, swallows, rubs his eyes '—so in love with you. Will you marry me?'

And he opens his other hand. A ring nestles on his palm — a vintage design with a green stone, an emerald maybe, and two small white stones set in gold claws.

# SEVENTEEN

I call Vivien the next morning, as early as I feel is decent, to share my news. She sounds as delighted as I feel, her voice warm and bubbly, laughing her soft, silvery laugh.

'Have you discussed any details yet?' she asks.

'Not really. It was quite late in the evening when he popped the question. I was ... I was overwhelmed. I really hadn't expected it. I mean, I like him a lot—' Should I tell her I love Jake, that I'd told him I loved him? It seems too intimate a detail somehow, which is ludicrous when I think about it given that I've discussed my virginity with Vivien. But I guess we all have our limits.

'I like him very much,' I resume somewhat lamely. 'But I had no idea that he'd planned it, had the ring — a beautiful ring, by the way, very unusual, vintage. He's got exquisite taste.'

'I'm so happy for you, Kate,' says Vivien. I suddenly remember about her fee.

'You must let me know,' I start, then stumble to a halt. I feel awkward raising money at this point, but she has a living to earn after all. 'You must let me know about the money, Vivien. I'm so grateful to you.'

'That can wait until after the wedding, after the honeymoon,' she says smoothly. 'You're going to have much more interesting things to think about, decisions to make, in the next few weeks. Any idea about the date?'

'Soon, is all I can say. We're both very keen. Why wait?'

'Why wait indeed,' she agrees, 'when you've waited all your life? That's what I always say. A whirlwind romance, like a fairy tale. Well, my dear, thank you so much for telling me — it's the news every matchmaker wants to hear, the phone call they're waiting for. And remember, I'm here if you need me.'

A whirlwind romance. The words stay with me, themselves whirling round my head. It has been very quick. But Jake seems so sure, so very much in love with me, and I'm quite sure about him, so as Vivien says, why wait? What can possibly go wrong?

*

'Kate called me earlier,' says Vivien. Max is stretched out on the sofa, feet propped up on one arm, head on the other, reading something on his phone. He glances up, raises his eyebrows in a question.

'Jake's proposed.'

Max swings his legs round, stands up and goes over to Vivien. He pulls her to him, kisses her forehead.

'You've worked your magic again, my love,' he says. 'My matchmaker made in heaven. That's speedy work by Jake.'

'It is,' Vivien agrees. 'Not that I'm complaining.' She thinks about the special fee, now coming sooner than expected.

'How does Kate feel?' asks Max.

'Happy. Thank god she's not a gusher like Stephanie so I didn't have the ecstatic tears and giggles and so on. But Kate's just as pleased.'

'We should have our customary toast,' says Max, opening the fridge. He takes out the bottle of champagne he put there that morning and starts to peel off the foil.

Vivien finds glasses and sets them on the counter beside him. 'It was very romantic, apparently.' Her eyes narrow for a second and Max interrupts his wrestling with the wire to pull her to him again. He kisses her, this time on the mouth, long and deep. Vivien kisses him back and feels the tension wash out of her. She disengages, steps back. 'He took her to the Walkie-Talkie building and proposed after dinner. She loves the ring.'

*

Even watching Stephanie's house, Carol soon realises, has its problems. She's taken to spending an hour or so in the vicinity of the house every day, at different times. Sometimes she strolls past, round the block, back again, up to Hampstead Village, window-shopping for unimaginably over-priced clothes and wine, browsing in Waterstones, returning to the house. At other times she loiters, poring over her phone, pretending to be on a long call with someone who barely lets her get a word in edgeways. On the fifth day, during another one-sided interminable conversation, an attractive, smartly dressed man is dropped off — by an Uber, she wonders? Or his own driver? — outside the house. He glances at his watch then up and down the street, strolls up the drive and lets himself in. She hears the bleep of the alarm and then silence. She's had more than a glimpse of his face — enough to see that he's good-looking, clean-shaven, with a decent head of dark hair — and noted that he's trim and tall. Not unduly so — maybe around six feet.

Carol waits. After ten minutes she's feeling self-conscious, visible and in need of a pee. Or a coffee. Or ideally both. But she's loth to abandon her vantage point.

She hears a car door slam above the background hum of generic traffic noise and glances behind her, half screening her face with her phone, to see a slim blond woman, also attractive and smartly dressed, flicking her keys at a small Fiat and setting off at a brisk walk, heels clicking on the pavement, towards the house. And turning into the drive, gently tapping the knocker.

The door opens promptly and Carol catches a glimpse of the hall as the woman slips in, the door closing behind her.

Is the man James Anderson, she wonders? And is the woman Stephanie's apparent replacement, come to rumple the bed again? But this is just supposition. She could even be

150

another viewer of the property and the man could be an estate agent. Not the one who showed Carol round though. Carol googles the agency and checks the staff at the Hampstead branch. One man, whom she met. Two women. Neither looks like the blond woman, and in any event she would have had a key while the man, if a client, wouldn't have done.

She's wondering whether she can risk sneaking up to the front window — the sitting room, she recalls — when she sees lights come on inside. She's surprised as it isn't remotely dark outside — if it had been, it would have been a perfect opportunity for her to draw closer as she'd have been harder to see from inside — but then she sees the curtains swish shut. She edges close to the window and hears the faint but unmistakable pop of a champagne cork, a brief but unintelligible murmur of conversation, then, louder though still muted, music. Slow, dreamy jazz. Not, she thinks, an estate agent and his client.

Carol glances at her watch. Ten past six. It looks as though the love birds — if that's what they are — are settling in for the evening. She decides to call it a day and come back early the next morning to see whether they — or the woman at least — are still there. She makes a note of the woman's registration number and has a quick look into the car, but there's nothing of obvious interest.

\*

My head's still in a whirl when I see next see Jake. As are my emotions. It's all so sudden, and even though this outcome is exactly what I hoped for when I took the plunge and approached a matchmaker, I still feel I need some time to prepare myself for my wedding and in particular my wedding night. Call me old-fashioned but it's a big first step. It's been a few days since his romantic proposal — we've both had a busy week at work — when I go to his flat for an aperitif, to be followed by dinner out in a local restaurant.

I arrive at Jake's building at about six and he buzzes me in. As before, I take the lift to the third floor and as I raise my finger to his bell he sweeps his door open with a dramatic bow then sweeps me into his arms, whirling — that word again! — me round as he nudges the door shut. I emerge, feeling somewhat dishevelled, from a long, needy kiss.

'Kate,' he says. 'It's been less than a week but it seems a lifetime! I've missed you.'

I lay my head on his shoulder and say, my voice muffled through his jacket, 'Me too.'

Jake gestures to the sofa. 'Come and sit down. I'll open the bubbly. We'll have a second celebration!'

He deftly opens the champagne with a subdued pop and pours it carefully into two flutes which he sets on the coffee table before sitting down beside me. 'Let me see the evidence,' he says, gently taking my left hand and running his fingers over the ring. 'It looks lovely on you.'

'It's beautiful,' I murmur. 'I love it. So unusual.'

We toast our engagement and then, hoping I'm not going to sour the romantic mood, I say, 'Jake, about the timing —'

Jake puts a finger to my lips. 'As soon as you like, my love.'

'That's just it,' I reply. 'I feel a bit — not rushed, that sounds as though I don't want it, which is very far from the truth. And I've always thought long engagements are a bit silly. It's just … it's all been so quick. No—' I add quickly, seeking his face fall '— I don't mean I'm having doubts. On the contrary, I can't quite believe my luck! Vivien's a miracle worker to have matched us so quickly.'

Jake smiles and tilts his glass at me. 'That she is.'

'All I mean,' I continue, 'is that I'd like a bit of time to prepare myself. Partly just get used to the idea, partly clear my desk at work.'

'Of course, darling.' Jake leans over and plants a kiss on my forehead. 'Let's discuss the details next time. I've got some work commitments coming up too — in fact the next time will probably be early next week. I need to find a job which doesn't involve so much time away! Anyway, we can look at diaries then, decide on a date that you're comfortable with.' He glances at his watch and tops up our glasses. 'We need to set off in 15 minutes or so. Not that we're going far.'

*

The following morning Carol arrives early at Stephanie's house. The woman's car is still there and the curtains still drawn. She decides that it would be a better use of her time to head over to the South Kensington flat rather than wait around in Hampstead. If James Anderson / Jake Andrews are the same person, and he wasn't planning to spend much time in the house, she may be able to spot him going in. And approach him about an interview. Reluctantly, conscious of her ever shrinking bank balance, she summons an Uber. No point risking being overtaken en route.

But there's no sign of him, or at least of James Anderson. Several men come and go but none is him, or at least none chimes with her recollection of the man she saw and assumed was him. Carol has brought her laptop and decides to settle in for the morning at a nearby Costa. She can't work and watch at the same time but she can check the main door of the block every couple of minutes. And between checks, she can resume skimming her old notes in search of another idea if James Anderson doesn't work out.

There's still no sign of him by midday and Carol wearily sets off home. She'll come back late afternoon, she thinks, and wait for another couple of hours. Maybe he and his lady friend have gone out for the day. Or indeed stayed in for the day. But presumably he won't want to stay too long at Stephanie's house, at least if what the estate agent said is correct. And it's such a desirable property that there are bound to be viewings in the pipeline. Surely he'll have to come back to his flat at some point? Of course she may have missed him, but there's nothing to be done about that now. She kicks herself for not seizing the moment the day before, brief as it was before his and woman's arrival.

At six fifteen Carol is back at her station, wondering whether it's worth it, when her eye is caught by a tall, flamboyantly dressed woman waiting at the door to the block. Flared russet trousers, a long navy cardigan and a floppy sixties-style hat. The woman is buzzed in. No reason to think she's anything to do with James/Jake, of course, and surely if James is Jake he's unlikely to have two women in tow in his period of mourning. Carol shrugs and goes back to intermittent glances at her laptop, on which she's now reading a True Crime blog.

Shortly after seven the main door opens and the tall woman comes out, followed by a man who was holding the door open for her. He's also wearing a hat — a Fedora, they look like a gangland couple from a Seventies film, Carol thinks — so she can't see much of his face. But none the less she thinks he may be the man she saw at Stephanie's house; certainly he has the height and the build. Carol slips from her chair and out of the café — good timing as the staff are pointedly starting to stack chairs — and follows them quietly down the street. As they pause to cross the road, the man looks carefully in both directions in an echo of James Anderson yesterday, even if now it's traffic rather than the pretty blonde that he's looking for. The gesture is enough to give Carol a clear view of his face. He is definitely James, and hence, presumably, definitely Jake.

*

James/Jake and the tall woman go into a restaurant called Vaut le Détour and Carol settles by the window of a pub diagonally opposite. If she'd had more money she'd have treated herself to a meal at the restaurant. James /Jake doesn't know who she is and would be unlikely to notice her, eating alone at another table. But the place looks both expensive and busy. The novelty of following people is rapidly wearing off — the films never showed the sheer tedium of seemingly endless waiting, trying to look both inconspicuous and occupied while also keeping a sharp lookout. But she hasn't much else to do, she's found James Anderson, knows — or is sure enough — that he's living in the South Ken flat under a different name, knows — or is sure enough — that he's in some sort of relationship with one woman, and now he is, apparently, wining and dining

154

another woman who, it seems, spent time in his apartment with him earlier in the evening.

When James/Jake and the tall woman come out of the restaurant, he has his arm draped loosely round her. He's still wearing his hat — well, he would, wouldn't he, he'd hardly leave it in the restaurant, but it strikes Carol as odd, so few men wear hats these days. And the woman is still wearing hers. They make an odd couple, somehow. James/Jake looks easy and relaxed. The woman, though, seems stiffer, somehow slightly clenched. Carol strolls along the opposite pavement a few steps behind them. They take a couple of turns into quieter streets but it's a Friday evening and there are enough people around for her to feel comfortable continuing her discreet shadowing.

At the entrance to another, much more affluent looking, block of flats — no, it's not a general entrance, it's a huddle of flats or maisonettes with their own entrances; the woman must be very well off, assuming it's her place — the couple pause outside the door, stark under the harsh security light that flicks on. They exchange a few words that Carol can't pick up; she's standing in an unlit segment of the pavement, ostensibly glaring at the map app on her phone. Lovers' murmurs? But James/Jake already has a lover, doesn't he? And is supposed to be mired in widowed grief. Carol watches from under her eyelashes. James/Jake gives the woman a long, lingering kiss. She surfaces, fumbles in her shoulder bag and pulls out a set of keys.

'Goodnight, Kate, my love,' says James/Jake, just loud enough for Carol to catch, and as Kate turns towards the door she wiggles the fingers of her left hand in a brief farewell to him. A gold band with a — maybe emerald? Some light-reflecting stone anyway — sparkles on her ring finger.

# EIGHTEEN

I've invited Jake to my flat for our next date — 'the wedding planners' meeting' we call it. Jake has said that while he'd love us to get married as soon as possible, he does understand my need for time. But I'm coming round now to a speedy wedding. I've thought through my anxieties about our wedding night and now can't wait, nerve-wracking though it still sometimes seems — I want to turn that page and start the next stage of my life as soon as possible. 'The sooner the better,' I say, beaming at my handsome fiancé.

But then we hit another, less solvable problem — Jake checks and we have to give 29 days' notice to the register office. I suggest that we elope to Gretna Green, only half in jest. Unfortunately we find out that we'd still have to give the same notice to get married in Gretna Green, so we settle on the more mundane but much more convenient Kensington and Chelsea Register Office. We're both disappointed, of course.

'There's nothing to be done about it,' I say, rubbing my eyes. 'We'll just have to wait. Gives us more time to plan the wedding at least.'

Though it turns out that there won't be much planning needed as Jake wants a very small, quiet wedding. 'My first wedding was like a circus,' he explains. 'Laura had a huge family. Both parents, numerous uncles, aunts and cousins, even her godparents. And several godchildren. And that's before the hordes of friends … It was a very traditional wedding — picturesque church, veil and train, confetti … you name it. The whole shebang. When we divorced I promised myself that if I married again it would be the polar opposite.'

I'm more than happy with that. Small and simple suits me fine. It's Jake I want, not a load of hangers on. I'll have fun choosing a dramatic, floor-sweeping dress but won't miss the full veil, train and confetti. Not my style. Though I'm tempted on reflection by a nifty little fascinator with a short veil. A nod to tradition. Jake's surprisingly enthusiastic about this compromise.

But he's adamant that he doesn't want a photographer. Something to do with some traumatic IT job he did ages ago, which involved seeing a lot of pornographic photos. But again I don't mind.

'I'm not much of a one for the camera anyway,' I say. 'I'd rather see things myself, and remember the most important. And there's no way I'm going to forget our wedding day.'

We decide that we won't see much of each other over the intervening month. Jake has another couple of out-of-town audits booked, which he confesses would have been tricky to postpone so maybe the notice requirement suits him better. And I can use the time to work longer days, make sure I leave everything in good order when I'm away on honeymoon.

'After all,' I reason, 'a couple of weeks ago we didn't even know we were getting married!' I rub my engagement ring, twist it round my finger, admire the light glinting off the emerald. 'We can survive another month being singletons. And it'll be a June wedding — so romantic!'

Jake's sitting at the dining table, his laptop open in front of him. I put my arms round him from behind and kiss the top of his head. He quickly closes the computer.

'Secrets?' I say playfully.

He turns and lifts his head to kiss me. 'Only honeymoon secrets,' he says.

'Ooh, darling, where are you planning to take me?' It's taken me a while to use the endearment naturally. It seemed to stick in my mouth at first — I'm not used to sweet talk — but I told myself to loosen up. I can come across as a bit stiff and certainly don't want to give that impression to my fiancé.

'Somewhere beautiful,' he says. 'Like you.' He kisses me again. I know I'm far from beautiful but Jake, unlike me, is bountiful with compliments as well as endearments. He says I've been neglected for too long and deserve to be cosseted.

I press him for more detail about the location.

'Somewhere beautiful,' he repeats. 'Beautiful, remote and tranquil. I was thinking Cornwall. I love it there. It's almost like stepping back a few decades.'

'That does sound wonderful,' I agree. 'Perfect for a honeymoon. But it's a long drive isn't it?'

Jake explains that he was thinking we could head down the day after the wedding. But I'm adamant. My wedding night is going to be very special and I want it in our secluded honeymoon cottage, not in my flat or his or at some anonymous hotel where we have to unpack and pack up again the next morning.

We go back and forth about it but of course Jake understands why my wedding night is so important to me. We agree on Dorset; I hug him again and he opens his laptop. It's one of those cool Macs with fingerprint ID. A quick Google search throws up numerous cottages described as remote, off the beaten track, secluded, isolated, secret. I'm happy for Jake to choose the cottage but make him promise to show me the photos once he's booked. I want to be able to think about my honeymoon, know where we're going, imagine what we'll be doing.

'We'll book a morning appointment for the marriage,' he says. 'Have an early lunch with just one glass of champagne to toast ourselves, and then drive down. I'll look for dates when the register office and the best cottage I can find are both available.'

'Wonderful, darling.' I squeeze his hand. 'I'm sure you'll find the perfect cottage. Do you mind — it would be icing on the cake for me if it had a lovely big bath. I adore a bath at night.'

'Of course! I'll see if I can find a bath big enough for two, even.' He wiggles his eyebrows in an approximation of a stage leer, and I smile back.

'And please — when you book it, can you call me Kate Andrews? I'll be married when we get there and it'll be my first outing as Mrs Andrews.'

Jake beams. 'Nothing will give me greater pleasure. Except …' He trails a finger down my arm, strokes the soft skin inside my elbow. I shiver with anticipation, then say, 'And also — sorry, these are just little ideas — could we drop in at my flat after the lunch? I know you want a very simple wedding but I'm going to treat myself to a special dress, and I won't want to wear it for the journey to Dorset. I'm also going to treat myself to a going-away outfit. And we can leave our cases in the flat and pick them up then. In fact why don't you leave the car in my parking place, with the cases and everything else we're taking already packed in the boot? Saves driving to the register office and restaurant.'

Jake pushes his chair back from the table and pulls me onto his lap. 'Excellent idea!' he says. 'We'll just have to pick up the food and wine from the fridge, and then we'll be off. Can't wait!' He gives me a long kiss, which I return with enthusiasm and mounting excitement mixed with apprehension. I can't wait either. But I've made it clear that there's no bed on offer tonight.

*

Vivien is so pleased that Kate is sorted, that Jake proposed so soon, that she has another deliriously happy client. She makes a note in her Liberty notebook and thinks that the fee will be welcome, even though she won't see it for a while. She's learned that it's better to be patient, not to fret about money.

She frowns, immediately smooths her corrugated brow. Tries to remember when she last did a home peel and facemask. She used to go to a beauty salon every week for a facial and a mani-pedi, back in the heady days after they'd set up the agency, collected the first big fee. The first special bride,

159

Paula. She'd left a fair amount of cash as well as her house and they'd put the money towards buying the maisonette. But then Max said they needed to pull their horns in, not spend conspicuously, and she'd regretfully given up her newly acquired spendthrift habits. She has no choice really; for obvious reasons, Max controls most of the money. With the second special — Belinda? No, Barbara — he'd managed to quietly siphon off some of her cash in the year they were married before he'd dealt with her. Even with Stephanie he'd got his hands on some of her money before their wedding and some more still by some financial sleight-of-hand immediately after she died; Stephanie was so credulous, so gullible, and in the latter case so dead, and Max was so clever with that sort of thing. Vivien just manages the routine income and expenses, balances the books as best she can, although of course her role in finding the brides is crucial. They're a perfect team. And they'll give it up in a year or two, she reassures herself, retire somewhere warm and sunny, never need to worry about money again.

Max was the brains behind the bride-grooming. He came up with the idea after reading a newspaper piece about a man who was widowed on his honeymoon when a van came round a blind corner too wide and too fast and ploughed into the car the bride was driving. She was killed instantly; he suffered multiple serious injuries but survived. The widower explained to the interviewer that they'd met through a dating agency.

*We were in our fifties, both divorced. We each wanted to find the right partner second time around. The agency was wonderful. And then, to lose her, to lose the rest of my life as I'd imagined it, so soon after our wedding. The irony is that she was far wealthier than I knew. She'd made a will leaving everything to her sister and nephews as she didn't have any children, but it turned out that it was automatically revoked by the marriage. It's the law, it seems. I don't know how she'd have left it if she'd made a new will, but she hadn't. And because she hadn't, and didn't have children, everything came to me under the intestacy laws. Apparently they changed recently. So I ended up with more*

160

*money than I knew what to do with but I'd lost the one person I loved. I'd gladly give it all away to get her back. Of course I gave some to her family, but still.*

Max pushed the paper across the table towards her. 'Read that, my love,' he said, pointing to the article.

Vivien read it. 'That's tragic. The poor man. On his honeymoon.'

They were in a café having leisurely Sunday croissants and cappuccinos. Max didn't say anything more until they were back at home that evening. He was opening a bottle of white wine when he said casually, tossing the words over his shoulder, 'You could do that, darling. Be a matchmaker, I mean.' He passed her the glass he'd poured her and picked up his own. 'You'd be brilliant at it.'

Vivien turned it over in her mind as she sipped her wine. Max was pecking at his phone. He gasped and she looked a question at him. He tilted the screen towards her. It was open at a *Daily Mail* article from the previous year. Vivien read the opening words: 'A high-end matchmaker, who charges clients £10,000 per year.' She stopped reading and met Max's gaze.

'It was set up by a thirty-seven-year-old woman,' he said.

Vivien was thirty-eight. She'd been working in a high-end clothes shop when Max found her a few years earlier. He'd come in for a final fitting of a suit. She went into the changing room to check the trouser length and came out twenty minutes later, flushed, slightly dishevelled and head-over-heels in lust and in love. She was fired for inappropriate conduct even though Max told her boss that he had no complaints, in fact he was delighted with the service, and they'd been trying to find something they could do together — apart from inappropriate conduct — ever since.

They set up MadeInHeaven MatchMakers a few weeks after Max saw the article, with the bare minimum of formalities. Max had looked into all that. 'Best not to go for a partnership,' he said. 'At least not that type of partnership. We'd have to register it with HMRC, appoint one of us as a nominated partner responsible for tax returns and so on, and we'd each have to register also. You should do it as a sole trader. You still have to pay tax of course but there's less bureaucracy. I'll be behind the scenes. A sort of sleeping partner.' He winked, and added, 'And if we keep the turnover below £81,000 you won't have to register for VAT.'

'That doesn't sound much,' said Vivien, disappointed. 'I was thinking we could make much more than that if we charge the sort of fee that article mentioned.'

Max drew her towards him, kissed her forehead. 'I was thinking that too, my love. But we won't declare every fee. We'll keep some off the books. The special ones.'

Vivien sighs, rubs her eyes, tries to shake off the memories. She flicks through her notebook, checking on her current client list. Enough to tick by for the moment, until they collect on Kate.

*

Carol is in her kitchen again, hunched over her laptop, staring gloomily at her online bank statement. It certainly makes for gloomy reading. She thinks back to — when was it, two or three months ago, March maybe — and her plans for pitching a new article or even a book. And what has she accomplished since then? Nothing, rien, nada. Spent a lot — relatively speaking — of money on petrol and hotels, coffee and more coffee, not forgetting the hardback edition of a historical romance whose title she can't now recall, even though she'd claimed to have written it. Something from a nursery rhyme? Pretty maids all in a row, or similar.

She's lost the trail. She had the makings of a good interview with James Anderson, the grieving widower whose wife had died on the first night of their honeymoon. She then had the makings of a much better story when she discovered that he had an alter ego. Which got even better when she realised he had something going with a pretty blonde, and then that he was apparently engaged to a quite different looking woman. Pretty maids maybe? Not the second one so much.

162

But since the evening she followed James / Jake and his apparent fiancée Kate, she's seen neither hide nor hair of either. Carol spent several more tedious and uncomfortable sessions watching the doors of his building and hers, to no avail. She then had what she thought was a brainwave and kicked herself for not having thought of it earlier — of course, James / Jake must have gone back to Stephanie's house. Perhaps with his pretty blonde. But when she checked on Rightmove she saw that the house had been sold. Fast work, she thought, but unsurprising given the location. She went for a last look. There was a sign and a van outside the house, both emblazoned with *Hampstead House Makeovers — kitchens, bathrooms, interior and exterior decorating.* Two skips in the drive brimmed with sinks, baths, fridges and other relics of what was clearly a major refurbishment. Carol sighed and slunk off.

Now she shakes her head to marshal her thoughts. Her mind is wandering. James / Jake has done a runner. She could go to the police, she supposed, who could doubtless track him down somehow or other, but after all as far as she knows he's committed no crime. A man who plays around and deceives women is hardly breaking news. She needs to accept that she's fucked up and find yet another Plan B. Or C, or D … Carol logs out of her bank and wearily opens the file of her previous articles. There must be something she can use.

*

Vivien always finds the weddings and the honeymoons difficult. The special ones anyway. She's roaming round the maisonette, unsettled, fretting. She pours herself a glass of wine, splashing it on the counter with uncharacteristic sloppiness as she does so, and opens a packet of smoked salmon to have with it, savagely impaling the almost blood-red strips — she must have bought wild salmon by mistake, she finds it a little strong for her taste — on a fork and slapping them onto a plate. She tries not to think about Max, about Kate, Max marrying Kate, driving down to the secluded cottage in Dorset, but can't shake off the unwelcome images.

When Max first came up with the idea of the agency, Vivien hadn't given much thought to what he meant by the 'special' brides. She assumed he was referring to particularly rich clients and left it at that. It wasn't till months later, when MadeInHeaven was up and running, or perhaps more accurately reeling in its first clients, that he expanded on his plan.

He'd been pivotal in setting up the agency, enthusiastic and engaged, full of ideas on so many fronts.

'No point wasting money on a long commercial lease, let's use one of those rent-an-office spaces,' he said at the outset. 'I think you should interview in the clients' homes anyway, gives you a chance to get a feel for them in a more natural setting. And you can do your debriefs and other meetings in cafés or wine bars or wherever — again, they'll feel that you're pampering them, they'll unwind and be more honest with you which means you can give them better service. Win win.'

Vivien had seen the advantages at once, and promptly took one of the cheapest Office Sweet options.

'Another thing,' Max suggested. 'A USP. Unique Selling Point,' he added when she frowned in puzzlement. 'Every business needs one. There are lots of dating agencies —'

'Matchmakers, darling,' reproved Vivien.

Max beamed. 'There you go. You've already got your first USP without even knowing what it means. Differentiating yourself from competitors who sound tacky and cheap in comparison.'

'Well,' smiled Vivien. 'They certainly will be cheap in comparison! The tacky ones anyway.'

'Yes. All that research will pay off. I'm sure we've pitched our prices just right. But what I was going to say is — keep it all offline.'

Vivien raised an eyebrow.

'Think about it, darling. We're aiming for wealthy, hopefully very wealthy, women. Or maybe … maybe not super-wealthy. Just well off. The men don't matter quite so much—'

Vivien looked another question at him. A couple of

questions, actually.

'I'll come to that,' he said. 'The men. But for our female clients, we're going to be angling mainly for widows and divorcees. And it works both ways — it's going to be mainly widows and divorcees who come to us. Of course the men we attract will also be wealthy, but … As I say, I'll explain later. So most of the women will be of a certain age, have maybe had a traditional marriage, not had a career or maybe given up work for their husband.'

Vivien snorted. 'We can't put that in our blurb! We'll be written off as sexist.'

'And worse,' agreed Max. 'I'm not suggesting we put it in our blurb. But what we do put in our blurb is that our commitment to discretion — no, our commitment to the optimal fulcrum — never mind what it means, it sounds good — between discretion and efficiency, or some such twaddle — means that we try and ensure that our clients leave no digital footprint. No one can track them down online and find out that they resorted to a matchmaker. We keep no computer records of them — no names, no addresses, no telephone numbers. And no note of their assets, their wealth. They'll be much more forthcoming if they know that.'

'Max, you're a genius,' said Vivien happily.

# NINETEEN

Jake was so right. The simple ceremony is perfect. I wear white, but it's nothing like a classic wedding dress. The top is fitted, with long sleeves and a boat neck, and below the narrow belt the skirt gently flares and falls to the ground in soft folds. The fascinator sits securely on my head, the fine veil soft against my face. I hold a small bouquet of white lilies and asphodel.

Jake's booked our early lunch at a restaurant a short walk from the register office. Several passers by cheer or offer congratulations as we make our way there. One woman raises her phone as if to take a photo but Jake ducks away, hiding his face — already partly shielded by his customary Fedora — behind his raised arm.

We stick to our resolve of only one glass of champagne each, and raise the flutes in a toast. 'To our honeymoon,' I say. 'To our honeymoon,' Jake echoes. He seems as excited as I feel, a slight flush to his cheeks, a gleam in his eye.

A taxi drops us back at my flat. I pause at the threshold and half turn to Jake, who sweeps me off the ground, one arm cradling my shoulders and the other under my knees. He carries me into the hall. We're both laughing, though I'm struggling not to lose my shoes when he sets me down. I change quickly while he takes the chilled food and drink out of the fridge. I hang my beautiful wedding dress in the bedroom and slip on my new going-away outfit — I found a royal blue crepe jumpsuit with the long, wide legs that I love. And white silk elbow-length gloves to match. Jake laughs at the gloves, says it's old-fashioned, but he says it in a nice way and I smile. 'It's a family tradition,' I say. 'Or was. Always wear silk gloves to match your going-away outfit. Until your wedding night.'

I'm glad I talked Jake out of Cornwall. It's a long enough drive to our hideaway in Dorset, and Jake only has a small Renault. He explained with some bitterness that he'd previously had a Jaguar but had had to sell it as part of his divorce arrangements. Still, the replacement gets us there. It's a solitary cottage set a mile or so outside the nearest village on a narrow lane that peters out beyond it. I've been to the area before so most of the drive is familiar to me, but I haven't seen the cottage. I gasp as we round the final bend and Jake brings the car to a smooth stop. It's so pretty — thatch, roses, an old pump in the front garden.

'The key should be under a black stone behind the pump,' says Jake, reading from his phone. 'I told the owners we didn't want to be disturbed. They're used to honeymooners it seems, so they were happy with that.'

'I'm not surprised it's popular with honeymooners.' I find the stone and retrieve the key. 'It's perfect. Like something out of a fairy tale.'

Jake takes the key from me and flings open the front door in a theatrical gesture. Inside, the cottage has been sympathetically modernised. A cosy sitting room, with exposed beams and a wood burner and an impressive collection of thriving houseplants. The kitchen diner looks traditional but closer inspection reveals state-of-the-art appliances and a well stocked fridge and store cupboard.

Jake carries our cases up the narrow stairs. 'You're travelling light, my love,' he laughs, hoisting my Osprey hold-all easily above his shoulder.

'You just think that because you're so strong,' I tease. 'Anyway, I didn't bring much. I thought we'd probably be spending most of our honeymoon in—'

'In here,' says Jake, flinging open the door to the left of the landing and revealing a large, light room with an enormous double bed strewn with red rose petals. There's an ice-bucket on the dresser in which a bottle of Taittinger nestles, with two champagne glasses beside it.

Jake sets the cases down and pulls me to him. He puts his hands either side of my face and kisses me hungrily. I feel the bulge in his crotch stiffen. I stiffen also.

'Darling,' I gasp, leaning away from him. 'Please. I'm so nervous. Can we — can we take it slowly? Maybe wait till later? Have a few drinks, a bite to eat?'

'Of course, my love,' says my handsome new husband. 'Anything you say.'

I move back into his embrace. 'Thank you. And I know what will relax me later, before we … before. A lovely hot bath. And I bet there'll be lots of yummy bath oils and things, it's that sort of place. And I brought a bottle of my favourite, in case not.'

*

As she's making coffee the following morning Vivien still can't shake off the mental pictures of Max and Kate, frolicking on their honeymoon. She tries to distract herself by picking up her train of thought from the previous evening, her memories of the birth of MadeInHeaven.

Max had waited a couple of weeks after he'd first started focusing on the wealthy widowed and divorced women the agency would want to attract before he elaborated further on his idea. He'd taken Vivien out to dinner and they were back in his rented flat. Vivien had moved in with him shortly after they met; it was a lot better than her bedsit, though she knew Max yearned to find something more private, quieter, with its own street entrance. But they didn't have enough money for anything like that. Not then.

They were in the antique love seat that Max had just bought to celebrate the launch of the agency, angled to face the other across the divide and holding a glass of brandy to round off the evening, when he asked, à propos of nothing, 'What's the worst thing you've ever done?'

Vivien frowned. 'What?'

Max shrugged. 'I'm just curious. We don't talk a lot about the past, our own past.'

'Who needs the past? That's what you said when we got together. That we should look forward, at our future, now we've found each other.'

Max leaned towards her and kissed her. 'I did. But now I'm curious. There's a reason, or might be. So what is it?'

Vivien thought for a few moments. 'You mean, the really worst thing?'

'I mean the really worst thing.'

'What if it's … really bad? So bad you never want to see me again?' Vivien shuddered.

Max gave her another kiss. 'That won't happen, my love. And maybe the worse the better.'

Vivien frowned again, puzzled. She reflected for a while, wanting to get this right. Max had been something of a saviour for her, rescuing her from the seemingly interminable dreary string of jobs as shop assistant, temp, waitress, shop assistant, temp, waitress that had followed her fall from grace as an escort girl. Well, woman really; by her early thirties she was already finding it harder to score the classier men and the classier tips. Max was generous and apparently had a fair amount to be generous with, though he was vague about how he earned it. But she was happy not to know as long as some of it fell her way.

Vivien gave a fractional shake of her head, trying to pull herself out of her reverie. Time to tell Max what he wanted to know. Or what she thought he wanted to know. She looked at him sideways, her eyes half-closed. 'I was working for an escort agency.'

Max leaned his head back and laughed. 'Darling, if that's the worst thing —'

'No, that's just what I was doing at the time. I mean, not literally at the time, but for my job. Well, actually, it was literally at the time. Almost literally. I stole £100 from a john.'

Max reached out, turned her head further towards him and gave her a long, full kiss. 'I'm sure he could afford it, sweetheart. And anyway, I already knew you'd worked for an escort agency. Even which one — Tassels without Hassles or something equally crass wasn't it? Don't you remember, you told me, quite early on in our relationship.'

Vivien did remember. He'd said he found it quite a turn-on and pressed her for details, but she'd resisted. Maybe he wouldn't in fact find it a turn-on.

'Yes,' she said. 'But it was the stealing I meant. That was worse than being a call— I mean an escort girl. He'd left his wallet lying around when he went to the loo.'

Max raised an eyebrow. 'Careless.'

'Yes. Unusual, also. Most johns never let their wallets out of their sight.'

Max laughed again. 'I wonder why?'

Vivien smiled. 'I could see all these £50 notes sticking out. The wallet was too small, probably bought before those big fifties were in use. So I just slipped out two. But when he was dressed and opened his wallet to pay me, he noticed. He counted them. Cheapskate. Made a huge fuss, complained, and I got a real bollocking from the agency. They threatened to kick me off their books but I pleaded with them, said it was a mistake, a moment of madness. They agreed to keep me but I had to change my professional name.'

'Bastards. But I wasn't thinking of that level of badness. What about what happened to Iris?'

The room seemed to freeze and become silent, though it had obviously not been moving or even noisy a moment before. But it took on the slight gloss, the sharp focus, of a movie still, a motionless pause before a dramatic moment. Vivien felt herself stop breathing, felt the colour drain from her face then rise again in a sudden, involuntary tide.

'I— Iris?' she croaked. 'How … Who's—'

Max narrowed his eyes. 'Don't pretend, Vivien. I know what happened. I just want to hear it from you. Remember what I said — maybe the worse the better.'

Vivien took a long, deep gulp of air. She came to a sudden decision. And felt empowered by it, as she had by the sudden decision she was about to reveal to him. Clearly there was no point in denying it; she had no idea how, but Max knew.

'OK, but it is really bad. Sometimes I try and pretend it was an accident, if I think about it and feel bad. But mostly I don't.'

'Don't pretend it was an accident? Don't think about it? Don't feel bad?'

'All of those I suppose.' She took a gulp of brandy. 'So I was in my twenties. I was here, in London I mean, and I was trying to get by. I'd fallen out with my parents — that's another story. I was trying different casual jobs but it was hard; I didn't have a degree or any qualifications. So that's how I ended up working as an escort. And I was sharing a crappy flat with a woman called Iris. Or that's what she called herself, I found out later she was a Jane. We were both working for the same agency, that's how I met her, and her flatmate had just moved out. I was sleeping on … er, I was between flats. I asked if I could stay with her for a few weeks while I found somewhere. At least she had a sofa bed. And I asked if it was OK if I paid the rent with cash. I did everything with cash then.'

Max got up, fetched the brandy bottle from the kitchen and gave them each a small top up. 'Very wise.'

'So Iris looked at me as though I was mad and said of course, surely I didn't do things via a bank. And I was a bit surprised, I said mostly I used cash but I did have an account for savings. Not that I had much of those.'

Vivien stopped and rubbed her neck. 'Let's go to bed,' she said. 'I'm getting a bit stiff, turned towards you all the time.'

'Let's do that,' agreed Max. 'You can carry on when we're comfortable. I'll give you a neck massage. As a starter at least.'

'You were saying?' prompted Max when they were lying on the bed, facing each other, propped on their elbows.

'She — Iris — told me I needed to get a safe deposit box for my cash. Do as little as possible through the bank account, otherwise the taxman would end up with most of my earnings.

171

She said she had one with the SafeBox Bank on Holborn, she'd researched it and talked to people and they were the best, charged the lowest rent and barely checked who was going in and out. She was going there the next day to "bank", as she put it, the cash from her last two johns. The agency paid us by transfer but most of the money came in big tips.'

Max eyed her appreciatively. 'I bet. And I bet you were one of the best, darling.'

Vivien lowered her lashes modestly. 'Well, I did OK on the cash front. Until I — well, I guess I got greedy. Anyway, Iris said I could come with her and see how it worked, and if I wanted to do the same I could set up an account at that branch — you had to have an account to get the box, but you only had to use it occasionally, just enough to keep it open. So I went with her. She had a little key on her main keyring and showed me how simple it was. She'd put her money in an envelope marked "old cheque books" because you weren't allowed to store cash, something to do with insurance. So I opened an account there and then — it was much easier in those days, you didn't need all the ID and stuff — and got my own box and key. Two keys actually, identical. Iris said I should keep the spare one somewhere safe, in case I lost my keyring; she said she kept hers in her bedside table.'

Max was watching her silently, intently. 'I didn't see how much she had in her box, obviously, but she told me that evening. We'd had a few drinks and she was boasting. Said she was going to get off the game soon, she was fed up turning tricks, and she'd saved nearly twenty thousand.'

Vivien took a swallow of brandy to give herself Dutch courage. 'A couple of days later we were waiting for the tube. We'd done a bit of shopping together and were heading back to the flat. It was rush hour and we were right on the edge of the platform, at one end. I usually go to the end because it's less busy, but not the Northern line at peak time, it was horrible. And then I heard the train coming and Iris was slightly in front of me and I — I just suddenly thought how I could have that money and I … I pushed her.'

Max rolled onto his back, folded his hands behind his head

and gazed at the ceiling, apparently deep in thought. Vivien gulped back a rising sob. 'I knew it,' she gasped. 'You hate me for it. I knew I shouldn't tell you. I've never said a word to anyone before.'

Max slid his eyes over to her. 'I don't hate you for it, darling. I love you for it.' He rolled back to face her. His hand caressed her neck, eased the delicate strap of her negligée a fraction down the curve of her shoulder, traced the dip and rise of her waist and hip. Vivien had opened her mouth to reply to him but her voice dwindled to a whisper and then a gasp as Max's hand slipped between her thighs.

Later, he asked her what had happened afterwards. She shrugged. 'Nothing really. It was chaos as you can imagine. Everyone trying to call 999 but there was no signal. A guard tried to get through but it was rammed. I just merged with the crowd.'

'Clever girl,' said Max approvingly. 'It's perfect. The perfect murder. And, I assume, the perfect heist?'

Vivien had the grace to blush, though really she felt warm, basking in his admiration. 'I went the next day, with her other key. Took out several of her cash envelopes, all labelled with different things like "pay slips" and "passport" and "air tickets". There was CCTV but only one camera and my box was quite near hers and I had my back to it and had sort of disguised myself, a big hat and dark glasses, so I felt quite safe. But I didn't want to be in there longer than necessary so I took the money with me and later opened another account and rented another box at a different bank.'

'Didn't you get asked anything? As her flatmate I mean, not as a suspect? As I said, you were clever.'

Vivien shrugged. 'Iris was the only one on the lease, she just let people use the sofa if they needed it, sometimes for ages. Charged quite a lot, but there was always someone desperate for somewhere to sleep. She always asked for cash, never told the landlord. But that was fine with me. And as soon as I was out of the Tube station I went to the flat, took my stuff — well, my stuff and her key — and cleared out.

Went to a cheap and nasty hotel for a few days while I found a bedsit to rent in a different area.'

'How did you feel?' asked Max. 'I don't mean about the money, I'm sure I can guess how you felt about that, but about — about what you did. Pushing her, killing her.'

Vivien chewed her bottom lip. 'I … it was so sudden. I took an instant decision. I just thought, I have as much right to that money as she does. And she was stupid, telling me about it and showing me where she kept it, where the key was. So I just … did it. And I felt …' She frowned, trying to think back. 'I felt empowered. Excited. As if I'd done something that most people wouldn't do, wouldn't have the nerve or the courage to do. I felt … on top of the world, really. But I never did it again.'

'That can be rectified,' said Max softly, stroking the creases out of her forehead, smoothing his hand over her hair. 'Except I'll do the dirty work this time.'

Later still, Vivien asked Max how he'd known about Iris.

'Everything's online these days. Including you and Iris. I googled the escort agency after you told me about it. Not a lot of interest came up, mainly saucy recommendations or complaints. But there were some comments from way back when about a girl called Iris who'd suddenly stopped being available. Dates cancelled at the last minute. There were a few complaints from disappointed johns. The agency apologised, said she'd died in a terrible accident. One guy kept pressing for details, said he'd been really fond of her. They told him how it happened. And then I found similar comments about you. Or rather about a girl who called herself Scarlett O'Hara. I found a couple of photos in their archive, which they probably don't realise they have. It's a very sloppy website. Anyway, I recognised Scarlett. Very sexy pics actually, darling. You must recreate some of those poses for me.' Max paused, running his hand down her thigh.

'But how …?' Vivien tailed off, frowning.

'There were similar comments, as I said. How you'd left suddenly. Only this time the agency just said you'd gone of

174

your own accord. One of the johns who was commenting — clearly a great fan, by the way — said he'd heard on the grapevine that you'd come into some money and were taking a break. I put two and two together, wondering if I was making five. But I wasn't.'

Max rolled over, half onto Vivien, and gazed down into her eyes. 'But it was the right answer, my love. I needed to know what you were capable of. Whether you'd be up for what I have in mind. To make us an unthinkable amount of money over the next few years. And then we'll disappear, go somewhere sunny and romantic and beautiful and never have to work again.'

*

We go back downstairs. We decide to leave the welcome bottle of champagne in the bedroom for later, and Jake opens one of the ones we brought.

'To tonight,' I say.

'To tonight.' Jake tips his flute against mine, then takes a long draught. He must be weary after the journey. I offered to share the driving but he says he's a bad passenger.

My flute empties quickly and often. Jake smiles, keeps us both topped up. We broach a second bottle while I fix a light supper of cold chicken and salads. Not very exciting for the first meal of our honeymoon but we both have other things on our minds.

I open a bottle of white Burgundy and pour us each a glass. I expected the kitchen to be well equipped, and it is, but I still brought two of my special Riedel Burgundy glasses. I had to wrap them so carefully they took up about a quarter of my case, but I felt it was worth it. Jake's impressed.

'They're my favourite wine glasses,' I say, 'and I wanted them for this special evening. They're big, I know, but the glass is so fine. The wine really does seem to taste better!'

'Big is good,' smiles Jake, and takes a slug of his as if to prove it.

The first wine bottle ebbs in companionable silence,

175

punctuated with increasingly passionate kisses. I pour us each a Riedel portion of a red he brought. When both glasses are empty I say, 'I feel so good, Jake. I'm relaxed and so happy and ready for the next stage of our marriage. Almost ready. I'm going to make one more drink for us, a champagne cocktail. Just a small one. My grandfather used to make them, it was a family tradition for happy occasions.'

I open the honeymooners' bottle from the bedroom. My grandfather's cocktail involved angostura bitters and a sugar lump. I'd forgotten the bitters but I make something similar and we have a last toast.

'Darling, are you ready?' he asks. I can tell he's getting impatient, and so am I.

'Yes,' I whisper. 'Just — be gentle. Later, I mean. I think we should have a bath first. Maybe together? It's big enough.'

'My thoughts exactly.' He pulls me to my feet and we go upstairs.

Jake starts to fill the tub. He's done so well to find a cottage with such a beautiful deep bath. There's a selection of bath products on the windowsill, including a large bottle of patchouli foaming bath oil. 'Ooh,' I squeal, handing it to him. 'My favourite scent. Let's have lots of it.' It smells divine as he sloshes in a generous slug.

'Darling …,' I start. Jake glances round at me.

'Will you — I need you to get in the bath first, while I'm not looking. Tell me when you're in, under the foam. I — I'm so nervous. I don't want to see … you until we're both in there together.' I swallow.

Jake gives me a hug. 'Anything you like, my love. I love it that you're so nervous, so coy. That it's your first time.'

'I tell you what,' I say. 'While you're getting in I'm going to get us one last glass of champagne. No cocktail, just a tiny sip so we can toast our …' I leave Jake undressing, go back down to the kitchen, open another bottle, rinse the flutes to take away any cocktail taste, fill them and take them back upstairs. I go via the bedroom where I finally peel off my silk going-away gloves and put on a pair of the disposable nitrile ones I tucked into my case. In the bathroom, Jake's head and shoulders and knees rise from a mountain of froth, like that scene with Tony Curtis in *Some Like It Hot*. His head is lolling slightly to the side and his eyelids are fluttering. 'Are you all right darling?'

'Feel — a little dizzy. Maybe drunk too much.' He gives a lopsided smile.

'This is ice cold,' I say, handing him his flute. 'Take a sip. It might help.'

He does, but he's moving awkwardly. The glass slips from his hand and his eyes drift shut. I kneel on the bathmat and stroke his hair. And then I lean against his forehead, pushing him back and down, back and down …

# PART FOUR – LUCY AND VIVIEN

# TWENTY

I keep Jake underwater for several minutes. He flaps about feebly at the start but the hefty dose of Rohypnol in the champagne cocktail combined with the copious amount of alcohol he's drunk takes effect as smoothly and efficiently as I'd hoped.

Once I'm sure he's dead I take his right hand and leave it draped over the elegant scrolled rim while I carefully dry his index finger. There's a painting I'm reminded of, Marat I think, his arm trailing to the floor after he was assassinated in his bath. But I need Jake's hand for something more modern than the quill that David's Marat is holding. I go into the bedroom and fetch a sticking plaster from my wash-bag and Jake's MacBook Air from the side pocket of his case. I ease the Mac's lid open until I can slide a finger in, and smooth the plaster over the camera — you never know who might be watching you — before opening the laptop fully and taking it through to the bathroom. It unlocks easily with Jake's finger print, and I ease his arm back into the water.

I put on a dry pair of nitrile gloves, balling up the used ones and tucking them, together with Kate's silk going-away gloves, into a corner of my case, take the laptop, still open, downstairs, draw the curtains and get to work. While I don't want to linger in the cottage with a dead body longer than necessary, neither do I want to leave in daylight, so I have some time in hand to sift through what there is on the laptop. Before I start, I swiftly frisk Jake's jacket and find his wallet — I'll retrieve the other pocketed items later. Apart from some cash, it contains only an Amex card and a Santander debit card, both in the name of Jake Andrews and issued in the last few months.

I go back to the laptop but there's nothing to see. There's no name visible in either the menu bar or System Preferences. I try to open the email app but I'm asked to type my bLOCKade password. I know so little about Jake that there's not a lot of fodder for guessing it, but I try JakeAndrews and MadeInHeaven on the off chance. Unsurprisingly neither works, and even if I could come up with another likely one I don't want to risk a third fail. This side of the bLOCKade stockade, Safari is as clean as a whistle — no history, no bookmarks, no favourites. No Photos. Nothing in Contacts. Calendars, Reminders and Notes all blank. The Messages app is also password protected. So near and yet so far; I bet his banking details are there. The only app Jake's visibly added to what the Mac comes with is a password manager, WatchwordVault. I use it myself and know that it's one of the best, a digital fortress. With little hope and no success, I try the two passwords again.

I push the laptop away with a sigh, but keep it open. It will need someone with considerably more experience and resources than me to mine it for information. He must have other bank accounts; I can't believe he's put all his inherited wealth behind a Santander debit card. But he's careful, admirably — in other circumstances — careful. The police would doubtless be able to find out more, but I'd rather get there first. I decide to take the laptop with me even though it's a risk with no benefit — I won't be able to open it again, but it will buy me time. I close the laptop down and take it upstairs.

Next, I go through Jake's case. There's nothing there apart from clothes, a wash-bag with unsurprising contents and chargers for his phone and laptop. I take both chargers but the one for the laptop snags on a trouser belt as I pull it out of the case. As I reach in to free it I see a slight bulge in the inside of a corner of the case. I probe with gloved fingers and find a small, basic mobile, not his usual smartphone and turned off, and a charger tucked into a slit in the lining; I put both, plus his wallet and laptop, into my case and take it downstairs.

In the kitchen, I load all the crockery, cutlery and glasses we used into the dishwasher and pour the remains of the two bottles of champagne I opened for the cocktails and the last flutes down the sink. Jake had brought in the wine and food, and when I put what needed to be kept cool in the fridge, knocked up and served the chicken and salad, opened, poured and drank the champagne and wine and made my cocktail, I was wearing Kate's going-away gloves, but I still use some of the bleach wipes I brought with me to clean the kitchen taps and the counter tops, the fridge and cupboard handles, the empty bottles — two wine and four champagne. What have I missed? Of course, there's also the flutes I took up to the bathroom. I run up to get them, and while I'm up there check the pockets of the trousers Jake had shed, which I find empty, and wipe the seat and flush of the loo and the taps in the basin. As I turn to leave the room, I see the bath-oil bottle, half empty, but I was wearing gloves when I bought it, brought it and handed it to Jake, so it will only have his prints.

Back downstairs I add the two flutes to the dishwasher, set it off on the hottest cycle and wipe the controls, put all the used wipes in one of the carrier bags that we'd brought into the cottage with the food and wine and slip it and the unused wipes back into my case. I go through the pockets of Jake's jacket again and find the car key, which I leave, and two Yale-type keys on a plain ring, which I take. Another pocket yields his passport, which like the bank cards was issued recently, and our marriage certificate.

Last, his smartphone. I open it using the passcode I clocked when he used it to open the lovey-dovey message I blushingly sent him in the Darwin Brasserie at the Walkie-Talkie on the day he proposed. Not that I had any inkling that he was about to propose; I sent the message so that I could watch, teeth gritted in Kate's usual idiotic smile, as he unlocked his phone. Fortunately the code's still the same. As

I'd expected, there's nothing on there apart from his brief WhatsApp exchanges and calls with Kate, which is telling in itself but I can't risk keeping it. I switch it into airplane mode, turn it off, remove the SIM card, put handset and card together with the passport, marriage certificate and keys in my handbag, and check again that I've left nothing behind. And then I change into my real going-away outfit.

Standing just inside the front door I take from my case the extra large plastic bin bag I brought, open it and flatten the rim as best I can, and step into it. Balancing inexpertly, I kick off Kate's three-inch wedge-heeled shoes, strip off her jumpsuit and wig and put on the jeans, T-shirt, fleece hoodie, socks and trainers that were in the bag. I add Kate's specs to her clothes, step out carefully onto the doormat, fold the top of the bag over itself, and cram it — her shoes make it a tight squeeze, that was one reason I'd brought the Riedel glasses though they had other uses also — into the case, scan the room to make sure I haven't missed anything, close the case and then turn it over and unzip the base to release the shoulder straps that turn it into a back pack.

Though I ditched the wig, I kept the close-fitting liner cap on to cover my hair, and now I stretch the beanie that I'd left in one hoodie pocket over it and leave the cottage after turning the thermostat just inside the front door right down and taking the key from its hook. I shut the door quietly behind me, lock it and post the key back through the letter box, peel off the gloves and tuck them in my pocket.

It's about an hour's walk to where I left my rental car yesterday, the key to which was in the other hoodie pocket. I meet no one on the route through fields and paths I'd mapped on that occasion; though I hadn't walked as far as the cottage then, I'd gone near enough to work out the way.

I just hope the house plants survive the onslaught of alcohol I gave them. And that I can keep the lid on my emotions for long enough to get home.

*

'Morning, Lucy,' says Deirdre as I stride into the office two days later. 'Good weekend? Do anything interesting?'

'Thanks, and yes,' I say with a smile. It's strange being Lucy again. On the train to work just now I'd heard a woman call out to a teenage girl, presumably her daughter, 'Kate! Don't forget your sunglasses.' My head had whipped round at the name. I need to be careful about that.

'I went to Paris. Treated myself to a break.'

'Very nice! Good food and drink?'

'Yes, excellent. And some culture too! But I'm just here briefly — I've still got a load of leave left so I've decided to take this week off. I've booked it online, and just popped in to pick up a couple of files in case I get any urgent queries I can deal with at home.'

The last few months seem to have made fiction my default mode. I'm not going to let on that I spent Saturday murdering my brand-new husband and Sunday disposing of evidence. Or that I plan to spend my week's leave collecting what further information I can about MadeInHeaven and Vivien Harrison.

*

I was on a strange combination of autopilot, emotional high and terrified incredulity at the enormity of what I'd just done as I walked from the cottage to the car. The first thing I did was remove Kate's blue non-prescription lenses, replace them with my usual clear prescription ones which I'd left in the glove compartment, put Kate's lenses in the container and slip the container into my case. Then I drove back to London. The Dorset Police website had helpfully confirmed what I suspected, namely that as it is a relatively small force it has relatively few Automatic Number Plate Recognition cameras (eighteen vehicle-based systems and fourteen roadside sites, to be precise). I kept to smaller roads as much as possible, and observed the speed limit throughout, and once I was in London I took a less direct route to avoid the Congestion Zone with its ring of cameras, but there was nothing in any event to link the car to Kate Andrews or Kate Lincoln. I'd rented it in my real name from a garage in Stoke Newington; I left it on their forecourt in the early hours and posted the key through the office door as agreed.

The first piece of evidence I disposed of was Jake's SIM card. I'd done a lot of research about phones and the trail they can leave and wanted to ditch the card as near the cottage as was safely possible. I'd thought about dropping it in a local carpark where it would be unlikely to be noticed and likely to be driven over several times, but the risk of CCTV was too high. But as I drove through the first village en route I kept an eye out for council rubbish bins. I soon noticed a roadside one with no other cars or people around, paused briefly and quietly slipped the card into it.

I never kept much personal stuff at the flat I'd rented, at considerable but worthwhile expense, in Chelsea — all those trappings of wealth that I'd seen Vivien, and then Jake, clock with greedy approval had come with the package. In fact I barely spent any time there, just when I was hosting Vivien or Jake. I took most of what there was — mostly clothes — back to Hackney in dribs and drabs over the week before the wedding.

I, or rather Kate, make one further visit on my first morning back in London, with long hair and wedge heels and blue contact lenses and her hat; wearing nitrile gloves, I retrieve my last few things, including Kate's wedding dress, and slip the key back through the letter box-when I leave. I'd rented the apartment in Kate's name and paid six months' rent up front from her bank account, which I'd set up months earlier and gradually funded with cash drawn out of my own account. The lease still had two months to run; the owners would find it in good order, if a little dusty. Otherwise spotless though; I'd asked the agency to send in cleaners the next day, saying I wanted a very thorough deep clean.

And then, back in my house, I say goodbye to Kate the bride, or some of her. I cram her wedding dress, going-away outfit and gloves, her first wig, the remaining Rohypnol tablets in their blister pack, the case that converts to a back-pack and the trainers I wore when I left the cottage, into a double black bin bag; tomorrow is rubbish and kerbside recycling collection day and I'll watch from my window as the contents of my dustbin are tipped into the chomping maw of the lorry. I hate waste but it's too risky to give them to a charity shop or keep them. And balanced against the waste of Steph's life, and Barbara's and maybe others', a few items of clothing are trivial. The Rohypnol tablets — or more accurately a generic version bought online using Kate's email and physical address and her bank card — are definitely better being incinerated for energy. The suppliers in India had conveniently not added the blue dye that some formulations include. I'd had to take a gamble when I ordered but had a back-up plan for an alternative champagne cocktail using blue Curaçao if necessary. I put the packaging with Kate's marriage certificate through my shredder and add the fragments to my food recycling caddy.

The basic second phone I found hidden in Jake's case has a different passcode from his smartphone, so after removing the SIM card I add the handset, his smartphone handset and their chargers to the rubbish bag, and will drop the SIM card down a drain when I next go out. I'm counting on it being a burner phone for emergency backup and hence unknown to the police.

I hesitate over the fate of Max's laptop, but come back to my initial instinct that it's too risky to keep. Google guides me through the process of erasing all the data on it, which alarmingly I can do without knowing the passcode (or having Max's fingerprint to hand), and further suggests leaving it overnight in a bath full of salty water, which seems a fitting last rite. It'll join his other devices and his wallet, with the shredded remains of his bank and Amex cards, in tomorrow's rubbish.

There are a few items which I hold on to for any necessary further appearances that Kate needs to make. I put the blue contact lenses and the heavy-framed glasses in a drawer where I keep my own spare and outdated spectacles and sunglasses, lenses and their paraphernalia, cleaning cloths and sprays. The Carly Simon hat is added to a jumble of hats and caps on a shelf above my bentwood coat stand, the wedge heels join the numerous pairs of assorted shoes cluttering up the floor of my wardrobe, and I keep one pair of bell-bottoms, slotting the coat hanger in among my jeans and trousers. The others I post into a street-collection charity clothes bin that's just been emptied, then I post the clothes I wore when I came back from the cottage last night into my washing machine and put them through a very unecological long, hot cycle. I'll add them to the charity clothes bin in a day or two.

And then there's the other wig. I'd bought two in the end. I'd been surprised how easy it had been to find mousy, grey-streaked ones — I guess if you're looking for a wig to cover up progressive balding, you'd want to reflect your natural colour and not everyone reaches for the hair dye at the first grey hair, though I confess I did. I 'treated' one of the wigs by trimming it — I'd thought of buying some pinking shears but then remembered I had a pair of multi-bladed herb scissors which did a brilliant job of mangling the ends. I wore that one for my initial interview with Vivien, my dates with Archie and Omar and my first couple of dates with Jake, then switched to the unmangled wig for the rest of our limited time together. I'm sure Vivien noticed that I'd made an effort, had gone to the hairdresser if not to the colourist she was doubtless itching to recommend. Although why would she care what Kate looked like? Jake didn't woo her for her beauty. I shudder, close down thoughts of Jake and cram the intact wig together with the wig cap into a drawer with brushes, combs, hairspray, scrunchies and clips.

As for Kate's ID trail, I dispose of it as best I can for the moment. I'd put the phone I'd bought for all contact with Vivien and Jake into airplane mode and turned it off just before Jake and I set off for the register office, and kept it that way since. Now I remove the SIM card, which will join Jake's two cards in a sewer somewhere while the handset will join Jake's two phones in the jaws of the rubbish lorry. I'd carried out a similar exercise at the outset, with the two very basic phones and cash SIMs I'd used for the Tooting and Chelsea rentals.

Trying not to think of how much I've spent on phones and

how much plastic and conflict mineral waste I've created with their disposal, I shred the passport and birth certificate I obtained for Kate, but keep her bank card — in the next day or two I'll find an ATM with no, or limited, CCTV and, wearing her heels and wig and hat and glasses, take out the small amount of money left in her account then close it online. And then I'll shred her bank card and delete her email address. I'd deliberately chosen a Yahoo one as it's the simplest and cleanest to close.

I hesitate over Jake's passport. It's tempting to shred it also, but it's evidence of his complicity rather than mine and something makes me hang on to it. It needs to be well hidden though, in case … well, I don't like to follow that train of thought. I decide to take it into work and archive it with an old file which I can retrieve at short notice if I need to.

Finally, Jake's keys. I add them to the tangle of old and duplicate keys that everyone has, which in my case is in one of the kitchen drawers. I have plans for them tomorrow, but for now they can hide in plain sight.

The only direct relic of Kate's match made in heaven I plan to keep for myself is her engagement ring, and that's because it's Steph's. Though probably also Barbara's and maybe others'. And it's not as though Jake's going to need it again. Or John, or James. I don't know what to do with it so for the moment I wrap it in tissue paper and put it in a small tin which I poke down to the bottom of my jar of ground coffee. In a Pavlovian response to the smell that's released, I make myself a double espresso, sit down at the table and think about what to do next. I need to do as much as possible as soon as possible because once the body is discovered the police will also be doing as much as possible as soon as possible. With luck, I have four or five days. But I may not have luck.

# TWENTY-ONE

On the following morning, after watching the rubbish lorry do its bit, I retrieve Jake's keys from the kitchen drawer. I suspect they're for his flat. I google the block to see whether the reception is manned 24/7. Fortunately it's a day-porter service, so I decide to go that evening; the sooner the better since I don't know when Vivien will find out what's happened. Or indeed what she'll do when she does, but I imagine she'll want to check whether there's anything in Jake's flat that connects him to her. As do I, and I need to get there first.

I wait till it's dusk, put on flat shoes, stretch the wig cap over my hair then cover up with a hat again — a floppy, brimmed one this time, though not as distinctive as Kate's. I put the keys in my pocket together with another packet of bleach wipes and pull on a pair of light cotton gloves over disposable nitrile ones. Scattering SIM cards like confetti over kerbside storm drains, I keep an eye out for CCTV: of course it's impossible to avoid but I can at least minimise my exposure, as I did with my infrequent comings and goings at the Chelsea flat.

There is inevitably a CCTV lens beadily trained on the main entrance. I turn my face away as best I can — it's probably half hidden anyway as I'm bent over the keys, trying the wrong one first. Once in, I stride purposefully to what looks like, and turns out to be, an entrance to the stairwell, and walk up to the third floor and along the corridor to the door of Jake's flat. I can't see a camera in the vicinity but again I tuck my head down, frowning at the keys, as I let myself in.

It doesn't take long to search the small, sterile, characterless space. I peel off my cotton gloves and stuff them in a pocket, leaving on the nitrile ones, and go through the drawers in the desk in the second bedroom where I find a different set of keys — two mortice, a Yale and a much smaller one, perhaps for a filing cabinet — on an unmarked fob. And a smartphone. Really, how many phones can one man have? I guess this is Jake's phone for when he's Max since the other smartphone had clearly been used only for Jake's communications with Kate. I try the passcode he used on Jake's phone but it doesn't work. Still, best not to leave it here for the police to find given that I don't know what's on it. I can use my recent knowledge of how to dispose of mobiles to get rid of it. Promptly, I think; the police will probably find his number soon enough. Once they've found his body, of course; I cross my fingers, hoping again that I've got a few days' grace. Though wouldn't Jake have used his Kate phone to book the Airbnb, keeping his two lives separate?

There's nothing else here apart from the photos of Jake's presumably fictional flat, which on reflection I decide to leave. I've checked all the drawers and cupboards, under the mattress and the sofa cushions, even in the fridge and freezer and cooker and microwave, feeling like a PI in a sleazy thriller set in LA. I'm initially surprised that Jake left his keys here, given the absence of anything else, but there's no identification or other information on the fob and I suppose he judged it preferable to be able to pick up his home keys, which I assume they are, when he was next able to go 'home' to Vivien, rather than 'home' with his new wife, at a time that was convenient for him, rather than rely on Vivien being at the maisonette to let him in. I'm making assumptions here, of course, but I'm guessing he shuttled between his two 'homes' for as long as each new wife was alive, using his alleged IT out-of-town audits and so on as cover for his pattern of absences.

But then I think again of the timing of Steph's murder — so much sooner and hence riskier than Barbara's — and wonder whether I'll ever find the reason for it. Had Steph found out something about him or he about her? Or had he simply changed his MO and intended to drown Kate on her honeymoon also? Even on her wedding night? It seems unlikely in the extreme, too risky, but still an ice-cold tide washes over me and I shiver.

I put the keys and phone in my bag then wipe every surface I might have touched as Kate before leaving the way I came, head bowed, eyes on my hand as it locks the door. As I'm stepping onto a zebra crossing over a busy road, I surreptitiously let the keys slip into a kerbside drain.

*

None of this is about the money, but I keep coming back to it. I've avenged Steph's death, and almost certainly Barbara's and quite possibly others', but their money bothers me. What will happen to it? It's probably offshore, where Vivien thought Kate banked her non-existent wealth. The Cayman Islands spring to mind, but there are doubtless other possibilities. Does Vivien have access to it? Is she married to her partner in crime, Max / Jake / James / John? She might inherit the lot if the police don't discover what he did. What they did, for Vivien was surely as involved as he. I've actually only partly avenged the deaths.

Will the police be able to trace Jake back to Max, and trace Vivien through him? If not, Vivien will go scot-free, with or without the money. Either way, the thought sticks in my craw. Vivien has to pay, somehow. But first I want to know more about the other brides and more about the money, and she's the only person who has that information. I think about her professed, but quite possibly and understandably genuine, paranoia about digital footprints. And her notebook with the Liberty cover, her silver pen swooping and dipping as she made note after note.

*

I have to start somewhere, so I call the MadeInHeaven office number again. Perhaps I should have kept Kate's handset or even Max's Kate smartphone, but I didn't and that was probably wise — it meant one, or even two, fewer links that could be traced back to me — so I bought the cheapest, nastiest handset from an appropriately dodgy looking walk-in phone shop and used that with a new pay-as-you-go SIM card.

'Good morning, MadeInHeaven MatchMakers. How may I help you?'

'Good morning. I'd like to speak to Vivien Harrison please.'

'I'm afraid Ms Harrison isn't in her office today. Can I take a message?'

I have my response ready. 'It's really important that I contact Ms Harrison,' I say smoothly. 'I'm a prospective client. A friend who was very pleased with the service gave me her mobile number and email but I've lost all my contacts. Is there any possibility—'

The voice drops a degree or two. 'I'm sorry, I cannot possibly divulge any confidential client information. We take our data privacy obligations very seriously.' Then it warms up a fraction, sounding interested. 'Could you not ask your friend?'

'She's, erm … on honeymoon. As I say, she was very pleased with the matchmaking. But I understand. Please could you ask Ms Harrison to call' — my response is not in fact as ready as I'd thought and I cast around wildly in my mind and dredge from nowhere … 'Avril Jacques-Smythe—'

'How do you spell that please?'

How the fuck do I know? And why didn't I choose a simpler name? I spell out some approximation. 'As I mentioned, I'm a prospective client. I've very keen to talk to Ms Harrison about signing up with her, so I'd be grateful if you could pass the message on ASAP.' I give her the new mobile number, grateful that I'd thought to write it down, and profuse thanks.

*

Vivien calls me from her 'No Caller ID' number shortly after I left the message. I answer, having turned on a YouTube video I'd found of construction site sound effects and draped a cotton hankie over the phone. Conversation is possible but strained. I would have used a voice-changing app had my new phone not been quite so cheap and nasty.

'How did you hear about MadeInHeaven, Avril?' Vivien asks after we're through the introductory formalities. 'You said a friend recommended us?'

I'd used the intervening time, brief as it was, to perfect my cover story. 'Well, I was simplifying slightly,' I shouted. 'She wasn't a friend, just someone I got chatting to in the queue for the Harvey Nicks changing rooms a couple of weeks ago. I don't even know her name. I admired her engagement ring — it was a beautiful emerald and gold one, very unusual. And she started telling me about her fiancé. I couldn't stop her, actually. They met through you, she couldn't praise you enough.'

There's a short silence from the other end, if not from mine. I wonder what's going through Vivien's mind, whether she'll ask for more details or decide it's safer to change the subject. Or perhaps she's simply surprised at the thought of Kate buying clothes at Harvey Nichols. In the event she asks me to tell her about myself, and I oblige. I tell her that I'm 46, recently widowed, and have the good fortune to have been left very well off by my late husband. I am very keen to meet a man with the potential to be a kind and loving life partner.

'I'm sure we can help you,' says Vivien warmly. 'What I normally suggest is that I meet a new client for the first time at their home, so I can—'

'I'm so sorry,' I interrupt. 'That's not possible. I'm having my kitchen redone — can't believe it's three years old already — and the place is like a building site. As you can probably hear. Ghastly. Can we meet at your office?'

'I much prefer not to,' says Vivien smoothly. 'It's so impersonal. Let's meet at a café then.' She suggests the place where she met Kate a few months ago and we agree a time tomorrow afternoon.

*

When she's finished the brief call, Vivien fetches her Liberty notebook from her desk and opens it at a clean page. Max would approve. 'No digital record unless it's unavoidable' was his mantra, and it had rapidly become hers.

But there's nothing much to write yet, apart from the potential new client's name at the top of the page. Avril Jacques-Smythe. Vivien rolls the name round her mouth, whispers it, says it out loud. It flows, sounds rich. Avril sounds highly suitable. Max will be pleased.

Vivien flicks through the notebook, smiling as she sees in passing the two strings of seemingly random numbers and letters that she's written on page thirty-eight. The Secret Key and the Master Password for their WatchwordVault account. The gateway to their wealth, their future, their escape. The one digital record that is unavoidable. But also, Max assures her, unassailable, at least as long as no one apart from them knows the two codes. They're not written down anywhere else; Max learnt the password by heart and the Secret Key would be needed only if one of them had to sign in on a new device. But Vivien never signs in; she's always been happy to leave the money side of things to Max. She just has the codes in case anything happens to him, and nothing will happen to him, he's far too clever, too careful. Vivien sighs, but it's a contented sigh, and runs through the list of current clients

Fiona: about to be married, at most a bit of phone support needed. She's paid the usual annual fee so there'll be no loose end there. And she's marrying Thomas, ditto for him. He took a while to match but Fiona seems besotted. No accounting for tastes. Vivien remembers that Thomas was Stephanie's second date. She frowns. Who was the first? Ah yes, Harry. He left the agency shortly afterwards, having met and proposed to a woman through friends.

Polly's also engaged, to a relatively new male client called

Xavier.

There's Charlotte, another recent client. Vivien frowns. She doesn't want to lose Charlotte but she doesn't have many unattached men on her books at the moment. But there's Archie, unsurprisingly still unmatched, and a pleasant recently widowed banker called Kenneth. She needs to set Charlotte up with Archie first, after whom Kenneth will seem delightful. Archie has proved very useful as a foil, as of course he did with Kate.

She brightens as she thinks about Kate's fee, which they'll collect after the honeymoon. And in due course, maybe in a year or eighteen months or a little more if the probate is slow, they'll collect a whole lot more. And that will be it; she and Max will be set up for the rest of their lives. Which they'll spend somewhere sunnier, more luxurious, more romantic than a poky maisonette in the backstreets of Camden.

Vivien closes the notebook, puts it back in the desk drawer and wonders whether it's too early for a glass of wine. She hates it when Max is away, especially when he's away on honeymoon.

*

Vivien sets off for the café feeling optimistic. She's pleased to see that her usual quiet table is free. She sits down with a cappuccino and a millionaire's shortbread and automatically puts her hand in her bag to pull out her Liberty notebook, ready to add notes to Avril's virginal page. Then she remembers that she left the notebook at home — Max always cautioned her against taking it anywhere public. 'It's too easy to forget things if you're in a café or restaurant. Too much distraction. Take it to their houses, but nowhere else.'

She finishes her coffee and biscuit and begins to feel impatient. Vivien is punctual herself and not tolerant of others who aren't. Except, of course, when they're wealthy clients.

Her phone chimes with an incoming text from Avril.

*I'm SOOOO sorry, I'm running late. Kitchen crisis. Should be with you in half an hour. Builders!! Sorry again, Avril*

Vivien tuts, but there's nothing to be done. She sends an emollient reply and orders another coffee.

*

Half an hour before our rendezvous at the café, I'm loitering outside a posh-looking restaurant up the street from Vivien's house, again ostensibly entranced by the screen of my phone. I see her leave, and when she's turned the first corner I rapidly shrug off my small backpack, take out the carrier bag containing a few cleaning items, including a rather classy feather duster which is poking rakishly out of it, walk briskly to her front door and let myself in. It's the sort of neighbourhood where plenty of people will have a cleaner and no one takes much notice of their neighbours, or at least that's what I'm counting on. The real risk — well, more of a deal-breaker than a risk, if I'm honest — is a burglar alarm, but to my relief there isn't one.

I use my elbow to close the door behind me then pull on the nitrile gloves I have in my pocket and work fast, keeping an eye on the time. It's a nice maisonette, if a little cramped. There's a small room that must be a home office, containing only an old-fashioned partners' desk, a couple of upright chairs and a filing cabinet. No computer — they must rely on Jake's — Max's — laptop for what records they keep. Or maybe not, maybe Vivien carries her apparent obsession with no digital trace to its logical conclusion. Certainly I've found virtually nothing about her or MadeInHeaven online, bar a few glowing testimonials and periodic links to her discreet classified ads in *The Lady*.

I need to find the Liberty notebook. When I saw Vivien with two of her clients in cafés she just had a small, black Moleskine, so I'm counting on her having left the bigger one here while she goes to meet Avril. I work fast, find it easily in a desk drawer and put it in my bag.

My phone pings with the reminder I set and I send Vivien

a quick text saying I'm running late.

The small key on Jake's fob is indeed for a — for this — filing cabinet, and I riffle through the neatly labelled hanging folders. The one marked 'car' helpfully yields a driving licence and MOT and car insurance certificates, all in the name of Max Carrington. Bingo — a surname at last. I'd wondered, after leaving the cottage, why there was no driving licence in Jake's wallet. I'd assumed it was in the car, but by then it was too late to check. The photo on the licence looks very familiar, though younger. I suppose Jake — Max — couldn't risk having the licence and papers in the car in case I saw them. The address, in W14, means nothing to me — it's neither Jake's flat nor the maisonette.

I'm about to take a photo of the licence but pause. I need to be much more careful about what I use my own phone for, what I keep on it, so I take the licence instead. Then, prompted by the thought of Jake's birth certificate, I flick through further folders until I find one marked 'JA'. My heart skips a beat; will this have IDs for all the other JA's as well? That would surely be too good to be true, and so it proves. The only document is Jake's birth certificate; Vivien and Max must have wisely destroyed all his predecessors' papers. I tuck it into the Liberty notebook and check my watch. It's already ten minutes past our meeting time.

A rapid run round the rest of the maisonette yields nothing more of interest apart from a small iPad on the coffee table. It's passcoded so I don't take it. I leave the house as purposefully and uninterruptedly as I entered it, and once I'm round the corner — in the other direction from the café — I text Vivien again.

*SOOOO sorry again. I'm still stuck at home with yet another kitchen crisis. I think it's best if we postpone meeting until the works are finished. I'll be back in touch in a couple of weeks, and sincere apologies again for messing you around. Avril*

I take the SIM card out of the mobile and drop it down another handy drain, along with the keys to the maisonette.

When I'm home I put the handset in the freezer — I'm not sure whether that makes it untraceable, but I reckon I've still got a day or two before the police find Jake's body and I'll smash it tomorrow, bundle it up in a plastic bag and slip into the skip that's currently blocking the road a few doors down.

# TWENTY-TWO

The following morning, I google Max Carrington. There's nothing there, or at least nothing in the first ten pages that appears to relate to the person I'm interested in, which is a lot more telling than finding reams of incriminating information. I throw another £3 at the Land Registry and check the W14 address on Max's driving licence. It's freehold and is owned by an Arthur Quinn whose own address is in SW6. Is he yet another incarnation of Max / JA? Perhaps he was an early alias, before Max had settled into the JA pattern. I find the W14 address on Street View. It's a typical London Victorian terraced house in West Kensington; three storeys over a basement with steps down to its own entrance. I zoom in and see a doorbell panel with six buzzers. Converted into flats then. Time to visit. Beanie and sunglasses again, with medium heels under boot-cut jeans. Neither Kate nor Lucy at first sight.

I check the names on the panel but there's no Max Carrington or any variation on that theme. There's also no answer from the bottom two buzzers, presumably the basement and ground floor flats, but the next one, which I guess must be one of two flats on the first floor, raises a deep, irritable 'Yes?'.

'Good afternoon sir,' I say. 'I work for the Cash in Your Hand debt collection agency and we're trying to trace a resident. Goes by the name of Max Carrington?'

'I only moved in a couple of weeks ago,' he barks. 'I don't know any of the other people who live here. I won't be able to help. And I'm flat out. Sorry.'

He doesn't sound it, and cuts the connection. There's no answer from the next bell but the one above it elicits a friendlier response. I repeat my line and the man says, 'I doubt I'll be able to help but come on up. Top floor, left.' He buzzes me in.

The house has an air of gradual decline. A stair carpet that looks as though it was good quality a long time ago. Tired magnolia wood chip on the walls. A rickety table in the hall littered with post and flyers. Everything needs a clean.

The door to the left of the narrow hall at the top of the stairs is open. A man who looks to be in his early twenties or so is standing there. He's wearing jeans and a faded rugby shirt; his feet are bare and he needs a shave.

'Hi,' he says. 'I'm Gavin.' Fortunately he doesn't ask for my name or evidence of who I am. He looks eager and interested. Perhaps for him, unlike for his neighbour below, I'm a welcome interruption of a tedious chore.

'Hello. It's just a quick question. As I said, we're trying to trace someone who uses this address. A Max Carrington?'

'No one of that name here,' he says with assurance. 'I've lived here for six months. The flat across the hall is between tenants, but the last one was a woman. There's Laurence Taylor below, just moved in — I think he's at home, I heard him banging about earlier, but I think I also heard him answering his buzzer just now?'

'Yes, that was me. He wasn't very friendly.'

'He hasn't said hello to me yet, though we've passed on the stairs often enough,' says Gavin then continues his virtual guided tour. 'Then there's a couple across from him, three sharers on the ground floor who moved in shortly after I did and another couple in the basement, who were here when I moved in.' He rattles off the names, none of which is a JA, and continues, 'There was apparently a gay couple — men — in this flat before me, but I don't know their names. And I'm sorry but I can't remember the names of the people who moved out of the ground floor but they were all women.'

'Thanks Gavin, that's most helpful.' I turn towards the door.

'You're welcome,' je says. 'I was desperate for an excuse to stop trying to finish my essay. Sorry, I didn't catch your name?'

'Avril Jacques,' I say before I can stop myself. It's the first name in my head and it just popped out. At least I cut off the Smythe. 'I'll see myself out.' And I scuttle down the stairs and onto the street.

I decide to try and catch the landlord at home, given that it's not far away. I'm pretty sure he can't be Max / JA, and that's confirmed when he answers the door. He doesn't look anything like him and, conclusively, he's very much alive.

I stick with my story. 'I'm so sorry to disturb you at home, Mr Quinn. I work for the Cash in Your Hand debt collection agency, and we're trying to trace someone who uses the address of your house in Stanwick Road, West Kensington. A Max Carrington. I understand that he's not a current resident but wondered whether you'd let to him previously, and if so whether you'd have a forwarding address, or his mobile number or email address?'

'Never heard of him,' says Arthur Quinn brusquely. He obviously makes enough out of his tenants to keep his own house in considerably better condition. The door is a glossy red with a gleaming brass knocker. The sash windows either side also gleam and the white paint on the frames and sills is spotless. The glimpse I have of his entrance hall — he hasn't invited me in — is like something out of *House & Garden* — original tiles, William Morris wallpaper, a Tiffany lamp.

'Thank you,' I gush, though I'm not sure for what. I resist the urge to ask him to check his records as I suspect he'd start to press me for ID. 'Would you happen to know who owned the house before you? The rented house, I mean,' I add, as he looks scandalised.

'Can't remember. It was an ordinary name. Definitely not Max Carrington. And now if you don't mind I must get on.'

He shuts the door in my face, firmly.

Back in my flat, I ask myself whether my visit to south-west London was just a wild goose chase. I suppose I needed to tick the box, to know that I'd looked in a corner which might have yielded some useful information even if it didn't. And I wonder why Max Carrington used that address for the driving licence and car documents. Perhaps he decided to keep an address that, once he'd moved away, was otherwise unconnected to his name. He could use it on ID or official documents that couldn't be easily or frequently changed. That would fit with my suspicion, which I confirm with a quick search, that driving licences are tricky. To change your name you need to surrender your existing licence and submit documents supporting the name change. To get a fresh licence you need to first apply for a provisional licence for which you need an identity document. If you were a serial murderer you probably wouldn't want to do either on a regular basis. Using your real name and an old address and setting up a redirection of post would be simpler and probably safer.

What isn't safe is for me to have Max Carrington's driving licence in my possession so I shred it, and then decide to start working my way through the Liberty notebook. I fetch it from the back of the desk drawer where I'd shoved it yesterday. As I open it, Jake's birth certificate falls out. Or at any rate a birth certificate for someone called Jake Andrews, born on 29 September 1972. Who, further online research reveals, tragically died at the age of twelve. I slip the certificate into the instruction booklet for my old toaster, nestled among numerous other manuals, receipts and guarantees that are crammed into an old Tupperware box in my chaotic under-stairs cupboard. Then, quite suddenly, I run out of steam, tipping from hyperactive to totally drained in a nano-second. The stress of the last few days, weeks, months catching up with me, probably. Time for a break. I pour myself a glass of wine and settle down in front of the TV, scrolling Netflix for a film. Any film as long as there are no murders.

*

I spend the next day going through Vivien's Liberty notebook with a fine-tooth comb. Vivien is very careful, very discreet. There are details of all MadeInHeaven's clients since 2018, or at least I assume they're all, but the information, while neatly set out in elegant, legible handwriting, is minimal. Name, age, address, sex, brief history (divorced / widowed / single too long), assessment of net worth on a scale of one to ten. I wonder how Vivien works that out? Presumably she forms an initial impression from the client's home — no wonder she's so keen to have an early meeting there — and teases out more detail with her delicate questions. Kate, of course, had been very upfront, almost vulgar in talking about her wealth. Steph … Poor, lovely, naive Steph. There'd have been no vulgar bragging but I'm sure she would have happily answered Vivien's questions. She was so longing to meet Mr Right, and so deserved it after marrying Mr Wrong. The first Mr Wrong.

I bite back my anger, my grief and keep reading. The final entry for each client is 'Matches'. There are usually two or three names, occasionally more, with dates, and a tick or a cross. I flick back, rewinding the agency's recent — perhaps its complete — history and my eye is caught by the name Paula Platt-Robinson at the top of an early page; unlike previous entries, hers is flagged with a capital S. Her tick, after two crosses, has a small M in a circle beside it and Joe Aston was her third match.

I move forward through the notebook again looking for Barbara Watson. Her third match was John Allen; there's a tick after two crosses, a circled M — and a capital S by her name. The same signs for Steph and James Anderson. I have to pause now, take a break, pull myself together.

Fortified by a strong coffee, I check the last few entries. I should have been expecting it, but somehow I must have blocked it out. There is Kate Lincoln. An S, two crosses, a tick and a circled M.

My hand is trembling as I go back to the beginning of the notebook and read each page in painstaking detail. It's stultifying after a while. Just the same old information about lonely men, lonely women. More women than men. I wonder how she pairs up her clients given the discrepancy; it's a small agency, she's never got many on her books at any given time. Then, with a wave of nausea, I realise that the answer, or at least part of it, is obvious. But there are still genuine ones, the Archies and Omars. Perhaps MadeInHeaven places occasional ads in classy men's magazines, if there are such things? Or The Spectator — maybe it has a Lonely Hearts column? But I don't dwell on the thought — it doesn't matter now, and I have more pressing things on my mind.

On page thirty-eight there's a change in format. No names or words or lists, just two series of numbers and letters. Like two passwords.

*

Vivien is surprised that Max isn't back by the end of the week. She knows the honeymoon cottage was booked for Saturday to Saturday, and normally he should have been back in London this afternoon. He'd have dropped Kate off at her flat and made an excuse to her about picking something up from his. He'd have collected his keys and his phone and called Vivien from there if he didn't have time to dash home and see her. But at least he'd have his phone so he'd have let her know he was back and could then keep in contact with her while he tried to work out a pattern with the new bride. Kate. He'd suggest, or probably have already suggested, that he move in with her, give up his serviced flat. Or maybe Kate has already invited him — she was desperate enough, after all.

Vivien tries not to worry; pointless, since she has no way of contacting Max; they've agreed that she won't call his phone until he's called her on it, and she would only call or message his Jake mobile if there was a dire emergency. There's his emergency burner, of course, hidden in the lining of his case, but that will be turned off unless he has to use it. And, she tries to reassure herself, he would have used it to call her, as he had used its predecessor when he'd had to tell her about

Stephanie, if anything had gone wrong. But she's disquieted enough that she tries to keep herself busy, to distract herself from the undertow of unfocused fretting that nibbles away at her. She decides to get out, walk to the office and pick up any mail, do a bit of shopping on the way back in case he turns up for supper. Though that's unlikely, she has to admit. Even for someone as creative and convincing as Max it won't be easy to explain to his newly minted wife that he's off to dinner without her on their first night back from their honeymoon.

But there's no post to collect from the office. Vivien stops at the local shops on the way home, picking up two salmon steaks and a bottle of Sancerre. She can always have the second steak tomorrow. She puts the wine and fish in the fridge and tries to think distracting positive thoughts. The potential new client, Avril, for example. Vivien is irritated about being stood up but can understand how disruptive and unpredictable refurbishment can be, and congratulates herself on being patient and accommodating to her. She should maybe give Avril a gentle prod in a few days if she hasn't heard back from her.

*

Later that evening, I flick back to the page in Vivien's Liberty notebook where she's noted what look like two passcodes. One of them has a similar pattern and combination of letters, numbers and symbols to my own WatchwordVault Secret Key code. I open WatchwordVault on my MacBook Air but instead of putting in my Master Password I use Vivien's other, differently formatted string. As expected, I'm asked to enter the Secret Key as a second step since I'm logging in from a new device; I peck out a series of careful keystrokes and I'm in to Max's WatchwordVault account.

As I'd also expected, it contains the details of several bank accounts. One UK high street bank — Lloyds — and two offshore accounts, both in Belize.

The passwords and memorable information are all neatly stored, together with the account-holder's name, the account number and direct links to the websites. But my luck ends there.

I try the Lloyds account first, which is in the name Max Carrington. But the bank site notes severely that I'm logging on from a new device and asks me to enter the OTP code which it has presumably sent to Max's mobile. I curse my lack of forethought for not keeping the phone, though it was probably a sensible decision.

The Belize accounts are in the names of Joseph Aston and John Allen. It takes me a moment to recall that Joe Aston was Paula Platt-Robinson's third match, husband and widower. Again, I can't delve any further.

I wonder why there's no account in James Anderson's name. Perhaps, quite simply, Max hadn't yet sold any of Steph's assets; whatever cash he inherited could be sitting in a UK account which for whatever reason isn't stored on WatchwordVault. Or, I suddenly think, perhaps he has sold some of her assets. I've been so preoccupied in the last few months that I hadn't given the Hampstead house much thought, but I run a quick search now and see that the sale went through a few weeks ago. While I'm at it I check Flat 10, and it was sold a couple of months earlier. Perhaps Max sold Stephanie's gemstones at the same time, and the cash is in an account which for a very specific reason isn't stored on WatchwordVault. Perhaps with the proceeds of Flat 10. Is Max double-crossing Vivien?

# PART FIVE – VIVIEN, HANNAH, CAROL AND LUCY

# TWENTY-THREE

When Vivien's still heard nothing from Max by the end of the following day, the day after the honeymoon, she starts to worry in earnest. She's also not sure what she should do. They never catered for silence. With all the previous special brides he's managed to contact her, however briefly, to let her know he's back in London, when he'll next see her. Or, in the case of Stephanie, to let her know what had happened.

Vivien has always fretted slightly, though she's never admitted it to Max and barely acknowledges it to herself, once the bride-grooming hits its first milestone and then continues through proposal to wedding and beyond. But of course Kate and Jake are different. Sex wasn't their first milestone; it was to come at the end, inverting the natural order of things. But that, if anything, makes it worse. She has to cope with the idea of the honeymoon, first sex, and how Max will manage to juggle his two lives until he finds, or more likely makes, an opportunity to cut off one of the lives.

If Vivien is honest with herself, which she occasionally is, her fretting has less to do with worrying about the progress of the current project and more to do with her deeply buried fear of losing Max. And her slightly less deeply buried fear of losing the money, over which of course Max has total control. The inheritances have to stay in accounts in each grieving widower's name. When she and Max retire from it all, when they've sold the last of the brides' properties and pocketed the proceeds, they'll both take new identities and he'll transfer the money to their joint new names. They know all about taking new identities by now.

Max wouldn't do that to her, would he? Run off with the money? Or even worse — well, perhaps not, but bad enough — run off with the bride? He's always assured her there's no risk whatever he'll fall in love with anyone but her, but she doesn't think he realises how hard that part is for her. Thinking about him having sex with the latest one. Although she has to admit that in retrospect each time it's a bit of a turn-on. But not all the romantic dinners, the proposal — thank god for his mother's engagement ring, at least they didn't have to fork out on one, and naturally it was recycled each time — the wedding and the honeymoon. Secluded cottages, rose petals, champagne. She feels a hint of bile at her throat and tries to shake off her shadowy thoughts.

But still, where is he? And what's going on? She can't call him, that's been a cast-iron rule since they started the bride-grooming. Unless there's a real emergency at his end as there had been with Stephanie, when even Max had had to break his own cast-iron rule.

Of course she has a note of Kate's number, but feels it's too early to call a client who's just back from her honeymoon. Too intrusive, almost prurient.

Restless, Vivien goes to the kitchen, opens the fridge, pours herself a glass of wine. She puts the TV on for the six o'clock news. It's a quiet day — no political scandals, no international incidents, not even any celebrity antics. She has her back to the screen, is plumping the cushions on the sofa, when she hears it.

*And lastly, some breaking news from Dorset, where a body was found earlier today drowned in the bath in a secluded holiday cottage in the village of Abbotsea. Police have been called to the scene and have sealed the cottage. It is not yet known whether any other persons were involved. That's all for now, we'll be back at ten o'clock.*

\*

It's Detective Constable Hannah Davies' first murder investigation and the photo projected onto the white board in the incident room at Bournemouth Central Police Station doesn't make for easy viewing. The adult male body in the bath is still mostly submerged, the thorax bloated, the skin on the hands and feet loose and wrinkled. But there's no blood or gore so on reflection she decides that it's probably easier viewing than most.

'First thing — we know that death occurred between sometime in the afternoon of 24th June — a week ago yesterday — when the victim, Jake Andrews, and his bride, currently only identified by her first name Kate and her very recent married name of Andrews, arrived at Honeysuckle Cottage, outside Abbotsea, for their honeymoon, and the discovery of the body yesterday,' says Detective Chief Inspector Neha Choudhury. 'The pathologist thinks from viewing the body in situ that it was probably in the first day or two of that time frame, but can't be certain. We'll know more after the PM. Second thing, there were signs of considerable alcohol consumption.'

Sniggers from the room. DCI Choudhury glares. 'Yes I know,' she says, 'the owner of the cottage who discovered the body thought it might have been a sex game gone wrong. And it's possible, let's face it. Realistically, there are only two possibilities. Either the drowning was an accident or it was deliberate. No defensive wounds, though, nothing under his fingernails. But either way, and this is the third thing, the bride scarpered with all her things. And maybe some of his. There's no phone, no wallet, no keys other than for the car. And the cottage — that was posted back through the front door, which was locked.'

Hannah clears her throat nervously. She's resolved to ask questions from the outset rather than sit quietly taking notes, which is her preference. But that's not a good way to get noticed. 'What sort of accident?' she asks.

'Well,' says the DCI. 'As the boys are busy fantasising, it could have been a sex game. It seems clear that Andrews got in the bath first. It doesn't look as though Kate joined him, but we're assuming that he was expecting her to given that by all accounts it was very early in the honeymoon. The only prints on the bath and the taps are his, as are the prints on the bottle of the foaming bath oil that was in the water.' She pauses, frowning. 'It's odd because there are no other prints on the bottle. The owner said she hadn't provided it. There were other bath products in the bathroom, for guests to use, but she was adamant that they didn't include that oil. So I guess the bride, Kate, must have brought it, in which case it's odd that there are no prints other than his.'

'Perhaps it was a present from him,' suggests Detective Sergeant Dave Stevens. 'Special prep for honeymoon night.' He gives a stage leer, and more sniggers and a wolf whistle follow.

DCI Choudhury rolls her eyes. 'Enough,' she says. 'To resume. So yes, it could have been a sex game. Equally, it could have been a more straightforward accident. They'd drunk enough to float — or do I mean sink? — the Titanic if the empty bottles are anything to go by. Not a good state to be in when you get into a hot bath.'

'If he'd poured in a lot of that bath oil it could have been slippery,' ventures Hannah, and feels her cheeks grow pink.

'Yes,' agrees the DCI. 'Although there's no sign that he slipped and knocked himself out. But he could have passed out with the combination of alcohol and hot water, and a slippery bath would make it more difficult to get out if he was conscious enough to try.'

Hannah is studying the photo, trying to focus on the bath rather than the body. 'It's quite a high bath,' she observes. 'And very curved. Nothing much to grab.'

'Yes,' says DCI Choudhury again. 'So an accident is certainly a possibility. And Bride Kate could have come into the bathroom and seen a body in the bath. Even he if wasn't dead yet she might have thought he was. She could have panicked and run off. But it would be an odd thing to do.'

The guys are quieter now, more serious. Hannah initially thought there must be a whole pack of them in the room but in fact there are just three, apart from DS Stevens: Detective Inspector Charlie Owens, Detective Constable Bill Evans and Detective Constable Zhen Li.

'How did she run off?' asks DI Evans. 'The car was still at the cottage when the body was discovered.'

'Bugger all CCTV around there,' says Bill. 'The owner said it was one of her USPs. For honeymooners, I suppose she meant.'

'And not much scope for house-to-house,' adds Zhen. 'Even in the village, where there are at least some houses, I can't see us getting very far with "Have you seen a woman, no idea how old she is or what she looks like, about a week ago but we're not sure about the date or time, or whether she was walking or in a car, no idea what make or colour of car if so by the way, and either way we've no idea what direction she was going in?"'

'Did you say there was nothing of hers left in the cottage? She must have packed up and walked out. Kept a very cool head.' Bill looks almost impressed.

'Maybe she hadn't unpacked much?' suggests Hannah. 'His clothes were still in his case weren't they?'

'They were,' confirms DCI Choudhury.

'Too eager to unpack first,' suggests Dave. 'Too busy prepping for honeymoon night.' He gives another stage leer, and more sniggers and a wolf whistle follow, but more subdued than before.

*

Carol reads through the latest draft of her article with a sigh. It's really neither very good nor very interesting. *Patterns in crime in northwest London over the last five years.* Even the title induces a yawn. But it's the best she's been able to come up with, and it's taken her long enough to write it. Partly, she admits to herself, because she's continued to waste time going back to

Jake Andrews' and the mysterious Kate's apartments and keeping watch. But though she sees plenty of people going in and out of the former, she sees no sign of Jake. And she sees no one going in or out of the latter.

She drags her mind back to her riveting article. Who's she going to pitch it to? Who, let's face it, will be interested? If she knew what to do, she supposes she could turn it into a blog, but she doesn't, and anyway she needs to make some money. Soon. She's desperate for a fag but has forced herself to stick to five a day — better than broccoli, at least — but she's had six already so far and it's not even noon.

At that point a Google alert flashes across her screen. Carol straightens, gripping the table till her knuckles are white.

### Honeymoon tragedy of bridegroom in bath
### Dorset Village Voice

*Jake Andrews and his new bride Kate drove down to Abbotsea, where they'd booked a week in Honeysuckle Cottage for their honeymoon, on Saturday afternoon a week ago.*

*The cottage is remote and it was only yesterday that owner Angela Williams discovered the horrific scene in the bathroom. The honeymooners should have checked out before noon, and shortly after that Angela went to the cottage to prepare it for her next guests. She was surprised and, she admits, irritated to see Andrews' car still parked outside. She knocked on the front door and, when there was no response, let herself in.*

*'I knew immediately there was something terribly wrong,' she told your reporter. 'It was the smell. It was horrible, like rotting food. All the windows were closed; the evenings have been cool for the time of year so that wasn't surprising. The heating was off, or at least turned right down; I suppose it would have been even worse, much worse, if it had been on or the weather had been warmer.' Angela takes a deep breath before describing what she saw in the bathroom.*

215

*'He, the groom, Jake Andrews, was submerged in the bath. Dead.
Drowned, they say. The bath was very full. The water looked oily
and there was an empty bottle of some brand of foaming bath oil.
Not one of mine, they must have brought it with them. And
downstairs … there were bottles everywhere. Empty bottles. Three
or was it four champagne bottles? A white wine and a red wine.
They must have been really drunk. Maybe it was a sex game gone
wrong? And no sign of her at all. The bride.'*

\*

Vivien turns so sharply that she knocks her shin painfully
against the corner of the coffee table. She stumbles, gasping
with the sudden needle of pain. The television has moved on
to the next programme. Vivien doesn't even register what it is
as she hobbles over to the dining table and opens her iPad.
Her heart is pounding, her mouth is dry. Is it another
Stephanie situation? Has Max had to act quickly again? But
wouldn't he have contacted her? Perhaps he couldn't. Perhaps
he's on his way back to London now, but the brief TV report
suggests it's not as neat as Stephanie. The police are there. Her
fingers shake as she stabs the keys and googles the frantic
string of 'Jake Andrews Kate Lincoln Dorset bath drowned'.
An article from the *Dorset Village Voice* comes up immediately,
though 'Lincoln' is scored out underneath the link. But the
other words are enough.

# TWENTY-FOUR

Carol sits immobile and reads the article again and again. Then she pulls up the article about Stephanie drowning in her bath on her honeymoon — on the first night of her honeymoon. She stands up, rolls her shoulders, lights a cigarette — what the hell — sits back down and starts to marshal her thoughts.

She knows — is as sure as she can be — that James Anderson and Jake Andrews are the same person.

She knows — is as sure as she can be — that that person, in his Jake Andrews persona, is in a relationship with and apparently engaged to a woman he called Kate.

And she knows — or at least strongly suspects — that that person, presumably in his James Anderson persona, is in a relationship with a different woman, a younger, prettier blonde. Carol has no name or other information about the blonde.

She glances back at the article about Jake. Drowned in his bath. No sign of the bride, Kate, who must surely be the woman Carol has seen. She should take what she knows to the police.

But … this could be her story. The big one. The one she was so sure she was onto until she lost the scent. The one that would kick-start her career again. Only this one is even bigger. And if she hands it over to the police it won't be hers anymore.

Carol reasons that the police are in a position to find out a

217

lot more than she can, and a lot more than she already knows, which after all is precious little. It's easy to persuade herself that she should start following her own threads, see where they lead. If she finds out anything that might help the police, why then of course she'll take it to them.

The problem is, how is she going to find out anything that might help the police? Or anything at all for that matter?

She needs to find Kate. She knows her address and her first name, and now her just married name, and what she looks like. But that's all. She can start by going back to the property. If Kate's recently married perhaps that's why she hasn't been there. OK, that only explains the last week, assuming the news article is correct, but maybe Kate was away on work matters before that, clearing her diary for her honeymoon. Maybe she's back now, hiding in her flat, recovering from her shock at … At what, exactly? Was Jake trying to drown her, as Carol now realises he must surely have drowned Stephanie, and it had gone wrong? She'd fought back? Or was it a genuine accident — too much alcohol, passing out in a hot bath — and she'd seen the body and panicked? Either way, it would be a fantastic scoop. Though Kate might not agree.

Carol's thoughts turn to Jake. Who was he? How can she find out more about him? She knows his address, but can't get any further with that. Though the police could, she thinks guiltily, before burying the thought.

She knows a little more about Jake in his James Anderson persona, but when she thinks it through it's nothing. Essentially she knows two addresses, one a serviced apartment from which he moved out ages ago and the other the house he owned and, she recalls gloomily, has sold. The house he inherited from his drowned bride. Where he entertained his blonde.

The blonde … Carol remembers with a jolt of excitement that she made a note of the registration number of her car. She finds it on her phone and starts scrolling through her list of contacts in the Met who've proved helpful to her in the past.

*

Hannah's wondering when they'll hear more about the fingerprints and other forensics. She knows some results must be in already because DCI Choudhury mentioned that Andrews' prints were on the bath and bath oil bottle. The DCI comes back to the prints when they reconvene later that afternoon.

'Right,' she says. 'Fingerprints are a fucking nightmare. His, Andrews', are in various places. Everywhere, really. They're on the bath and bottle and bedroom and downstairs. Except in the kitchen, where most of the surfaces have been thoroughly wiped clean. As have the loo seat and flush and basin taps in the bathroom. But there are numerous prints from numerous people everywhere. The owner, of course. Mrs Williams. She came in to clean at the end of the week. She says she hardly touched anything before finding the body and dialling 999, but obviously there are lots of her prints from before. She was a bit defensive actually, thought I was criticising her cleaning. I didn't like to say we much preferred really sloppy cleaners on these occasions.'

Polite laughter ripples round the room.

'But she didn't clean on the day they arrived. She lets out two places and asks her teenage daughter to help out if there are changeovers at both on the same day. And the teenage daughter was behind with her homework so asked a friend to help her. So their prints are everywhere. We can eliminate all three, of course, but it'll take time. And she got the chimney sweep in the week before so he'll have left some; we haven't taken his yet. Hannah, can you get onto that?'

Hannah nods and makes a note.

'With any luck there'll be some unaccounted for after elimination and we can assume they're the bride's.'

'Presumably Andrews' aren't in the system?' asks Zhen.

'No trace in the PNC of anyone matching the name Jake Andrews of around that age.'

'What about on the wine glasses?' asks Hannah. 'Prints, I mean.'

'Good question. Bad answer. The bride was cool-headed

219

enough to load the dishwasher with everything they'd used.'

'You said there were empty bottles …' This from Zhen.

'Wiped,' says DCI Choudhury grimly.

'Hairs? Fabric?'

'A few hairs. They're at the lab.'

'If those girls are anything like my daughters,' says Bill gloomily, 'they'll be leaving a trail of hair everywhere.'

'Footprints?' suggests Zhen. 'When she left the cottage?'

'Nothiing. It was dry, had been for days, and she probably stuck to the gravel path and then the road. Assuming she walked, though we've got no idea where to.'

'The car,' says Bill suddenly. 'Andrews' car. Presumably they drove up together. She must have left prints?'

'Looks as though she wore gloves. Plenty of his — our body's — but bugger all else of use. But I was going to mention the car next, because it's given us what's so far our only real lead.' DCI Choudhury runs her fingers through her hair, takes a deep breath and continues, 'As you'll have realised by now, we haven't got much to go on for either the bride or the groom. To recap: the elusive bride's first name is Kate, we don't yet know her maiden name or any middle name, or indeed her full first name assuming Kate's an abbreviation. We don't know where the marriage took place until the details are in the central registry, which they're not yet. They should be, but there was some problem with data entry last week. Fucking typical.'

'Didn't they have the marriage certificate with them?' asked Hannah. 'They usually give it to you after the ceremony I think.'

'They do — usually give it to you, I mean — but there's no sign of this one. The mystery bride must have taken it with her. Anyway, the marriage details should be online any day now — Hannah, can you keep checking the GRO?'

Hannah nods again and makes another note.

'In the meantime,' says DCI Choudhury, 'we're looking at the groom, Jake Andrews. At least that's the name he booked the cottage under, I'll come back to that. Mrs Williams, the owner, has a mobile number for him but no address.

Apparently that's the norm for lets through Airbnb. Airbnb won't necessarily have his home address, but of course they have his bank details, and we've put in a request for those, and with the mobile provider for whatever they've got. In any event, the mobile's not in the cottage and it's not responding. So for the moment we have bugger all except the car.' The DCI pauses and takes a long swig of water.

'Which is owned by a Max Carrington. We should get his photo from the DVLA tomorrow, but the PNC has the registered owner's address, which is a rental in London W14. Carrington is helpfully not in the PNC in any other context — no convictions or cautions or anything so no fingerprints, no DNA. And so far the address is a dead end as well. The Met sent uniform earlier today and they've reported back that it's a house divided into flats which are rented out and neither the current tenants nor the current freeholder have ever heard of Max Carrington. Although —' DCI Choudhary pauses, with a frown. 'Apparently one of the tenants told uniform that a woman called at the property a few days ago, also asking after Max Carrington. The freeholder said the same. Hannah, can you see what more you can find out please?'

*

As Carol expected, there's no answer when she rings Kate's doorbell. She's had enough of watching it and now tries the neighbouring flats, with only one hit. A young woman opens the door, revealing an open-plan kitchen with a toddler screaming in a playpen and a baby screaming in some sort of bouncing swing contraption. The woman, understandably, looks harried.

'Yes?'

'I'm sorry to disturb you,' says Carol with some truth, as she tries to block out the crescendo of noise. 'I'm trying to contact the woman at number three. It's rather important. Do you happen to know when she's likely to be home? She was expecting me,' she adds with somewhat less truth.

The woman glances distractedly towards the kitchen. 'No

I don't. I've hardly seen her, just going in and out occasionally. And not for — oh, I don't know, certainly the last week or so. Though that might mean nothing, I might just have missed her. Sorry, I must —' The woman calls behind her, 'Camellia! Thelonius! Stop that bloody racket NOW' and shuts the door.

Carol revels briefly in the relative quiet and heads for the tube home.

# TWENTY-FIVE

Vivien has read the article again and again, trying to parse it for some shred of hope, some sign that the body in the bath isn't Max. But there's nothing to be gleaned. She's barely slept and now, in the morning, she wanders round the apartment, draped in Max's striped dressing gown, her eyes like pandas' with the tear-smudged make-up she hasn't bothered to clean off. She feels cleft by grief, like a conjoined twin who's been surgically separated from her other half. And she has no idea what to do next.

She can't claim the body, organise an undertaker, register the death, arrange the funeral. All the practical formalities that distract others who mourn their loved ones. She assumes that the police are involved and won't be releasing the body for a while, but what will happen when they do? Jake had impeccable ID, which will be in Max's 'Jake' wallet; his own one is here, she's checked. She feels the glimmer of a fleeting smile — Max always insisted on wrapping his wallet in foil and leaving it in a Tupperware container in the fridge. Vivien would tease him about his paranoia: why, or even how, would anyone else get into their home?

She comes back to Jake's ID. When they started bride-grooming, they planned that he'd simply change his name by deed poll each time. But they realised that he'd need a birth certificate or passport when giving notice of marriage, and although he could apply for a passport in the new name by submitting the deed poll with the application, he'd lose his own. And, simple and informal as that process was, it would still leave an information trail back to him, and repeated applications for a new passport might trigger a red flag or whatever. So they adopted the old-fashioned method, beloved of golden-age crime novels: apply for a copy of the birth certificate of someone born at the right time for the new persona, someone who tragically died young, and use that certificate to obtain a passport. Either could then be used for the marriage formalities, together with utility bills or the rental agreement in the new name and showing the relevant serviced apartment address. The first birth certificate, she recalls in a fleeting moment of amnesiac fondness, was for a Joseph Aston, and they'd chosen subsequent bridegrooms with the same initials. Max said it helped him stay in that persona, separate the two identities, remember who he was. Vivien shakes her head, dragging herself back to the present. There will be nothing at the honeymoon cottage linking Jake with Max. Which is, of course, exactly as they intended.

Vivien opens her iPad to do some googling, though she's not sure what to search. But as she does so, she remembers with a horrified start that Max's laptop will be at the cottage. It was the one duplication he drew the line at. 'I can't get a new Mac each time,' he said. 'And I need my laptop with me if I'm away for a week or two. But don't worry, darling, I'll keep it in my case, she won't even know it's there.'

Then, lurching from panic to relief, she remembers that his current Mac has fingerprint ID so no one else can open it. And even if they did, he's downloaded some app that means his emails and messages are password protected, she remembers him showing her. She tries to recall what else is on the laptop. Mainly the banking stuff, but he's got a password manager for that, and she has the codes written down in her notebook, with nothing to indicate what they're for. Though maybe the police can bypass or break through all these barriers? If they find the money … They weren't married, so ironically she can't claim as his widow. Even apart from all the other impediments.

Vivien closes the iPad and takes a deep breath. There are some things she can't do anything about, at least for the moment. Max's laptop is one of them, but there's also the body. Will they trace Jake Andrews back to Max Carrington? What happens if they do? What happens if they don't?

There is something, however, that she can do something about. Find Kate.

*

The marriage has finally been entered at the General Register Office. The bride is down as 'Kate Lincoln' and under 'Age' it just says 'Of full age'. She's described as single and as a venture capitalist, whatever that is. But as well as her maiden name the form gives an address for her, in London SW3 which Hannah finds is Chelsea. It also indicates that the marriage took place on 24 June 2023 at Kensington and Chelsea Register Office.

Hannah calls the register office and asks whether they have additional information on file. Ten minutes later a scanned copy of the Notice of Marriage pings into her inbox. She opens the table of information on Kate Andrews which she's compiling and adds her maiden name, date of birth (20 April 1973), nationality (British) and period of residence (five years), which the register office assistant explained means the period during which the bride had resided at her given address. She's googled 'Kate Lincoln' and 'Kate Lincoln Venture Capital' but it's a needle in a digital haystack — literally millions of hits. Filtering the search by adding references to the wedding date and venue brings up nothing and adding 'Jake Andrews' simply generates the article in the online *Dorset Village Voice* which the police are already aware of. But Hannah has two other possible, even probable, details about Kate from the registrar who officiated at the wedding.

'She was very tall. I'm almost certain it was her. We have so many ceremonies, especially on Saturdays, that I couldn't swear to it, but her wedding was the last one before I had a break so I'm pretty sure I'm remembering right. She must have been nearly six foot. Or maybe that's an exaggeration, but certainly unusually tall for a woman. Otherwise not very striking, even on her wedding day. Oh, except she had very blue eyes. I'm almost sure it was her,' the registrar repeats. But she had no particular recollection of the groom.

Hannah opens the table she's started on Jake Andrews and adds the new details from the marriage forms: his date of birth is 29 September 1972 and he's single, British and an IT consultant, resident for three months at an address in London SW7, which is South Kensington. Hannah takes printouts of the official documents and her tables to DCI Choudhury, who asks her to find out what she can about Jake's and Kate's properties and to put in urgent applications for both passports and for search warrants for both addresses. She's already run Kate Lincoln through the police database and, like Jake Andrews and Max Carrington, she has no police history.

Hannah sets the passport and warrant applications in motion then logs on to the Land Registry website. Jake's address is an apartment owned by Swordfish Corporate Rentals Ltd. A phone call elicits the information that it was let to him as a furnished, serviced flat for six months, terminable on two weeks' notice, from 26 March 2023. And that Swordfish takes its data protection and client confidentiality obligations very seriously and can't divulge any further information without a court order. Hannah shrugs as she puts the phone down — they should get Jake Andrews' passport details from the passport office promptly, without needing to go to court to squeeze them out of Swordfish.

The Land Registry site reveals that Kate's address is a flat owned by Janet and Richard Ogilvy. Hannah googles the names and eventually, after ploughing through the usual irrelevant hits, is directed to myriads of Tweets and Facebook postings rhapsodising about the beauties of Marlborough Sounds. The couple are travelling round New Zealand in a rented VW camper it seems. She googles the address of the flat and finds it listed on an up-market rental site, Central London Listings. Hannah salivates briefly over the photos — it's luxurious, spacious, light, beautifully furnished, and even has its own underground parking space. And it's marked 'LET!! Another success story for our owners!'

Hannah calls Central London Listings and is passed to the agent dealing with that property, Frances, who informs her that it was let in March to Kate Lincoln and that the agency handles the letting for the Ogilvies.

'Are you sure about the date?' asks Hannah. 'Our information is that Kate Lincoln resided there for the last five years.'

'Definitely not. I've got the rental agreement in front of me. It was signed on 14 March 2023.'

Hannah frowns as she double checks the marriage certificate, which clearly states five years rather than five months. Could the Registrar have transcribed it wrongly from the information Kate Lincoln provided? Or was it a simple error on her part? Perhaps she was so excited by her impending wedding that she muddled months and years.

'It's a bit odd, though,' says Frances. 'I can see from our records that she paid the full six months' rent, and the deposit, in advance. I remember now, I asked her about it and she just said it was easier for her book-keeping or expenses claims or something. And … wait a sec, there's something else here.' Hannah hears the subdued tapping of electronic keys 'She asked us to give it a very thorough clean last week. I was on holiday myself, a colleague dealt with it. Says here that she said she'd be away and it was a good opportunity.'

Hannah's heart sinks. 'Has it been cleaned?' she asks.

'Yes, it was done on Tuesday. I've got a note here, "Full service, extra deep clean". Our cleaners are excellent,' Frances adds proudly. 'I see that she also asked for all the bedding to be stripped and sent to be laundered as well as the towels and kitchen linen. And for the rugs and curtains to be steam cleaned — apparently she has an allergy and the dust was accumulating.'

Frances gives Hannah Kate Lincoln's mobile number and email address and the details of the bank account in her name from which the initial transfer was made, and emails a scanned copy of the photo and signature page of Kate's passport. It's poor quality but usable, and with the passport number Hannah will be able to get a clean electronic version from the passport office. She puts in the request, finds Kate Lincoln's mobile provider and applies for her records, and goes back to DCI Choudhury with what she's found out.

*

Vivien has a long, scalding shower, cleans her face, makes it up again, finds clothes that even in her distracted state she thinks match and look OK, makes herself a strong coffee and sits down with a mobile. She's decided to call Kate. There's a risk, it's another link, but she'll use the burner phone she bought for her communications with Kate so she's not really adding much. And she'll probably have to get rid of that phone soon anyway. What would Max say she should do? She quells the rising panic. Max has gone, she has to make her own decisions now.

But Kate isn't picking up, which is probably not surprising. Vivien tries a few times but just gets an impersonal recorded message saying that the subscriber's phone is not accessible. She remembers Kate's address though and sets off.

Vivien rings the doorbell several times but there's no answer. Feeling faintly ridiculous, she crouches down and looks through the letter box, but it must have one of those draught excluders or whatever they're called and she can't see anything.

Frustrated, she rings the bell of the flat next door. It's mid-morning so most people will be at work, but after a pause, a woman opens the door with a toddler balanced on her hip.

'I'm sorry to disturb you,' says Vivien, trying to smile at the child. His lip wobbles and he turns his head away. 'I urgently need to contact the woman who lives at number three.' She gestures. 'Have you seen her today?'

The woman narrows her eyes as if trying to recollect. 'Tall

woman?' she asks. 'Glasses? Longish hair?'

Vivien nods eagerly.

'No,' says the neighbour. 'To be honest I've only seen her a couple of times. And not for — I don't know, maybe a week or two? Hasn't she moved out?'

'I don't know,' says Vivien helplessly. 'Has she?'

The woman shrugs. 'I'm just the nanny here, didn't know her at all. I suppose Julian and Penny might have spoken to her, but I doubt it to be honest. I think she only moved in a few months ago. Penny told me the flat was rented.' She starts to close the door, then pauses with a frown. 'There was another woman asking for her though. Only yesterday.'

'Who?' barks Vivien urgently. 'What did she look like? Do you know her name?'

The woman shrugs again. 'Dunno. About your age maybe — fifties or so? Casually dressed. Didn't give a name.' The door shuts definitively this time.

Vivien is so appalled to be thought to be in her fifties that she barely registers the lack of useful information. Grief and stress must have taken their toll on her face, she thinks with a flicker of despair.

\*

DCI Choudhury has asked Hannah to draft an appeal to the public for information. They still have no photo of Jake Andrews when he was alive, which doesn't help. But the DVLA has sent the licence photo of Max Carrington, who may be the same person as Jake Andrews and is at least similar in appearance to the body in the bath, and they're waiting to hear back from the passport office with details of any passport in the name of Max Carrington or Jake Andrews and a clearer copy of Kate Lincoln's. In the meantime Hannah has a stab at some wording.

**Do you know this woman or this man?**

*Dorset Police are appealing for information on sightings and the whereabouts of Kate Lincoln, Jake Andrews and Max Carrington. Max Carrington and Jake Andrews may be the same person.*

*Kate Lincoln, a venture capitalist aged 50, and Jake Andrews, an IT consultant aged 51, were married at Kensington and Chelsea Register Office on 24 June 2023. That afternoon they drove down to Abbotsea in Dorset in a grey Renault Captur 2019, registration plate LW69 QIZ, registered to Max Carrington, aged 52.*

*If you have any information about any of these people, please immediately contact the Dorset Police hotline on the number below.*

Hannah sighs. It wouldn't look good to say that the police have no idea what she was wearing or other aspects of her appearance. But it's the truth. The details the registrar mentioned — the blue eyes, the height — are too uncertain and could be counter-productive in an appeal. She'll have to see what the DCI thinks, and if the wording's OK they can release it and then release an update as soon as they get the additional photos. And then follow up the address on Max Carrington's driving licence. Where, she recalls, someone else was recently asking about Max Carrington.

*

Back in the flat, Vivien opens her iPad again, intending to google Kate. Surely she can find out where she works?

But when she starts to type 'Kate Lincoln' she pauses. 'Kate' is almost certainly an abbreviation. But for what? Katherine. Katharine. Kathryn. Kathleen. Katerina. Catherine. Catharine. Catherina. Catharina. Catarina. Caitlin. Vivien tries to think back to their first meeting, Kate's interview. She must have asked to see her passport. But she knows that she won't have noted any details, still less taken a photo, particularly since Kate seemed as though she might be a special. Looking at the passport is just a formality, really, to make her and the agency seem more professional. She'd have picked up if it was in an obviously different name from the client's, but otherwise wouldn't have registered the detail.

Vivien pushes her tablet aside, pillows her head on her folded arms and weeps. Almost immediately, her mobile rings and she jerks upright, but it's not her Kate phone, it's her normal one. Fiona, she sees. She sighs, sniffs back some tears and answers. It's not the right time for Fiona's babbling questions about wedding planners. Fiona's all right, but her enthusiasm can be irritating. The Mills & Boon gushing reminds Vivien of Stephanie, though the two are very different in other ways. In particular, Fiona has parents and siblings and so many friends she's having a problem finding a big enough venue. She could never have been a special. Very uncharacteristically, Vivien cuts her client off mid-babble. 'I'm so sorry, my dear, but I really must go; I have an urgent appointment. I'll give it some thought and get back to you later. I'm so pleased for you,' she adds, her voice sliding automatically into her customary warm murmur.

She ends the call, turns back to her iPad and googles 'K Lincoln venture capital'. 'About 8,720,000 results' instantly pop up. There's a global investment bank called Lincoln International. It purports to 'combine investment banking advisory expertise with unique perspective to help venture capital clients maximize value and opportunities'. Vivien has no idea what that means, except that it makes searching for a K Lincoln who works in venture capital a lost cause. And a C Lincoln even more so.

Surely the police will find her though? They'll be looking for her, they have the manpower, the resources. So Max's killer will be brought to justice. Taking some comfort in the thought, Vivien makes herself a coffee. She's raising the cup to her lips when she's struck by a realisation so obvious, and so terrifying, that she can't believe she missed it. She sets the cup back on the counter, her hand trembling. If the police find Kate, she will tell them everything she knows. Vivien doesn't know exactly how much that is, but she's sure that it's more than enough. The police will come for her. She has to find Kate before they do.

*

Carol doesn't hear back from her police contact until the following afternoon. She'd had to dangle the lure of a tasty dinner out, possibly followed by a tasty digestif in — they'd been casual lovers once or twice when their paths had crossed in the past — but Will has come up with the goods. He calls as she's walking back from the corner shop with a packet of fags she'd promised herself not to buy, but she's been nervy and impatient all day, worried that she's losing valuable time to find her only lead. She'd called at Kate's flat again that morning but it was another fruitless trip.

Will understandably doesn't want to email or even text her the information, so Carol squats gracelessly on a doorstep and scrabbles in her bag for a pen and paper. Ever the journalist, she has both to hand.

Deborah Susan Yule, with an address in Kensal Green.

Carol searches it on Google maps. It's a manageable journey and she decides to go straight there once she's done a quick turnaround at home — she should arrive in the early evening, when with luck — and surely she's due some luck? — she might catch the blonde coming home from work, whatever that is.

And for once Carol has some luck: Deborah Susan Yule is at home. She opens the door a slit, a chain clearly visible, with an unwelcoming 'Who are you? What do you want?'

'I'm a journalist,' says Carol, with the fleeting thought that telling the truth feels distinctly odd. 'Carol Turner. I'd like to talk to you — erm, to interview you for my paper. About someone you know. There could be something in it for you.' She's warming to her theme.

Deborah Yule at least doesn't close the door in her face. 'About who?' she asks.

Carol glances behind her. 'It will be easier if I come in,' she

232

says. 'It's — there's some rather personal stuff involved.'

Deborah almost closes the door but then unhooks the chain and eases it part way open again. Her stance is somewhere between unwelcoming and aggressive but after staring at Carol for a minute or two, she grudgingly steps back and lets Carol in. She shuts the door and stands, arms crossed.

'Well?'

Carol would have preferred to do this sitting down but Deborah's had her chance.

'I want to ask you about someone you know. I have some news about him, which you should know.'

'Who?' There's a flicker of interest on Deborah's face now.

'James Anderson.'

'Who?' says Deborah again, neither her voice nor her expression giving any hint of recognition or curiosity.

'James Anderson. You may know him as Jake Andrews I suppose.'

Again, no sign that the name means anything. 'I don't know either name. You must have got the wrong person. Whatever it is, it's clearly nothing to do with me.' Deborah moved back towards the door.

Carol frowns. Either Deborah is an excellent actor or she, Carol, is barking up the wrong tree. She can at least test the first hypothesis. She pulls out her phone, finds the *Dorset Village Voice* article and passes the phone to Deborah.

Deborah scans the article and thrusts the phone back to Carol.

'I've already told you, I don't know a Jake Andrews. Nor anyone called Kate.' She moves nearer the door, reaching towards the Yale lock.

Carol thinks rapidly. She needs to show Deborah a photo. Would the police have released an appeal yet? They must have some information by now — it's only a couple of days since the body was discovered, but she knows that it will have been all hands on deck from that moment.

'Wait a second,' she says. She pulls out her phone and googles. There it is. She does a fleeting mental double take

233

when she sees yet another name but the appeal's so short that she still reads it in what is little more than a literal second — the police clearly have very little information, and she pushes aside the small spark of guilt that briefly flares — before holding her phone out to Deborah.

Deborah's eyes flick to the screen, the headline shrieking *Do you know this woman or this man?*, and she gasps — no, it's more of a squawk, thinks Carol. An anguished squawk. She grabs the phone and stares at it, biting her lip as if willing it to say something else. 'Max,' she manages, her voice weak and trembling. 'I don't know the other names. But I know Max. And it's his photo.'

# TWENTY-SIX

'Shall we sit down?' asks Carol. 'Can I get you a glass of water? This must be a shock.'

Deborah nods and staggers through the open door of what is clearly the sitting room. It's a mess — clothes, magazines and shopping bags scattered haphazardly on the sofa and chairs, dirty plates and mugs on the table. Deborah shoves a sweater off one side of the sofa to join a pile of ironed blouses on the other and gestures to one of the chairs. 'Just put the bags on the floor,' she croaks. Carol does so, then goes through to what is an equally disordered kitchen, finds a clean glass with some difficulty, fills it from the tap, hands it to Deborah and sits down. She pulls her notebook and pen out of her handbag and says, 'Who's Max?'

Deborah takes a gulp of water, puts the glass on the floor and hands Carol back her phone. She finds her own in a pocket, pecks a few keys and evidently finds the appeal. Tears well in her eyes and she wipes them angrily, leaving a trail of mascara.

'He is — was —' her voice wobbles again — 'my partner. Boyfriend. Lover. We were going to get married.'

Carol blinks. She looks down at her notebook and makes a meaningless squiggle while she tries to order her thoughts.

'Shall we start at the beginning? How did you meet him?'

Deborah takes another gulp. 'At the dentist.' She stares at

her phone as if trying to find some meaning in the words. As well she might, thinks Carol. Then Deborah suddenly frowns, narrows her eyes, and says, 'What's it to you anyway? Why are you here? How did you — how did you know about me, my address?' Her voice has risen dangerously.

'I'm a journalist,' says Carol again. 'I'm working on a story about a man I know as James Anderson and Jake Andrews. He uses both names. I didn't know he also goes by Max Carrington.'

'I think that's — was — his real name. Though—' Deborah pauses, screws up her eyes. 'He did tell me once that it wasn't. But it's on his dental records.'

'Are you his dentist?'

'I'm the receptionist. We were leaving the surgery at the same time one evening. He was the last patient. We got chatting as we went down the stairs and he asked me if I'd like a drink. Said he always needed one after seeing the hygienist.' Deborah stops suddenly, fumbles in her pockets and produces a crumpled tissue, starts to blow her nose then dissolves into tears.

Carol finds a packet of clean tissues in her bag — another habit she'd formed after interviewing hundreds of emotional witnesses over her career — and hands it to Deborah, who uses several of the contents to staunch her eyes — now piebald — and nose — now red.

Carol waits quietly and eventually Deborah resumes.

'He asked me out again. Several times. He said he wanted to marry me but he was in a relationship that he needed to get out of. A bad relationship,' she adds defensively, then frowns again and says, 'How did you know my address? And that I knew Max? We were so careful. He said he had to be very careful until he'd got rid of Vivien. His partner.'

*

It's odd seeing a photo of myself on the TV. The wording of the appeal is intoned by an intense-sounding woman. It's short, which isn't surprising. There's one other photo, of Max

236

/ Jake. Not from Max's driving licence; it looks more recent. I think it's from Jake's passport.

I turn back to mine, still up on the screen. I'm not too worried about being recognised. Kate's passport photo looks nothing like Lucy. In fact, Kate's passport photo looks nothing like Kate. I'd used a spray-on wash-out black hair dye, scraped my newly coloured locks back in a tight bun, worn dark brown contact lenses and used a foundation that gave an olive tint.

The only link to the real me is so tenuous that after all this time I feel almost sure that it won't be unearthed. Because it was Kate's first passport, the application and one of the photos I submitted with it had to be countersigned by someone who'd known her for two years and their passport number had to be on the form. I couldn't risk involving even the closest of friends in my scheme, so I'd invented a counter-signatory with a fictitious passport number, an ephemeral email address and a disposable and long since disposed of phone with a PAYG SIM card. I'd gambled on HM Passport Office relying on random rather than routine checks, and it had paid off.

I suppose it's possible that Kate's two first MadeInHeaven dates might recognise her name or — though much less likely — face from the appeal. But the nuclear werewolf author, Arnie or whatever he's called, showed so little interest in anything but himself that it seems improbable. The other one, the more charming teetotal vegan, is more of a risk but not one I can do anything about.

I can do something about Vivien though. She'll recognise the name even if not the photo. She'll surely be panicking now, and if she's got any sense she'll be looking for me, or rather for Kate. She'll want to find Kate before the police do. And if she's got any sense she'll also have realised that the only way she can save her own skin is to silence me permanently. What she doesn't know, though she may suspect, is that I have come to the same conclusion about her.

*

Carol pauses for a moment to process yet more new information and yet another new name. She needs to decide how much to give away to Deborah. She briefly curses that she didn't prepare better before knocking on Deborah's door, but of course at that point she hadn't seen the appeal so there wasn't much she could have done. Except wait, she supposes, but that's never been her forte and in any event now is the time for moving fast not sitting about. And she's had enough unavoidable waiting as it is.

'It's a long story,' she starts, her brain whirring as she tries to sort the kaleidoscopic facts, or assumptions, that she's gathered into some more digestible arrangement. 'Do you smoke?' she adds hopefully, though she knows she'd have picked up the signs by now.

'Sorry, no. Do you want a glass of water?'

'Good idea, thanks.' Carol goes to fetch one from the kitchen and refills Deborah's glass while she's at it. She settles back into her chair and starts again.

'A long story, which started when I stumbled, by chance, on an article in a Cornish newspaper. About a woman who'd drowned in her bath on the first night of her honeymoon.'

'A *woman*?' Deborah frowns.

'Yes. It happened in October last year. The husband — widower — was James Anderson. He was out of the honeymoon cottage when it happened. They'd been drinking a lot and there was oil and soap in the bath. The coroner ruled it to be an accident and there was no police investigation.'

'But what's this got to do with Max?'

'I don't know,' confesses Carol. 'Apart from its being a mirror image. But the thing is, James Anderson inherited his wife's estate. Most of which was a house in Hampstead. In Flask Avenue.'

Deborah jerks upright, spilling most of the glass of water that she was raising to her lips.

'I was watching the house,' continues Carol. 'I was trying to find James Anderson. Thought if I could get an interview it would make a good human interest story. He was very elusive though. I'd got the address off his deceased wife's probate. Anyway, I happened to be watching it when you arrived just after him — I suppose about six weeks ago. And stayed the night.' She decides to leave out the stuff about the estate agent and the reclusive widower allegedly stricken with devastating grief.

Deborah shifts in her chair. 'That was Max,' she says. 'I've never heard of James Anderson. Max said he owned the house and it was on the market. He had another property he was selling and we're — we were—' She gulps, and pauses to blow her nose and rub her eyes again. 'Going to use the money to, to run away together. Once he'd left Vivien. Get married and go and live in the Caribbean somewhere. Somewhere with sun and sea.'

And offshore banking, no doubt, thinks Carol. She resumes.

'I carried on following James Anderson, or the man I knew as James Anderson. He was living in an apartment in South Kensington under another name. Jake Andrews. And I saw him, I think when he was using that name, with another woman.'

'Vivien,' says Deborah scornfully. 'He hates her. He's just waiting for the right time ...' She tails off, evidently realising that there was never going to be a right time now.

'What does Vivien look like? Or don't you know?'

'Oh, I know. She comes to us — the dental surgery — also. Though not so often. Her teeth are perfect, apparently.' Deborah sounds as though she regards this as a personal affront. 'She's pretty. If you like that sort of thing. A bit dated, petite, hair in a bob.'

'The woman Jake Andrews was with,' says Carol, 'was very tall and not very pretty. She was wearing an engagement ring. And Jake called her "Kate". "Kate, my love," actually.'

'But ...' Deborah stops, chews her lip. 'I don't understand.' But it looks as though she's beginning to. 'I can't take in any more,' she says. 'Are you really saying Max was that man? Engaged to a woman called Kate?'

'Married,' corrects Carol. 'I'm sorry, this must be very hard for you, but the police will have checked before putting that in the appeal.'

'But you say he'd married someone else in … when did you say, last October, who died on her honeymoon in an accident …'

The natural colour, though not the smeared mascara, ebbs from Deborah's face.

Carol waits for a few moments then says gently, 'Were Max and Vivien married?'

Deborah shakes her head vigorously. 'No. Max was so grateful that they weren't. Much easier to leave, he said, but he still had to sort the money.' She pulls out another tissue and starts sobbing quietly. 'You think, don't you, that Max killed that woman? The one who had the house?'

'I do,' says Carol. 'And then married Kate Lincoln ten days ago. And there was another fatal accident on the honeymoon. But I suspect not the one Max, or Jake, or James, had in mind.'

\*

Vivien is pouring herself a glass of Sancerre when she hears the appeal. She's thinking that she's drinking too much. Even though she and Max enjoyed a glass or two of wine most evenings, they usually kept it to a reasonable quantity. Max always said he didn't like to risk losing control; it was too easy when you were lubricated by liquor to say something that was best unsaid, to give something away by an unguarded reaction. Again Vivien finds herself wondering what it was that had made Max so shadowy, so secretive. She'd asked him a few times, early in their relationship, about his past, but he was always vague and evasive. 'The past is past,' he'd say. 'We're the future, my love. Let's look forward not back, plan for the next adventure.' The next adventure was usually a new idea for making money. Some worked better than others. The agency and the bride-grooming were more lucrative by far than any of their earlier, abortive schemes. Until now. Vivien turns and heads restlessly into the sitting room. She's beginning to worry about the money, where it is, how to get hold of it, the questions drumming a relentless beat in her head.

She snaps out of her reverie when she hears the names Kate Lincoln, Jake Andrews and Max Carrington. She drops onto the sofa with a gasp, slopping wine out of her glass, and crouches forward, eyes riveted to the screen. To the photos on the screen.

Max. Where did they get it? The driving licence? The passport? Both documents were obtained using his old rental address — just the house number, no indication of which flat it was — and he'd always told her that the tenants in that building changed so often, and the landlord was so casual about paperwork and references, that there was no risk of anyone making the connection. The forwarding instruction, showing their home address, would be somewhere in the bowels of the Post Office's system but would anyone think to look? With the previous brides, Max managed to keep the publicity very low key, but this time there was no grieving widower to plead for privacy, wringing his hands, choking on his sobs. And of course the police had never been involved before, or not seriously, as he'd always arranged it so convincingly as an accident.

Vivien puts her glass down, her hand trembling, and rubs the tears for Max from her eyes. Or are they tears for herself? She tries to listen to what's being said. There's nothing she doesn't know from the newspaper article, so she turns her attention to the photo of Kate.

Except … it doesn't look like Kate. Vivien goes closer to the TV, but that doesn't help, she's too close to focus so she returns to the sofa. The hair's different, the eyes look darker, duller, not that brilliant blue which was her Kate's only arresting feature. Apart from her height, of course, though there's no mention of that in the appeal. But Vivien's good at faces. She looks carefully at the features. Cheekbones, nose, chin, eyebrows, mouth. She's pretty sure now that it is her Kate. People change their hair colour and style all the time of course. But you'd only change your eye colour if you were deliberately trying to look different.

Clearly her Kate is even more devious and dangerous than

241

she thought. She has possibly, probably, killed Max, or at best abandoned him when he died by accident, and that's not a very worthy best. And she's disappeared. The police are looking for her and are better equipped than Vivien to find her. If they do, she, Kate, will obviously be in deep trouble, but she can almost certainly give them enough information about MadeInHeaven for Vivien also to be in deep trouble. Vivien needs to find her first. She's thought it already, just a day or two ago, but hasn't done anything further about it because she couldn't think of how to go about it. But now it's urgent. And Vivien realises — well, she knew already, she thinks, but she faces the fact, articulates it to herself — that when she finds Kate she needs to kill her. I've killed before, she tells herself grimly. I can do it again. She raises a shaky glass to Max. 'For you, my love.'

*

Deborah carries on sobbing for a few moments then starts hiccupping. She reaches for her glass but can't drink while she's sobbing, so she stops crying. She takes a gulp of water but still hiccups. She takes a long breath in, presses her lips together and doesn't inhale again for a long minute but still hiccups.

'Can I get you anything?' asks Carol. 'Or do anything, like slap you on the back? I've never found any of those supposed remedies helpful.'

'How about giving me a shock?' says Deborah with a bleak laugh, punctuated by hiccups. 'Except that you've probably — hic — run out of shocks, and anyway they seem to have — hic — caused the hiccups.' She drains the last drops of her water to no avail, and adds, 'How did you find out about — hic — the Dorset drowning?'

It sounds like a Trollope title, thinks Carol irrelevantly. Or, perhaps more relevantly, one of a series of murder mysteries.

'I set up a Google alert for deaths on honeymoon. At that point I didn't think there was anything suspicious about Stephanie's — James Anderson's wife's — death. But I did think that if there was something similar it would make a good story. Sorry, I mean good for a journalist. I'm on the rocks to be honest. Made redundant a couple of months ago when my paper merged with another. No other source of income. I was scraping the barrel I suppose, casting around for a juicy story I could sell, or even turn into a book. Or a blog or a podcast,' she adds, though she still has little idea how to set about either of those, still less make any money from them.

Carol takes both glasses into the kitchen and refills them. 'I don't suppose you've got anything stronger have you?' she asks as she hands the water to the still hiccupping Deborah.

Deborah shakes her head; she looks as though she's holding her breath again. Carol takes a quick decision.

'Do you think Max was planning to murder Vivien as well?'

Deborah lets out her breath in a gasp. She stares at Carol, her racoon-like eyes wide, the face chalk white. Carol waits for a couple of minutes before saying, 'Well at least that's stopped the hiccups! Which is the only reason I said it,' she adds not quite truthfully. 'I don't know anything about Vivien. Had they been together long?'

Deborah shrugs. 'Max never said much about her. Just that he wanted to be free. Free to be with me.' She bites her lip. 'But — it's been a shock, everything you've said. I need to think about it. Why should I believe you?'

'Well,' says Carol. 'I assume the police haven't made it up. And why would I?'

'To get your story?'

'You can't sell a story — especially one suggesting murder — which is made up. Not unless it's a novel, I suppose, but I was looking for something to sell quickly. Something to make my name again as an investigative journalist.'

Deborah narrows her eyes. She's mulling it over, thinks Carol. She could be famous. Or so she thinks, perhaps correctly.

'How about you interview me then? For your paper. I mean your article or whatever. Or your book.' Deborah brightens visibly. 'I could come on your podcast. I could help you with it,' she adds kindly, giving Carol a doubtful glance.

'I could interview you,' agrees Carol. 'It could be a big

splash—' Not a good image. 'Erm, a hit. But I, we'd, have to be careful. There are restrictions, legal restrictions, on what we can say. But I can write something that would get round them.' Something very short and not very interesting, she thinks. But Deborah won't know that. And if she can forge some sort of working relationship with the girl — woman, she automatically corrects herself — she can probably put something together later. Much later. When all the dust has settled. Though Carol's still not quite sure what dust there is.

Deborah starts to speak then sags without warning, clutching the sofa arm. 'I'm sorry,' she mumbles. 'I'm exhausted. It's just hit me again. You can interview me, but tomorrow.'

Carol calculates rapidly. Is Deborah likely to do a runner? She could do without another disappearance. On the other hand, Deborah's clearly keen on being interviewed. And has a decent job. Which is how she met Max and—

'That's fine,' she says. 'You must be shattered. I'll leave you in peace for now. Just one last question. Do you know Vivien's address?'

Deborah looked confused. 'Well, she lives — lived — with Max of course. Until he could get away from her. It's somewhere in Camden. Max said I must never go there, it would risk messing things up for us. I can get the address from work though.'

'And the phone number?'

'Of course. I'll call you tomorrow.'

They exchange numbers and Carol heads home.

# TWENTY-SEVEN

Hannah and Zhen are on their way to London with a busy schedule. The warrants for entering Kate Lincoln's and Jake Andrews' flats have come through, and they're also going to try and trace Max Carrington through the address on his driving licence; although the Met has already paid an initial, fruitless visit, DCI Choudhury feels it's worth a follow up, especially as they now have the better quality passport photos of Max Carrington as well as the other two. They reissued the appeal last night as soon as the photos arrived.

They're on the Hammersmith flyover, with Zhen at the wheel, when Hannah's mobile rings. It's DCI Choudhury, her voice buzzing with excitement.

'This may be nothing,' she warns, but it's clear that she's hoping it's something. 'An interesting call just came through on the appeal line. A woman who claims to recognise Max Carrington. She doesn't know him, or even his name, but says she was stopped outside Camden Register Office by a woman who was about to get married. The bride asked her to take a photo of the groom for her. I said you'd come and take a statement as you'd be in London anyway, so I don't know more.'

'Camden?' asks Hannah, surprised. 'Is she sure?'

'So she said, but she must be remembering wrong.' The DCI gives Hannah the woman's name and mobile number and the address of an office near St Paul's and suggests they go there first.

Parking's a nightmare in the City so Zhen drops Hannah at One New Change and heads to the nearest NCP. Hannah's already spoken to the woman, Grace Reed, who's an associate lawyer at a firm of solicitors.

'There's a load of cafés and so on here,' Grace had said, 'on the retail floors. We could meet at one of those?'

Hannah thought for a moment. 'Is there any chance we could use a meeting room or empty office?' she asks. 'As you can imagine from the appeal, it's quite … delicate. And it's an ongoing investigation. I'd rather we spoke in private.'

'Of course,' said Grace. 'I'll ask reception to find a room for us and tell them to expect you.'

The building is modern, a brooding hulk of smoky brown glass, all planes and angles. Hannah checks in with the street level reception and is directed up to the fourth floor. There, the receptionist at Mainwaring & Cox takes her through lavish corridors with stunning views over St Paul's and beyond and shows her into a small meeting room with a low, slanting ceiling. A striking black woman is sitting at the table, checking her phone. She looks up with a smile and Hannah introduces herself.

'My colleague Zhen Li should be arriving shortly,' she tells the receptionist. 'He's gone to park the car.'

'I'll bring him round when he arrives. Would you like a coffee?'

Hannah could kill for caffeine and accepts the offer with alacrity, as she does the indication of the Ladies across the corridor. A few minutes later, facing Grace across the table with the first much needed mouthful of strong coffee inside her and a basket of tempting mini croissants between them, she pulls out her notebook.

'My colleague has told me very little,' she says. 'Just that you recognised the photo in the appeal. You took a photo at a wedding?'

'Yes,' says Grace. 'It's odd, really. It was a while ago — I've just checked the date of the photo, it was 8 October 2022.'

Hannah's head snapped up. 'Nine months ago? Are you sure?'

'Yes,' says Grace patiently. 'Look.' And she hands over her phone. There's a photo with a location (Camden) and date (8 October 2022) above it.

Hannah stares at the photo and then at the passport photos of Max Carrington and Jake Andrews. Grace's photo is somewhat askew but there's enough detail to see that the man is almost certainly a slightly older version of Max Carrington. It's also almost certainly a much the same age version of Jake Andrews. And of their body in the bath, though their body looks considerably worse for wear.

\*

Max would know what to do. He always did. Vivien feels the absence of him like a lost limb. She misses his physical presence, not just the passion in bed but the small kisses, the caresses, the arm round her shoulder. She misses the company, the conversations and conviviality, the hand pouring her a glass of wine or bringing her a cup of coffee. And most of all, at least right now, she misses his mind. He was always one step ahead, knew how to plan, how to change course swiftly if the plan didn't work out. Though it always had, until now. Even the blip with Stephanie hadn't fazed him; he'd just dealt with it as and when he'd had to, and everything had been fine.

Vivien has thought and thought about Max's final moments at the cottage in Dorset and still doesn't understand what can have happened. Was he trying to replicate Stephanie's death? But that was unlikely in the extreme. Stephanie had only died on her honeymoon because Max had seen his photo on her phone and decided he had to take immediate action, just in case. He would definitely not want to echo that murder so precisely, nor would he want to dispatch another bride on her honeymoon, or so soon after the last one. In the normal course of things, Kate would have died in a year or so. And Vivien, and Max would have retired shortly after. To the sun, and leisure, and luxury …

Vivien snaps herself back to the present. Max in the bath. Max. It must have been another emergency, prompted by something Vivien would probably never know. But even if Max had had to make another swift change of plan for any reason, it should have been Kate in the bath. Like Stephanie. But again, she thought, it was very odd that he replicated the method.

He must have tried to encourage Kate into the bath and she must have insisted he got in first. Probably something to do with her ridiculous virginal coyness. Which would almost certainly mean it happened on the first night. It sounds as though they had a lot to drink; again, probably her wretched pre-wedding night nerves. Vivien brightens briefly at the thought — if she's right, it means Max never had sex with her. But she plunges quickly into gloom and grief again; Max is dead, what does that matter? Her thoughts flip back to the scene in the bath. Maybe it was something to do with all the alcohol and the hot water? The article had reported the owner of the cottage as saying there were numerous empty champagne and wine bottles. It was unlike Max to drink to excess, but perhaps he makes — made — an exception on his honeymoons. Perhaps Kate needed Dutch courage for her wretched deflowering. Perhaps Max did. Vivien shudders, bats the thoughts aside.

She opens her iPad and googles 'alcohol hot bath': the very first result shouts *Never Mix Hot Tubs and Alcohol*. She reads on. 'Hot tubs can lower your blood pressure, and if you have been drinking, both combined can cause you to stumble, have slow reaction times and possibly slip into the hot tub.' And further down, under 'Is it bad to drink alcohol in the bath?', she reads 'The combination of alcohol and the bubbles of a hot tub can make you too relaxed. With too much alcohol in you, one can easily fall asleep or pass out while in the hot tub. This can lead to extreme dehydration, heat exhaustion, and even drowning. If you're alone, passing out in a hot tub can be a very dangerous thing.' That must be what happened. And Kate panicked and fled.

Vivien tells herself she must focus on what to do now. On her own. That's what Max would want. Would have wanted. She rummages in her handbag for her Liberty notebook, but it's not there. She frowns, thinks back to when she last had it. Of course, it must have been before she met, or rather didn't meet, that new client who never turned up. Avril Jacques-Smythe. Avril hadn't wanted to meet in her home and Vivien, again well schooled by Max, had taken the notebook out of her handbag before going to the café the first time. She came back from the café, she remembers, and checked the status of her current clients, so she had the notebook then. No, that's not right, that had been before she first went to the café — it was after she'd called Avril back, she'd opened the notebook to start a new page for her and then flicked through her current clients. But she's barely thought about the agency or her clients since then, or at least in the last few days; she's been too worried, imagining dreadful scenarios and persuading herself that everything was fine, and then finding out that it wasn't fine at all. She goes through to the home office, but the notebook's not in its usual place. Vivien checks all the drawers, the filing cabinet, her bedside table, the bookshelves in the sitting room. But it's disappeared.

Vivien tries, unsuccessfully, not to panic. Surely the notebook will turn up? She needs to focus on Kate, on what to do about her. That's what Max would do. She fetches a pad of paper. Half an hour of hard thinking later and she's pleased that her list is so short.

*What Kate knows*

1. *My name.*
2. *Agency name.*
3. *Office address and phone number.*

Vivien scratches her forehead, then automatically smooths away the crease between her eyes. There's no way Kate can know any more. She can't know about Max, or their home address, or about the bride-grooming and the special brides, or about Max's other identities as the special brides' grooms, or about the money — how much there is, where it is, how to access it.

Max said that if ever anything about the bride-grooming came to light, they needed to be able to disappear. Fast. The virtual office that Vivien had rented on a rolling monthly contract in Bloomsbury was a perfect fit. She kept nothing there — she didn't even strictly have anywhere to keep anything as she only had access to an office if she paid extra by the day — but it gave the agency the professional veneer of a posh — well, almost posh — address and she had the use of a conference room and a business lounge. Not that she used either much, any more than the optional day office at a discounted rate, preferring to see clients, particularly the special ones, in their own homes or in the more convivial atmosphere of a café, bar or restaurant.

Vivien logs on to the agency's Office Sweet account — another digital trace, she realises, but it was unavoidable. The company had stressed how seriously they took their obligations of confidentiality and data privacy when she first approached them, and she has no reason to doubt the earnest assertions. She gives notice of termination of the contract with effect from the end of the current month, and that's it. No more MadeInHeaven office. Kate may have a note of the office phone number, and in any event it's on the brochure and in the advertisements in *The Lady*, but it's a generic Office Sweet one. Then Vivien remembers that Kate knows her mobile number, or at least the number of the burner phone she used for her after their first meeting. She adds a fourth point to the list then removes the SIM card from that phone, wraps each in a plastic bag and puts the two small packages on the table by the front door. She'll post them into different council bins later, as soon as it's dark.

Which reminds her that she still has her normal mobile that she uses for all the non-special clients, and of course there aren't any special ones at the moment — well, apart from the one at large, she thinks grimly. She and Max always left an eighteen-month gap between them, although it might be longer if no one suitable for bride-grooming turned up, but of course Stephanie's unplanned end had disrupted that schedule. Does she need to change her mobile number, her handset? She would have called Kate from it before their first interview. Max would know what to do. Vivien feels a rising tide of despair. She has no idea how to cope on her own. Then she remembers that when she uses her normal mobile for someone who's not yet a client, she always blocks her number from showing. So she doesn't need to worry about that.

But there's no shortage of other things to worry about. She stands up, paces back and forth. Focus, she tells herself. Kate. The appeal. Will anyone recognise Kate and make a connection to her, Vivien? She stumbles, grabs the back of the love seat for support, edges round it and collapses on one of the cushions. Her cushion. The other is empty and always will be. She pushes the thought away, though the thought that replaces it, the one that nearly caused her to fall, is even more disturbing. Kate's two first dates.

What if Archie sees the appeal? Would he recognise Kate's name, her photo? The photo was thankfully not at all like Kate. What about the name? Kate, as Vivien discovered to her cost, is a common enough name, and Lincoln, while not so usual, isn't particularly memorable either. And Archie has had several, unsuccessful, dates since, and is so self-absorbed that he probably never took it in anyway. She tries to shrug off the chilly fear; this is something she can't do anything about. And after the date with Charlotte, maybe she'll have to tell Archie that she's closing the agency. She can wait till shortly after his next annual fee is due and waive the payment, useful as it would be, as a sweetener.

And then there's Kate's other warm-up date. Who was it? Of course, Omar. Omar married his next match, Diana, and as far as Vivien knows they are now living in blissful teetotal — if that is possible — harmony in Nepal and probably don't spend much time reading or watching UK local news.

Her thoughts stray back to her other clients. Of course there should have been that new one, April. No, Avril. That was all rather odd but again, nothing to be done about it. Maybe she'll get back in touch when her builders have finished. Vivien has no idea whether she'll be in a position to take on new clients in the future, or even what she'll be doing or where she'll be. She panics again as she remembers that she's misplaced her Liberty notebook, and a shiver of icy apprehension ripples through her.

# TWENTY-EIGHT

Hannah calls Zhen, who's only a couple of minutes away, so she and Grace wait for him to arrive. Hannah continues to gaze at the photo as she downs the rest of her coffee and nibbles on a croissant. She doesn't understand.

The receptionist shows Zhen in and brings fresh coffee. Hannah takes a deep breath and passes the phone to Zhen.

'This is a photo that Grace took on 8 October 2022 at Camden Register Office,' she says.

'Camden? But …'

'Yes. And it was nine months ago, more or less, with no possibility that that date's wrong. Grace, now my colleague's here could you tell us how it came about?'

'Sure,' says Grace. 'I was walking past the register office with Steve. My husband. And this woman comes running down the steps. Really pretty, radiant, wearing a red dress. Well, you can see a sliver in the photo, here.' She leans over to Zhen and traces her finger down the side of the photo. 'She asked us if we would be witnesses to her wedding. She looked so happy, and we said of course we would. Then she asked me if I'd do her a favour. A big favour, I think she said. The man she was marrying had a phobia about having his picture taken or something. So they didn't have a photographer but she wanted a photo of them, or just of him if that was easier for me to take without him noticing. She gave me her mobile number written on a piece of paper. And I took that picture and sent it to her.'

Grace breathes out a long sigh. 'But I don't understand how he can have got married last week. And the photo in the appeal of the bride — well, she's definitely not the same woman. Quite different.'

Hannah finds the recently received photo of Kate Lincoln on her phone and holds it out towards Grace. 'The one in the first version of the appeal was poor quality,' she says. 'We've now got a much clearer version.'

Grace shakes her head. 'Definitely not the woman I saw.'

Hannah and Zhen look at each other, eyebrows raised.

'Honestly, Grace, we don't understand either,' says Hannah. 'But this is really important information, whatever it means. Thank you so much for coming forward. Do you know the name of the bride in your photo? Well, partly in your photo!' She attempts a laugh but can't quite manage humour at the moment.

Grace shakes her head. 'No, she didn't tell me.'

'Do you still have her mobile number?'

'I didn't bother putting it into my contacts. But—' She frowns, reaches for her phone and starts scrolling. 'I texted it to her. It should be … Ah, here it is.' She offers the phone back to Zhen, an unnamed mobile number showing on the screen.

'Thank you,' says Hannah again as Zhen makes a note and asks Grace to send him the photo. 'Grace, we need to take a written witness statement from you — it shouldn't take long. And after that, do you think Zhen and I could stay here for half an hour or so? I just need to call my boss, and the Camden Register Office, and send the photo across. They should be able to give us names and addresses.'

Grace smiles. 'Technically, I'm not sure, as you're not staff or clients or prospective clients. But I'll let Susie on reception know and I'll clear it with my boss. He can hardly say no to the police, can he?' She shudders slightly, looks shaken. 'It's only just sinking in. That man she married, whose wedding I witnessed, married again nine months after that wedding. And he and his new bride have disappeared? Are they dead, as you're involved? Sorry, I know you probably can't say, but there's something weird, something wicked going on.'

'I think there is,' agrees Hannah. She hands Grace a card and Zhen does the same. 'But you're right, we can't say more at this stage. Here are our details. Don't hesitate to call if you remember anything.'

'I won't,' says Grace. 'And … well, I don't know how it works, but when you find out what's happened, when you can, will you let me know?'

'Of course. But it may not be for a while.'

Grace stands, straight and elegant, an embodiment of her name. She shakes hands with both of them and glides out of the room, the beads in her braided hair whispering, as Hannah's sending Grace's photo to be added to the appeal and Zhen is googling the Camden Register Office.

*

'Busy afternoon coming up,' says Hannah. 'I think we should go to Jake's flat first. It's here, in South Kensington'. She points to a pin she's dropped on the map she has open on her phone. 'And then Kate's. We'll need to go via the letting office — they'll give us the keys now the search warrant's come through. They're in Chelsea, above a bathroom fittings shop called The Chelsea Shower Flow.' She rolls her eyes then moves her finger on the screen a fraction and says, 'Kate's flat's here, not far from the office. And also not far from Jake's.'

'Handy,' says Zhen. 'Or suspicious? Or am I just turning into a paranoid old bobby?'

Hannah shrugs. 'They might have bumped into each other at the local Tesco Express, who knows?'

'In Chelsea?' scoffs Zhen. 'Little Waitrose more like.'

Jake Andrews' address is a flat in a modern block on the edge of South Kensington which Zhen pronounces to be classy. It's a portered building, at least by day, and the porter on duty can't

255

offer much. 'Never saw him,' he says, after a cursory glance at the photos Zhen shows him. 'Not to my knowledge anyway. I must have seen him come and go I suppose, but there are 96 flats here. Quite a few are owned by agencies who rent them out as serviced apartments, usually to companies, so there are always new faces. I remember someone if they come to me with a query or to collect post, or I take a delivery for them, but I never came across Jake Andrews. Nor that woman either.'

They show him the warrant, which had come through at the same time as the one for Kate's address, and he lets them into Jake's flat, which is bland and impersonal. There are two books and an old edition of a magazine called *The Decanter* on the coffee table, a few clothes in the wardrobe but nothing giving any clue to the identity of the occupant. Even though there's a desk in the corner of the second bedroom there are no documents, no laptop or tablet or mobile, no keys. There's one photo, though, or rather one folding frame holding two photos, of the exterior and interior of what looks like an apartment. Hannah scrutinises them, her eyes narrowed in concentration. 'That's odd,' she says. 'When I googled Kate's address and found the letting agent, there were still photos on their site. The flat in this photo's very similar.' She takes photos of the photos then slides the frame into the evidence bag that Zhen hands her, seals it and slips it into her daypack.

At Central London Listings Hannah has a quick word with the agent, Frances, who hands her the keys to Kate's flat once she's been shown the warrant. 'It hasn't been re-let, I assume?'

'The lease is still current,' says Frances. 'So no. We've updated the owners but I don't know when they'll read my email or get back to me. It's something of an unusual situation for us.'

For us too, thinks Hannah, but doesn't say it. Before leaving, she asks Frances whether she recalls anything about Kate's appearance. Frances looks puzzled but frowns as if thinking back then shrugs and says, 'Sorry, it was months ago and we have so many clients in and out. And she probably did some of it by phone or online, most people do these days, just come to sign and pick up the keys.'

'It does look like that photo in Jake Andrews' flat, doesn't it,' says Hannah when they're outside Kate's apartment. She gets out her phone and finds the photos she took of the two pictures in the frame. Zhen squints at the one of the exterior then glances up at the building in front of them.

'Similar,' he agrees. 'Same style, I guess. Maybe the same period? I don't know much about architecture. But there's definitely a resemblance.'

Unsurprisingly, there's no answer when they ring the bell. Nor had there been any answer earlier when Hannah called the mobile number the letting agency had given her: she'd been put straight through to a generic recorded message saying that the phone was inaccessible. She's put in a request for the phone to be traced and the records released but nothing's come in yet. There's no answer either when they knock on the doors of the two nearest neighbours, and the couple of slightly further flung residents who are at home say they never met Kate or even to their knowledge saw her.

The similarity to the photos in Jake's flat is more striking inside. High ceilings, tall sash windows, lots of light, wood floors, bright rugs and art and blinds.

Hannah frowns. 'It's a bit like a stage, isn't it? Everything's here, in place, even though no one's living here.'

'Well, there was someone living here. We don't know what her plans are. Among other things we don't know.'

'I went through the brochure with Frances,' says Hannah. 'The online particulars from when they let it out. All this goes with the flat. The paintings, the soft furnishings, the rugs. All the high-end kitchen equipment and the artistic vases and so on.'

'It's also very clean,' says Zhen gloomily. The bathroom is devoid of towels and the bed has been stripped.

'There are bound to be a few fingerprints, a bit of DNA,' says Hannah. 'We'll get SOCO in. Frances has another set of keys so we can keep these ones for the moment. Not that

257

prints or DNA will help much if they're not in the system.'

'Like Max Carrington,' says Zhen, sounding ever more Eeyore-like. 'Can't wait to visit yet another flat, in his case almost certainly completely pointless.'

\*

True to her word, Deborah calls Carol the following morning.

'I've got what you need,' she says in a conspiratorial whisper.

'Can you speak?' asks Carol, playing the game.

'No.'

'Shall I come round to you this evening?'

'Yes. I'll be home by 6.30.'

'How about if we order a takeaway?' says Carol. 'And I'll bring some wine or whatever you like to drink. We can't really eat out, too much risk of being overheard.'

Deborah was looking better when Carol arrived, bearing a bottle of cheap red for herself and a half bottle of not very cheap rum plus a litre of Coke for Deborah and trying not to think about her credit card. The sitting room and kitchen were less chaotic and Deborah was wearing tight black jeans, a clingy fuchsia pink sweater and what looked like freshly applied make up. Had she, like Max / James, recovered so rapidly from her recent bereavement? For different reasons, though, thought Carol charitably. Deborah was young and clearly bright enough, at least in the sense of streetwise and savvy, and if she'd decided to put her broken heart behind her and try and salvage something for herself from the fallout, who could blame her? She was probably expecting a flattering photo to accompany the flattering article.

Carol poured a generous rum and coke for Deborah and, ruefully, a very ungenerous glass of wine for herself.

'Shall we start with what you know about Vivien?' she asked. 'Her address and phone number? Anything else?'

Deborah gave a moue of apparent distaste. 'I hope this interview isn't going to be all about Vivien.'

'Of course not. It'll be about you and Max. I just need to get the housekeeping out of the way before we start properly.'

Carol noted down Vivien's address and mobile number and spent the rest of the interview with Deborah, which didn't yield anything further of significance — the essence being older magnetic man meets younger impressionable woman — thinking about the best way to approach Vivien tomorrow.

*

DCI Choudhury suggests that Hannah and Zhen find a cheap hotel and continue the following morning. Apart from Max Carrington's flat, there may be other investigations to pursue in London when they've found out more about Stephanie Sarah Anderson, previously Faulkner. So far Hannah has the details which Camden Register Office gave her: Stephanie's date of birth (20 April 1981), nationality (British), her address (in London NW3) and period of residence (seven years). She's described as widowed and as a housewife. They have her mobile number also of course, courtesy of Grace. As for the bridegroom, James Anderson, he is — or was — single, British and an IT consultant, resident at a different address in London NW3 for three months. His date of birth is 28 February 1980.

Zhen books them into a Premier Inn and once they've checked into their characterless but clean and adequate rooms they find a decent-looking pub with a quiet corner table set away from the bar and most of the other customers. Over drinks, Hannah continues her research on the General Register Office website while Zhen searches the Land Registry site.

'Stephanie's maiden name was Hawkings,' says Hannah, rubbing her eyes which ache from more screen work after an early start and a long day. 'Faulkner was her first husband's surname. She's got an adopted sister. Lucy Susan Hawkings, birth name Wright. Eight years older than Stephanie. And Stephanie's mother was forty-two when she had Stephanie.'

Zhen glances up and takes a long draught of bitter. He wipes the trace of a foam moustache from his upper lip and says, 'Something similar happened to my aunt. She and her husband couldn't conceive, or so they thought, and adopted, and a couple of years later she got pregnant. Naturally. Apparently it's not uncommon.' His eyes go back to his laptop, following the cursor as it swoops across the screen. 'The address Stephanie gave on the notice of marriage or whatever it's called? It's in the name of Bernard and Claudia Taylor now,' he says. 'They were registered as the owners on 9 June this year. I suppose she, Stephanie, must have left it—'

He's interrupted by Hannah who, eyes wide as the next piece of information pops up on her screen, starts what's almost a shout. She cuts off immediately though not before a couple of heads have turned towards them from the nearer tables. 'What the fuck?' she says in a much quieter voice. 'Stephanie died the day after her wedding.'

Hannah angles her laptop towards Zhen. It shows Stephanie's death certificate. 'Accidental drowning and submersion in bath tub,' she reads from the cause of death section.

Zhen is already googling 'Stephanie Faulkner James Anderson drown'. 'What the fuck?' he echoes, and turns his own screen towards Hannah so they can read the article together. *Honeymoon Tragedy of Bride in the Bath*, the headline screams.

\*

Hannah comes back from the bar with another pint for Zhen and a glass of wine for herself. She's picked up a menu and puts it on the table as she sits down, but they're both too focused on Stephanie's death to think seriously about eating.

'He must have been planning to do the same thing,' says Zhen eagerly. 'Jake Andrews. Well, I know he must be the same guy, and they're both presumably Max Carrington, but you know what I mean. With Kate. But it went wrong, for whatever reason.'

'Maybe he did just drink too much and passed out briefly in the hot bath and drowned,' says Hannah, attracted by the dramatic irony, but she's frowning, unconvinced. 'Kate could then have come in and panicked. As DCI Choudhury suggested at that first meeting.'

'We need to find Kate,' says Zhen. 'To state the bleeding obvious. And I've no idea how, it's just another series of dead ends.'

'We can contact Stephanie's sister. Not that that'll help with finding Kate, but we should talk to her about what happened to Stephanie. Tomorrow, if she's at home, after the last few properties. We need an early start.'

# TWENTY-NINE

Vivien finds herself sitting up in bed, shaking with some unknown terror. She's wearing one of Max's T-shirts — no point in any of her slinky black negligées now — and the cotton is soaked in night sweat, cold and clammy. She shivers, peels it off, pads over to the chest and finds another one. Knowing she won't get back to sleep easily, she heads to the kitchen to make some hot milk, her usual panacea for a broken night, but finds herself pouring a brandy instead. She sits in the love seat, the balloon glass cradled in her hands, the empty cushion across the divider a stark reminder of her solitude.

She takes a sip of the spirit and feels the amber warmth of it spread from her mouth down to her stomach, relaxation in its slipstream. What was it that woke her? She tries to navigate the wispy memories of her dream. Or nightmare. Max, naturally. Telling her what to do if there's a problem. She's had no practice, of course, as this is the first problem. Or at least the first problem apart from Stephanie, but he was there to deal with that one. But surely she's done everything he said? Or as much as is possible in this unforeseen, and particularly problematic, situation. Move the agency, hide the trail. Keep a low profile. Keep the clients onside or let them go painlessly, on good terms. Give notice on the office, on his—

Vivien jerks upright again. Brandy splashes out of the glass and pools on the velvet. Vivien ignores it.

Max's — Jake's — flat. The current rented service flat. The bank where he opened Jake's account will know the address and his debit card is in Jake's wallet. And his Amex card. They'll be in police hands now. The address will also be on the marriage certificate, and she assumes the register office will have noted it when they, Max and Kate, gave notice of the marriage. Bile rises at the back of her throat. She washes it away with a gulp of brandy.

She desperately tries to think whether there's anything in the flat that could point the police to her, or Max, or even Kate. But Max is — was, she stifles a sob — so careful, he wouldn't have left anything in the flat that could identify him, Kate, Vivien. His laptop is, or was, at the cottage, impregnable. Or maybe not to the police; she shudders and shuts down the thought. All his Max ID is here, at the maisonette. Did Jake have a passport? He must have had, for the bank account and Amex card, and perhaps for the marriage. Vivien doesn't know whether Max took it to Dorset or whether it's at the flat. If it's at the flat, would Max want her to find and destroy it?

His mobile, she thinks with another brandy-slopping start. Not his throwaway Kate phone, that'll be at the cottage. Unless Kate took it. Vivien finds herself hoping Kate has taken it; at least that would mean the police won't have it yet. In fact, maybe Kate's also taken the other stuff, his laptop, Jake's passport if it was there, Jake's wallet. But what would she do with them? Vivien's head aches with the relentlessly circling thoughts. Back to Max's own mobile. He always leaves it at the flat — no risk of the bride finding it, and it means he can call her, Vivien, as soon as he's back in London and has managed to slip away. The police will obviously be able to find her once they have it. She needs to get it first.

She remembers the burner phone hidden in the lining of his case. She can't see how Kate could have known about that, so unless she took his case it must still be in the cottage. But the police won't find anything on it; he'd only ever had to use his emergency phone once before, for Stephanie, and he'd got rid of that one afterwards and replaced it with another cheap burner which has never been used.

263

What about his driving licence? Vivien tries to remember what he said about that. Changing the name and address on his own each time would have left a very visible trail, and there were also problems in getting a new one in the new groom's name each time. Something to do with proof of address, she thinks. Address, of course. She remembers now — Max's driving licence still shows the address of the rented apartment he was living in when they met. They bought the maisonette after the first special bride — Pauline, was it? No, Paula. Vivien had added the cash — or most of the cash — that she'd stolen from Iris, which she'd been careful not to squander though it had been tempting. Max had been so generous, saying it should just be her name on the deeds. When they moved, Max said he was going to set up a redirection of mail and keep using the old rental address for what limited post he couldn't avoid. 'No business of the government where I, we, live, darling.'

He was always like that, trying to keep under the radar. She found it part of his exotic charm, his mystique, his Sean Connery persona. Now, Vivien wonders what exactly he was trying to hide. She realises she never asked him all those years ago — five or six, maybe? — about the worst thing he ever did. It's too late now. And it's almost certainly been overtaken anyway by what he's done since.

Vivien shakes her head like a dog. Her mind is wandering. What was she thinking about? The driving licence. She looks in the filing cabinet but though the paperwork for his current car — they changed it for each special, Max bought a second-hand one of some unremarkable model and colour and used it as little as possible — is there, the licence isn't. Is it at the cottage or in Jake's flat? Or in the car? Even if the address is unlikely to give much away after several years, it carries Max's photo. Also several years old, but still. Nothing to be done if it's in Dorset or the car but she needs to check in the flat.

And for his keys, she suddenly thinks. The keys to the maisonette. He always left them in the current bridegroom's flat when he was on honeymoon or holiday as he never knew exactly when he'd be back. Vivien's sure there's no name or address on the fob, but they're still a link. She'll have to go to the flat first thing tomorrow and pick them up, and Max's phone and Jake's passport and driving licence if they're there. She's got a set of keys. For a moment she wonders whether there's a burglar alarm, then remembers that this rental is in a portered block so there won't be. Max distrusts them anyway, saying he'd rather rely on good locks than have the police start poking around their house. Finding things that are no one else's business.

Vivien feels a fraction of her tension, her distress, roll away with the relief of a decision made, and takes another soothing sip of brandy, wondering whether she might snatch another hour or two's sleep. And then realises, in a sudden ice-cold wash of awareness, that the police will almost certainly already have been to the flat. Might be watching it. She mentally kicks herself for her stupidity. She can't manage this without Max. Nor, clearly, can she go to the flat now.

*

Vivien has, against all her expectations, managed a few more hours of sleep. Tossing and turning, sweating and dreaming, but still mostly sleeping. She showers, forces herself to put on make-up and smart clothes, styles her hair. After a strong coffee, she tries to take stock.

Clients. Does she need to contact anyone, have a chat, an update, a debrief, suggest a meeting? She opens the top right-hand drawer of her desk, then remembers with another wash of cold fear that her Liberty notebook is missing. She buries the thought and tries to recall the list of clients she ran through — when was it? Before she knew about Max, about Jake and Kate. When she thought her life was rolling along on its usual well oiled wheels, trundling towards the sunny future with Max, no more agency, no more clients, lots and lots of money. Was it really just a week ago? It seems much longer; something odd has happened to her sense of time. Perhaps it's a common feature of grief, particularly after sudden death. She stops herself just in time from savagely rubbing her freshly mascaraed eyes. No point revisiting the problem of being unable to claim the body and set in motion the normal steps after the death of a loved one. Even less point in letting herself think about what the police will do if — surely when — they conclusively identify the body. She needs to keep on top of her immediate clients for the moment — Max would have wanted her to do that — while readying herself to disappear if — surely when — she needs to.

Vivien's chain of thought is rudely interrupted by the ring of the doorbell. Is it always so loud, so sudden, so insistent, she wonders? She's on her way to the door, on autopilot, to answer it then stops dead in the hallway. It might be the police. It might be Kate. It's one thing to want to find Kate, but she definitely doesn't want Kate to find her. Yet another sign of her new life, her changed circumstances. She turns and slinks silently back to her chair, grateful for the muslin curtains which she never much liked but which Max insisted on. 'No point letting any old passers by gawp at us, darling.'

Clients. She can easily redo the list, from memory. She runs through it in her head, decides there's nothing that needs doing, at least for the moment. But she should make some notes; realistically, she should probably start gently shedding some of the unmatched ones. She fetches the pad of paper from her desk. And sees the other list she wrote the day before.

### *What Kate knows*

1. *My name.*
2. *Agency name.*
3. *Office address and phone number (from brochure).*
4. *My Kate mobile number.*

Vivien frowns at the words. She knows, deep down, that it must be Kate who has somehow taken her Liberty notebook — who else could it be? Vivien definitely didn't take it to her abortive meeting with Avril; she remembers automatically feeling for it in her bag and reminding herself that, as always, as per Max's instructions, she'd left it at home. But how could Kate have got into her home? Or even know the address? And again her chain of thought is interrupted — her mobile, her personal and MadeInHeaven mobile, is ringing. Again she reacts automatically, reaching out to answer it, and again she freezes. No caller ID. It could be the police. It could be Kate. She almost weeps with the frustration, the fear, the increasing awareness of how difficult her life will now be. She lets the call ring out then turns the phone off. Get a grip, she tells herself. You were thinking about Kate. She frowns, tries to pick up her earlier train of thought. So annoying to be interrupted by — And then she remembers that strange call, around the time Max came back after — after having had to deal with Stephanie much earlier than planned. Someone asking about Stephanie, or was it about James Anderson? Anyway, the call must have been a day or two after Max had rung her from Cornwall on his emergency burner phone to tell her what had happened, because she remembers freezing in momentary panic when the caller mentioned Stephanie, or maybe they asked about James Anderson first. She'd still been reeling from the shock of Max's call — the mere fact of it, and then the contents. She's tried not to think too much about it since, but now the memory of his call floods back.

It had been the first evening of Stephanie and James's honeymoon. Well, the first proper evening — Vivien knew they'd spent the previous night at Stephanie's house, and that they'd spent earlier nights together. But that evening would have been the romantic coupling — doubtless rose petals and chilled champagne in the bedroom, she knew Max loved to choose perfect settings for the honeymoon and the little holiday treats that followed, celebrations of an anniversary or a similar excuse. And she knew it was just sex. But still, it was hard sometimes. She'd tried to distract herself, Vivien remembers now, started a couple of films, a box set, but nothing drew her in. She was thinking she might have a relaxing bath — the irony — and an early night when a phone rang. She automatically reached for her mobile then paused, hand extended. It wasn't her ringtone. She stood, frowning, and followed the harp chords to her office. It was the blue phone on her desk, the burner phone she used for all her communications with Stephanie. And the screen said 'No Caller ID'.

The harp chords stopped after five, she'd thought, though she wasn't sure — she hadn't been consciously counting before she realised which mobile was ringing. She hesitated, supporting herself with a hand on the edge of the desk, working her way round to the chair then sinking into it. She and Max have — had — an absolute rule, even more absolute than the usual quirky no-digital-trace policy she has with all her clients. When it comes to the special ones, it's essential that there's no record of any contact between her and Max when he's not Max. It's another expense, getting him a new smartphone each time, but it's not worth the risk of fiddling with different SIM cards. Too easy to make a mistake. And not foolproof even if you don't. But they have — had — a code for use in a dire emergency. Max always takes — took — a second phone, a no-frills burner, with him. He'd never had to use it before.

Vivien had eyed her blue mobile as if it were a scorpion. She jumped as it started to ring again, even though she was expecting it in a cocktail of fear and prurient curiosity. Something must have gone wrong.

The second time she definitely counted five chords before it cut out. She'd forgotten to bring her own phone with her to set the countdown timer — she was out of practice, even though Max makes — made — them rehearse the drill before each honeymoon or holiday. She checked her vintage watch, a gift from him after their second special. Barbara. It was vintage enough to have a second hand which her eyes followed as it described an impossibly slow circle. The phone rang for a third time after 58 seconds.

Vivien's hand trembled slightly as she reached for it and accepted the call. She said nothing; that much she remembered from the drill.

'I've had to bring things forward.' Max sounded breathy, edgy, but also, she realised, excited. She knew that lustful timbre.

Vivien exhaled deeply; she hadn't realised that she'd been holding her breath. 'Why? What happened?'

'I checked her phone. I've been doing it whenever I can, since I got her passcode —'

'How—'

'I've seen her open it often enough. Doesn't matter anyway. But there was a photo on it. Of me. At the wedding.'

Vivien gasped. 'But—'

'No photographers.' Max's voice was soothing, reassuring. 'Usual reason. She agreed. But somehow there's a photo. She must have asked one of the witnesses. She pulled them off the street.'

'Do we know who?'

'Their names are on the certificate. I've checked. No address though. But they definitely didn't have her phone. I'd have seen her get it back. We went straight from the register office to the restaurant. So one of them must have taken the photo and sent it to her. She must have asked them to.'

'So we can—'

'We can't. I've checked. She must have deleted the text or email or whatever. There's nothing. So the fact that there's no record of her sending it to someone else isn't conclusive. She's cleverer than we thought, clearly.'

'She might not have suspected. It could just be that she wanted someone to see her new husband.'

'Who though? She's got no family, no close friends. Anyway, I didn't think we could take the risk. I had the perfect opportunity. It's done. I need to destroy this phone now.'

'What about hers?' Vivien's voice was panicky. 'They can trace—'

'I'm not a fucking magician, Vivien. I've done what I had to, as soon as I knew.' Max took a long breath. 'Sorry, darling. It's just been a bit — stressful. I don't like doing it on the spur of the moment. But I didn't have a choice. Too big a risk.'

Vivien thought for a moment. 'You're right. And sorry also. You did what you had to, when you had to. Thank you.'

'I'll need to stay down here for a few days. You need to

destroy your Stephanie phone ASAP. And I can't contact you again till I'm home. I'll have to go via the flat, pick up my house keys. It might be the middle of the night.'

'Of course. I'll expect you when I see you. Love you, darling.'

'You too.'

Now, Vivien rubs her forehead, trying to think back to the mystery phone call. First the caller had said they wanted to get in touch with James Anderson. Vivien had given her much rehearsed but never previously used stock response. Then the caller said something about knowing Stephanie, though Vivien had known that Stephanie had no friends. Known from her own mouth and from what Max said once he was dating her. But then — she strains again at the elusive memory; the call was a while ago and she hasn't thought about it since. The caller finished by saying she must have got it wrong, she barely knew Stephanie and hadn't seen her for ages or something similar. She'd mentioned the agency though hadn't she? But then backtracked, said she must have got the name wrong and had advised Stephanie against it anyway. Could it have been Kate? There's no reason to think so really; perhaps she's just thought of the possibility because if it was, it could be a way — the only way — of tracing Kate. The real Kate.

Vivien makes herself another coffee, her thoughts whirling. She'd put the call out of her mind at the time — Max came back from Cornwall a few days after he'd phoned her, earlier than planned, of course, and without his bride, and — yes, the mystery call had come that same day, before Max had walked into the maisonette, and she hadn't wanted to worry him. He'd been on edge, restless, she remembered.

In fact it hadn't been the middle of the night when he came back. It was late afternoon, and Vivien was in her home office planning the following week's client meetings. She ran to the hall when she heard the key in the lock, and into his arms once he was the right side of the closed door.

He'd almost crushed her, swooped in for a long, hungry

kiss. But she could feel the unaccustomed tension across his shoulders, see the tiredness in his face.

'I could murder a G&T,' he said. Vivien flinched at the word, and Max laughed softly. 'It's OK,' he whispered. 'It's all fine. I fixed it. But I could have done without it. I don't like ad libbing.' He nibbled her earlobe, swirled his tongue in the whorl. Let out a sigh, and Vivien felt something ebb, or perhaps float, away from him.

She fixed a strong drink for him and a more measured one for her. They went through to the sitting room where he dropped heavily onto the sofa and drained a good third of his, the ice cubes clinking, what little condensation had had time to bead on the glass glistening on his lip.

He took a deep breath and another draught. Vivien sat next to him, nestled against him. He put his drink down, cupped her face in his hands and leant in for another kiss. She could taste the gin, the lemon, the tonic.

'It's OK,' he repeated. 'Obviously I had to make it up as I went along, but I was lucky. We were lucky. You and me, I mean.' He gave a harsh laugh. 'I had to drown her in the bath. Thank god I'd chosen a cottage with a decent one, I had a vague idea she liked them. Then I drove to the village to pick something up at the shop, which was of course closed. I'd plied her with drink, more than she realised — of course I hadn't planned for this, but there was a good selection of spirits at the cottage and I invented a special champagne cocktail. And there was loads of bath oil and stuff in the bathroom, so it was plausible that she slipped and knocked her head, briefly lost consciousness. Well, she had slipped, with help. And lost consciousness, but not briefly.'

Max drained his glass and held it out to Vivien, who mixed him another and topped up her own.

'Will we … do you think we should stop now?' she asked. 'Call it a day?'

Max rubbed his mouth reflectively. 'Let's see. If another perfect bride — a special bride — turns up after a decent interval, let's go for it. Last tango in wherever. If not, we'll let it go. We've had a good run at it. And I'll get everything of

Stephanie's — she hadn't made a new will, though we'd talked about it. She raised it, in fact.'

Vivien had turned her thoughts to the money, to the prospect of retiring with Max somewhere distant and sunny. Perhaps they should start quietly selling the properties. Barbara's, now Stephanie's. Just in case. She'd raise it with him when he was more relaxed. She smiled, tipped her glass towards him and drank to their future. And, she realises now, pushed the mystery call out of her mind.

Vivien drags herself back to the present, sits down with her coffee. The call had probably been referred to her from the office, which is the number in the advert in *The Lady*. She'd have assumed it was a prospective client — there were always a few who preferred to phone, despite the suggestion in the advert about making the first approach by letter. So she'd almost certainly have rung her back using her MadeInHeaven mobile, the legit one. Though with No Caller ID set for all calls. She only lets clients know her number when she's vetted them. And the number she gives them, of course, depends on the outcome of the vetting.

Vivien opens her MadeInHeaven mobile and the phone app. As she expected, there are a lot of calls out, but knowing the approximate date means she can scroll back rapidly. She finds what she thinks must be the number; she doesn't recognise it. Can she muster the courage to call it, she now wonders? She doesn't have to speak, she can just listen. Maybe the woman, like some of her clients of a certain age, will recite her name when she answers. And surely she'll say something and give Vivien the chance to compare her voice to Kate's. She starts the Rev Call Recorder app — her clients would be horrified to know that all their conversations with Vivien are recorded; Max thought it was a good idea to avoid misunderstandings. Although not, of course, for the specials, where they definitely didn't want to avoid misunderstandings — but stops before she touches the call icon. The sight of the recording app reminds her that her conversation with the mystery caller will have been recorded.

Vivien feels like banging her head against the table. Her mind is so clouded with a toxic cocktail of loss, grief and panic, compounded by lack of sleep, that she can barely function. She gives herself a mental shake — the main thing, surely, is that she has remembered. She scrolls back through the in-app recordings and finds the conversation.

# THIRTY

'Hello, am I speaking to Lucy Hawkins?' Vivien hears herself say, in her best professional mode. She's always been proud of her voice, her diction, her intonation, relics of the posh school and good education that her parents had shelled out on before everything fell apart.

'Yes. Is this MadeInHeaven?'

Vivien's attention quickens. The voice sounds familiar.

'Vivien Harrison, owner and manager of the agency,' the recorded Vivien replied smoothly, silkily. 'How can I help you?'

'I'm trying to get in touch with James Anderson.'

There's a pause. Vivien remembers her stunned silence while she tried to assemble her thoughts, marshal the agreed and rehearsed response, sound puzzled. She'd succeeded. 'I'm sorry, but I don't know that name.'

'Isn't he one of your clients? Or ex-clients?'

'I'm afraid not.' Her voice sounds assured, and she congratulates herself on keeping her cool. If only she could hold herself together so effortlessly now. Of course, it wasn't really effortless at the time. It's the effect, the veneer, that counted. She must cling on to that thought, to the fact that she did it against all the odds before.

'What about Stephanie Faulkner?' Vivien hears. Her heart lurches back into panic arrhythmia, as it did at the time.

'Who?' she managed. Again, Vivien present thinks Vivien past sounds unruffled, in control.

'I'm sure she told me …' There's another short pause, then 'I'm sorry.' The woman sounds unsure now, muddled, a bit of an airhead to be honest. 'I'm getting confused. I heard some tragic news about Stephanie. Someone I used to know back in the day. I didn't know her well, lost touch ages ago, but I ran into her, oh, a few months ago I think. She told me she was planning to try a dating agency but I must have remembered the name wrong. Or maybe she decided not to use an agency at all, I have to say I advised her against it. So sorry to have bothered you.'

'Not at all, my dear. Have a nice day.'

There's a grudging 'Thank you' and the call ends.

Vivien listens several times to the recording. She's good with voices as well as faces and now she's sure that it's Kate Lincoln speaking. She opens her iPad and googles 'Lucy Hawkins', knowing it's another pointless needle-in-a-haystack exercise, which it duly proves to be. But something snags at her. She listens to the recording again. It's Hawkings, not Hawkins, that she says. The office receptionist must have correctly heard and passed on the name, though Vivien had forgotten the detail.

Not that that narrows down the Google search significantly. She needs something more. She tries adding 'venture capitalist' and, despite the usual grandiose claim of millions of results, none of the hits in the first few pages contains all the words.

Vivien's head starts to throb and she realises that she hasn't eaten for … she can't really remember. She finds some stale bread and cheese and puts together a late lunch, makes herself take a break from the screen, forces herself to eat.

Slightly fortified by the sandwich and another coffee, Vivien tries LinkedIn. She doesn't have an account of course but knows that you can search without one. It's bound not to be a full search, leading to a full bio or profile or whatever it's called, but it might give her something.

Two Lucy Hawkings come up on the screen. One is a town

planner and the other a solicitor. There's no indication of where either works, but googling the name plus solicitor finds the second one easily. She's a professional support lawyer, whatever that is, at Leadbeater & Johnson whose office is in Gresham Street, EC2. And the icing on the cake is the headshot on her profile on the firm's site. Lucy is, beyond doubt, Kate. Her hair is neater, brighter, worn a bit shorter, her eyes are grey, not blue, and she's not wearing glasses. But all those details — unlike the bone structure, the set of the eyes, the mouth — can be manipulated. Max tried the coloured contact lenses for his first bridegroom, but got fed up with the fiddling around and worried that he'd forget to take them out when he transitioned between his two lives. He'd used glasses once, she thinks. She can't remember now — did he have them for James, for Jake?

Looking back at the photo, Vivien feels a flare of hope, the fleeting satisfaction of something achieved, for the first time since she found out about Max. Which, she realises with the now familiar shock at the disconnect between actual and perceived passing time, is only five days ago. She writes 'Lucy Hawkings' on the notepad, then finds Lucy's Twitter account and scrolls through her recent tweets. Nothing as handy as an address, just 'London, EU', but there are a couple of photos which appear from the taglines to have been taken in her home. Which is nothing like Kate's Chelsea flat.

The doorbell rings again twice but Vivien ignores it, tries not to let it worry her. She has a plan of sorts forming. She can do this.

*

'Another three viewings today,' says Hannah, taking a long draught of her coffee at the EAT near their Premier Inn. 'I'm beginning to feel like a letting agent myself. And then Stephanie Faulkner's sister before we head back to the sticks.' She's got Google maps open on her phone again, zoomed in to show a narrow north/south slice of London, and angles it towards Zhen. 'I think we should go to Max Carrington's address first. Or at least the one he uses. Or rather, used,' she corrects herself. 'It's here.' She puts her pain au chocolat down and taps the screen with a finger, then points with the corner of a paper napkin before using it to wipe off the buttery smear over West Kensington. 'The freehold's owned by someone else who lives in Fulham, which isn't far from Carrington's. So he probably rents out Carrington's address. We should speak to him also.'

'So that's two houses plus Faulkner's sister.'

'There's a flat as well,' says Hannah. 'I managed to get Kate Lincoln's previous address from the agency. I suddenly realised they should have it from the money-laundering checks. It's here.' She gestures at the very bottom of the rectangle. 'In Tooting. And after that, Lucy Hawkings. She lives in Hackney. Off the map, I couldn't get them all in at a manageable scale.' She gestures vaguely to the right of the screen.

Zhen looks more closely at the map then checks a note on his own phone. He's been working on the addresses from James Anderson's and Stephanie Faulkner's marriage records while Hannah focused on Kate's and Max's.

'Can you find NW3 4UY?'

Hannah put it in the search field and tilts the screen back towards Zhen, who says, 'That's James Anderson's flat. Stephanie Faulkner's — Stephanie Andrews' — house isn't far.' He points.

Hannah frowns. 'A bit of a coincidence if Anderson and Stephanie also met in the local Little Waitrose. Do you think he was maybe stalking her or something?'

Zhen shrugs. 'I guess we'll never know, it's too long ago and they're both dead now. We'll need to get forensics into both properties once the warrants come through.' He'd started that process the previous evening. 'Not sure there's much point though.'

Hannah looks a question at him.

'We know Stephanie's house was sold recently. I spoke to the agents and apparently the new owners were planning to gut it. And Anderson's was a rented serviced flat. Guess who

277

owns it.'

Hannah tries to remember the name. 'Something fishy?'

Zhen laughs. 'Spot on, in both senses. Swordfish Corporate Rentals Ltd. Coincidence ... not, I think. But that apartment's had a shit-load of people in it since Anderson was there.' He checks his phone. 'It was rented a couple of weeks after he left by a Japanese company for various employees visiting its newly acquired UK subsidiary. There've been 17 occupants, each for a short period. And Swordfish confirmed that they had the flat deep cleaned between Anderson and the Japanese company, and he took everything of his when he left.'

Hannah groans. 'There'll be nothing of him there now, that's for sure.'

Zhen frowns. 'I've just thought — he might not even have spent much time at Stephanie's house, given that he had another address when they were married. Maybe they were traditional and he was going to move in after the honeymoon?'

'Third time lucky?' suggests Zhen hopefully. 'After nothing at Kate's or Jake's flats, I mean.' He and Hannah are outside the address in West Kensington where, according to his driving licence, Max Carrington lives. Lived. It's a large terraced house that has clearly been divided into flats. Six of them, by the look of the doorbell panel. There's no mention of Max Carrington or indeed Jake Andrews. Hannah starts pressing the buzzers.

There's no answer from what she assumes are the basement and ground floor flats, but there's someone at home on the first floor. A hostile voice snaps, 'Yes?'

'It's the police,' says Zhen. 'Nothing to worry out. We're trying to trace a Max—'

'What the fuck? There was some debt-collector here the other day looking for him. And your lot too. As I told both of them, I've only just moved in and don't know any of the other people who live here.' He cuts out.

Zhen raises his eyebrows at Hannah, who shrugs. 'Let's try the rest,' she suggests. 'We know one of the first-floor tenants is home, we can go and see him later, if we need.'

Zhen tries two more buzzers, with no answer, but the last is answered by a friendlier voice and Zhen starts his spiel. Again, he's interrupted after a few words, though in a more courteous fashion and with a breath of excitement.

'There was a debt-collector here last week,' he says eagerly. 'Looking for him. At least I assume it's the same man. And more police two, no three, days ago, though I wasn't in, just heard on the grapevine.'

'Can we have a word?' asks Zhen.

They're buzzed in and go through the dingy hall and up the grubby stairs. The left-hand door at the top is propped open by a young man leaning against it, a quizzical expression on his face. He gestures them to enter.

Hannah and Zhen introduce themselves, showing their warrant cards, and the man says he's Gavin Robertson. 'We're trying to trace a Max Carrington who we think lives at this address, or at least used to,' says Hannah.

'As I told the debt-collector, there's no one of that name here,' says Gavin. 'I can give you the names of the other tenants though if that helps?'

'Thanks, that would be great' says Hannah, and Zhen notes them down. 'Do you recall the name of the debt-collecting agency?'

'Sorry, no. She said it downstairs — over the intercom I mean. It's never very clear. Something about cash, but I don't suppose that narrows it down much.'

'What about her name?'

Gavin frowns, screws up his eyes. 'I can't remember that either I'm afraid. Something unusual. Oh, wait, I think it was April. April Jack, or similar. We just had a quick chat. I told her about the other residents, same info I've given you.'

'Do you recognise any of these people?' asks Hannah, showing him the photos of Kate, Jake, James and Max, but Gavin shakes his head.

Zhen makes a note of Gavin's name and mobile number. 'In case we need to follow up further,' he explains. 'Thank you so much for your help.' He and Hannah shake his hand in farewell and head down the stairs, via the first floor whose surly occupant doesn't respond to their knock, and out of the building.

They get the same story from the landlord, Arthur Quinn. He answers the door guardedly, doesn't invite them in. When Zhen says they're from Dorset Police and are trying to trace a Max Carrington, Quinn cuts across them.

'What is it with this man?' he says with heavy irritation. 'I had some debt-collector at the door last week. And some cub policeman a couple of days ago. I've never heard the name. Or at least hadn't until she came asking.' He starts to close the door, but Zhen blocks the movement with a braced hand.

'Please look at these photos,' he says. 'Is this the debt-collector? And do you recognise the man?'

Quinn glances at the photos, clearly without much interest. 'No,' he says firmly.

'Are you sure?' asks Zhen. 'Could we check your records? You do keep records, I assume?'

Hannah watches in fascination as Quested's face turns a shade of what can only be described as puce. 'Certainly not,' snaps Quinn. 'I mean of course I keep them, but that's my business. Since when is an Englishman's home not his castle? Wasn't that the point of Brexit?' He slams the door shut.

'We could get a warrant, I suppose,' says Zhen. 'But if he says he doesn't recognise the name he probably doesn't. It's a memorable name. I suspect he's under-declaring his rental income though.'

'We could get a warrant just to irritate him,' suggests Hannah, though she's not being serious, tempting as it is. She pauses, chewing her lip. 'It's odd that someone else is looking for Carrington,' she adds.

Zhen shrugs. 'He's obviously a very dodgy character. Probably has debt-collectors after him all the time. And there's no chance of finding the collection agency without knowing the name.'

'Not dodgy enough to be on the PNC,' says Hannah.

'Could be very dodgy and very clever,' counters Zhen.

The next stop, the last of the suspects' various past and present addresses, or at least the ones they know about, is Kate's previous rented flat in Tooting. It's above a kebab shop and the owner is reluctant to show them the room.

'I don't remember,' he keeps repeating. 'It's just a bedsit, I have one person after another in there, students mostly. They come and go, no one stays long. I don't remember names. I don't recognise the person in the photo.'

Eventually he takes them up to the bedsit and opens the door. It's a far cry from the sumptuous Chelsea pad: a small studio with a stained, threadbare carpet, faded curtains, a lumpy futon sofa bed. There are dirty dishes in the cramped kitchen and a pile of damp towels and what looks like running gear in the tiny bathroom. Hannah and Zhen know from Central London Listings that Kate moved into her Chelsea flat over three months ago so the chances of them finding anything useful here are negligible. They decide to have a late lunch somewhere — not kebabs — before hoping to catch Lucy Hawkings at home.

*

As it happens, Carol doesn't have to decide how to approach Vivien the day after Deborah gives her the address. She watches it — a small maisonette in Camden — from 8 a.m. till 6 p.m., with brief periodic escapes to one of the local cafes, but no one leaves or enters, at least not that she notices. She can't see anything through the ground-floor windows either, they're screened by some sort of net curtain, so she has no idea whether Vivien is at home. Carol tries the doorbell on several occasions but there's no answer. She calls the mobile number, withholding her own, but it goes through to an impersonal voicemail each time. The second and third times she calls, Carol is standing on the doorstep and can't hear a ringtone; it's possible that she wouldn't be able to, or that it's set to vibrate only, but Carol suspects it's been turned off.

At six o'clock she decides to call it a day. There's a limit to how much watching one person can do, even when the stakes are high. She thinks about putting a note through the letterbox but decides there'd be too much risk of rattling Vivien so much that she runs. No, she'll come back tomorrow and resume her sentry duty.

# THIRTY-ONE

I was assuming the police would make a connection to Steph at some point, though I wasn't sure how. I didn't think it would be so soon though. But as I walk round the corner on my way back from a few hours in the office and see two people sitting in a car parked outside my house, I know who they must be. And if I'm right it means I need to move fast vis-à-vis Vivien, before the police join the rest of the dots and find her. Or find Kate. I blot out the thought.

They — a man and a woman — get out of the car as I open my front door.

'Hello?' I say.

'Good evening,' says the man. 'I'm DC Zhen Li and this is my colleague DC Hannah Davies, from the Dorset Police. We're looking for Lucy Hawkings.' They show me their warrant cards.

'I'm Lucy Hawkings.' I hope I look puzzled rather than apprehensive. 'Dorset?'

'Yes, but we want to talk to you about something that happened in Cornwall last year.'

'Steph,' I gasp. It's a gasp of relief but I suspect it will pass as a gasp of surprise and sadness. 'Do you want to come in?'

I take their coats and hang them up along with mine. 'There's a loo in there if you need it,' I say, gesturing to the door. 'Just in case you've been waiting for me for hours.'

Hannah then Zhen thank me and use the facility.

In the sitting room I invite them to take a seat and ask whether they'd like a drink. They both want water and, with a rueful glance at the white wine chilling in the fridge, I pour myself the same. Best to keep my wits about me.

'We're investigating a murder, or probable murder, that occurred ten days ago or so in Dorset,' starts Hannah. 'But that's not directly why we're here. We found a report of a similar death in Cornwall in October last year. Your sister.'

I nod. Tears rise to my eyes and they're not fake or even conjured up. Suddenly everything feels like a huge weight crushing me and I want to howl like a baby. I compose myself after a few sobs, fetch a sheet of paper towel from the kitchen and rub my eyes fiercely.

'Can you tell us about it?' asks Hannah gently.

I swallow, take a sip of water. 'I don't know much,' I say. 'We were estranged, hadn't spoken for ages. It's a long story, which I wish I could change.'

'Take your time,' says Hannah. 'Anything you can tell us may help.'

Would it be normal to ask what happened in Dorset, I wonder? But I'm clearly — and genuinely — upset, they're probably not expecting me to behave normally.

'I'm several years older than Steph,' I start. 'Eight years. But we were always close, despite that. We fell out, oh, it must be eleven or twelve years ago now. She got engaged to Robert. Her first husband. I couldn't stand him. Not that that on its own would have made me interfere, it was her choice, her life, but I had a really bad feeling about him. I'd recently finished with a boyfriend who was very controlling, to the point of being abusive. Coercive control they call it now. Anyway, I could see the signs. I tried to warn her but she wasn't having any of it. Steph is — was—' I gulp and rub my eyes again '— a born romantic. She wanted the whole fairy-tale marriage and I could see she was heading to the Brothers Grimm rather than Hans Christian Andersen. I couldn't let it go, I kept on at her and eventually she just cut me out.'

'That must have been very hard,' says Hannah.

I nod. 'It was. Especially as it became clear that I'd been right. They got married and Robert began to prise her away from all her friends and family. Well, I was her only family by then really, our parents had died shortly before and otherwise there were just a couple of not very close cousins, but he essentially imprisoned her. Gradually. She invited me over once or twice, just for lunch as I refused to go there when Robert was at home, but that was very early days. Then she stopped working — she'd had a job at an art gallery — and said she couldn't see me anymore, Robert had explained how controlling I was — I guess he should know. How toxic our relationship had become, how I hated him and she couldn't have us both. She stopped answering my calls or texts. Robert probably saw to that if she wavered.'

I go to the kitchen, bring back a jug of water and top up our glasses. 'He died a couple of years ago. A heart attack. I thought it might be an opportunity for us to make up, which we did briefly. But she was dead set on getting married again. I told her to wait, said it was too soon, she'd get hurt again. But she was adamant. She'd missed out on one fairy-tale marriage — not that she'd admit I'd been right, but I could always read her like a book —'

I stop, choke back another sob, chase it down with a swallow of water and press on. 'She was determined to have another go. Said she'd found a dating agency and I just lost it. Steph was such an ingénue, she'd be a sitting target for the sort of people who use Tinder and whatever. She said I was as bad as Robert, trying to control her every move. I couldn't take that. We both said things that hurt, things that I anyway deeply regretted. Even more of course since—'

I blow my nose on the soggy and mascara-smeared paper towel and toss it into the waste-paper basket. Then I remember there's a packet of tissues in my handbag; I dig around till I find it and put it on the table in front of me.

'I tried to get back in touch with her,' I resume. 'But she blocked my calls and my texts, wouldn't answer the door even when I was sure she was home. She could be very childish, very obstinate. To be honest she'd always been spoiled. She was the magic gift, the child who arrived even though my parents — my adoptive parents — were convinced they couldn't conceive. It often happens, apparently. Anyway, end of story, almost. I knew she remarried.'

I haven't worked out what led Hannah and Zhen to me, but decide to be honest about Steph's text. It's too risky not to mention if they know about it, though I don't know how they could given the passage of time since Steph's death. Murder. And James / Jake / Max will surely have destroyed her phone. But still.

'How did you know?' asks Zhen. 'Were you invited to the wedding?'

I give what I think would be described as a hollow laugh. 'No chance. She didn't even let me know in advance. In fairness, I'd refused to go to her first wedding, and that was another nail in …' I trail off. Bad metaphor. 'But she texted me a photo of the groom on what must have been the wedding day. Her second wedding day I mean, last year. She wasn't in the photo, or only a bit of her, but she followed it up with another photo, showing her left hand and her wedding and engagement rings. Just so I'd know.'

'How did that make you feel?' Hannah sounds genuinely curious.

'Mixed feelings. I was angry that she hadn't told me, angry that she'd married someone who was probably from the dating site or agency or whatever. She was quite wealthy, you know. Robert may have been a bastard but he was a bastard who made a lot of money. Precious stones. Steph was just ripe for the picking.'

I feel more tears brimming and rub my eyes, this time more comfortably with a tissue.

'But I also felt hopeful that maybe when she was back from her honeymoon' — more tears, more tissues — 'we could make it up. Even though I thought her new husband might be a gold-digger, I didn't imagine he'd be another Robert. So I was looking forward to mending fences when she came back. Except she didn't.'

Again I feel swamped by the tide of emotion that I've

largely kept in check over the last few months. I sit with my head cradled in my hands, sobbing and hiccupping, for several minutes. Hannah tops up my glass from the water jug and offers it to me.

'Thanks.' I take a swig, use another tissue. 'I'm sorry. It's just brought it all back, telling you about it.'

Hannah nods. 'Understandable. Can we see the photos Stephanie sent you?'

'Sure.' I delve into my bag again and find my mobile, scroll back to the two photos and hand it over. Thank god I'd put so much thought into phones, among other things, before I started my scheme, and never used this one to contact MadeInHeaven, at least as Kate, or Vivien or Jake.

'It's the same one,' says Zhen. I look a question at Hannah.

'It was the appeal we made,' she says. 'About the death in Dorset. We had a photo of the — the victim. And of the woman who disappeared. Didn't you catch the appeal?'

I shrug. 'I hardly ever watch the news on TV. I follow politics and international news closely, but through the *FT* and *The Economist*. And, to a lesser extent, the World Service. I just use the TV for films and the occasional series. So no, I didn't.'

'The woman who took the photo that your sister sent you, who was a witness to the wedding—'

I look up sharply. 'Did she know Steph? Was she a friend?'

'No. She was just walking past the register office with her husband and your sister ran out and asked if they'd be witnesses. And then asked the woman if she could take a photo of the bride and groom, or just the groom if that was easier. Apparently he had some phobia about being photographed. Anyway, she did see the appeal and she recognised him, so got in touch with us.'

My mind races. Now the police know about Steph and have her mobile number, they'll get the phone records. Which will almost certainly lead them to MadeInHeaven. To Vivien. And perhaps to me, though I can't see how. Even so, I can't risk failing now; I need to bring this saga to a rapid close.

I also need to know how much they know about Jake. In any event, I can't keep putting it off without it looking odd.

'What … what happened in Dorset?'

'We'll come to that,' says Hannah. 'But first, can I ask a bit more about your sister. How did you hear about her — about what happened on their honeymoon?'

'I set up a Google alert on her name. When I realised that she really wasn't going to speak to me anymore. I still hoped, as I said, that we could mend our fences in due course, but I wanted … I suppose I wanted to keep an eye on her, as best I could. I'm, I was, the older sister, and always felt responsible. But she was never into social media and never did anything newsworthy, so the first alert I got was an article in a Cornish newspaper about her death.' I shudder, and stand up. 'I'm going to get a glass of wine,' I say. 'Can I offer either of you anything?'

They both decline. I pour myself of slug of cold Sauvignon blanc and sit back down.

'And after?' asks Hannah. 'The funeral? I assume the husband, widower, James Anderson, got in touch?'

'He didn't. I didn't really know what to do. I was grieving terribly, as you can imagine, and struggling at the same time with the conflicting — but very strong — feelings that on the one hand I should have been more forceful, stopped her getting married, locked her in my house or whatever it took, and on the other that I should have been … kinder, I suppose. Gentler. Let her do what she wanted. She was a grown woman after all.' I take a calming swig and blot more tears away. 'I was in a terrible state for weeks. I was waiting for him to contact me but I never heard anything. I didn't have any contact details for him. I went to her house but there was no one there. I put a note through the letterbox with my mobile number, but still nothing.'

'Perhaps he didn't realise who you were?' suggests Hannah. 'He may not have known Stephanie's maiden name I suppose, as it was her second marriage.'

I frown. 'But he must have known Steph had a sis—' But maybe he didn't. Maybe Steph really had disowned me, cut me out of her life. I hadn't thought about that, but of course it would have added to her attractiveness as a potential

MadeInHeaven client. I heave a genuinely heartfelt sight. 'I don't know,' I confess. I try and think back. 'I think I just signed the card "Lucy", didn't explain who I was, assumed he'd know.' I'd always wondered what had happened to that card. Presumably Max had found it, and while it was obviously a link to someone who knew Steph, perhaps he took the view that by then it was too late to worry about it. Perhaps he'd just torn it up, vowing not to answer her door or landline unless he knew who it was.

'What about … would you have expected your sister to leave you anything?' asks Zhen.

'I'm a lawyer,' I say simply. 'It did cross my mind but I knew that any will Steph had made would have been automatically revoked by the marriage. Unless she'd made a special sort of will, in expectation of that specific marriage, but most people don't know about that possibility. In fact plenty of people don't even know about wills being revoked by marriage. And Steph never had anything to do with the law, I don't think she'd have known.'

'So James Anderson inherited everything?'

'I assume so. I mean I know that he should have done. I did check that because I thought maybe some would come to me as Steph's sister, and I could use it for some memento for her, give it to a charity she'd have supported or whatever, but they changed the intestacy law a few years ago. Simplified it. If someone dies intestate with no issue, the surviving spouse gets the lot.'

'Thank you for your openness,' says Hannah. She and Zhen both stand up. 'We really appreciate it. It must have been very hard for you. At the time, I mean, and then again reliving it all again now.'

'I'm pleased if I could help,' I say, getting to my feet also. 'But I don't understand. What happened in Dorset and what's Steph's death got to do with it?'

'We can't say much,' says Zhen, 'as it's an ongoing investigation. But the bare facts will be all over the internet anyway. A man going by the name of Jake Andrews, who also uses the name Max Carrington, married a woman called Kate

Lincoln ten days ago. They rented a secluded cottage in Dorset for their honeymoon. At the end of the week the owner found Jake Andrews dead, drowned in his bath, and no sign of Kate Lincoln.'

I wonder how I should react, but I'm feeling so drained by reliving the last few years that I'm not sure I have the energy to put on an act even if I wanted to. I know I must look wrecked, pale face mottled with the flush I sometimes get when I drink white wine, eyes smeared with mascara, and hope that will do. I grab the arm of the sofa for support, then sink onto the cushions. 'I … I don't know what to say,' I whisper. 'That's … that's terrible.'

'I'm sure you understand we can't tell you more at the moment,' says Hannah, her voice kind. 'But if we do find that there's a connection with your sister's death, we'll be sure to let you know. Thank you again for your honesty.'

Zhen cuts in. 'You mentioned that your sister used a dating agency. Do you happen to know which one?'

I'd thought I'd got away with having carelessly let that piece of information slip. I'd let my guard down once I was in full flow about Steph. It was a relief, really, to talk about her openly, but I'd been too open.

'I'm sorry,' I say. 'She may have said but I don't recall.'

'If you do think of it, please let us know,' says Hannah. 'You never know, there might be a connection. Thank you again for your time, we'll leave you in peace now. Will you be all right? Would you like us to call someone, a friend, to be with you?'

'Thanks, that's kind. I'll be OK,' I say, truthfully. And, less truthfully, 'My partner will be home soon.'

# THIRTY-TWO

Vivien has never followed anyone before, at least not in the sense of a sleuth shadowing their movements. She's seen it done on films; it can't be rocket science, surely? Make sure you can keep them in sight and make sure they don't see you, at least not close enough to recognise you.

If Vivien's right, and she's almost certain that she is, and Lucy is Kate, then Lucy knows exactly what Vivien looks like. She'll have to disguise herself in some way. Her rush of confidence about the simplicity of tracking someone, her heady belief that this is something she can do, evaporates. Max would know. The lack of him, his Machiavellian cleverness, his cool head, pierces her like a sharp blade opening a wound.

But she sits straighter, clenches her fists. Max isn't here and won't be ever again. It's down to her now. She needs to … to *deal with* Lucy. Again, Max would know what to do, in fact he'd go and do it. But again, it's her now. In fact it's her or Lucy.

Vivien thinks about her appearance. She's used to doing that, but this requires looking at herself from another angle. She's always dressed neatly, professional but not drab, bright colours, tailored jackets, fitted skirts that finished above the knee — sometimes quite a way above the knee, Max always said she had lovely legs. Stockings, sometimes with a seam — he loved that, said she was showing her seamy side. High heels. She never wears trousers, isn't sure she even has any — oh, there are the loose linen ones that are so cool in summer, but they're too striking, chalk white with a turquoise motif. She needs jeans. Those things that used to be called sweatshirts but are now hoodies or something. And a hat, or a cap. Her hair is quite distinctive; black, in a bob, always well cut. And, these days, well coloured. She wonders whether she should have it cut differently, but that seems a step too far. Max loved that cut. It's part of her identity. It's also just about long enough — she's got a hair appointment next week — to tie back. She'll have to buy some of those scrunchies or whatever they're called. She'll go shopping first thing tomorrow; it's too late now. She's no idea whether anyone is watching her house — surely if it had been the police at the door they'd have persisted, called through the letterbox or something? She'll stay in for the evening and hope that whoever it was doesn't come back in the morning and see her leave or return.

*

'I'm not sure we're much the wiser,' says Hannah, settling into the driving seat and waiting for Zhen to buckle up. 'Except that it's consistent with James Anderson being the same person as Jake Andrews. And Max Carrington. Which it looks like anyway from the passport photos.'

'It makes it very likely that he murdered Stephanie Faulkner,' says Zhen. 'Even though he was supposedly not in the cottage when she drowned. I checked with the police in Cornwall, and his story about popping to the village to pick up eggs, or whatever it was, held up. The shop was closed but a couple having a drink outside the pub saw him park and get out of his car, then get back in and turn it round. And he called 999 ten or fifteen minutes later, which fits with what he told that journalist.'

'It's hardly conclusive though,' objects Hannah. 'At least I imagine. The TOD window can't have been that narrow. But he must have played the grieving widower to a T.'

'And the coroner was comfortable with his version of events. No investigation was opened so it's not even on

Holmes. And Stephanie was cremated. Not that her body would tell us much now anyway.' Zhen shakes his head irritably as Hannah moves into the left lane and they head back towards Bournemouth.

*

My ex-partner, Eddy, hasn't in truth been home for a while. I haven't missed him much over the last few months to be honest. Our relationship had always been semi-detached and we'd both liked it that way, living independent lives some of the time and joint, though not cohabiting, lives at others. He's a journalist, a foreign correspondent, and is often away, often at a moment's notice. We'd been together in that loose sense for several years, had never moved in together but rubbed along happily between our two houses, our two lives. But six months ago I instigated a gentle separation of the ways. Once I'd found out what I had about MadeInHeaven, Vivien Harrison and Max Carrington and decided to set myself up as a potential wealthy client, I couldn't risk involving anyone else. I had plenty of friends, some close, but everyone's busy with careers, difficult teenagers or new grandchildren, ageing and ailing parents, and I knew no one would question, maybe even notice, my temporary disappearance from the social scene, especially given what had recently, tragically happened to Steph, my only immediate family.

But Eddy was more of a problem. He was, by nature and profession, observant and inquisitive and I'd never have got it past him, even though the number of evenings, the amount of time generally, I spent as Kate turned out to be limited.

When I first approached MadeInHeaven as Kate, I didn't know how it would play out. By that point I knew a fair amount about the agency and suspected a great deal more, but all my suspicions were just that, and each time I circled back to them I couldn't quite convince myself that they were more than my befuddled fantasy. It seemed implausible, incredible even, that an old-fashioned matchmaking agency could be a screen for murder for money, and I was conscious that my grief was almost certainly affecting my rationality and powers of analysis. But circumstantial evidence is still evidence, and I reasoned that if my suspicions were justified, Kate would find out soon enough. Which of course she did, when she heard Jake Andrews' name, when she first saw him. And if and when she did, she'd act — as she did — and Eddy needed to have no knowledge of what really happened to Steph, of MadeInHeaven, Vivien and Jake, of Kate and her Chelsea flat and what Katy did. So once I'd decided what to do, I finished our relationship, as kindly as I could. Which inevitably was not very kindly, but it would have been far unkinder to put Eddy at risk.

After we split, I'd been so caught up in preparing for my sting and then executing it — ha — that I had neither time nor energy for anything else apart from holding down my job. And of course grieving for Steph and, at a much greater emotional distance, for Paula and Barbara.

Should I have continued once I was sure about MadeInHeaven, about James and Jake? Should I have handed it to the police then? Probably. But I knew Max at least would have had a prompt and failsafe escape route planned; the first hint of police interest and you wouldn't see him for dust. Or Caribbean sand. Or so I justified my actions to myself.

My planning was exhaustive. I wrote my list over several days, maybe weeks, on pages torn off a pad; when each became scarred to the point of illegibility with deletions, additions, cross-reference, I started a new one and shredded the old. I destroyed the final version also, but by then I'd refined it, pared it down enough to remember every word. Though in retrospect I should have mentioned SIM cards and phones in the plural.

*What I need*

1. *New SIM card and phone.*
2. *Wig.*
3. *Tinted non-prescription contact lenses and clear-lens glasses (can use my reading glasses as necessary).*

4.   *Dedicated email address.*
5.   *Wedge heels, long bell-bottoms, floppy hat.*
6.   *New fictional career (nobody wants to date a lawyer, and MIH definitely won't want a lawyer client!).*
7.   *High-end flat rental.*
8.   *New ID and bank account.*
9.   *PAYG Oyster card*
10.  *Short rental of cheap flat with, or instal, landline*

Of course there was quite an outlay, but I'd still got most of the money I'd inherited from my parents. At the time, I'd thought maybe I'd buy a secluded cottage in the country somewhere, but rural cottages have somehow lost their appeal. And after Steph died, I'd thought I'd maybe use it to fund something in her memory. Which of course I did, though not quite the sort of thing I'd had in mind.

I'd planned to use my original birth certificate, on which I have my biological mother's surname. But I decided on reflection that if I was going to go through with this, I couldn't take any unnecessary, avoidable risks. There must be a digital link somewhere between that certificate and the adoption certificate, so I applied for a copy of the birth certificate of a woman born in the same year as me who had sadly died when she was nineteen. I'd chosen a woman with a common name and in my application for the certificate I'd used a fictitious name, a temporary email address and a prepaid cash card (thank you Martin Lewis), and then obtained a passport on the back of that.

I'd had to research the money-laundering requirements. I hadn't known the details but one advantage of being a lawyer is that I knew how to find them, and I ploughed wearily through The Money Laundering, Terrorist Financing and Transfer of Funds (Information on the Payer) Regulations 2017. I started by renting a miserable studio flat above a kebab house in Tooting whose owner was happy to take rent in cash with no paperwork — more KFC than KYC. I installed a landline, and once I had the first bill in Kate's name and her new passport, I — or rather Kate — opened a bank account and rented a high-end flat. And the rest, now, is history.

As, sadly, is Eddy. I could really do with him now, after the emotionally draining session with the police. A warm, comfortable shoulder to cry on, a friend to pour me a drink and cook me a meal, a lover to share my bed. But I'll be OK, being alone is a small price to pay. And I've still got more to do until this is over so it's best this way.

# THIRTY-THREE

Vivien lurches in fleeting panic as she automatically checks the long mirror strategically placed just inside the front door. For a moment she thought there was a stranger in the house, an intruder, maybe Lucy come to find her and … do what? And why? A moment later and she recovers her composure and recognises herself in the glass, takes the opportunity to check her appearance. Jeans — how can people wear them all the time? So stiff and cumbersome compared to tights or stockings. The shop assistant had seemed amused at Vivien's evident unfamiliarity with denim, and assured her that they'd soften in the wash. But Vivien has no time to wash and dry her disguise. She'd left the house at eight, hoping that if yesterday's doorbell-ringer returned they wouldn't be so early. She'd originally intended to shop at the nearby Brunswick Centre but, trying to think like Max, she realised that that was too close. She might see someone she knew; she's shopped there often. So she decided to go to one of the big anonymous malls, Westfield Stratford. Annoyingly the shops don't open till ten but she waited it out over coffee and a croissant. By the time she'd finished her shopping and returned, it was too late to think about laundry.

A zipped fleece with a hood; at least that is comfortable, but the grey she deliberately chose drains her face of any colour. Especially without make-up. In fact she looks like a ghost. Good cheekbones, though, she thinks, tilting her head to catch the light. They're more obvious now with her hair painfully pulled back off her face. But she supposes she'll have to pull the horrible baseball cap, or whatever they call it, down so her face won't be very visible anyway.

Her shoes are a lot easier than her usual high heels, which are fine for her regular walks to her office and favourite client cafés — it's how she keeps fit and trim — but definitely wouldn't do for journeys of unknown distance and speed. She'd drawn the line at trainers, but found a pair of flexible slip-on ballerinas. Reluctantly she'd passed on the scarlet, the electric blue, the leopard print and gone for a dingy brown.

If Vivien barely recognises herself, that must be a good sign, she reasons. It's four o'clock and she's heading to Lucy's office, to loiter outside or, hopefully, in a conveniently placed café. It may be a long wait, she knows, and there's no certainty that Lucy will go straight home from work, but it's the only way she can think of to find out where she lives.

She nearly misses Lucy because she's expecting her to be unusually tall. But the woman she sees coming out of the office building just after six o'clock is average height. Certainly taller than Vivien, but then she's on the petite side herself.

Vivien is sitting outside a Pret across the road from Leadbeater & Johnson. She arrived later than she'd planned, having suddenly realised after leaving the maisonette that she hadn't checked the street before she opened the front door, or looked around when she set off. She's not used to thinking like a criminal. She tries to channel her inner Max again — he would have checked. And then he would tell her to do something unexpected to lose anyone who was following her. So en route Vivien suddenly veered into a Sainsbury's Local that she was passing. She knows the shop and it has a separate exit via the small carpark. She walked briskly through the busiest aisles, left the supermarket, took a couple of quick turns in the network of narrow streets — keeping a careful mental note, she knows her weaknesses and doesn't want to get lost now — and almost ran into Camden Town tube station. She was lucky, a train was just coming into her platform and she slipped into a crowded carriage with a sigh of relief.

Now, sitting with a cooling and unwanted coffee, she feels self-conscious in her unaccustomed outfit but is glad of the disguise: the price for an excellent view is that she's more visible than she'd like to be. The woman looks very like her profile photo on the firm's website, though truthfully Vivien can't see a lot of detail. Shoulder-length hair, a bright chestnut brown tied back in a scarlet silk scarf. No glasses, but she was expecting that. And a skirt and jacket. She wasn't expecting that. Kate always wore trousers.

But the cast of the woman's features and the way she moves is definitely Kate's. Some things you can't hide. Vivien watches Lucy turn left as she comes out of the office, then slips away from her Pret table and follows at a short distance as Lucy heads towards the Bank of England. Vivien's heart sinks — if she goes into Bank tube station in the rush hour there's no hope of keeping her in sight. But Lucy carries on along the north side of the Bank of England, bears left into Throgmorton Street and then into Old Broad Street towards Liverpool Street station.

Vivien's heart sinks again, but Lucy goes into the main concourse rather than down one of the tube entrances. She pauses to glance at the main arrivals and departures board then makes her way to wait by the barrier to platform one. The concourse is busy but not impossibly so, and Vivien can still keep her in sight without too much difficulty. She silently thanks Lucy for her thoughtfulness in choosing the bright red scarf.

The barriers open as a Chingford train draws in. It disgorges a handful of counter-commuting passengers, then the waiting crowd surges through. Vivien sticks close to Lucy, thinking that she's unlikely to look round as she's carried forward. She watches her get into the train and follows after letting a few thrusting commuters push past and into the carriage first. Lucy has grabbed a seat and promptly pulls a phone out of her handbag and starts doing something on it,

Vivien can't see what. Vivien squeezes through people until she's behind Lucy and strap-hangs for what turns out to be a mercifully short journey. As the train approaches the second stop, Hackney Downs, Lucy puts her phone back into her bag and stands up. A number of people scramble out and Vivien follows, keeping her eyes firmly locked on the moving red dot of Lucy's scarf.

Lucy walks briskly, turning left and right through a maze of streets. There are still enough people around for Vivien to feel reasonably safe from discovery, but the crowd is thinning and when Lucy slows, fumbles in her bag and lets herself into a terraced house, Vivien breathes out a long sigh of relief. She stops before she reaches the house and crosses the road for what she hopes is a discreet look. It's narrow and on two storeys, the sort of place an estate agent might describe as a cottage with the subtext that it's small rather than rural or quaint. But the windows are clean and the paintwork, if not fresh, is at least not chipped and peeling like some of the neighbours'. The front door is a bright, glossy blue and there's a pot of jasmine to one side, twining untidily up a crooked trellis. There's a tiny front garden, only just big enough for the plant and a couple of bins.

Vivien makes a note of the address on her phone and tries to navigate herself back to the station using Google Maps. She finds it difficult, having neither a good sense of direction nor natural digital skills, but manages eventually and works her way home.

Later that evening, Vivien is sitting on the love seat nursing a glass of wine and wondering how she can do what she knows she must do. Now she has found Lucy and tracked her to her address she has no further excuse for putting it off. And the longer she leaves it, the more likely the police will find Lucy first. And then they'll come for her. She'll do it tomorrow.

She'll have to use the element of surprise; Lucy's taller than her, though thankfully not as tall as she'd thought, and probably heavier, stronger. And she'll have to do it in Lucy's house. At least she has her disguise sorted.

Vivien shudders as she thinks about the knife, but no better, safer method comes to mind. The news is full of reports of fatal stabbings by impoverished, and presumably uneducated, teenagers; surely if they can do it, she can?

\*

Carol's luck, what little there was of it, has well and truly run out. Her tube that morning was delayed and she doesn't get to her lookout point outside Vivien's maisonette until after half past eight. She tries the doorbell again, to no avail, and the mobile, ditto. The house has an air of emptiness. Carol thinks back to the previous day. Does she know for sure that Vivien was even at home then? She saw nothing, heard nothing. Still, Vivien's her only lead — she must know something, someone, who could be a link to her story. And what a story it's turning out to be. Vivien's a wronged woman, doubly so. No, triply — Stephanie, Deborah, Kate. And her partner is a murderer, and now a murderee. So Carol waits and watches for another tiresome few hours. And finally hits pay dirt.

At about four o'clock, the door of the maisonette opens slowly and a woman comes out. Carol steps quietly back towards a shop window and pulls out her phone, puts it to her ear but in reality she's watching not listening. The woman's petite but otherwise quite unlike Deborah's description. Her hair's hidden under a baseball cap — it must be pulled back, piled up — and Carol can't see what colour it is. The woman's face is somewhere between chalk-white and grey, gaunt and apparently unmade-up. She's wearing jeans and a hoodie and flats.

Carol is torn. Is this Vivien? It could be a cleaning woman, for example, who'd arrived during one of Carol's unavoidable brief coffee-and-pee breaks. Or a friend, come to offer Vivien moral support. But again, the woman was the only potential lead, so Carol follows her. For all of ten minutes, or maybe even less if she's honest. The woman suddenly darts into a Sainsbury's Local. Carol trots in after her but the shop's busy and the woman's been swallowed up in the tide of shoppers.

301

She sees a baseball cap and hoodie and runs to catch up but it's a teenage boy who gives her a surly look when, without thinking, she grabs his shoulder.

'What the fuck?' he spits. 'Watch yourself, lady.'

He pulls away and Carol turns round, fruitlessly scans the aisle, notices and follows a sign to an exit. She's disgorged into a small carpark milling with people laden with trolleys and bags and trying to find their cars. Furious with herself, Carol gives up. Some PI she is. Maybe it'll have to be plan C after all, though she's now forgotten what that was. She'll give Vivien's address one last chance tomorrow and if that fails … she doesn't know what.

# THIRTY-FOUR

It feels strange, becoming Kate again. It's been a while and, worried that I've missed something, I stand in front of the full-length mirror in the hall and check my reflection top to bottom. Floppy hat. The surviving wig. Blue contacts. Glasses. Flares. Wedge heels. I've lost the high-heel habit, got used to my trainers and ballerinas again, and hope I don't have to run.

I tick off the things I need to take with me. Vivien's keys. The single sheet of single-spaced (the list has grown much longer since the original four bullets) paper I'd printed out then photocopied at the busy local newsagents. And a pair of nitrile gloves. I'd fleetingly regretted having thrown out Kate's going-away gloves, but keeping them would have been an unnecessary risk and it's not as if they're hard to come by. I'd worn inconspicuous cotton gloves when I took the copy out of the photocopier.

I'd left work early, planning to give myself time to change at home then set off to Vivien's in the rush hour, my hat pulled down over my face. Not that anyone's going to recognise Kate from her passport photo that was publicised in the appeal, but still. I cast my mind back. Does anyone apart from Vivien know what Kate looks like? I suppose it's possible the police have spoken to someone who's seen her. Archie, but he was so absorbed in himself that he's unlikely to remember. Omar, possibly, I suppose, but we only met once. The registrar, but she must have conducted numerous marriage ceremonies that day. The letting agent, but that was months ago. The woman I saw occasionally in the next-door flat in Chelsea, a nanny or child-minder I think, but our encounters were brief and she was usually preoccupied with the toddler and/or baby. Jake, of course, but he's in no position to make a positive identification.

But sod's law decreed that my train home was held up between Bethnal Green and Hackney Downs because of some signalling problem. The delay felt interminable, and was all the more frustrating as I could have walked home from where we were stuck, but we weren't at a station so couldn't leave the train. So I'm running late and won't have the security of full rush-hour travel when I head to Vivien's in a moment. Who'd have thought I'd be yearning for that unseemly crush I normally tried to avoid! But I'm not too worried about being seen; the tail end of tired commuters will all have their eyes anchored to the screens of their phones or tablets or Kindles.

I'm not entirely sure what I'll do when I get to Vivien's house. Assuming she's at home, of course, but that's not within my control. If she's not, I'll just have to start watching the maisonette again. For a long time, or at least it seems a long time, I suppose it's only months really, I'd planned to kill her, but I don't think it's in me to commit a second murder or to kill a woman. I know in my head that she's as culpable, or at least almost as culpable, as Max, but I'm still not sure I can bring myself to do it. And the more I've thought about it in the last couple of weeks, the more I've realised that Vivien has lost everything already. Max, who she was due to lose anyway, it seems, to the faux air hostess. The money, ditto. Her livelihood in all probability — realistically, how can she carry on the business? And, perhaps, she was due to lose her life at Max's hands. Ironically, I may have saved her from slaughter only to find that I can't after all take that last step myself.

But I have to bring this — what? Quest? Narrative? Revenge tragedy? — to an end. The best I've been able to come up with is to confront her, ideally in her own home where she'll be off guard, tell her what I know, show her my list of what I've found out. I'll leave a copy with her and explain the steps I've taken to protect myself. And mention the sort of things that are likely to happen in prison to a woman who goes down as an accomplice to three murders of innocent women. Maybe more, but that will be for the police; I'm done with detecting.

So I'm about to head to Vivien's for the final reckoning. I flick on a playlist so the house doesn't seem empty and reach for my bag and keys.

*

Vivien sets off in the late afternoon. She's planning to travel in the rush hour; well, it's unavoidable really if she wants to arrive at Lucy's house shortly after she's back from work, but it also makes it unlikely that anyone will remember her. There's a risk she'll be seen ringing at Lucy's door, but her plan is to charge straight in as soon as the door's opened and pin Lucy against the wall, behind the door, while she kicks it shut. She's not sure it will work but it's the best she's been able to come up with, and it will mean that she's not loitering on the doorstep arguing with Lucy and more likely to be noticed.

She's got the knife in her handbag. It's one of her kitchen set, good quality stainless steel. She checked the blade when she chose it and was glad she'd done so with caution; it's razor sharp. Max sharpens — she gulps, almost breaks when she thinks of him, then squares her shoulders, she can do this, she has to do this, Max would be proud of her — used to sharpen her knives regularly, bending lovingly over the table where he'd put newspaper to protect the polished cherry wood, swiping the blades carefully across his whetstone. Vivien realises it's still sharp because she's barely used it recently. She doesn't cook much when she's on her own, when Max is — was — on honeymoon for example, and she's hardly even eaten in the last few days.

This time, before she leaves the maisonette, she opens the front door just enough to check the street. There's no one in the immediate vicinity apart from a woman standing outside the shop diagonally opposite, talking animatedly into her phone. Vivien edges out of the front door, clutching her handbag, and makes her way to Camden Road station, from where she takes the Overground to Hackney Central. Once on the platform she gives herself a mental shake, squares her shoulders and strides through the covered walkway to Hackney Downs as if she's planning to get on a connecting train on another line but instead leaves the station and emerges onto the street. She could almost certainly have walked from Hackney Central, the stations are close to each other, but she's hoping that, even though she'll be guided by Google Maps now she knows Lucy's address, the navigation will be easier if she's following the route from Hackney Downs that Lucy took the previous day. It's already looking a little familiar — Vivien may have no sense of direction but she's observant. Voices. Faces. The way someone moves.

She walks at her usual brisk pace and realises as she turns into Lucy's road that she's earlier than planned. She hopes she doesn't have to wait too long, risking being noticed as she loiters nearby. But as she's about to pass Lucy's house, thinking that she'll walk along the street in search of somewhere she can half hide while still being able to watch Lucy's door, she hears music. She pauses. Lucy could have left the radio or a playlist on for security, she supposes, to give the impression that there's someone at home, but she hopes, or part of her hopes, that it means that Lucy's back early. Only one way to find out.

As Vivien turns into the tiny front garden she wants more than anything to run away, to go home, to turn back the clock. But she knows that none of those options are possible, so forces herself to stride purposefully — all two steps — to the front door. She tucks her right hand carefully into her bag and grips the handle of the knife as she rings the bell with her left. She's poised, leaning forward slightly, her right hand now out of the bag clutching the knife, her left shoulder tilted ahead to push the door forward as she rushes in as soon as Lucy opens it.

The door is opened almost immediately. By Kate. Vivien

lurches, almost crumples to the ground with the shock. She's swaying on her feet, gasping like a goldfish. And just as if she were a fish, Kate grasps her right wrist with one hand, her left arm with the other and reels her in.

*

Carol is fighting the temptation to give up and go home, but suspects she won't be able to hold out much longer. It's nearly five and she's been watching Vivien's maisonette since 8 a.m. Maybe Vivien's done a runner, she thinks. Again, there's been no sign of her and no visible or audible sign of any activity in the maisonette. And Carol is conscious that she can't continue to stalk Vivien — or try to do so — day after day, without fruit, indefinitely. Especially as she doesn't even know whether Vivien will yield any interesting information. Though it seems unthinkable that, as Max's partner, she won't, or at least can't. But still.

And then the front door opens slowly. Carol retreats to the shop window and clamps her phone to her ear, talking excitedly into it while keeping her eyes on the door. Vivien emerges. She's hunched over her handbag, looking even gaunter and paler than the previous day, and dressed in what look like the same clothes.

Carol stops talking once Vivien has set off down the road and follows at a discreet distance, determined that this time she won't lose her quarry.

At Camden Road station, Vivien takes the eastbound Overground. The train isn't sufficiently crowded for Carol to keep an eye on Vivien without Vivien being able to see her, but she stands by the door they came in through, strap hanging and, as ever, apparently engrossed in her mobile but with half an eye on the huddled figure sitting a few seats down the carriage.

At Hackney Central, Vivien stands and shuffles past Carol and onto the platform. Carol follows as Vivien picks up speed and scurries through the covered walkway — thankfully in the company of enough transferring passengers for Carol to be able to stay close without, she feels, much risk of exposure — to Hackney Downs. Carol doesn't know this part of London well but had checked the maps of the Overground lines in the carriage and assumed that Vivien would change to a train on one of the two lines running through Hackney Downs, northbound from Liverpool Street. But instead Vivien leaves the station and walks, looking from behind as tense as a taut wire, through the narrow streets, turning left then right.

Carol is starting to worry that Vivien will spot her — again, there aren't enough people out to give her the cover she'd prefer. On the other hand, that works both ways: it makes it much less likely that she'll lose Vivien again. And Vivien, in fact, seems focused on the road ahead, her shoulders rigidly squared, her bag now hanging, still tightly clutched, against her right hip.

Vivien turns into another quiet street then pauses, tilts her head and cranes forward as if listening for something. Whatever she hears — or doesn't hear — seems to impel her forward again, into the tiny front garden of a small terraced house. At the front door she puts her right hand into her bag and rings the bell — somewhat awkwardly — with her left hand.

Carol, watching from a few steps along the pavement, frowns. Vivien is leaning forward slightly, as if she wants to rush through the door, or push it open. But when the door opens, which it does almost as she rings the bell, Vivien instead takes an unsteady step back, stumbling as if about to fall, swaying on her feet.

The woman who opened the door — she's wearing a floppy hat and flares and Carol just has time to realise she's the elusive Kate — reaches out and grabs Vivien's still outstretched arm. There's a brief flash of sun on metal as she does so. Carol thinks for a second it's Kate's engagement ring, but instantly realises that it looks much more like the blade of a knife.

Kate snatches Vivien's left arm, pulls her into the house and slams the door shut.

It takes me a few seconds to recognise Vivien, but even before I recognise her I see a slight woman holding a knife and automatically seize the wrist of her knife hand and then her other arm. My conscious mind catches up with my instincts and I realise who it is and drag her into the hall.

She looks terrified and terrible. She's lost weight and, trim and petite to start with, now appears almost skeletal, a shell of the svelte, slender woman I first met. The anomalous baseball cap she was wearing fell off as I pulled her in; her hair is mussed and the roots are beginning to show. Without her usual elegant makeup her eyes look smaller. They're red and swollen.

'K — Kate?' she whispers.

I shrug. I'm done with pretence. 'If you like.'

I twist the knife from her — she yields it without demur, her grip limp. I take her handbag from her shoulder and she relinquishes that too without fuss, as if all the energy has drained out of her.

There's a small downstairs loo in my house with an old-fashioned lock and the key sitting in the inside keyhole. I put the knife in the basin and the bag on the floor, take the key, close the door and lock it.

'You'd better come through,' I say to Vivien, tucking the key into the back pocket of my jeans. I hope I've judged this right. I can't envisage her being a danger to me now, unless she has some fiendish small weapon hidden in a pocket of her own, unfashionably new-looking, jeans. But it seems unlikely. She looks defeated, frail, older than her years or at least older than I'd thought she was. I realise that I wouldn't have been able to kill her even if I'd set out to do so.

I gesture towards the sofa and she sinks down, letting out a long breath. 'Would you like a drink?' I ask, realising how absurd this is. I'm offering hospitality to the co-conspirator of the man who killed my sister, the man I married — albeit voidably, since the marriage was unconsummated — and then murdered. 'A glass of wine? A coffee?' I'm about to add a jokey assurance that it's not poisoned, but decide on balance not to. Vivien doesn't look as if she could cope with humour, especially of the black variety.

'Wine, thank you,' she says, and part of me is grudgingly impressed that she remembers her manners despite all.

I pour us each a glass and scan the fridge for a rapid snack, something to absorb the alcohol — not so much for myself, though I prefer not to drink on an empty stomach, but Vivien looks as though she hasn't eaten for days. I put some hastily cut chunks of cheese and a few olives on a plate, tear off a couple of squares of paper towel and take the wine and food, inexpertly holding the two glasses in one hand, through. Once I've set them on the coffee table, I sit at the other end of the sofa from her and kick my shoes off.

'Oh,' she says, looking at the chunky wedge heels. 'I wondered why you always wore those awful bell-bottoms.'

'They were at least comfortable, but the shoes were a nightmare.'

We share the ghost of what might in other circumstances have been a smile.

'How did you find me?' I ask, taking a sip of wine. As the crisp chill of the first mouthful washes through me, I realise how pent up I am, my shoulders rigid, my breath shallow. I consciously relax my muscles, inhale deeply.

'You made a mistake.' There's a vestige of triumphalism in her voice. She also raises her glass, takes more of a glug than a sip. But then, she probably needs it more than me. Even more than me.

I frown. I'd planned this so carefully, from the beginning. The beginning ... The beginning was that first phone call to MadeInHeaven's office, the ensuing conversation with Vivien. Before I realised anything was wrong. I just wanted to speak to my sister's widower, offer condolences, ask if I could choose a memento.

'I gave you my name. My real name. In that first call.'
'Yes.'

I frown again. 'I didn't see it written down. In your Liberty notebook, I mean.'

Vivien's eyes widen, but she doesn't look very surprised.

'You weren't a client,' she says without batting an eyelid. 'I assumed it was you. Who took it, I mean. Though I couldn't work out how.'

'It was when you were at the café, waiting for Avril Smythe-Jacques, or whatever she was called. The one with the problem builders.'

Vivien narrows her eyes. 'That was you too?'

I nod.

'How did you get in?'

'I had Max's — Jake's — keys.'

At the mention of Max, Vivien starts. No, more than starts, almost jumps in her seat. Shies like a startled horse. It's as though she's suddenly remembered what happened, remembered why she's here.

'You killed him!' she spits out, her face a rictus of hate.

'He killed my sister,' I say simply.

Vivien's face is a canvas of emotions. Fear, no, terror. Confusion. A flicker of curiosity.

'Who are you?' she asks eventually.

'Stephanie's sister.'

Vivien gasps, rocks back in her seat, slops her wine. 'But she said … you said … you don't look … I'm good at faces.'

'Adopted sister. I know Max killed her. And Paula and Barbara and maybe others before. And the plan was to kill me, wasn't it? For my non-existent offshore wealth and my glitzy Chelsea flat. Rented, by the way.'

Vivien drains her glass, puts it on the coffee table and sits hunched forward with her head in her hands, her elbows on her knees. I go into the kitchen and fetch the bottle, top us both up. She starts to weep, tears rising and slowly spilling. She seems unaware of them as they dribble down her cheeks. She looks around, her head in jerky motion like a bird. 'She lied to me,' she says with venom. 'Your sister. If she hadn't said she was an only child—'

'She wouldn't have been married off to Max and killed by him? Lying by the victim is not a recognised defence to a murder charge I'm afraid.'

311

'It was Max,' she says desperately. 'All Max.'

I keep my eyes on her, say nothing.

'Max did everything.'

I raise an eyebrow. 'You procured the victims, and so aided and abetted the commission of murder, which makes you liable to be tried and punished in the same way as the murderer. Which means life, if you're convicted.'

'He made me do it. He forced me.' She makes it sound like an offer. Perhaps it is.

'Ah, duress.' My voice is icy. 'Unfortunately, murder is one of the few crimes for which it's not a defence. *R v Gotts*, if you're wondering,' I add helpfully, glad of my earlier research. 'And the other crimes for which it's unavailable are attempted murder — so you'd have been on the hook for me as well in due course — and treason involving the death of the sovereign. Just in case you were thinking of branching out. Though it's a bit late for that to be honest.' I take a sip of wine.

Vivien frowns, chews her lip. She's stopped crying. 'But I didn't murder anyone. Or attempt to. That was Max.'

I raise my glass to her. 'Full marks, Vivien. You should have been a criminal lawyer. Instead of stopping at the halfway mark. But to get back to your failure to murder anyone, as I said earlier you aided and abetted, and that's enough.' I wonder whether to tell Vivien about conspiracy and encouraging or assisting an offence, but decide it might be overload. Then I remember one detail which is relevant.

'There's also conspiracy to murder,' I start. 'What's interesting is that husband and wife aren't guilty of conspiracy if they're the only parties to the agreement. Were you and Max married?'

'No.' Vivien chews her lip again. I keep quiet, wait her out. 'He didn't want to. Said we'd have to give the state a lot of private info about us, and it would all go on record somewhere. He liked to stay hidden. And he said it was just as well, his subsequent marriages were valid so he was entitled to the money. I mean we were, I'm sure he said we.' Vivien stops abruptly, and a red stain washes over her cheeks then ebbs. She must realise she's said too much, or is she more concerned about what Max had intended? She starts crying again. 'It was all his idea.' There's a note of desperation in her voice. 'The agency, the bride-grooming.'

That was possible, I concede, though I don't voice it. I nudge the wine bottle towards her and watch as she shakily tops up her glass. Then she changes tack, retreats from passing the buck. She crumbles back into her defeated slump, starts crying again. 'I've lost Max. That's the only thing that matters.'

Apart from at least three deaths, I think. And as for Max … would it make it better or worse for Vivien to know that he was planning to ditch her, probably to kill her too, to run off with the faux air hostess into the sunset lined with his victims' wealth? Which Vivien had evidently thought was their joint spoils. I decide it would make it worse and keep silent.

'What are you going to do with me?' she asks eventually, her voice trembling. And her glass, I notice.

I sigh. 'Nothing. I was planning to kill you too, complete the revenge. Avenging really — Paula, Barbara, Steph. But I can't do it. You've lost everything. You need to go home, Vivien. I don't want to see you again, obviously. But I won't go to the police —'

'But I will,' interrupts Vivien, though without much conviction.

'Feel free,' I say generously. I fetch my bag from the hall table, put on the nitrile gloves that I tucked in there earlier for use in my original plan for Kate's last outing and pull out the sheet of paper. It's the latest and final version of my *What I know* list — considerably longer and more detailed, of course, than the original four bullet points that I'd set down all those months ago.

I'm about to go back to the sitting room when I remember Vivien's bag. And the knife. I unlock the loo door, open it and retrieve the bag, then lock the door again leaving the knife on the right side of it. I check the bag but there's nothing untoward there. I put it by the front door then go back to the sofa and hand her the list.

She reads it slowly, her eyes flicking from side to side as she scans each line. Her face seems to lose even more colour, though I wouldn't have said that was possible a few minutes ago. Her skin is like chalk, then a hectic red flush begins to bloom on her cheeks. She crumples the list and tosses it on the coffee table, but it's a feeble gesture, as if the paper's too stiff and too heavy.

'How …?'

'It's a long story and it was a lot of very tedious work. I'm a solicitor — oh, of course you probably know that.' I understand now, how she found my address. 'You must have googled me once you realised you had my name and followed me home from work.'

'Yesterday,' says Vivien, a glimmer of pride in her voice.

Deserved, I think, and throw her a crumb. 'I never noticed you.' I try and think where to start with my long trail of following her, seeing her with Max, following him, delving into the ownership of the properties he visited, finding the deaths and the probate details, seeing Max with the faux air hostess and hearing their conversation, going to Jake's flat and finding his home keys, setting up and implementing the search of Vivien's house, finding the Liberty notebook and Max's driving licence and birth certificate, probably other steps I've forgotten. I feel suddenly drained, fed up with it all. Vivien can work it out herself, or not. For now, I've had enough. I glance at my watch. It's less than ten minutes since Vivien arrived, but I can't face any more of her.

'Keep the list,' I say. 'But know that I've already given my solicitor a copy. She's also got your Liberty notebook and Jake's fraudulent birth certificate and passport.' I pause, thinking rapidly. This is not the time for sticking too closely to the truth. 'And Max's laptop and phone and Jake's phone. I've instructed her to send everything to the Met if anything happens to me. Including if I'm even questioned by the police. So you'll go down too, Vivien. Do you really want to spend the rest of your life in a cell? Word gets out in prison you know. I don't think you'll be popular. Except for providing sexual services no doubt.'

Vivien flinches. 'I'll go away,' she says. 'I've got money, three properties. I'll just go away and hide and never come back.' She pushes herself unsteadily to her feet, supporting herself with a hand on the back of the sofa.

Three properties?

'Are you sure about that? Did Max forget to mention that he'd sold Stephanie's house and Flat 10?'

Vivien blanches. 'You're lying,' she screeches. 'He wouldn't have.' But she looks as though she's beginning to realise that he would have.

Whatever, this is no time for sympathy. I stand up also and we move into the hall. 'Don't forget what I said,' I say. 'Remember what my solicitor knows.'

And as we approach the door, a voice shouts through the letterbox: 'I know you're both in there. I know who you are. I know there's a knife. Let me in before I call the police.'

# THIRTY-FIVE

Carol has her ear to the letterbox. When she saw Kate haul Vivien into the house, she had stood rooted to the spot for what seemed like several minutes but was probably less — she felt frozen in time, trying to process the wildly spinning wheel of her thoughts. Then she moved to the front door, unsure what to do.

What she needs, wants, for her own purposes is to know more, to know everything, to have a scoop, write a best-selling true crime book, even turn it into a novel. But Vivien has a knife, Carol is sure that's what it was, and Kate may well be in danger. Or maybe Kate now has the knife and Vivien is in danger. She strains to hear anything beyond a hum of background music and murmuring voices. It doesn't sound as though anyone is being murdered, but still.

Carol hesitates. She waits for five or ten minutes — she has no idea what time Vivien rang the doorbell but it can't have been much more than that — as she continues to listen at the letterbox, learning nothing more than that the conversation is continuing. But then she hears the sound of a key being turned in a lock, sounding very near the front door. She squints through the slit and sees a slice of what looks more like Kate than Vivien, moving away. She resumes her listening pose — Jesus, her back won't take this much longer. There's a pause, then more indecipherable words followed by an all too decipherable eldritch screech 'You're lying! He wouldn't have!' She squints again, and this time the slice is moving towards her.

Carol takes an immediate decision. If Kate and Vivien, or one of them, is about to leave the house, she'll lose the prospect of cornering them together. She shouts through the letterbox, 'I know you're both in there. I know who you are. I know there's a knife. Let me in before I call the police.'

\*

Vivien and I both stop dead. Not a good expression, I think automatically. Vivien half turns towards me, her eyes huge and terrified in her spectral face.

I make an instant and instinctive decision. I can't risk the police being called. All my carefully constructed house of cards would come tumbling down. Vivien would get her comeuppance but so would I, and that was definitely not part of the plan.

Of course this woman may be the police, but that's a risk that I have to take. It can't, after all, be worse than the alternative, and if she isn't the police it can only be better. At least I suppose so, though thinking through the possibilities of who she is, what she knows, how she knows it and what she wants would take a lot longer than the seconds I have. Only one way to find out. I open the door.

The woman on the other side is maybe in her early fifties, casually dressed with no makeup and hair showing not unattractive streaks of grey. She enters rapidly as if worried that I'll change my mind and slam the door shut again before she's crossed the threshold.

'I'm Carol Turner,' she says before I have a chance to ask. 'I'm a journalist. I know that you're Kate Lincoln—' she nods at me '— and you're Vivien Harrison.' She juts her chin at Vivien. 'And I know something about what's been going on. With James Anderson aka Jake Andrews aka Max Carrington. I want to know more. Otherwise I'll—'

'Go to the police,' I intoned. 'Yes, you said. I'd prefer that you didn't do that, and I'm sure Vivien would also. You'd better come through.'

*

Vivien and Carol follow Kate into the house. Carol frowns: Kate is shorter than she recalls and is shuffling in overlong flared jeans. In the sitting room, Kate wearily gestures at the others to sit down. 'Wine?' she asks. 'I don't know how you know what you know or what you want to do about it, but a glass usually helps.'

Vivien shakes her head, looking regretful, but Carol says, 'Thanks. And can I use your loo please? You've no idea how difficult it is watching someone all day.'

'As it happens I do,' says Kate. 'Yes, it's— oh, wait, you'll have to use the upstairs one. You can't miss it.'

Carol is quick and when they're all sitting in a surreal tableau of a convivial gathering, two holding wineglasses, she says, after an awkward silence, 'OK, shall I start then?'

Kate shrugs. 'Why not?'

Carol takes a long breath followed by a long draught of wine. 'It's a long story,' she begins. 'I stumbled by chance on the newspaper article about James Anderson losing his bride on the first night of their honeymoon. I thought it was a good story—'

She breaks off, seeing Kate's face darken with fury.

'Sorry,' says Carol quickly. 'I'm a journalist, as I said. Out of a job. I just mean I thought it was something that I could maybe write about. I was — still am — desperate to find something to sell. Anyway, this was a couple of months ago. And the honeymoon accident was a while before that. I thought I could interview Anderson, make something of it. But I couldn't find anything about him online. Nada. It was unnerving. But I thought I could keep trying, and in the meantime I set up a Google alert for other examples of honeymoon deaths. It might make for a human interest—'

Carol breaks off. Kate is pale, her mouth set, her eyes — a vivid blue — blazing with fury.

'I'm sorry,' says Carol again. 'Look, I'm broke. Made redundant except with no redundancy money. Trying to earn a crust before I'm bankrupt. It's what I do.'

'It's OK,' says Kate after a pause. 'But James Anderson's short-lived bride was my sister.'

Carol gasps, stares at Kate. 'But you — you married him afterwards.' She takes another swig of wine. 'And you — you murdered him.'

Vivien, until now a silent huddle in her chair, suddenly lets out another eldritch screech. 'Max,' she wails. 'She killed Max.'

'Shut up,' says Kate. 'No one's interested in your feelings, believe me.' She turns to Carol. 'How did you find out about Max?'

'The Google alert told me about his drowning on the first night of his honeymoon, with no sign of the bride. I already knew that that was how his first bride died.'

'Stephanie,' snaps Kate. 'That's her name.'

'Sorry, yes, Stephanie. But — I'm not telling this in order. I'd continued trying to find James. I found the address of his — of Stephanie's house, that he inherited. I went to see it, posing as a potential buyer. As if — I can barely afford a sandwich at the moment. Anyway, I found an envelope addressed to a Jake Andrews at another address. And later I saw Anderson at the house with a young woman. I watched the other address and saw the same man — Anderson, Andrews — coming out of the block with you.'

Carol nods at Kate, who says nothing.

'I saw your engagement ring. And heard him call you "Kate, my love".'

A guttural, throaty squawk breaks from Vivien. Carol ignores her and continues, 'When I got the Google alert I knew what must have happened, but I didn't know why.'

'How did you find out about Max?' asks Kate.

'I found the young woman. I'd made a note of her number plate and, well, I have contacts in the police. I've been a crime reporter all my life. I tracked her down and she told me — well, it was all a bit complicated but the gist is that she was in a relationship with the man who goes by the names of James

Anderson, Jake Andrews and Max Carrington. She knew him as Max and he told her he was going to leave his partner—'

'She was lying,' cries Vivien, but again Carol ignores her, as does Kate whose eyes are fixed unwaveringly on Carol.

'I told her he was dead,' Carol resumes. 'Showed her the police appeal, with the photo. And the local newspaper article which was more graphic. She's a smart cookie. Saw the writing on the wall I guess and decided to move on. By giving me Max and Vivien's address. She's the receptionist at their dentist.'

Another squawk from Vivien, who starts to mumble something about patient confidentiality and data protection.

'Shut the fuck up,' snaps Kate fiercely, at the same moment as Carol barks, 'You can't be serious.'

There's a pause, and Kate and Carol look at each other as if about to speak. Carol takes an instant decision and gets in first.

'Listen,' she says. 'Kate. I know nothing about you except this address, and believe me I have a terrible memory and no sense of direction. Let's keep it that way. Tell me nothing—'

'She's called Lu—' Vivien spits out.

'I'm deaf,' says Carol swiftly, cutting across her. 'Selectively deaf. Something to do with the pitch of your voice. Can't hear a thing. I suggest you do what Kate advised and shut the fuck up.'

'Or go,' adds Kate. 'As you were about to do when Carol showed up.'

'No, wait,' says Carol urgently. 'I need to go in a minute, we can leave together. What I want to say to you' — she dips her head at Kate — 'is that I know enough from my own inquiries to write a good story. I've dotted some i's and crossed some t's here, but I don't need to know more.'

'You do,' says Kate grimly. 'Check out these names — Paula Platt-Robinson and Barbara Allen, previously Watson. Before she married John Allen. And Joseph Aston, who married Paula. I only found out about Paula very recently and couldn't face digging up more filth.'

'I can dig up filth,' says Carol, 'it's what I do.' She pulls her notebook out of her bag and notes the names. Her pen slows as she writes John Allen and Joseph Aston, and she looks a question at Kate.

'Yes,' says Kate. 'And if you don't know this already, then Max and Vivien ran a dating agency—'

'Matchmakers,' croaks Vivien automatically.

'Dispatch makers more like,' says Kate. 'It's called MadeInHeaven.'

Carol is scribbling furiously. She closes her notebook, drains her glass, and stands.

'Thanks for the wine,' she says to Kate. 'And the info. I'll flesh it out through other means. I'm a good researcher. I won't need to mention you. I've got the scoop of the century.'

Carol grabs Vivien by the elbow and marches her out of the room. She's struggling to open the Yale lock on the front door when Kate calls 'Wait' and thrusts a crumpled piece of paper at her. 'You might find this useful,' she says, neatly unlocking the door. 'Good luck.'

*

Carol's plan to leave with Vivien — or, more accurately, to frogmarch her out of Kate's house — was a spur-of-the-moment decision. She has no desire to engage further with Vivien, in fact she folds her arms tightly to prevent herself from impulsively pushing her under a passing bus, and she already knows where Vivien lives. But she isn't sure whether Vivien still has the knife and, given her deranged appearance and wild statements, Carol thinks she might lash out at some innocent passerby. Or somehow force her way back into Kate's house. Quite apart from the fate of the innocent passerby or of Kate, Carol has some concern, which she recognises as heartless in the circumstances, for the fate of her book — if Vivien attacks someone, the police will be involved and … well, that'll be the end of Carol's scoop.

So she thinks she'll just follow Vivien back to her maisonette and see that she goes in. There isn't much she can do beyond that but at least it will give Kate a chance to think things through and presumably come to the same realisation that Vivien might storm back and prepare accordingly.

Of course, Carol suddenly thinks, Vivien might well lash out at her, Carol. In fact, isn't that more likely than attacking a random stranger? Or even Kate? Killing Kate would be inspired by revenge, but killing Carol could bring Vivien the more concrete benefit of killing Carol's story.

Carol hangs back a little while keeping Vivien in sight and trying to work out what to do. But in the end she doesn't have to do anything.

She follows Vivien, as she expected, to Hackney Downs Overground station, through the walkway to Hackney Central and onto the next westbound train. It's too crowded to sit but Vivien slumps against a corner of one of the narrow cushion rests either side of the doors, her shoulders hunched, her face in her hands. Then, as the train pulls out of Caledonian Road and Barnsbury, she suddenly lifts her head, sits up straight, squares her shoulders. Carol's ready for her to get off at the next stop, Camden Road, which she does, but as she leaves the station Carol is surprised to see her turn right, away from the maisonette, rather than left, towards it. She's walking briskly and purposefully and Carol, who's already a few passengers behind her at the exit barriers, struggles to keep her in view. She just sees Vivien turning into Camden Town tube station and promptly loses her in the crowd of commuters pouring out.

\*

### *The Standard, London*

*A person has reportedly been killed on the London Underground tracks.*

*Vivien Harrison, 45, was seen on CCTV entering a Tube station at 19:05 last night before taking her life.*

*Police and paramedics were called to Camden Town Tube station at 19:15, following a report of a casualty on the tracks, according* to British Transport Police, who said the death was not being treated as suspicious and evidence would be sent to a coroner.

'Sadly a person was pronounced dead at the scene,' the force added.

The Northern line was suspended after the death.

# PART SIX – LUCY AND CAROL

# THIRTY-SIX

It's been six months now since Vivien and the reporter walked unsteadily out of my house and I've slotted back into my Lucy life. Slowly and shakily at first — I felt drained and fragile after it all. But I have generous and sympathetic friends and colleagues who understand that I've been grieving for Steph. One or two people have asked whether I'm still in touch with her widower. I shrug and say sadly not, he obviously didn't want to keep in contact. Too painful for him probably.

I'm gradually relaxing. I think the only mistake I made was to give my real name to Vivien in that first phone call, before I knew how black was the hole I was about to step into. And, I realised more recently, I must have missed Max's wallet when I searched the maisonette, as it definitely wasn't in Dorset or in Jake's flat. It must have been well hidden, and admittedly I'd been under some time pressure. But while that was an oversight with no obvious consequences for me, I may have made other more serious errors, and they may still be my undoing. I imagine the police investigation is dormant, if not formally closed — if they'd found something linking Max's murder to me, I'd surely have heard about it by now. Lucy Hawkings isn't hiding, isn't hard to find. But she's never been convicted of an offence, or arrested or charged or even questioned, so neither her fingerprints nor her DNA will be in the police database, and now that I've disposed of the remnants of Kate's wardrobe and accessories, I can't think of anything that could conceivably link the two names.

At least I don't have to worry about Vivien anymore. I'd thought that she might consider suicide once she'd digested all that had been said the last time we met and faced the implications. And once she'd taken that decision, what would stop her from leaving a note identifying me as Kate Lincoln? But the day after that last time, I found someone, presumably the reporter Carol, had posted a copy of the Standard through my letterbox while I was at work.

Max's offshore money is still in Belize. I'd included the account details in the *What I know* list I gave to Carol and assume she'll pass them on to the police, though I have no idea whether the long arm of English law can reach that far. As for the rest of Max's money — Stephanie's estate, the proceeds from Flat 10 and probably other funds I don't know about — that never made it to Belize, I don't know. It's presumably in some account I didn't find, perhaps — as I'd tentatively surmised — hidden from Vivien. I suppose eventually the account will be declared dormant and the money used for charitable causes. Similarly, I imagine, with whatever Max, as James Anderson or his predecessors, had deposited in his self-storage unit on the Finchley Road.

My phone vibrates with an incoming text from Eddy. I'd got back in touch with him after what I think of as the showdown, apologising for our split and blaming it on the stress and grief of having my only close relative dying so unexpectedly and horrifyingly. He was generous and we've resumed something of our former semi-detached life. His message says he's running a bit late for dinner, delays on the Northern line.

# THIRTY-SEVEN

It took Carol a while to write *MadeInHell* but boy, she thought, was it worth the wait. It was snapped up and now, a year, give or take, from that day she followed Vivien, she's staring, disbelieving, at the note of her first royalties.

There was a lot of research, of course. Carol knew she must have been duplicating much of what Kate — or rather Lou — Louise? Lucy? Lucinda? Lucille? — had already done, but she was determined to honour her side of their implicit bargain and dig out what she could by her own research, though admittedly using Lou's *What I know* note as a springboard. That way she could almost truthfully say that she'd searched long and hard for Kate Lincoln and drawn a blank but found enough information about the other players to put it all together. Max Carrington and his alter egos Joe Aston, John Allen, James Anderson and Jake Andrews — murdered. Vivien Harrison — deceased, by suicide. Paula Aston, née Platt-Robinson — deceased, probably murdered. Barbara Allen, née Watson — deceased, probably murdered. Stephanie Anderson, née Hawkings — deceased, probably murdered. And MadeInHeaven — dispatch makers, as Lou had called them with grim humour.

There were times when Carol felt she was going cross-eyed with tedious legal research into properties, deaths, marriages but she got there in the end. Or at least got enough to flesh out a story so dark and evil that she thought she'd have a problem billing it as true crime. But the public appetite for dark, evil true crime was gargantuan enough, and now she sees the cover everywhere, in bookshop windows, in huge adverts at tube stations, in the review sections of the Sundays.

Towards the end of her research, Carol had asked one of her old crime-beat contacts at the Met to put out feelers to the Dorset Police and ask if she could speak informally to the team investigating — or as it turned out no longer investigating — the murder of Jake Andrews and the disappearance of Kate Lincoln. The message came back that Dorset had more or less conclusive proof that James Anderson, Jake Andrews and Max Carrington were the same person and suspected, though without concrete evidence, that he had murdered Stephanie Anderson. However, as James / Jake / Max was well and truly dead and as all evidential leads to Kate had been exhausted, it was clearly not within the public interest to continue with the investigation and they'd formally closed the case.

Carol had pushed her contact for more detail, and he'd relayed the police's evident frustration. Forensics had found a few residual fingerprints and DNA traces in the honeymoon cottage, Jake's serviced apartment and Kate's rented flat which were unaccounted for, and hence might have been Kate's, but which didn't match anything on the database. The mobile number which Jake had used to make the honeymoon Airbnb booking was a prepaid SIM card bought and topped up with cash, no longer active; the record showed no calls or texts ('WhatsApp has a lot to answer for', she was told darkly). The mobile number which Kate had used for communicating with the letting agents for her Chelsea flat was similarly a prepaid SIM card bought and topped up with cash, no longer active; the record showed no other call or text history. As for CCTV, the police had checked records around Kensington and Chelsea Register Office and both Jake and Kate's flats, and though they had identified glimpses of of a tall woman they were almost sure was Kate, in each case she was either wearing her wedding veil or a big floppy hat or looking away from the camera.

Carol had wanted to tell them about her brilliant idea of how to trace the proceeds of the sale of the house in Hampstead, which surely belonged to Stephanie Anderson's sister. She'd noticed that the name of the solicitor who 'extracted', as the grant stated, the probate — it sounded painful, and reminded Carol of the serendipitous dental services sought by Max and Vivien — was set out on the form. They, surely, would have details of the account to which they'd transferred the proceeds of the subsequent sale, on which she assumed they would have acted, and the money could be followed. But Dorset was ahead of her and the National Crime Agency had already used its powers under the Proceeds of Crime Act 2002 to recover the funds and restore them to those entitled. What Dorset hadn't known, however, was that James Anderson was suspected of having deposited valuable gemstones at a self-storage unit on the Finchley Road. Carol said she'd sworn to protect her source for that piece of information — which in a sense she had — but they said they'd follow it up. So with luck Stephanie's sister, the mysterious Lou, will have had another nice windfall, or will do soon. With more to come for others perhaps, as she'd given the police the numbers of Max's bank accounts in Belize.

The dental reference reminds Carol of Deborah, who has a bit part in *MadeInHell* — a chapter she persuaded Carol to entitle 'My brush with death — I was nearly killer Max's next victim'. But she added some colour to the fruits of Carol's dry research, and she's dead (not literally for once, and no pun intended) set on the two of them doing a podcast about true crime reporting. Or was it a blog?

# ACKNOWLEDGMENTS

I am fortunate enough to have many generous and tolerant friends who kindly, carefully and critically read through a late draft of The Matchmakers, gave me extraordinarily astute and helpful comments and suggestions, and drew my attention to many embarrassing typos, inconsistencies and infelicities. Sincere thanks to Alan, Andrew, Beverley, Caroline, Diana, Heather, Lucy, Lynn, Pat, Paul and Sal: without you, this text would be a lot more ragged. Many thanks also to my son Fred and his partner Courtenay for their unwavering interest in and enthusiasm for my writing, to my late parents who by example and encouragement showed me that I could be a fox rather than a hedgehog, and to Helen for the concept and much early support. And finally thanks to Graham Bartlett for his clear and informed answers to my numerous questions on police procedure and phones. All errors are of course mine.

# ABOUT THE AUTHOR

Vanessa Edwards is a former solicitor who lives in London with her Border collie Elvis. The Matchmakers is her second novel; her debut The Grass Widow is available as a paperback from Amazon and all bookshops and as an ebook from Amazon and other platforms. Her website is vanessaedwardswriter.com and she can be found on Facebook and X as Vanessa Edwards, Writer.